D0826567

ALSO BY SUSAN GABRIEL

FICTION

The Wildflower Trilogy:

The Secret Sense of Wildflower

Lily's Song

Daisy's Fortune

Temple Secrets Series:

Temple Secrets

Gullah Secrets

Trueluck Summer

Grace, Grits and Ghosts: Southern Short Stories

Seeking Sara Summers

Circle of the Ancestors

Quentin & the Cave Boy

NONFICTION

Fearless Writing for Women:

Extreme Encouragement & Writing Inspiration

Available at all booksellers

in print, ebook, and audiobook.

TEMPLE SECRETS

SUSAN GABRIEL

WILD LILY ARTS

Temple Secrets

SECOND EDITION

ISBN 978-0-9835882-7-6

Cover design by Lizzie Gardiner, lizziegardiner.co.uk

Wild Lily Arts

Printed in the United States of America.

CHAPTER ONE

Queenie

Iris Temple has been threatening to die for three decades, and most of the people in Savannah who know her want her to get on with it. Queenie looks up from the crime novel she's hidden within the pages of *Southern Living* magazine and takes in the figure of her half-sister, Iris Temple, across the sunroom. Everything about Iris speaks of privilege: the posture, the clothes, the understated jewels. Not to mention a level of entitlement that makes Queenie's head ache. An exasperated moan slips from her mouth before she can catch it.

Iris's gaze shifts to Queenie. Her eyes narrow, the adjoining crow's feet forming a close-knit flock. The look delivers the message that even though Queenie is solidly middle-aged, she is to be *seen and not heard* like a child.

As Iris Temple's companion for the last thirty-five years,

Queenie lives the lifestyle of a Temple instead of a Temple servant like her black mother, grandmother, and great grandmother. With the precision of a Swiss clock, Queenie is reminded daily that she is not a *true* Temple—though they share the same father—any more than Sunny Delight orange drink is considered *real* orange juice. She is simply a watered-down Temple—albeit several shades darker.

As she does every morning, Iris studies the local newspaper from headlines to classifieds in the lavish sunroom facing the prominent Savannah square. Wicker furniture with rich fabrics mingles with antiques and tropical plants, as gold elephants the size of laundry baskets offer their polished backs to hold Iris's porcelain teacup.

Focused on the society section, Iris licks her lips as though relishing the fact that the Temple family is one of the elite families of Savannah. Their photographs appear in the newspaper with a regularity that Iris's constitution rarely achieves. As if on cue, Iris's stomach rumbles, and she fidgets in her chair. If treated more kindly, Queenie might feel sorry for Iris's discomfort and offer to make her life easier in some way.

For years, Iris Temple's unpredictable illnesses, usually of a gastrointestinal nature, have manipulated everyone around her. Just last week, a stomachache canceled a Daughters of the Confederacy charity event, and gas pains dismantled a family reunion planned for over a decade. Other social events Iris deemed unworthy of her time were aborted by attacks of acid reflux. To what does Iris Temple attribute these ailments? Gullah voodoo.

Within seconds, Iris's stomach rumbles again. Yet her attention has not left the newspaper.

"Oh my word, listen to this," Iris says.

Queenie exhales as Iris begins to read.

"Miss Iris Temple, of the Savannah Temples, will be hosting the 20th annual charity bazaar for the Junior League this coming Saturday. The grand matriarch, also known as Savannah's grandmother—" Iris balks and looks as though she's swallowed something bitter. "Savannah's grandmother? Is that supposed to be a compliment?"

"Oh, I'm sure it is, Iris," Queenie answers, all the while thinking, *Savannah's grandmother, indeed. Never mind that you're eighty years old and have one grandchild who you've never even met. Or that you don't have a nurturing bone in your body.*

Queenie anticipates what will follow: Iris's angry letter to the newspaper on embossed Temple stationery that will insist that the reporter be dismissed and Queenie called upon to hand deliver the bad news.

Voodoo or not, most people—including Queenie—consider Iris Temple to be a first-class fake. What she blames on folk magic is merely an excuse to bring the fancy families and institutions of Savannah under her control.

And if that doesn't work, there's always that damn ledger, kept in a safe at the bank, documenting secrets about rich and powerful Savannah families. Secrets, Queenie has been told, that their great-grandfather began collecting before the Civil War and that every Temple has contributed to since.

Well, not every Temple. Iris has never asked my thoughts on anything, never mind what I'd like to put in that "secret" book.

It's true. Iris has noted every affair of prominent men, their illegitimate children, mental illnesses of wives, and any dishonest money dealings she's ever become privy to. According to Iris, two entire pages are devoted to Queenie. Given the Temple family's inclination to lie if it benefits them, Queenie questions how many of those so-called "secrets" are true. But she does have one that could do some serious harm if it got out.

"Did you call the restaurant about tomorrow night?" Iris asks.

Queenie looks up from her crime novel and gives the expected response. "Yes, Iris, it's all been arranged." And then thinks: *Only you, Iris, would counteract a voodoo curse by following a strict diet that consists of no sauces, no spices, and no intermingling of foods. You might as well be eating the Temple Book of Secrets!*

Part of Queenie's job as Iris's assistant is to make certain that chefs in downtown establishments follow these strict dietary restrictions. Chefs hate being told what to do. But if any fail to meet her requirements, Iris will make sure that they never work in Savannah again.

"And did you tell them about my special condition?" Iris asks, turning to the classifieds. "You know how delicate I am," she adds. "Fragrances make me nauseous."

"Yes, Iris. I made them aware," she says, thinking that Iris is about as *delicate* as a piranha.

Fragrances include perfumes and scented body powders, soaps, shampoos, and detergents. Every maître d' in town has been alerted not to sit Iris next to anyone who might fall under the scrutiny of her superior olfactory system.

"What about the Catholic charities meeting tomorrow?" Iris asks. She takes a sip of tea, the sunlight bouncing off the gold inlay of the cup.

"I'll see to it, Iris." Queenie resists rolling her eyes. *It would be more of a charity for Savannah if Iris didn't show up.*

For the privilege of living in the big house and being Iris Temple's companion, Queenie pays a steep price. Among other things, she is required to arrive thirty minutes early to every meeting of the Junior League, the Daughters of the Confederacy, and any other event that Iris Temple is sched-uled to attend to ensure that they are fragrance-free. It's on these days that Queenie feels like little more than a trained bloodhound, sniffing at the heels of Savannah's elite. More than once, she has had to approach a prominent Savannah resident and request she go to the restroom and scrub off expensive fragrances dabbed behind her ears and on her wrists. This seldom goes over well, leaving Queenie to feel blacker than she already is.

Queenie knows how the rich women of Savannah feel about her. She has overheard their whispers, their cutting remarks about her color, her place. No matter what she does, they—like Iris—will never see her as legitimate. They never see her for the woman she is and never think of the burden Queenie carries because of Iris's insistence that she play Prissy to her Scarlett O'Hara to have a decent life.

Yet deep down, Queenie knows that she's more real than any of them and is as entitled to her life as Iris is. She is well aware of what their daddy left behind when he passed over. Not that she's seen a penny of it. Yet Iris has promised to leave her the house when she finally passes to the Great Beyond. And for that, Queenie will tolerate just about anything.

"I smelled one of those horrible dryer sheets, yesterday," Iris begins again, her nose upturned.

Queenie sighs, thinking of her periodic sleuth for scents while strolling the beautiful Savannah square where the Temple house stands. During this surveillance, Queenie must ascertain whether any housekeepers in the area are using scented dryer sheets. If so, said housekeepers risk losing their jobs, and their employers risk having their secrets revealed. Secrets Iris has told them are stored in the bank vault.

As a result, most of Savannah—regardless of race, class, gender, or age—is waiting on Iris Temple to die. If for no other reason, so that life can return to scented bliss. Fantasies of Iris's demise have indeed graced Queenie's thoughts many times. It is time for Iris to step aside so Queenie can head the Temple clan. She looks around the room, thinking of how she might redecorate, adding more color.

"I know it doesn't bother you to smell the dryer sheets," Iris concedes. "But if you were a *true* Temple, you'd understand. You just don't have our level of sophistication."

There it is, Queenie thinks, *as predictable as Old Faithful, and just as full of toxic vapors.*

To distract herself from doing Iris harm, Queenie thinks back to when she came to live with her thirty-five years ago in 1965. She was twenty-two years old when she made this fateful choice. Iris was forty-five. It was Mister Oscar's idea —Iris Temple's husband—that Queenie join the staff because of a particular fondness he had for her. A fondness which extended to the bedroom.

Queenie lifts an eyebrow and studies Iris. *Did she really never know what Oscar was up to right under her nose?*

The Temples are one of the richest families in Savannah, Georgia. Iris's father—also Queenie's father—made a fortune in the invention and production of prosthetics. A generation after his father, a surgeon in the Civil War, removed thousands of limbs that his son seemed destined to replace.

Though Queenie has seen none of the Temple money except for a meager monthly allowance, she and Iris live in a large Victorian house listed on the national registry of historic homes. A house used at the end of the Civil War by Union officers reveling in their victory during General Sherman's March to the Sea. As the story goes, these Union soldiers were told to burn the mansion to the ground, but they refused to do any damage to it, given its rare beauty.

The extinguished torch is now encased in the Temple foyer, where it was left all those many years ago. It is also the house where the present-day Junior League conducts annual house tours to raise money for orphans in a country many of them cannot pronounce, and none would ever dream of visiting.

An oil portrait of Edward Temple, Iris and Oscar's only son, glares at Queenie from across the room. Their daughter Rose's portrait was taken down and stored in the attic twenty-five years before, replaced now by an original Audubon. Queenie keeps in touch with Iris's estranged daughter, Rose, who lives on a horse and cattle ranch outside Cheyenne, Wyoming. Rose has one child, Katie, who graduated from college and now works in Chicago and is Iris's only grandchild, whom she has never met. Queenie pulls a photograph from her pocket that arrived in the morning mail of Rose and Katie in Chicago. She smiles.

"What are you looking at?" Iris asks.

"Nothing, Iris," Queenie says. She slides the picture back into her pocket. Of all the Temples, Queenie likes Rose best. Yet Iris has forbidden Queenie to ever speak of her. Rose's existence has been totally erased. No photographs. No memories. Nothing.

Rose was ten years old when Queenie came to live here, and Edward was seventeen and away at boarding school. Queenie's mother—fondly called Old Sally by everyone who knows her—was still working for the Temples then but would be replaced by Violet in 1980. Violet, Old Sally's granddaughter, spent a lot of time at the Temple house when she was growing up and was Rose Temple's best friend.

Queenie glances at her watch and then at Iris's empty teacup. She always calls her mother after Iris finishes her tea and retires to her bedroom for her morning constitutional—a ritual that easily lasts until noon. Queenie would never call her mother in front of Iris unless she wanted to aggravate her half-sister for the rest of the day. The two women are like fried okra and a dainty watercress sandwich and do not mix.

At one hundred years of age, Queenie's mother, Old Sally, lives on the coast of southernmost South Carolina in a house she has lived in her entire life. She was born in the year 1900 and has seen a century's worth of change. Yet Old Sally still practices the family trade of root doctoring and folk magic in the way her Gullah ancestors did. Just yesterday, she got a call from someone in New York City who is flying to Savannah to have her work her spells and cure their environmental illness. This kind of thing happens all the time. Queenie has never practiced the family trade. Perhaps it is the Temple blood in her that refuses to participate. But her mother is quite versed in it.

Seconds later, Iris screams, and Queenie bolts upright, her book and magazine flying, as Iris's teacup crashes to pieces on the marbled floor. Queenie has never heard Iris screech and has to admit it is an interesting change from the silent roar of her half-sister's delicate constitution.

"What is it Iris, what's wrong?"

Iris's mouth gapes as though she is reading her own obituary. She points a boney, bejeweled finger at a section in the classifieds, her hand shaking.

Queenie comes to Iris's side and leans in to read:

FOUND. One Book of Temple Secrets.
First Secret to be revealed tomorrow.

"Sweet Jesus," Queenie mutters under her breath. "The shit has just hit the fan."

Iris's stomach gurgles in ready agreement.

CHAPTER TWO

Violet

As the grandfather clock in the hallway strikes seven, Violet serves dinner in the grand dining room. Miss Temple sits at the head of the elongated table while her Aunt Queenie takes her place at the far end of the mahogany monster Violet has polished so often she now has tennis elbow without ever lifting a racket. Violet and her aunt have always been close. Like sisters almost, though Queenie is seventeen years older.

The evening meal always looks like a BBC mini-series Violet would never watch. Sepia tones surround an efficient servant (that would be her) serving a grand dame and her half-breed sister elaborate meals while standing nearby to meet their every need. The room is lit by a cumbersome chandelier—one she can only reach with a tall ladder when she dusts—that was an original feature of the house before it was converted to electricity a hundred years earlier. Violet can't imagine what it was like to work here then, yet her ancestors would know. Her grandmother, who people call Old Sally, has told her stories about washing all the clothes and dishes by hand. Violet shudders with the thought.

After she serves Miss Temple her usual bowl of clear broth soup to begin, the meal can easily last a solid hour while her employer grinds every morsel of food to a lifeless pulp to aid her uncooperative digestive system. In contrast, Aunt Queenie finishes her meal while it is still hot—a lovely piece of flounder, with rice and mixed vegetables—which Violet makes separately.

While Violet stands stationed at the door, she remembers her youngest daughter Tia's question to her this morning:

"Mama, when will I have to start working for the Temples?"

Tia is fourteen, and the question shocked Violet. As she told Tia, she will never, *ever*, let either of her daughters work as servants. Never. Violet gives her foot a strong tap now to seal the promise. She will be the last of a long line. Her children will never know what her life has been like, and she is glad. *Never*, she tells herself again, standing straighter. If she can save enough to open her own business, she won't be at this job much longer anyway.

Life is too short to spend it waiting on rich white people, she thinks. At the same time, she is grateful for the job.

When Iris isn't looking, Violet winks a hello to her Aunt Queenie. In return, Queenie gives a brief nod and hides a smile behind her napkin. Queenie makes the entire situation of waiting on Miss Temple bearable. They are like two soldiers in a foxhole together, their fates linked by a common foe.

Shadows grasp the corners of the room, winning out in a tug-of-war with the light. The dark wood of the doors and moldings adds a veil of heaviness to the room. Period furniture, heralding the time the house was constructed, gleam with over a century's worth of lemon oil rubbed into the grain by her ancestors, and now by Violet. History, in this house, is as heavy as the curtains that cover the floor to ceiling windows. Every day, Violet yearns to throw open the curtains and let some fresh air into the rooms. She is convinced air from the last century is still trapped in the corners.

As far as she knows, Miss Temple is the only member of Savannah's upper class who still insists that they dress for dinner. Violet is also the only housekeeper and cook still required, even in the year 2000, to wear a blue uniform with a starched white apron on top and white shoes. A look meant to remind Violet of her place and perhaps the 1940s. As Violet has observed, things are slow to change in the Temple household.

However, on this particular evening, Miss Temple has not changed from the clothes she wore that morning when Violet cleaned up the spilled tea in the sunroom. Something from the newspaper had Miss Temple practically in tears. Not that Violet has ever seen her employer cry. Violet isn't that fond of crying, either, but at least she knows she can do it when a situation warrants. Yet Miss Temple's lack of dinner etiquette strikes her as odd.

Violet lifts an eyebrow to ask Queenie *what's up?*

Queenie shrugs and widens her eyes with the message to stay alert.

No one speaks during meals—another of Miss Temple's dinner rules—so Violet is left to listen to the old grandfather clock ticking away the seconds of her life and the click, click, clicks of silver on china, along with Miss Temple's persistent chewing, accompanied by her guttural rumblings.

Violet pulls a small tincture bottle of vanilla, cinnamon, and ginger root from the pocket of her apron to dab underneath her nose. A scent, oddly enough, Miss Temple never notices. The tincture is the only thing Violet has been able to find to counteract the smell of the potent exotic meats and Miss Temple's occasional reaction to them.

Tonight's reactions are more forceful than usual. Perhaps because of what was in the newspaper this morning. After the first course is finished, Miss Temple lets out a belch found more often at a Georgia Bulldogs game than at the table of one of Savannah's most prominent families.

It remains a mystery what causes Miss Temple's ailments. No matter how many specialists she sees or what radical changes she makes to her diet, her condition does not improve, making Violet believe that it is entirely possible that her grandmother deserves more credit.

"Are you reading during dinner?" Miss Temples barks at Queenie as if she's caught her buying sweatpants at Wal-Mart.

Violet snaps to attention.

"Answer me," she insists. If Violet had the nerve, she would tell Miss Temple to quit being such a bully. But, for now, she can't risk losing her job. Besides, Queenie knows how to take care of herself.

"If you must know, Iris, I was praying," Queenie says.

Miss Temple pauses as if aware that even she can't trump God.

"No need to worry, Iris, I'll put in a good word for you." Queenie glances heavenward, whispers a few words, and then winks at Violet.

In response, Miss Temple's stomach roars like a thunderclap. Anticipating what's next, Violet dabs another application of her tincture to her upper lip. Over the years, Violet has become as adept at reading Miss Temple's dark moods as the experts on the weather channel are at predicting hurricanes. In the current forecast, her employer's stormy disposition has changed from a watch to a warning.

Miss Temple coaxes into her mouth a piece of rattlesnake that Violet sautéed in butter and onions. In the last decade, she has learned to cook things she would have never dreamed would end up in her kitchen. Miss Temple chews with so much vigor it makes Violet's jaws hurt. Her Gullah ancestors would much sooner run from a snake than to eat one. When Violet was a girl, her grandmother told her stories about whip snakes, which were said to bite their tails and roll like a wheel to overcome their victims. At that moment, she pines for her grandmother's stories, as well as her red rice, okra soup, and shrimp and grits. She has come a long way from her Gullah roots, though she's not so sure this is a good thing.

No one expected Miss Temple to live this long. Her physical woes have plagued her since before Violet started working here and have intensified over the years. Meanwhile, Miss Temple's face takes on the color of a confederate gray uniform worn by one of her ancestors in the portrait gallery. Violet is smart enough to fear what is coming, but luckily it doesn't seem to be about the food.

"I was at my attorney's office today trying to sue the newspaper when I received some alarming news of a different nature," Miss Temple says.

Violet and her aunt exchange a quick look.

"Sometimes those closest to us betray us," Miss Temple says, sounding like a Hallmark greeting card gone wrong.

Her eyes narrow and change from tired blue to a steel gray. A pause follows, the distance between lightning and a thunderclap.

Violet fears for Queenie more than herself. Miss Temple can be spiteful when she wants to be, especially to Queenie.

"It seems my attorney has found a most distressing letter," Miss Temple says.

"A letter?" Queenie asks, appearing calm. "From whom?" Both Violet and Queenie know it is safer not to react.

Miss Temple tightens her lips and then wipes her mouth on a silk napkin graced with a prominent monogrammed "T" in gold thread that Violet has laundered and ironed hundreds of times.

"Did everyone know except me?" Miss Temple asks Queenie and then turns the question toward Violet, who takes a step back. It is not like Miss Temple to notice her.

"I've fought my entire life for the recognition I deserve," Miss Temple begins again. "My father would have much preferred his only child to be a son. It doesn't matter that I've solidified the Temple dynasty during my tenure."

Violet has never heard the Temple matriarch talk like this. Does it have anything to do with the threat in the newspaper this morning? Something to do with the secrets?

"Are you okay, Iris?" Queenie asks, as if she, too, has noticed the change.

"I've been thinking about the past more than usual, that's all," she answers. "Nothing good can come of it, of course. It's probably because of those damn secrets."

"Do you want to talk about it?" Queenie asks.

Miss Temple's eyes widen like confiding in Queenie is about as appealing as desegregation. "Must you be so common," she says to Queenie, her words coming out in a huff. "Of course I don't want to talk about it, especially not with someone who isn't a *true* Temple. How could you possibly understand?" She sighs, as though putting Queenie in her place isn't as satisfying as she hoped.

Violet hates it when Miss Temple takes out her frustration on her aunt, and she opens her mouth to tell her so, but Queenie shakes her head to stop her.

"My father was a brilliant man except for sleeping with the servants," Miss Temple begins again. "But I have to put up with you as a constant reminder of his indiscretions. Have you ever thought about what it's like for me to deal with my father's bastard child for over half a century?"

Violet steps closer to defend Queenie, but Queenie shakes her head again. In most cases, it's best to just let Miss Temple's rants play out, like a tea kettle releasing its steam. It doesn't help that someone is threatening to leak secrets to the newspaper. However, this latest news seems to have distracted her from even that.

"Of course it was Oscar's idea," Miss Temple continues. "He could be quite persuasive when he wanted to be." She rubs her temples as though smoothing a splitting headache. "Did I ever tell you that I married him just to make my mother angry? He was from a family of tailors." Iris gives a short laugh. "*Beneath us*, my mother said."

Violet always wondered how Mister Oscar ended up with Miss Temple. He seemed way too nice for her.

According to Queenie, Miss Temple refused to take his name when they married, so she could remain a Temple. She also insisted that Edward and Rose keep the Temple name. Queenie told Violet that Miss Temple treated Mister Oscar's parents horribly, as well. They were never invited to the Temple mansion, and she didn't even attend their funerals.

To Violet, family is sacred. Having never known her parents, she doesn't take family for granted.

"I shouldn't have changed it," Miss Temple says, talking to herself.

"You shouldn't have changed what?" Queenie asks.

Within moments Miss Temple's mood shifts, like the wind has changed direction and the storm downgraded. However, Violet and Queenie know better than to relax just yet.

Miss Temple turns to Violet again. "You are lovely," she says.

Violet stands straighter. Her employer never pays compliments. She gives a quick, "Thank you," wondering what this has to do with a found letter.

As Queenie can attest, to capture Miss Temple's attention is rarely a good thing. She has observed more than one casualty from her employer's venom. Violet thinks of Rose, Miss Temple's daughter, who hasn't returned to Savannah in decades. Venom goes a long way when used to poison a relationship, and Violet never wants to pass on anything like that to her girls.

"Are you married, my dear?" Miss Temple asks her.

Violet looks at her aunt and then back at Miss Temple. Should she refuse to answer?

"Iris, leave her alone," Queenie says, but Miss Temple waves her comment away.

"I'm married to a man named Jack," Violet says, hoping her response will end the tension.

"What does this Jack do?" Miss Temple asks.

"He teaches English at the community college." Violet lowers her eyes.

"Do you have children?" she asks.

Violet hesitates. Then she thinks about how hard it will be to find another job without a reference from Miss Temple.

"Two daughters," Violet says. "Sixteen and fourteen."

Miss Temple looks thoughtful.

Violet's face feels hot, and her heartbeat races. She steps toward Queenie's end of the table, wanting to flee. Under the table, Queenie makes a slight motion with her hand, as if guiding jets onto a tiny aircraft carrier at her feet. In their foxhole, Queenie and Violet have developed a type of Morse code, using a series of eye and subtle hand gestures to relay Miss Temple's moods. If not for the seriousness of the situation, Violet would feel foolish making these gestures.

Meanwhile, Miss Temple scrutinizes Violet, as if overcome with great curiosity. After the main entrée is finished, Violet gathers the empty plates and goes back into the kitchen. She returns with crystal dessert goblets, each filled with a scoop of blackberry sherbet. Violet waits near the kitchen door. Beyond this door is her territory, her safe place. The heightened tension in the room causes goosebumps to rise on her arms. Queenie must feel it, too.

In their agreed-upon mayday signal, Queenie winks twice and jerks her head left, like the return on an old typewriter. Through gestures, Queenie tells Violet to save herself. Violet, however, refuses to abandon Queenie no matter how many times she winks and returns her carriage.

Not only are Violet and Queenie bonded as niece and aunt, but they are close like people who survive natural disasters are close. When Miss Temple has nothing for her to do, Queenie often helps Violet in the kitchen and knows intimate details about her and her husband, Jack, and their two daughters, Tia and Leisha. Sometimes Tia and Leisha come over for the day if they don't have school, and Queenie and the girls have Parcheesi tournaments in the kitchen, just like Violet, Rose, and Queenie did decades before.

After taking her last bite of sherbet, Miss Temple nods, a signal to Violet that she is finished.

As Violet clears the table, Miss Temple pats Violet's hand and thanks her.

Violet swallows a gasp and shoots an alarmed look in Queenie's direction. Miss Temple never touches anyone, especially not a servant. Nor does she thank anyone for anything. If saved from a raging river, Miss Iris Temple of the Savannah Temples would expect her rescuers to thank her for the privilege of keeping her alive. Hubris she may have inherited from her father, a man who supposedly never liked children and made a daily practice of ignoring her. It is this fact alone that helps Violet tolerate her.

Queenie signals for Violet to save herself, but Violet refuses to leave. Miss Temple is up to something big. Something that feels dangerous. After having observed her employer for over twenty years, Violet knows one thing for certain: a predator is still a predator, even with claws retracted.

Miss Temple stands and stares at Violet like she is seeing her for the first time.

"Iris, are you sure you're all right?" Queenie asks. "You've had a big day with the threat of the *Book of Secrets* getting released."

"Of course I'm all right," she says, her tone dismissive. But she doesn't look *all right* at all. This crisis seems to have cracked her hard exterior, at least for now.

Violet and Queenie follow Miss Temple into the foyer, where she announces she's going to bed early because she has a big day tomorrow.

At the base of the grand staircase, Miss Temple gives Violet a quick, tight embrace in a rare act of affection that feels more like a frontal version of the Heimlich maneuver that Violet learned in a Red Cross class. In response, Violet gasps, waiting for her ribs to crack, and then lowers her eyes, wondering if she should be terrified or relieved.

Miss Temple lets out another belch to rival her other emissions for the day and says, "Damn voodoo curse," glancing back like she holds Queenie responsible.

Ascending the spiral staircase, Miss Temple releases a long, slow sigh that sounds like a lonely train whistle fading in the distance.

CHAPTER THREE

Queenie

The next morning Queenie chews a fingernail as she wonders who is behind releasing the coming secrets. Iris picks up the morning paper, skips the society section entirely and goes straight to the classifieds. Queenie lost sleep the night before, worrying that her secret might be the first one revealed. She imagines there are many people in Savannah with this very same fear.

As Iris runs a finger down the column, Queenie covers her ears awaiting the scream but hears a shriek instead. Iris's lips disappear into her scowl.

"Who is doing this?" Iris points at Queenie as if she should know.

Queenie has no idea who is behind it. If she did, she would offer them every penny in her savings account to keep her biggest secret out of the newspaper. Meanwhile, in all the years she's known Iris, she has never seen her this unnerved. In a way, she finds it as refreshing as those scented dryer sheets Iris hates so much.

Iris throws the newspaper at Queenie and pieces cascade to the floor. Despite a personal visit to the head of the paper and another trip to her attorney, the first secret has appeared anyway.

"Get the car," Iris orders. She walks out of the sunroom and climbs the stairs, heavy-footed like a child having her second tantrum in as many days.

Queenie quickly gathers the newspapers and reads the first secret in the classifieds:

Several Savannah patriarchs have mixed-raced children. Contact Iris Temple for more information: 912-944-0455.

Queenie lets out a guffaw to go along with the relief she feels that the secret released is not one of her own. Even though she is of mixed-race, that scandal is old news. Almost immediately, the phone rings in the hallway, and Queenie answers it.

"Keep your damn mouth shut," a male caller says before a loud click severs the call.

"Uh, oh," Queenie says. She'd better warn Violet not to answer the telephone today.

AN HOUR LATER, Queenie sits in the waiting room of Bo Rivers, Iris's attorney, someone who probably has his own share of secrets in Iris's book. Queenie wonders if he's someone who actually might have access. It would be just like Iris to store a copy with her legal representative in case the banks failed. Iris could be a little paranoid sometimes.

Behind a heavy door, Queenie can hear Iris's raised voice and the low mumblings of Bo Rivers as he tries to calm her. Seconds later, Iris appears from behind the door and slams it and then strides past Queenie, who scurries to follow. For an old lady, Iris has some pep. It reminds Queenie of when power walks were in fashion. Not that she ever did one. *Wouldn't want to ruin my girlish figure,* she says to herself and slaps her large hip. She has never understood why white women have to be skinny to be happy. Even Oprah falls for it from time to time.

LATER THAT AFTERNOON, Queenie waits in the grand foyer, where the telephone has not only been unplugged but removed entirely. It is Queenie's job to accompany Iris to the Piggly Wiggly grocery store across town. All household errands are relegated to Queenie, except for one, which Iris insists on doing herself. This errand is to order exotic meats from Spud Grainger, the butcher at the Piggly Wiggly, with whom Iris had a storied affair in the 1970s. An affair—Iris told Queenie after having too much sherry on All Souls Day in 1983—that she blames on an article she read in *Vogue Magazine* concerning the free love movement.

Free love or not, what that man ever saw in her, I will never know, Queenie thinks.

"How do I look?" Iris asks, her scowl softened. She joins Queenie with purse and keys in hand and dabs at her hair as though it might actually move.

"You look, uh, stately," Queenie says. *And pissed,* she thinks, but she's not about to say that to Iris.

"I've decided to put the morning behind me and go to the market as planned," Iris says. Her face twitches, the closest she comes to a smile.

Queenie doesn't voice her skepticism. She's never known the Temples to keep the past behind them, and they have a house full of ghosts to prove it.

Though she can afford a multitude of chauffeurs, Iris insists on driving herself. Queenie follows Iris out the front door and around the side to the carriage house. Although cutting through the kitchen would make much more sense, Iris refuses to use any door that might be considered a servant's entrance.

Once inside the car, Queenie buckles up and says a silent prayer that they reach their destination unharmed. Then she kisses the sweetgrass bracelet her mother gave Queenie for protection. Between the good lord and her mama's Gullah magic, she figures she has her bases covered.

Despite the snail-paced speed, a drive with Iris always proves harrowing. As far as Queenie can tell, Iris has never once used the rear-view or side mirrors on her black Lincoln Town Car. Instead, she uses the sidewalks in town as a kind of bumper car railing, to keep track of the edge of the road. All because Iris is so vain that she refuses to wear her eyeglasses in public. What Iris lacks in accuracy, she makes up for in spite. Anyone she endangers with her recklessness, she deems somehow deserving. Some days it is all Queenie can do to not hang out the window and scream, "Get out of the way!" to unsuspecting pedestrians on sidewalks up ahead.

In the fire lane near the entrance of the Piggly Wiggly, Iris brings the Town Car to an abrupt stop and ejects herself from the car while leaving the engine running. The persistent alarm from inside the Lincoln does nothing to remind Iris that she may want to turn off the car and take the keys out of the ignition. Queenie completes the task and reminds herself that someday she will have to take the car keys away from Iris on a permanent basis, an action she looks forward to about as much as back-to-back root canals. Iris is not the type to give up control of anything, especially large, life-threatening motor vehicles.

With the sophistication of Savannah royalty, Iris enters the Piggly Wiggly. Queenie follows not far behind as store employees exchange their usual looks, as well as a few new ones. Queenie guesses that word has spread about the *Temple Book of Secrets*. Although Savannah is not a small town, it has some similarities. Gossip is savored, chewed, swallowed, and then digested until it comes out the other end as compost, which is then used to create more secrets.

Iris walks down aisle three toward the meat department in the rear of the store. Despite being eighty years of age, her posture is impeccable, as if a flag pole extends from crown to coccyx. And though she is of average height, perhaps five feet, seven inches, she seems much taller than everyone else. Even her wrinkles appear to align themselves properly, and her solid white hair is coiffed to perfection like she and the Queen of England share hairdressers.

Queenie serves no particular function on this outing except to fulfill her half-sisterly duty as a companion and keep her mouth shut. Afterward, she will get her hair washed and relaxed at the Gladys Knight and the Tints Beauty Parlor located in the shopping center adjacent to the Piggly Wiggly, a reward she looks forward to all week.

Iris arrives at the meat counter and gingerly clears her throat to get Spud Grainger's attention. When this doesn't work, Iris crescendos her query from *pianissimo* to *forte*. He turns around, causing Queenie to think: *If there was ever an example of love's blindness, it is Spud Grainger's affection for Iris Temple.*

Their affair began two years after Iris's husband, Oscar,

died unexpectedly of a massive heart attack while in a compromising position in his office with Queenie. Spud Grainger was a bag boy at the Piggly Wiggly at the time and a part-time jazz musician. The affair ended after six months, at Iris Temple's insistence. Heartbroken, it is rumored that Spud Grainger never played the saxophone again.

"My dear Iris Temple," Spud says, his southern accent smooth and lilting. "You get more beautiful every day."

"Oh, Mr. Grainger. How very kind of you." Iris radiates a smile that has received minimal exercise over the years, and her bottom lip quivers with the effort. Once weekly, Queenie marvels at her half-sister's transformation into a somewhat pleasant human being while in Spud Grainger's presence. Not to mention, it is extra impressive that Iris can do this amidst the hullaballoo around the *Book of Secrets*.

Spud Grainger is not a day over sixty and has aged well. A solid white mustache hides his slightly crooked front teeth. He also has an affinity for bow ties. Today's tie is lime green, with thin red stripes that match the beef tips on special, displayed in the glass case in front of him.

At least he doesn't mind a little color, Queenie thinks.

The elegant butcher wipes his hands on his perfectly clean white apron and steps into the aisle to kiss Iris's extended hand. A girlish giggle escapes her octogenarian lips.

When Queenie is unsuccessful in hiding her smile, Iris shoots her a look that could stop a wildebeest in a dead run. No matter how many times she gets these looks from Iris, they always shock her. Iris returns her attention to Spud and her face colors slightly from Spud's consideration. She tilts her head upward as if this noble gesture might command the color to recede. They speak affectionately about the weather.

Damn, y'all, how many different ways can you describe hot?

Queenie wonders, for Savannah is as hot as a furnace in Hades for six months out of the year.

Iris hands Queenie her leather handbag, heavy enough to contain the wildebeest from earlier. As instructed, she reaches inside the bag for a linen envelope containing an order written neatly on Temple stationery. She hands it to Spud Grainger, who thanks her kindly.

Exotic meats, Iris Temple will tell anyone who has the misfortune to ask, are the only thing her delicate, voodoo cursed constitution can tolerate. Whether the strong medicine of these exotic animals is meant to counteract the spell she is at the mercy of, remains a mystery.

Antelope, alligator, buffalo, elk, kangaroo, and ostrich are flown in from all over the world at great expense. Not to mention iguana, llama, rattlesnake, and yak. Exotic animals associated with nursery rhymes or the stars of animated Disney movies Queenie watched with Violet's daughters. Animals that would have fought harder if they knew their capture would result in ending up in Iris Temple's gullet.

Spud Grainger studies the list. He smiles and pets his mustache, as if Iris's exotic orders, as well as her exotic nature, have captivated him.

"The caribou may take a while," he says thoughtfully. "But I'll give Violet a call as soon as it comes in."

A line of Savannah housewives forms behind Iris. Queenie overhears at least one mention of secrets and that Iris should be ashamed of herself. Luckily, Iris doesn't hear them, but that doesn't stop her from eyeing their khaki shorts and New Balance sneakers before inclining her chin heavenward like she's on the trail of an unacceptable scent. She wrinkles her nose and furrows her brow. Though the 4th of July is three months away, Queenie anticipates the upcoming fireworks.

"Chanel," Iris says to Queenie in a whisper that can be heard from the front of the store. The look on Iris's face reveals her complete and utter disgust.

Chanel no. 5, as Queenie has been told countless times, is the fragrance of the terminally middle class. Iris abhors the wannabe rich or any other kind of rich that doesn't involve money that has been around since the Confederacy.

Spud Grainger gives Iris an apologetic look and motions to the line forming behind her. Iris stops mid-sniff and thanks Spud, another kindness reserved only for him. Before leaving, she turns to the gaggle of Savannah housewives and gives them a parting hiss, like the rattlesnake she had for dinner the night before. Queenie offers the women a quick apology, but the final word comes from Iris as she departs. Meanwhile, two children holding a box of Lucky Charms cover their noses and run in search of their mother.

Back at the car, Queenie gives Iris the keys to the Lincoln and Iris drives—at the speed of a handicapped snail—the 500 yards to drop Queenie off at the hairdresser.

"I'll be back in two hours," Iris says. "You'd better be finished."

Queenie nods as the grand matriarch drives off to conduct another errand, running over the curb and missing by inches a stop sign at the end of the parking lot. Queenie never questions the nature of Iris's other errands, but just last week when returning to the car to retrieve her crime novel, she found a bucket of Kentucky Fried Chicken bones crammed under the back seat, the bones picked clean, like an exotic jungle animal had feasted on them while lying on the plush leather seats.

So much for voodoo and special diets, Queenie thought at the time, as she held the bucket of bones and smiled back at Colonel Sanders' emblazoned image. If Iris keeps this up, hardening of the arteries may take her out, but Queenie's not so sure she has the fortitude to wait for natural causes. Although violence isn't really in her nature.

HER HAIR RELAXED AND STYLED, and all the latest gossip discussed—most of which has to do with the *Temple Book of Secrets*—Queenie puts the charge on Iris's bill and waits outside, fanning herself with a real estate flyer pulled from the box in front of the beauty shop. Queenie has only seen the *Temple Book of Secrets* twice, both times while in Oscar's office, before the ledger was moved to the safety deposit box. No matter how much Queenie begged, Oscar refused to let her look at it, saying Iris would kill him, which she probably would have. The book was kept in the bottom desk drawer that locked with a key Oscar kept on his key chain. It was moved to the bank vault a few years after his death.

Within minutes, the shiny black Lincoln rounds the corner, rolls over the sidewalk, and hits a green trash can that bounces off a silver Toyota wagon before coming to rest at the north end of the parking lot.

"Good lord, this woman is an accident waiting to happen," Queenie mutters.

Queenie is an excellent driver herself. Oscar, Iris's husband, taught her when she was sixteen in an equally big Lincoln Continental. In exchange for the driving lessons, she agreed to climb into the back seat with him and show him her breasts. At the time, this gesture seemed a small price to pay to use the Temple cars. *Of course, this is a secret I doubt ever made it into Iris's precious book.* But others might have. She wishes now she had caught a glimpse of that secret book, but Iris keeps the key to the deposit box locked up, too.

If Queenie's own secrets are revealed in the classifieds, she might be looking for a new place to live. She gulps with the thought. While some southerners follow the motto: *What would Jesus do?*—seen on car bumper stickers as *W.W.J.D?* —Queenie is more prone to ask *W.W.O.D.? What would Oprah do?* Having watched nearly every episode of Oprah since the early 90s, Queenie's best guess is that her hero would put a team of lawyers to work on it. Unfortunately, Queenie doesn't have that kind of money.

The Town Car rounds the final corner and veers in Queenie's direction as if Iris is playing a game of geriatric "chicken." Queenie debates whether to jump aside but decides to hold her ground.

"Just try it, old lady," Queenie says, her teeth gritted in determination. She locks her ample knees in place, grateful she has some substance to her. "If it's my fate to go to the Great Beyond at the hand of that smelly witch, then so be it," she adds. "But I refuse to be the first one to flinch."

The Lincoln lurches twice before screeching to a halt and then stops only inches away from Queenie. So close that heat drifts from the engine and further relaxes her hair. Queenie gets inside and slams the door while Iris's wrinkled lips glisten in the sunlight from her latest rendezvous with the Colonel. The grease relaxes her face like a kind of Botox injection while the smell of his secret recipe of eleven herbs and spices permeates the closed car.

After several attempts, Iris coerces the Town Car into drive and hits the curb three times before reaching the main road, causing a family of four to frantically scatter into the good hands of an Allstate Insurance office.

"God in heaven," Queenie shrieks. "Watch where you're going!"

"Keep your commandments to yourself," Iris says with a sneer.

ON THE SLOW RIDE HOME, instead of worrying what secrets of hers might end up in the newspaper—a legitimate concern—Queenie entertains herself by daydreaming of Iris Temple's accidental death while choking on one of the Colonel's chicken bones.

CHAPTER FOUR

Violet

Violet rubs her left shoulder that has ached all morning. The day before her daughter Tia broke her leg in 4th grade, this same shoulder predicted it. It happened before Mister Oscar—Miss Temple's husband—died, too. Since she was a girl, Violet has known her arm is hooked into a higher level of consciousness. As a result, the minute it begins to ache, she automatically breaks into a sweat.

A sense of urgency accompanies her drive to the Temple house as she wipes a thin layer of perspiration from her upper lip. She has taken this route through Savannah hundreds of times, yet something about this morning feels different. Nearing the house, a blast of pain radiates up her arm. She rubs it and sighs her anguish.

"What are you trying to tell me?" she asks.

Anyone who heard her talking to a body part would

assume she was crazy. *But I guess I'm only crazy if I hear it talk back.* Violet smiles despite the pain, as the throbbing continues. Meanwhile, she catches every traffic light and is still five minutes away from the Temple mansion.

When Violet pulls her car into the carriage house, the throbbing intensifies, and her blouse is soaked straight through. Her deodorant works overtime as she turns off the car and gets out. Even though she grew up in Savannah and has never lived anywhere else, to go from air-conditioning to the sweltering Georgia heat is shocking at first, like stepping into a pre-heated oven.

After she walks into the kitchen, she stands still and listens, purse still in hand. The house seems quieter than usual. Violet has the family *sensitivity*, as her grandmother calls it, a sense of invisible things, like the different entities in the Temple house. Now that the *Temple Book of Secrets* has been in the news, the ghostly presences have seemed especially strong. Violet can usually tell where the spirits are that live in the house, by the energy they give off. It's like tuning into a distant radio station. Violet turns her head to intuit her next move while the entire house appears to be holding its breath.

"What's going on?" she asks any spirits listening. She's never known them to answer back. *But there's a first time for everything,* she tells herself.

Having read once that so-called *sensitives* often come from tragic backgrounds, Violet wonders if her psychic ability has anything to do with her being an orphan. She has no memory of her mother, who died in an automobile accident when Violet was a baby, and she never met her father, who left town when he found out her mother was pregnant with Violet. For whatever reason, her grandmother never speaks of either of her parents. And even though her grandmother and her Aunt Queenie raised her, at times, Violet feels all alone in the world.

Now that she thinks about it, her Aunt Queenie seems worked up about that secret book, too. While Violet used to always retrieve the newspaper from the front porch, it is now Queenie who gets it before she even arrives.

Mysteries are everywhere, she thinks. But this is nothing new.

Out of habit, she checks the kitchen counter for the note Miss Temple always leaves. In the two decades Violet has worked there, her employer has critiqued every meal, leaving detailed feedback on Temple stationery for Violet every morning. In all that time, she's never been told she did a good job. If something is prepared well, it simply isn't mentioned. To Violet's credit, Miss Temple's communications have become shorter over the years, but she doesn't know what to think about there not being a note at all. She looks around the floor to see if it might have dropped. Sometimes if the Temple ghosts get rowdy in the middle of the night, things get moved. But nothing is there.

After retrieving two aspirin from the cabinet, she fills a glass with water, takes the pain reliever, and then glances at the clock. Queenie is usually already downstairs by the time Violet gets here, but not this morning. Her shoulder tells her again that something isn't right.

Violet leaves the kitchen and walks into the dining room. With every step, her shoulder tells her she is getting closer to whatever she needs to find, like in a childhood game of hot and cold. She steps into the grand foyer, which could use a touch up with the dust mop.

"Queenie?" she calls. "Miss Temple?" She waits and listens again. The only sound is her old friend, the large grandfather clock ticking in the entryway that smells of the lemon oil she rubbed into the wood yesterday.

Upstairs, Queenie's bedroom door opens and then slams. "Is that you, Queenie?" Violet calls.

Queenie steps to the railing wiping her eyes.

"My heavens, that's the deepest I've slept in years," Queenie says. "You would have thought I took one of mama's elixirs."

Violet exhales her relief. "With all these nuts worked up about those secrets, I was worried," she says.

"There's still plenty to worry about," Queenie says. "For one thing, Iris is going to give me hell for sleeping so late. Is she in the sunroom yet?"

"I haven't heard a peep out of her," Violet says.

They turn to look in the direction of Miss Temple's room at the end of the hallway.

"Maybe she's overslept, too," Violet says.

"That wouldn't be like her," Queenie says. "She's usually up at dawn doing her calisthenics on the balcony." Queenie approaches Miss Temple's room and knocks on the door. "Iris?" Queenie says.

Violet winces as her shoulder sends her an urgent message that perhaps she relaxed too soon. "Be careful," she calls after Queenie. She waits downstairs in the middle of the foyer as Queenie knocks again and then slowly opens the door.

"God in heaven!" Queenie shouts, disappearing into Iris's room.

Holding her shoulder, Violet runs up the stairs to find Queenie shaking Miss Temple, who lies lifeless on the bed.

"She's not waking up, Vi." Queenie's voice sounds an octave higher than usual. "All this mess about the *Temple Book of Secrets* has gone and pushed her over the edge."

Violet has never heard Queenie sound this frantic, and it scares her. She seems to be the one over the edge. Moving closer, Violet notes Miss Temple isn't breathing. The left side of her face droops like it has somehow melted from the heat. Violet dials 911 from the telephone by the bed. She gives the address to the operator, who assures her that someone is on their way. Meanwhile, Queenie is giving Miss Temple mouth-to-mouth resuscitation, evoking Jesus and Oprah as she pumps her chest.

"Don't you dare die on me, you old witch," Queenie says.

Given how Miss Temple has treated Queenie over the years, Violet considers her care heroic.

"Help is on the way," Violet says to Queenie, who repeats the message to Miss Temple.

"She's been so stressed about those silly secrets," Queenie says. "Plus, all that reminiscing and speaking in riddles last night at dinner. And asking you all those questions? What was that about?"

"I don't know, but look," Violet says.

A note rests on the nightstand that is written in Miss Temple's handwriting. In all capital letters, it reads: MAKE APPT TO SEE BO RIVERS ASAP. CHANGE THE WILL!

"Do you know anything about this?" Queenie asks.

"Nothing," Violet says. "But it looks like that's one appointment Miss Temple won't be keeping, at least not today."

Sirens approach in the distance and stop in front of the house. Violet runs downstairs and opens the door for paramedics. As abruptly as it started, the pain in her shoulder stops. In the next instant, she feels the whole house breathe, the Temple spirits offering a collective sigh of relief.

CHAPTER FIVE

Rose

Y*ou finally got your way, Mother, I've come home.*

Rose Temple pulls the rental car in front of the Temple house and takes in its stoic presence. Despite the car air conditioning running on high, she begins to sweat. Courage is called for, but it is also mid-April in Savannah, and temperatures are already approaching ninety degrees. When she left her house in Wyoming that morning, there were eighteen inches of snow on the ground.

It has been twenty-five years since Rose returned home to Georgia. In its grandeur, the house she grew up in always seems unapproachable to her, an architectural replica of her mother. It belongs to an earlier time, when gentlemen strolled the squares with ladies wearing bonnets and carrying parasols, mirroring the aristocracy of Europe. The house rests among mature palm trees, magnolias and live oaks. Spanish moss clings to the oaks and waves in the warm breeze. The pink camellias, having already dropped their blooms, make way for abundant pink, white, and red azaleas that hold onto their last blossoms of the season as if to prove their resilience. She could use some of this resilience herself right now.

Rose gets out of the car, and it feels good to move. After spending the entire day sitting in cars, airports, and planes, her back has been complaining.

A small group of tourists stand on the sidewalk and look up at the house.

"Hey, do you live here?" a lady asks. Short, perky, and middle-aged, she wears a T-shirt that reads: *I Heart Savannah.*

"I used to live here," Rose says. "A long time ago."

"I can't even imagine," the lady says. She nudges her friend with an elbow as if Rose is some kind of celebrity.

Just because you grew up in a mansion doesn't mean you had a happy childhood, Rose wants to tell the woman. Yet, there were moments of her childhood that were incredibly happy. They just didn't involve her family.

Five days ago, Rose received a frantic phone call from Queenie at six in the morning. Rose's mother was unconscious, having suffered a massive stroke. Queenie had gone into a long explanation over the phone about how the *Temple Book of Secrets* had caused her mother's collapse. In a weird way, it made sense that her mother might fall on the same sword she'd been wielding all these years.

Rose considered not coming to her mother's death bed. After all, she lives far enough away that she almost has a legitimate excuse. But for some reason, she feels the need to see her mother one last time. For closure, if nothing else.

The Temple mansion looms above her. In the shadow of the live oaks, Rose feels herself become more protective.

Twenty-five years ago, she broke off contact with her mother for reasons of self-preservation. Given the amount of inheritance she chose to forgo, most people would not understand her choice. Luckily, her husband, Max, had spent enough time with her mother to understand and be supportive.

After walking through the black wrought-iron gate to the east side of the house, Rose follows the groomed pathway through the garden. She pauses outside the kitchen door, looking back over the mature landscaping and dense shade sprinkled with handfuls of sunlight.

"God, I've missed shade," she says aloud. She could have saved a fortune on sunscreen and moisturizer if she'd never moved to Wyoming.

The magnolias emit an aroma reminiscent of her childhood. The garden, lush with growth, resonates with vibrancy. This is the part of the house that Rose was always drawn to. As a girl, she imagined it her secret garden after she read the book by the same name. The garden is hidden from the street and has a high brick wall around it.

A stone fountain graces the east wall, an impish looking gargoyle spouting water from its center. Moss covers the stones at its base and climbs upward, a green beard stretching to connect with the face. Koi fish live in the broad base of the fountain and flash like golden gemstones through the murky green water. Sounds of the trickling water almost lull Rose into the belief that nothing bad could happen here.

The salty smell of the sea travels on the breeze. Compared to the dry air of Cheyenne, Savannah drips with moisture. It clings to Rose and pulls her clothes close. She closes her eyes and takes in the faint smell of salt water, the ocean only a few miles away. Whenever she smells the sea, she thinks of Old Sally. She wants to see her again.

Rose fans her overheated face and chides herself for

forgetting about the heat. It is too hot for blue jeans, a cotton shirt, and her cowboy boots. At least she left her Stetson at home. Her clothes help her remember who she is now. She isn't the lost young artist who left here twenty-five years ago. She is the woman who co-owns a thousand-acre ranch and sells her art in a prominent gallery in Santa Fe. Yet as soon as Rose exited the plane in Savannah, she felt herself weaken. It is as if her past has been waiting in the baggage area to be claimed, and she is now saddled with it again.

Memories greet her everywhere. She looks up at her mother's bedroom window, half expecting to see her standing there. In the heat, a chill crawls her spine. Walking the garden path, she takes in the regal live oak she played under as a child that stands in the center of the garden. Branches of the oak are as thick as entire cottonwood trees at home. The oak's massive limbs touch the ground in places. The roots rise up to greet the limbs, and it is hard to tell which are which. Moss carpets cover the ground underneath. As a girl, Rose and her best friend, Violet, created a doll hospital under this tree. They made beds out of twigs and moss and wrapped bandages around her doll's arms and legs and spent hours nursing the dolls back to health. Perhaps she gave them the care she never got from her mother.

Don't start this, she tells herself. *No pity parties allowed.* She forces herself to stand straighter.

Near the carriage house, someone moves out of the deep umber and forest green shadows. Rose emits a slight gasp, but when the man smiles—looking pleased to have startled her—she realizes it is her brother, Edward. His hair graying at the temples makes him look distinguished, and his clothes convey the same attitude. Even Edward's smile is a tool of intimidation.

"Should have known you'd show up," he says. Edward, who is six years older, puts his hands on his hips as if to reinforce his dominance.

Rose and her brother have never been close. The last time she saw him was two decades earlier at the Denver airport during a two-hour layover for a flight from Los Angeles.

"I suppose you've come back to make sure you don't miss out on the inheritance," he says with a smirk. Even in middle age, he has managed to throw Rose off balance. But she has no intention of letting him know.

"Actually, I've come to pay my respects," she says.

"Right," he says. "I know exactly how much you respect our lovely mother."

His sarcasm sounds so much like their mother, he could be channeling her.

Don't let him get to you, Rose tells herself. She's only been back to Savannah for an hour, and already she's talking to herself.

When they were young, she did her best to avoid Edward. She wishes she could avoid him now.

"You haven't changed," Rose says.

He tucks his light blue oxford shirt into his tailored navy pants. Does he think her comment is about his boyish figure?

A ghost of a memory taps her on the shoulder, and she remembers another sword that has nothing to do with secrets. Rose glances at her left hand where the tip of her little finger used to be, severed at the first joint forty years before. She lost it when she was almost five years old, Edward ten. He convinced her to play Cowboys and Indians. Rose was the Indian.

"We had some good times in this garden, didn't we?" Edward's smirk changes to a smile that appears almost genuine.

Is he serious? she wonders. "I don't remember them as good times," she says to him. "You used to lock me in the garden shed."

"It was the stockade," he says. "You were an Indian. It was where you belonged." He smiles again.

Interesting that he would bring up belonging, she thinks. For the last twenty-five years, she hasn't felt like she belonged anywhere.

"You had no business getting Grandpa Edward's sword," Rose says. It has taken her forty years to address her brother's recklessness.

Their grandfather's collection of weaponry dated back to the Civil War. Elaborate cases for these weapons extended down a hallway in the back wing of the house. Old Sally always mumbled to herself when she polished the dark wood of the cases, saying incantations to protect her from the evil these weapons had been used for.

"Oh, come on, it was fun," he says.

"Fun?" she asks. *Since when is severing body parts—even small ones—fun,* she wonders.

"When you tattled to Mother, she smiled, remember? It was weird the things that would get her attention." He laughs as though it is a treasured memory. A treasured memory that gave Rose nightmares for years.

A scream replays in her mind. A scream that brought Old Sally flying out the kitchen door, and sent Edward running back into the house. She wrapped her hand tight in a kitchen towel and ran with Rose in her arms all the way to the doctor's office, several blocks away. Whenever her various therapists asked for her earliest memory, it was always this one she recalled.

Old Sally kept the fingertip wrapped in wax paper in the freezer. A week later, she and Queenie, with Violet still in a stroller, gave a funeral for it in the garden. Queenie sang a moving rendition of *Swing Low, Sweet Chariot*, while Old Sally unwrapped the wax paper to reveal the severed fingertip. Before its internment, she poured a black root concoction over it and said a spell. As far as Rose knows, the tiny bone is still buried under the live oak in between two of the most prominent roots.

"It wasn't that bad," Edward says, glancing at her hand. "Simply a casualty of war."

"We weren't at war, Edward," Rose says.

"Weren't we?" Edward asks. "Mother and Father pitted us against each other."

Now that she thinks about it, they did. Their parents were embroiled in their own version of the War Between the States, and Rose and Edward were required to take sides. It was like each parent took a hostage while they were growing up. Perhaps to take the focus off how unsuited they were for each other. Edward was her mother's favorite, and Rose was her father's.

The Temple women were never good at nurturing their offspring. Although her relationship with her daughter, Katie, is a healthy one, it is mostly due to Queenie and Old Sally's influence. It also helped that Rose refused to be anything like her mother.

Her father was the kind one, the gentle one, to the extent that someone pickled in bourbon could be. He died during her freshman year at Smith, and she skipped an entire semester to grieve. Yet her mother's pending death seems entirely different. Rose's grief at never having her mother's love has filled much of her life already. In fact, her mother's impending death almost feels like a relief. At the very least, it will mark an end to Rose's lifelong dubious hope that her mother might become a different person—someone who is kind, loving, and tolerant.

For as long as Rose can remember, Edward wanted their mother to be proud of him. Unfortunately, she valued ruthlessness in her males, and even as a boy, he tried to become what she prized.

"Don't think you can waltz in here after twenty-five years and get any of Mother's money," Edward says, his words pulling her out of the past. "I'm the one who stuck around and protected her interests."

In your endless pursuit of her approval, Rose thinks.

However, before Rose can respond, Edward exits the garden and gets into a silver Mercedes next to the carriage house. For several seconds she waits for her breathing to return to normal. She didn't anticipate seeing Edward, at least not right away, and it has shaken her. Facing her mother again was a big enough challenge already.

What will it be like to see her mother again? She was her daughter Katie's age when she last saw her, and now she is middle-aged. Rose can't imagine she will derive pleasure from her mother's vulnerability. When both parents die, you realize you are next in line.

Rose wishes her husband, Max, hadn't been needed at the ranch. Max is the antithesis of Edward. A solid, kind man who can make sense of things. Though she wonders if anyone can make sense of her family.

Rose takes another deep breath telling herself to relax. After all the therapy she's had, at least she's learned to breathe. When she's calm again, she continues through the garden to the kitchen door. It feels odd to knock at the door she used daily for the first two decades of her life. A woman answers, of early middle-age and with a glowing smile. At first glance, Rose thinks it is Queenie, but then she realizes it is Violet, who was four years younger than Rose yet a best friend for most of Rose's childhood.

"Should we do the Sea Gypsy handshake?" Violet asks.

"Oh my, I haven't thought of that for years," Rose says, returning the smile.

As girls, Rose and Violet created a secret society called the Sea Gypsies, complete with secret handshakes and rituals. Rose and Violet decided that Queenie was the Sea Gypsy *queen,* and they were princesses. Up until then, Queenie's name had been Ivy. One entire summer, they wore only blue clothing because it was the sacred Sea Gypsy color. For years she has added that color to everything she paints, if only a single brushstroke.

Old Sally made them all special swimming caps with sparkling blue, green, and silver sequins. She still has that old swimming cap back home in Wyoming. This is part of the past that she doesn't mind remembering.

Violet, a pretty child, has now blossomed into a striking woman. With skin the color of coffee with extra cream, she looks like a walking advertisement for the Coppertone perfect tan. In comparison, Rose feels old and leathery. The Wyoming dryness and long winters have done nothing to preserve the little bit of beauty she thought she possessed in her 20s and 30s.

In her early years, Rose spent hours in the kitchen with Old Sally, Queenie, and Violet. Old Sally seemed to be raising everybody in those days. Then Violet came to work for Rose's family shortly after Rose's father died, and it got a little strange. Plus, Rose went away to college to major in art and to avoid her mother. She soon figured out ways not to come home. Friends in New York and Boston invited her to stay for the holidays. Friends whose families impressed

Rose's mother enough that she didn't complain. During that time, Rose and Violet somehow lost touch.

Violet ushers Rose into the kitchen, and the two women have an awkward moment of deciding whether or not to embrace. The embrace wins out.

"It must be strange to be back," Violet says.

"You don't know the half of it," Rose says, remembering Edward's appearance in the garden.

Rose glances around the kitchen. She has fond memories of this room. Except for newer appliances, and a darker shade of taupe on the walls, it has changed very little in the last twenty-five years. Her kitchen at home is chaotic. Dishes need washing, the mail is stacked to read, and groceries need to be bought. Rose forgets how smooth things run when someone else is in charge of a house—someone whose entire job is to maintain order and keep things running smoothly.

What a luxury, Rose thinks, although she lived with this luxury the first twenty years of her life.

"I spent most of my childhood in this kitchen," Rose says. "How is Old Sally? The last I heard, she was still going strong."

"Grandmother just turned one hundred," Violet says. "We had a birthday party for her last month. She lives in the same place on the coast."

"I'd love to see her while I'm here," Rose says. "Is Queenie around?"

Their conversation, though warm, feels hesitant, as if the past is scrambling to catch up with the present.

"She's in her room," Violet says. "She's been looking forward to seeing you."

"Any change with Mother?" she asks, realizing she has relegated her main reason for coming to an afterthought.

"I'm sorry, there's not," Violet says. "They're bringing her home from the hospital in an hour. She'll have a nurse, 24 hours a day until..." Violet pauses, as though concerned about being insensitive.

"Until she dies?" Rose asks.

Violet nods and lowers her eyes.

Should Rose tell Violet that the possibility of Rose's mother's death holds no emotional charge for her? In a way, it's like her mother has already been dead for twenty-five years. But Rose hesitates to reveal this to someone she is just getting to know again, even if she is a Sea Gypsy.

"Evidently, your mother left detailed instructions on how to conduct her final days," Violet continues. "She made lists of things to be done in the event of her incapacitation, as well as instructions about her funeral."

"She thought she might get decapitated?" Rose asks, confused.

Violet laughs. "No, silly. *In*capacitation, not *de*capitation."

Rose rolls her eyes at her mistake and laughs, too. It feels good to laugh at such a serious moment.

"I guess I'm more jet-lagged than I realized," Rose says. She set the alarm for four that morning so she could leave the house by six and get to the Denver airport by eight. Weary doesn't begin to describe how she feels.

"I saw Edward in the garden," Rose says, her pinkie vibrating with the memory.

"What was he doing in the garden?" Violet asks. "I didn't even know he was in town."

"He's good at lurking," Rose says. "He probably appointed himself as head of my welcoming committee."

The look on Violet's face confirms that no love is lost between her and Edward.

"Your mother's stroke has been bad enough," Violet says.

"Edward sure doesn't help things. He's like a vulture circling."

Footsteps approach, the kitchen door swings open, and it's like the sun breaks through thick clouds.

"I thought I heard you," Queenie says, her smile aimed right at Rose.

Seeing Queenie is like coming home to the best part of Rose's past. Queenie wears a flower print dress of bright pink and orange. Colors so vivid it looks like they might attract hummingbirds.

I wouldn't dream of wearing something so alive, Rose thinks. But just being around Queenie again makes her wonder if she should try.

"Sweet Jesus, there's a cowgirl in the kitchen," Queenie says, slapping her thigh.

Rose welcomes Queenie's embrace—a woman who was more like a mother to her than anyone else. On her desk at home is a framed photograph of Queenie carrying her around after she was born, a twelve-year-old toting a baby. She is the one person in Savannah that Rose has kept in close contact with, having exchanged letters several times a year for over two decades.

When they end their embrace, Queenie pulls Violet into their circle, and they are all young again and inseparable. Yet as much as Rose wants to relax into their reunion, the closeness feels almost unbearable. It is too much of what she's missed. Too much of what will be hard to leave again.

"How's Mother?" Rose asks as if she knows the question will serve to separate them. It does.

"I talked to her doctor this morning," Queenie says. "He says she doesn't have much time left."

"Do they think she'll wake up again?" Rose asks.

"Unlikely," Queenie says. "But you never know with Iris.

She's probably writing a letter to God on Temple stationery as we speak. She hasn't given all that money to Catholic charities for nothing." Queenie lets out a cackle that makes Rose laugh. There was a lot of laughter in her childhood. She has missed that, too.

"I'm sure it's not the way Mother would have wanted to go," Rose says, serious again.

Queenie agrees. "To lose all control must be killing her." She lifts an eyebrow at her choice of words. "You know how much your mother likes to be in charge," she adds.

"That's the understatement of the century," Rose says, putting her purse on the kitchen table.

"Perhaps the millennium," Violet says.

They pause as if each realizes how much Rose's mother would disapprove.

"They're bringing Iris home this afternoon," Queenie says. "Her wishes were to die here, and it would be just like Iris to haunt me after she's gone if I don't follow her requests to the letter."

"The famous Temple deathbed requests," Rose says. "I'd forgotten about those."

"She wouldn't be the first apparition to live here," Violet says. She glances up like she's listening for confirmation.

Queenie clucks her agreement.

"I can't say that I've missed the ghosts," Rose says. "There's nothing quite like seeing your dead great-grandfather in the garden on your way to school. Of course, he seemed harmless enough, but it was always a little startling when he first showed up."

"He's the one with the surgeon's bag, right?" Violet asks. "He's always out by the oak tree."

"He was a doctor during the Civil War," Rose says. "When my mother was a little girl, he was ancient and told her stories about the war. He said he had sawed off more limbs than all the limbs on that live oak in the garden."

"That's why Iris refused to go near that old tree," Queenie says. "She told me once that she always imagined amputated arms and legs dangling from its limbs."

It occurs to Rose that only in Savannah would the first real conversation she's had in twenty-five years include an update on the Temple ghosts. From Rose's experience, sometimes the living can be scarier than the dead. In a way, her mother has haunted Rose her entire life.

It's also been years since Rose thought of curses and spells and the magical Gullah arts. When she was a girl, Old Sally told her stories that intrigued her, about how Old Sally's grandmother was a slave owned by the Temples, as was her mother before her. Old Sally's mother was the first woman in her family born free, and she was very proud of that fact.

Rose has never told anyone that her ancestors owned slaves. Not even Max. It is Rose's secret. Growing up, she related much more to being owned than to being an owner. Sometimes she still feels like she's waiting to be liberated. Maybe that's part of the reason she's here.

"You look like you're a million miles away," Violet says.

"I was." Rose turns to look at her and Queenie. "Remember that time when I was six, and I covered myself with mud from the garden to darken my skin?"

Queenie laughs. "You wanted to be black like Mama and me," she says.

"I thought you were magical," Rose begins. "Old Sally knew all these Gullah potions and spells, and you had these deep roots that extended all the way back to Africa," Rose says.

"I'll never forget the look on Mama's face when you

showed up in the kitchen," Queenie says. "She laughed until tears came and was still laughing when she put you in the bathtub. Remember that?"

"She was always so patient with me," Rose says, thinking of how much she looks forward to seeing Old Sally again. But first, she needs to play the dutiful daughter for one last time.

CHAPTER SIX

Violet

M iss Temple would not like that Rose is back home, standing in her kitchen, which makes no sense to Violet given how kind Rose is. Violet remembers why she and Rose were friends now. Unlike some in Savannah, she doesn't see color as a reason to reject someone.

"Have you told Rose about our latest drama in the newspaper?" Violet asks Queenie. Her aunt has been acting strange the last several days. She practically races Violet to be the first one to grab the newspaper off the porch. Then the rest of the day, she mumbles about who must be behind telling the secrets.

"You mean someone is still releasing secrets from that old book?" Rose asks.

"One a day," Queenie says. "At this rate, whoever it is will be at it for years." Queenie's eyes widen.

"Mother must have had a fit when this first started," Rose says.

"Actually, she had a stroke," Queenie says, with a grimace.

Violet retrieves the newspaper from the counter and reads Rose today's entry:

> **Temple Secret: Downtown Jewelry Shop**
> **Does Money Laundering for Millionaires.**
> **Contact Reeves Bartow.**

"Do the Bartows still live here?" Rose asks. "I was in school with the son."

"He's probably calling his attorney as we speak," Queenie says. "All of Savannah is standing in line to file lawsuits. And nobody can figure out who is doing it."

"God, I hope I don't have any secrets in there," Rose says, her brow creased.

"Me, too," Violet says, although her only secret is how much she hates working for Miss Temple, and she doubts that is newsworthy. "Would you believe I found a designer poop bag at the front door this morning filled with doggie you-know-what?" Violet says, wondering why she's using *you-know-what* for its actual contents.

"Who would do something like that?" Rose asks.

"No telling," Violet says. "But I just thought you should know in case someone approaches you."

"It's probably good Mother's in a coma," Rose says. "She couldn't bear to see the Temple family name tarnished."

"She brought it on herself," Queenie says. "That *Book of Secrets* was how she kept everybody in line. Including me."

"This morning, I pulled a couple of posters from the

fence," Violet says, "with not very flattering pictures of Miss Temple."

"That's the least of it," Queenie says. "You should have heard some of the phone calls."

Aware of how tired Rose looks, Violet interrupts: "Let's get your things," she says, taking Rose's arm. "Unfortunately, our resident ghosts don't carry luggage from the car. But I can do that. Then you can settle in a bit before your mother arrives."

"I can get my own luggage," Rose says, but Violet insists.

Violet retrieves Rose's suitcase and then ascends the spiral staircase toward Rose's old bedroom. Violet has trudged up and down these stairs thousands of times. At least it keeps her legs in shape. She's also memorized every detail of the maroon carpet runners on the wooden steps, the polished banisters, as well as the Temple portraits lining the walls. As girls, whenever the Temples weren't around, Violet and Rose slid down the railings as the Temple ancestors watched in framed silence. They watch her now. Do they remember Rose?

Violet meets Rose at the doorway to Rose's room as Rose places her suitcase on the bed. Violet seems to always be standing in doorways these days as if tempting herself to exit from the Temple lives for good. Rose's bedroom is frozen in time from before Rose left for college. The dark antique furniture, too heavy for a child's room, makes Violet feel claustrophobic whenever she cleans in here. The furniture and heavy draperies over the windows do their best to suck the oxygen from the room.

"I'm surprised she kept my room intact," Rose says. "I noticed my portrait was gone from downstairs."

Violet doesn't tell Rose that when Violet started working here, Miss Temple forbid her to ever speak Rose's name. But she did keep the room as it was. Over the years, Violet has discovered that Miss Temple is as complicated as her meal choices.

"I forgot how dark this room is," Rose says. "I could never paint in here."

"Do you still paint?" Violet asks. Rose was quite good by the time she went away to college.

"I do still paint," Rose says. "Mostly Western scenes now, but I'd love to paint more of the landscape around here."

Violet's creative side comes out in her cooking and baking. She walks over to the window and tries to open it, but it won't budge. A large crepe myrtle twists upward outside the second-story window. At least the blossoms offer a touch of cheerfulness to the drab room. As girls, they rarely spent time here and played in the kitchen or in the garden while her grandmother worked.

"It looks like a museum or something," Rose says. "No wonder I could hardly wait to leave home."

Violet resists confessing that she can hardly wait to leave, too.

"I'm surprised a security guard isn't stationed at the door to make sure I don't touch anything," Rose says.

"I can get you one if you want," Violet says, and they both laugh.

A small photograph of Rose and her mother at Rose's college graduation sits atop her antique bureau. Rose looks sullen in it, as she always did when photographed with her mother. Miss Temple doesn't look that thrilled, either, her chin tilted upward in typical Temple fashion. As teenagers, Rose talked to Violet about how she was a constant disappointment to her mother. That's also when their friendship began to fade.

Queenie calls from the foyer that the ambulance has arrived.

"Should I go downstairs and greet her?" Rose asks.

"It's up to you," Violet says. "She won't know the difference." *Or will she?* Violet thinks.

Violet follows Rose downstairs, where two men wait with a stretcher next to Queenie. Strapped onto the stretcher covered with a white blanket, Miss Temple appears small and vulnerable, the opposite of the critical force she usually is.

Violet, Queenie, and Rose follow the men carrying Miss Temple upstairs. It feels ceremonial, in a way, as if they are practicing for the funeral, not that Violet would be part of the procession. Violet never knew her own mother, so she can't imagine what this is like for Rose. She imagines it is like witnessing a fire-breathing dragon whose flame is going out. She is surprised her arm isn't hurting since it usually announces a death or injury. Does this mean Miss Temple isn't ready to die?

Two technicians join the crowd in Miss Temple's bedroom to set up the various machines. A hospital bed is where the four-poster antique used to be.

"Mother won't like this," Rose says to Violet and Queenie. "She would want to die in a Temple bed."

"I know," Queenie says. "But this is the only way her doctor would agree to let us bring her home."

Even the Temple beds have lineages. Miss Temple was born in the same bed in which her grandmother and grandfather died. Working for Miss Temple meant Violet had to know the history of every piece of furniture in the house as if it somehow might make her dust and polish everything with more care.

Why anyone would want to sleep where numerous relatives

have died is beyond me, she thinks. At the very least, it verges on weird. But to Miss Temple, tradition trumps weird. Tradition trumps everything.

Stories about the Temples are given on every carriage ride tour that passes the house. Most famously, the story of Rose's great grandfather, one of the more eccentric Temples, who took to his deathbed, requesting a final visit from his pet pig, Salty. According to legend, Salty lived on the Temple family's plantation near Charleston and was transported the hundred miles between Charleston and Savannah and led up the stairs to say his final goodbyes.

Violet overheard Miss Temple tell Queenie one day about how much she liked that "dumb old pig."

Evidently the same evening the grandfather died, the grandmother condemned Salty to their dinner table. *Revenge for his transgressions,* Miss Temple said, of which there were supposedly many. To this day, Violet is to never serve Miss Temple pork of any kind.

The front bell chimes. Violet goes to answer it. She spies another fancy doggy-do bag on the porch. A nurse arrives, a young woman who introduces herself as Ava. She wears a white uniform, her dyed black hair pulled back in a rubber band. A green lizard tattoo crawls up the middle finger of her right hand, a detail that hints at a different personality hidden beneath the young woman's professional appearance. Violet knows what it's like to wear a uniform that's meant to obscure your personality, but she's never considered a tattoo. Maybe she should. It would certainly surprise Tia and Leisha.

Just outside the door, Violet, Queenie, and Rose wait for the flurry of activity to cease. Rose's face drains of color, and Violet steps closer. On the hospital bed a few feet away is the person her former friend has spent the last twenty-five years of her life avoiding. Even Violet's chest tightens with the thought. She decides to stay close in case Rose needs her.

The ambulance drivers leave first. Then after several minutes of testing the various machines, the two technicians leave. Ava, the nurse, straightens the sheet over Miss Temple's body and then motions for them to enter.

"Miss Temple is ready for visitors," Ava says, sounding older than she looks. If she is aware of the secrets that have caused such a fuss for the last ten days, she doesn't let on.

Rose approaches the bed and Queenie and Violet file behind her. Queenie rests her hand on Rose's shoulder as if to offer emotional support. Queenie can be counted on in a crisis. She was the one Violet called upon when darker girls said hateful things to her at school because Violet was lighter-skinned. Queenie was also there the time Edward attacked her when he was home from college.

"She looks strangely peaceful, doesn't she?" Queenie says. "It's like the *Temple Book of Secrets* never existed."

Peaceful isn't a word Violet would ever use to describe Miss Temple. "I guess we'd all be better off if we hadn't heard of that book." Violet reminds herself to pick up the second batch of dog poop on the porch and wonders what might come next.

"Look at it this way," Queenie says, her eyes sporting a twinkle. "It only took a devastating stroke and a coma to achieve this serenity."

Queenie's humor helps compensate for the gravity of the moment. Violet is seldom close enough to study Miss Temple's face. Instead of the usual tight line of irritability, her lips are relaxed and droop slightly. A drop of spittle collects in the corner of her mouth. Rose pulls a red bandana from her blue jean pocket and uses it to soak up the drool.

"It's so odd to touch her again after so many years," Rose

says. "I half expect her to snap out of the coma and slap my arm away."

Violet gives Rose's other shoulder a squeeze, aware that her own shoulder isn't reactive at all. She turns to look at Violet, and Violet wonders if she and Rose might someday renew their friendship.

"You know, I think this is the longest I've ever spent in a room with her without getting criticized," Rose says.

"Iris is one tough cookie," Queenie says. "That woman should have come out of the womb with a warning label."

"I hope she can't hear us," Violet whispers.

"We listened to her bellyache for years," Queenie says. "Now it's her turn to get a little of what she dished out."

Violet isn't so sure this is wise. The energy is shifting in the house. The Temple spirits seem to be waking up irritable after a long nap.

Across the room, Ava unpacks a small backpack and arranges different nurse-related items on Miss Temple's vanity. With this task complete, she steps over and checks the IV drip that flows into Miss Temple's hand. A thin line of black eye-liner accentuates Ava's small green eyes, the same shade of green used on the lizard tattoo on her finger.

Nice touch, Violet thinks. If she gets to know Ava a little better, she will ask her about the lizard. There has to be a story there.

Ava sits on a Victorian loveseat in the far corner of the room and pulls a *People* magazine from her purse. Johnny Depp graces the cover. A person admired by her younger daughter.

Power and money haven't protected Miss Temple from this moment. She is dying just like everyone else, and with a scandal afoot.

The telephone rings and Violet jumps. Until recently, the

phone had been unplugged because of all the crank calls they were getting, but with Miss Temple this ill, they need a line out. As Violet answers the phone, Queenie gives Rose a brief hug and excuses herself. Violet is relieved to hear no death threats or cursing when she answers.

"It's for you," Violet says, handing the cordless to Rose.

Apparently, it is Rose's daughter Katie on the phone. Rose cuts the call short, but not before telling her daughter how strange it is to be here.

Without looking up from her magazine, Ava smiles, as if she is no stranger to strange.

Rose hands the phone back to Violet and sits by her mother's side. "You don't have to stay," she says to Violet.

Violet appreciates the offer to leave and excuses herself to go make dinner. Rose talking to her daughter reminds Violet that she has two daughters of her own she needs to get home to. She descends the grand spiral staircase with a fantasy of sliding down the banister like she and Rose used to do, but then Violet realizes how many decades it has been since the last time she pulled this off. Long enough for broken bones or traction to result.

Past and present mingle as she crosses the foyer to the dining room and then into the kitchen, her constant refuge as a girl when she came to work with her grandmother. Like a game of hide-and-seek, the kitchen was always the place to run to that was deemed "safe." Otherwise, she was to stay out of Miss Temple's sight. A talent she still relies on to get through the day.

When Violet enters the kitchen, she finds Queenie sitting at the large, oval oak kitchen table drinking a cup of coffee. The difference between the kitchen and Miss Temple's bedroom feels like the difference between life and death.

"How are you holding up?" Queenie asks, motioning for

Violet to join her. "Can you believe Savannah's biggest tyrant might actually die?"

"Why limit her to Savannah?" Violet says and then apologizes. "Rose isn't anything like her," she adds, and Queenie agrees.

"They say an apple doesn't fall far from the tree, but in this case, it fell in a totally different forest," Queenie says.

Violet makes herself a cup of tea. She isn't much of a coffee drinker—she prefers the smell of it more than the taste and only drinks it if she adds enough half and half and sugar to mask its bitterness.

Rose enters and sits at the table with Queenie. "I'm not sure how long I can just sit there and watch," Rose says.

Violet pours her a cup of coffee, which she accepts and drinks black.

"Would you like to visit Mama tonight?" Queenie asks Rose.

"I'd love that," Rose says.

"We can go right after dinner if you're not too tired," Queenie says. "I was going to drive over anyway and bring her back. She says your mother's crossing is tonight, and she needs to be a part of the transition."

Violet has never witnessed one of her grandmother's end of life rituals.

"Crossing and transition aren't words I usually associate with death," Rose says. "They sound more fluid and less final. Although with Mother, the more 'final', it is the better, I suppose."

"I'm not sure the Temples know when to go," Violet says. She waits for the resident ghosts to agree or disagree, but they are quiet for now.

"Mama and Iris have quite a history," Queenie says. "It almost seems fitting that they would be together at the end."

"Does Mother still believe that Old Sally put a curse on her?" Rose asks.

"Good lord, yes," Queenie says. "Several curses, in fact. I'm not sure how much of it is true, but Iris is at the effect of something. As I've mentioned in my letters, the last place you want to be when your mother is having one of her attacks is downwind. It's enough to kill a moose."

"And then have it for dinner," Violet says, offering another quick apology. She is starting to sound like her Aunt Queenie.

"No need to apologize for something true," Rose says.

"Mama would say that laughter and misery go together," Queenie says. "They're flip sides of the same coin."

Violet wonders how Queenie can still laugh. It's no secret how badly Miss Temple treats her. Sometimes Violet wishes Queenie would stand up for herself more. This is the part of her lineage she doesn't understand. The part that thinks nothing of staying under the Temple's rule. If Violet gets her way, this will all come to an end with the next generation. Maybe even before that, if Violet can finally save enough money to realize her dream. She glances at the spare cookie jar, where she keeps her life savings. With the Temple security system, this is as safe a place to keep it as any bank. And definitely safer than Violet and Jack's apartment, which was broken into several summers ago.

In the twenty years she has worked for the Temples, Violet has saved fifteen thousand dollars. She just needs a little more money for a deposit on the modest storefront she found downtown and to buy the equipment and inventory she'll need. But first, she must say goodbye to Miss Temple.

CHAPTER SEVEN

Rose

The machines keeping her mother alive breathe and beep in an oddly comforting way, a lullaby of technology. Ava, who is stronger than she looks, scoots one of the Queen Anne chairs from the corner of the room to the side of the bed. Rose thanks her and sits stiffly next to her mother as if anticipating complaints about her posture. At first, Rose looks at everything else in the room except her mother: the lavish draperies, the expensive antiques, and a small gold clock ticking loudly on the nightstand near her bed. Then Rose turns her gaze to the body in the hospital bed.

Her mother must have been fifty-five the last time Rose saw her. She is old now. Etched with wrinkles, her mother looks more like Rose's grandmother, who lived in the house when she was a young girl. A woman who scared Rose and always smelled of camphor and mint. Sometimes the old woman would yell at Rose for no reason at all. Her grand-mother Temple was a woman who possessed a coldness that made her mother seem full of warmth. Years after she died, the smell lingered in the hallways and in the corners of the rooms. She can almost smell it now.

At five o'clock, a woman named Lynette arrives to replace Ava. Rose is the only person in the room. Closer to Rose's age, Lynette is almost as wide as she is tall and wears a traditional white uniform. Her pantyhose rub together as she walks and creates a synthetic swishing sound. Because of her height and width, she resembles a linebacker in drag. Rose likes her instantly.

"I'm one of those people who believes people in a coma can hear everything that's going on around them," Lynette says.

Lynette's southern accent is as thick as her plentiful waist. To her surprise, Rose has missed hearing such a vibrant rendition of her native tongue. In the West, the language is crisp and to the point, seeing no need to waste its time. A southern accent, on the other hand, is in no hurry. Every syllable entertains the luxury of an afternoon stroll or a balcony evening on the front porch.

Lynette asks Rose if she would like to help give her mother a sponge bath. Rose doesn't answer at first. How can she tell kind Lynette, that besides the earlier spittle removal, she can't remember the last time she touched her mother? *Or Mother touched me, for that matter.*

Lynette encourages Rose to join her. She coaches her on how to move the washcloth gently down her mother's arms and hands and avoid the needles that force fluids into her aged veins. Washcloth in hand, Rose stands motionless, looking down at her mother's body.

How can she be kind to someone who she could never

please? Someone who didn't know the meaning of kindness, perhaps because nobody ever treated her that way, either.

"Oh, sweetie, I know it's hard to see your mama this way," Lynette says.

Rose has never, in her entire forty-four years of life, called her mother *mama* or *mom*. The terms are too endearing. She always called her Mother or simply said, 'yes, ma'am,' like Old Sally and Queenie did.

Lynette swishes her way to Rose's side of the bed. "Just follow my motions, sweetie," she says.

Following her instruction, Rose glides the moist white washcloth down her mother's slender arms sequined in liver spots. Colors she's used in western landscapes. She makes a long, soft brushstroke of care across her mother's skin. Skin does strange things as it ages. It loosens, puckers, spots, and blotches. Rose notes the beginnings of this process on her own body. Thankfully, it doesn't scare her. She has always felt older than her years. Growing up in the Temple household required a certain amount of toughness.

As Rose mirrors Lynette's motions, she pretends she is someone like Lynette who genuinely cares about the person on the bed. To her surprise, the washing of her mother's unconscious body carries unanticipated emotions for Rose. Hidden within the folds of discomfort is a secret longing for her mother's touch. Perhaps this reaction is brought on by her fatigue, combined with the onset of hot flashes and all the memories that have been waiting for her here. Whatever it is, she is too tired to resist it. It's like she's been running away for twenty-five years only to end up at the same place.

Unexpected tears rush to Rose's eyes. *More needed moisture,* she thinks. Like the droughts out west, she has had a drought of tears over the years. She takes a deep breath and welcomes the rain. Yet with the quickness of a sword cutting through flesh, all emotions cease, as her brother, Edward, steps into the room.

CHAPTER EIGHT

Queenie

After Queenie adjusts the seat and air conditioning vents so they'll blow straight on her, she backs the Lincoln out of the carriage house and waits at the gate for Rose to join her. The drive up the South Carolina coast to her mama's house will take thirty minutes, twenty if she has good luck with the traffic lights and is generous with the gas pedal. In the past, in return for the use of one of the Temple cars, Queenie had to run an errand for Iris. Perks like cars and cash have always been at her half-sister's discretion. But Queenie has other reasons for putting up with Iris. Reasons that nobody else knows about. Not even Rose.

Toilet paper is wrapped around the garden gate and thrown into the trees. *Good lord,* Queenie thinks *we've become a college frat house.*

The secrets have brought all sorts of undesirables to their

doorstep. When Queenie gets back, she'll remove the toilet paper, so Iris won't wake from her coma to complain. At least the crank calls have stopped. Calls plagued them all evening until Queenie finally called the phone company to have their phone changed to a restricted number. She taps the steering wheel, worn out from worrying that her biggest secret will end up in the classifieds, too. She's also tired from getting up so early to get a first glance at the secret of the day. So far, several Savannah adulterers have been revealed, as well as a cross-dressing oil tycoon and a mentally ill banker. All deceased, and mostly forgotten, but still. Whoever is doing it likes to throw in secrets from the present-day every now and again just to keep people interested.

Meanwhile, not a single one of Iris's so-called society friends visited her in the hospital. Not one. For a week, Queenie has spent every day at the hospital with Iris. Her only visitors were Violet—who stopped by every evening on her way home— and Spud Grainger, who stopped by twice a day, once in the morning before going to the Piggly Wiggly and then afterward to relieve Queenie. Although she has a hard time understanding it, she appreciates Spud Grainger's loyalty to Iris.

Rose walks out of the house and latches the gate behind her. She looks tired. In an earlier conversation, Queenie and Violet discussed how difficult this trip back to Savannah must be for Rose. To come home after an absence of twenty-five years, her mother in a coma—a woman too stubborn to show any love—must be hard. Not to mention, seeing Edward again after all these years.

Queenie can't believe he showed up at his mother's bedside. When she called her half-nephew after his mother's stroke, he seemed indifferent and inconvenienced. At least tonight, he didn't stay long. Just enough time to give Rose a prolonged sinister look before rushing off to meet someone at the country club. Queenie has never liked Edward. He acts more like a spoiled brat than a man. Edward and Rose are about as different as two siblings can be.

Rose gets into the car and buckles herself into the passenger seat, giving Queenie a faint smile.

"Seeing Mama will be good for you." Queenie pats her hand. "You two have a special bond."

"I've missed her," Rose says. "I don't think I realized how much until now."

"She's missed you, too," Queenie says. "You're family."

Twelve years separate Queenie and Rose in age, but because of her mama's influence, they have similar sensibilities flowing through them.

With Rose silent next to her, Queenie lets her mind wander. She has driven this route thousands of times and never tires of it. The Talmadge Bridge stretches across the Savannah River, a ribbon of concrete reaching toward the horizon. The water fans out in every direction, and the late afternoon sun glistens across the grassy marsh.

Crossing this bridge suspends time for Queenie as if the bridge itself is a timeline for her family. Her ancestors made this crossing, at first in boats, and her descendants will make this crossing long after she is gone. At the highest point, where the bridge arches upward, she feels weightless, a water bird soaring up and out on a heavy wind. She wishes this part could last longer. But then the bridge delivers her to the land on the other side, as waterways skirt off in different directions.

Her mama never learned how to drive a car. Her entire working career, Old Sally caught rides into Savannah with different maids and housekeepers who worked the same hours. A wide assortment of family and friends are available to call upon whenever she needs a ride. But for Queenie, learning how to drive a car was a statement of independence.

Daughters need their differences, even if their mamas are wonderful, she tells herself.

As they near the ocean, Rose sits straighter. "So many memories," she says. "You used to drive us out here all the time."

"Mama loved bringing you and Violet to the beach," Queenie says. "I think it gave us all a break from your mother."

"Do you remember how we used to sing while we crossed this bridge?" Rose asks. Her eyes sparkle with recollection.

Queenie hums the melody of *Michael, Row Your Boat Ashore.* Her alto voice resonates, tickling her cheeks. Her hum becomes words, and to Queenie's surprise, Rose joins in on the chorus. After they finish, Rose smiles.

"That was wonderful," Rose says. "I forgot how well you sing."

"Violet is the real singer in the family," Queenie says. "A few years back, the preservation society in Beaufort did a recording of her singing some of the old Gullah songs Mama had taught her."

"I never knew that," Rose says, her tone thoughtful.

For several seconds they ride in silence until Queenie breaks the quiet. "I have a confession to make."

Rose turns to look at her. "You know I love confessions," she says.

"Well, sometimes I do more than sing when I cross this bridge," Queenie says.

"Like what?" Rose asks, sounding intrigued.

"Sometimes I do a kind of primal scream," Queenie says. "It's a technique I read about in the *Psychology Today* magazine while waiting on your mother to finish a plate of yak."

"Weren't primal screams big in the 80s?" Rose asks.

"They're still big for me. I do it whenever the frustration of living with your mother becomes too much," Queenie says. *Or whenever the shame and pressure of keeping secrets become too great,* she thinks.

"I'm convinced if everybody screamed while crossing bridges, the world would be a better place," Queenie continues. "Maybe we'd all break free of whatever holds us back. Maybe people right here in Savannah could break free of the past."

It occurs to Queenie that maybe whoever is leaking the secrets to the newspaper is trying to break free, too, and get out from under Iris's thumb. Once all your secrets are out in the open, nobody has power over you. She wonders if maybe it's time for her to tell hers, too. Her lips tighten as if they've already decided this isn't a good idea.

"If I started screaming, I might not stop," Rose says, leaning into the door.

"That's everybody's fear," Queenie says, "but from my experience, you do it for a while, and then you just get all tuckered out. It's like sprinting to a finish line. Not that I know anything about sprints." Queenie smiles and pats her thighs. "These old gals wouldn't know what to do if I took off running somewhere." Her giggle turns to a laugh.

"Has anyone ever seen you scream?" Rose asks.

Queenie grins. "Lord yes, honey. Sometimes a car full of people will pass me while I'm yelling my lungs out, so I just smile at them and wave. If they're from Savannah, they probably don't think anything of it. You're allowed to be crazy here, as you well know. And if it's tourists from out of state? Well, I figure I've just given them a good story to tell their friends when they get back home." She gives Rose a wide smile.

"You are so much braver than I ever could be," Rose says. "It's not about bravery. It's about not caring what people think," Queenie says. "Besides," she begins again, "I may be responsible for Savannah being considered one of the premier tourist destinations in the South. Maybe everybody's heard of that crazy woman down in Savannah screaming her head off in her car while crossing that bridge, and they come here to see it for themselves." Queenie cackles her signature laugh. "Hell, for all my efforts, I may be getting a key to the city any day now," she adds.

When she opens her mouth and pretends to scream, Rose doubles over in the front seat to catch her breath. Her story has worked. Rose looks rejuvenated. Laughter does that. It's like a secret elixir Queenie uses whenever life gets too heavy. And it gets heavy a lot.

After their laughter fades, they settle into a comfortable silence. The bridge is now in Queenie's rear-view mirror. She likes the idea of having Savannah behind her, at least for a while. The road to the barrier islands gives her breathing room. She doesn't have to worry about what rich white people think of her out here. Different rules apply. You are judged by the quality of person you are, not by big houses and fancy cars.

Rose sniffs something in the air. For a second, she looks like Iris on the scent of a rogue fragrance. "Do you smell fried chicken?" Rose asks.

Queenie laughs a short laugh. "Well, I don't see any harm in telling Iris's secret now," she says.

"Mother has a secret?"

"Your mother has lots of secrets. Too many to get into

right now. Of course, your mama's secrets never made it into that stupid book. That would defeat the whole purpose. That book is all about having power over prominent families in Savannah. But if they knew some of Iris's secrets? Oh my. Now that would cause a stink." Queenie chuckles, enjoying her pun.

"Tell me the one you're thinking about," Rose says, her eyes are bright with what could be mischief.

"Well, it seems your mother has a thing for Kentucky Fried Chicken," Queenie says.

"Mother eats junk food?"

"Uh-huh." Queenie smacks her lips together as if the secret is delicious.

"I thought she was on this strict diet and couldn't eat anything except water buffalo or something."

"The jury is still out about your mother's special dietary needs," Queenie says. "But it seems the Colonel's secret recipe is the exception."

"Are you saying Mother has been faking it all these years?" Rose asks. "What about the Gullah curse?"

"I'm not sure anymore," Queenie says. "Mama doesn't talk much about her spells. But if Iris is sneaking around eating KFC, she may be causing some of it herself."

"It's hard to picture Mother going to a fast-food restaurant," Rose says.

"Let me just say, I found a bucket of bones crammed under the front seat week before last. Picked clean like a buzzard had eaten them."

Rose's soft giggle grows into a full-fledged laugh, and before they know it, Queenie and Rose are laughing so hard Queenie has to pull over to the side of the road.

"For the first time in my life, I wish I wore Depends," Queenie says, which causes more laughter.

Smiles linger on their faces when Queenie pulls back onto the highway and drives east toward the ocean, to an area where her mother's family has lived for seven generations. She signals to turn and then drives down an unpaved road. Pine trees line the right side with an open field on the left. Sand billows behind the Town Car like choppy waves made by a motorboat.

"I've never known anyone who is a hundred years old," Rose says.

"Sometimes I think Mama's winding down. She spends hours looking out over the ocean now. Perfectly content."

"I owe her a lot," Rose says. "I don't know how I would have survived my childhood without her."

"Well, she loves you like you are her very own child," Queenie offers.

"I never asked if that bothered you," Rose says.

"Of course not," Queenie says. "Mama has enough love to circle the globe twice. I never felt cheated. Not for one instant."

Early on in life, Queenie learned to share her mother. People always needed her. If not for spells and cures, then for advice on everyday things. She has frequent visitors, some of them total strangers, and some of them the people her mama looks out for. *She is a mother hen with a lot of chicks.*

The ocean waits in the distance—the blue-gray water fading toward an invisible horizon. Rose rolls down her window and leans out to smell the salty air. Seconds later, Queenie parks the Lincoln in the backyard of her mother's house. Flowers are everywhere and overflow their makeshift containers: large truck tires, a child's rusty red wagon, a washtub filled to the brim with purple, white, and yellow petunias.

Queenie and Rose take the wooden walkway to the

house. Her mama sits in her rocker on the front porch and smiles as if she's been expecting them. Over the years, her mother's skin has darkened from the sun. Queenie has always been lighter-skinned than her. Every generation of her family seems to have a little more white mixed in.

As they approach, Old Sally claps her hands with joy. She looks weathered but strong, her gray hair clipped short, an inch from her scalp. The creases of age on her face make her look wise, an elder of their clan. A strong presence, even in her advanced age, she reminds Queenie of a lighthouse lighting the way for weary travelers, steering them to safety.

Queenie can't imagine her mother not being there anymore, and even now, she forces the thought away. Yet her mother's death is as certain as the ocean's ebb and flow. She squeezes Rose's hand and leads her up the steps, as though bringing her mama a long-awaited gift. One of Old Sally's daughters has come home.

CHAPTER NINE

Old Sally

"She be getting closer," Old Sally says aloud. "I can feel her."

Old Sally stands and faces the sea. The knowing starts out as a vibration in the center of her chest that grows in strength as Rose nears. It won't be long now before she can see her sweet Rose again.

Children get unlucky sometimes with who their parents are, and it creates bad medicine, like chemicals that shouldn't be mixed. As soon as Old Sally realized how bad the medicine was between Rose and her mother, she knew Rose was hers to watch after.

Old Sally glances out over the ocean that feels like an old friend, its waves racing to pound the shore. The rhythm of the tides is etched in her. To Old Sally, the land is living. The waterways and marshland along the coast are living. The oak trees are living. For Old Sally, everything she touches, everything she sees is alive. Even her Gullah ancestors, who some would say have gone out with the tide of time, are still alive and talk to her.

A memory is carried in on the breeze. Her grandmother, Sadie, was a slave for the Temple family until freed in 1865. Old Sally touches the small broach pinned to her simple dress that used to be Sadie's. Sally was only twenty when she learned the Gullah spells and potions from her grandmother, who was well into her eighties at the time.

"I be remembering what you taught me, Granny Sadie," she says.

The Gullah ways are as much a part of Old Sally as her heart that ticks away inside of her. She mixes medicines to protect the people she loves from bad things that might happen to them.

On the porch of the house she grew up in, Old Sally rocks in her wooden rocker. She lives twenty miles north of Savannah on a small island off the South Carolina coast. A place where the Atlantic Ocean bathes the islands and coastland, where waterways work their way inland like fingers grasping to hold onto the edge of the coast. A place where pungent marshes are home to shrimp, crab, and alligator and where oysters grow in terraced colonies like pearl necklaces scooped along the neck of the land. A place where osprey and cranes search the brackish water for their supper while seagulls squawk and hover above shrimp boats heading out to sea. The beauty here is seductive. It is deep and sometimes dark. Just like the Temple secrets that have begun to float up from the depths and come to light.

A melody comes to her. She hums a song taught to her by her grandmother about the crossing between this life and the next. A bridge we all cross, some early and some later.

"Iris Temple be making that crossing soon, and I been called on to help," she says as if her grandmother Sadie is sitting right next to her. "I remember everything you taught me, Granny, and it would please me if you could help, too."

For centuries, the Gullah people have carried the mysteries of life. In addition to being guides between the two worlds, her ancestors wove sweetgrass baskets. They made medicine from herbs and grew all their own food. When it came time to give birth, they delivered their own babies. They fished the surrounding waters with nets they made themselves. They lived off the ocean and land.

Another memory comes. Memories visit Old Sally often these days so she can review her long life. This memory is from thirty-five years earlier, in 1965, a time when certain things were set in motion that are about to be made complete. The scene sweeps over her like a warm ocean wave, and she closes her eyes to receive it. The voices of children come.

"LET'S GO, CHILDREN," Old Sally says. She ushers Rose and Violet into the back seat of the Temple car.

Around the age of sixty, the 'old' was added to Sally's name. She never complained. Having worked as a housekeeper all her life and raised three children of her own, there are days she feels older than the land she lives on. Her youngest, Ivy, still lives with her. Lately, everybody calls Ivy, Queenie, a nickname given to her by Rose and Violet that has stuck like the Savannah humidity.

Queenie drives them to the island. Mister Oscar is good about letting her use one of their cars if she needs it. He has a fondness for Queenie that Old Sally and her daughter don't talk about.

Just like her mama was and her mama before her, Old Sally is the Temple maid, housekeeper, and nanny. Iris Temple and Mister

Oscar have two children. Edward is nearly grown and away at boarding schools most of the year, and Rose is ten years of age. Rose is Iris Temple's only daughter. A child handed over to Old Sally to care for when she was days old.

Today, Iris Temple is busy with meetings, and Old Sally has the time to bring the girls to her house on the shore. She loads her ironing into the trunk, so as not to get behind in her chores. The drive is familiar and comforting, like putting on slippers after wearing shoes all day. As they approach the island, she feels her breath deepen. This coastline is where Old Sally feels the most connected to her ancestors.

After they arrive, the girls run to the beach to build sandcastles, and Old Sally opens the doors and windows of her house to catch the ocean breezes. In the kitchen, she refills a coke bottle with water and twists the sprinkler cap on the top so she can moisten the wrinkled sheets before ironing them. A portrait of Dr. Martin Luther King Jr. shares a wall with photos of her children, grandchildren, and great-grandchildren. She greets him, calling him Martin.

"I MISS YOU, MARTIN," Old Sally says, making the leap from then to now. "A lot of people do."

As she rocks, the boards of the porch crackle to the beat of the rocking chair, adding background noise for the memory. Her eyes remain closed as she travels back to the past.

OLD SALLY TURNS *on a burner on the stove and stirs the roots soaking in a pan. The water has already turned as black as the swamps where she collects them. She is conjuring up a new batch of a protection spell for Rose. Protection spells were one of her mother's specialties. Old Sally's mother lived past the age of 90 as an independent woman, still chopping her own firewood, washing clothes in a tin tub, and cooking on a cast-iron stove. Old Sally has this same sturdiness.*

From the front porch, she keeps an eye on the three children in her charge—two brown and one white, one older and two younger—while they build a sandcastle on the beach. Although Queenie is no longer a child, she is still hers to protect.

Violet, the youngest, is six years old. She is Old Sally's grand-daughter, with a complicated history, who Old Sally has agreed to raise. Old Sally will raise up whoever needs rearing. It is in her nature. It doesn't matter if they are her own blood or not.

Without warning, tears come as she remembers her daughter, Maya, who died the same year Violet was born. It doesn't matter how long it's been, the pain is still there. The only thing that made that year bearable was Violet's birth a few months before.

Earlier that morning, Old Sally braided Violet's hair and added colored beads to the end of the tightly woven rows. Despite her circumstances of coming into this world, Violet is a happy child. She often sings or hums, the beads in her braids keeping the beat as she moves her head with made-up melodies. Old Sally often finds her with her head back, eyes closed, feet stomping and hands clap-ping as she hums and sways with the music. Someone much older resides in her. Someone who has stories to tell.

Rose Temple might as well be an orphan, the way her mother treats her. If Old Sally lives to be a hundred, she will never under-stand how somebody like Iris Temple, given so much in this world, can be so stingy with her love. The ancestral line of Temple mothers be like a drought that changed the landscape from the lush low country marshland into a desert.

Queenie, Old Sally's grown daughter, her waist and hips already thick with good eating, helps the girls carry buckets of seawater to fill the moat around the sandcastle. In some ways,

Queenie is like a girl herself, though grownup things have happened to her. Secret things.

Old Sally turns off the boiling roots on the stove and makes egg salad sandwiches and sweet tea. From the front porch, she waves and calls the girls to lunch. It is spring and the perfect temperature with the sea breezes blowing. Something sweet is in the air, blooming in the dunes. She closes her eyes to identify the flowers, but it is gone before she can catch it.

Hearing the call, the girls run through the dunes and up the steps to Old Sally's small beach house painted white with its blue trim to scare off evil spirits. The girls' bodies and bathing suits are covered with sand. Queenie follows them, her sleeveless cotton dress blowing in the sea breeze as she brushes sand off her brown arms and legs.

"Queenie, please wash the girls off before they come inside," Old Sally says.

"Yes, Mama," Queenie says. She uses the green garden hose at the side of the house to rinse them off, and the girls squeal in ecstasy as Queenie covers the end with her thumb and sends water spraying in all directions. She can count on Queenie to get them giggling.

Old Sally returns to her ironing in the front room.

If I hurry, I can get one more piece done before lunch, she thinks.

The sound of Rose's laughter makes her smile. She is much too serious for a child, nagged by her mother for every little thing—the way she walks, the way she talks, the way she should always be doing something other than what she's doing.

At least out here she be getting a little peace today, *Old Sally thinks.*

The two younger girls wrap themselves in towels hanging on the porch railings and come into the living room where Old Sally is ironing her fourth full sheet of the day. She has four more to go. At *home, she irons in front of her three large windows, where she can keep an eye on the sea. She sprinkles the wrinkled sheet with the sprinkler bottle. Her iron sizzles as it hits the damp sheets. Steam rises. Sweat dots Old Sally's brow.*

Rose leans into Old Sally's wide hip. Birthing hips, she likes to call them, perfect for bringing children into the world. She smoothes Rose's wet hair with her hand and notices again how thin she is. Old Sally is always trying to fatten Rose up. Yet Rose could eat chicken and dumplings every day of her life and stay skinny. She's tall for her age, too, most all legs. Her mother keeps her hair styled and permed like Rose is some kind of prize-winning poodle. Rose always tugs at it to try to make it straight.

"Baptize me," she says. Rose stands nearly as tall as Old Sally's shoulder and looks up at her, her eyes filled with playful pleading. She asks Old Sally to do this every time she irons like it is the food she needs most.

Old Sally nods, and Rose turns toward the sea and bows her head about to receive a sacred anointing. When Old Sally sprinkles the water on Rose's head, the child's laughter rides on the salty breeze that sweeps through the house.

Violet begs to be next. Old Sally repeats her christening ritual, and Violet and Rose collapse in giggles on the sofa. Queenie shakes her head as if she is too old for such nonsense, so Old Sally aims a few sprinkles in her direction, too. Her daughter, who also seems much too serious these days, laughs a little.

"Lunchtime," Old Sally announces.

The four of them enter the kitchen where the food is set out on her round wooden table. The girls and Queenie each eat two sandwiches that Old Sally has cut into triangles like finger sandwiches at the fancy parties Iris Temple throws. Big slices of watermelon are piled high on a plate in the middle of the table, and they devour these, too, collecting all the seeds in a bowl for Old Sally to plant later. The thirsty girls drink a gallon of sweet iced tea to go along with lunch, a slice of lemon perched on the lip of each glass. Meanwhile, Old Sally reheats some shrimp and grits from her dinner the night before and then joins the girls.

"What's that smell?" Rose asks. She wipes her mouth with a napkin all proper as if her mother might be watching.

"That be something your Old Sally conjuring up," Old Sally says.

She walks over to the stove, her bad hip already stiff from a few moments sitting, and gives the root mixture on the back of the stove a stir with a wooden spoon. Then she spreads the roots on towels on the kitchen counter and pours the black brew into a brown bottle with a stopper. The spell will be complete when she goes back to the Temple house and adds some of Iris Temple's hair to the mixture pulled from Iris's hairbrush while cleaning her bathroom later on this afternoon. This is one of Old Sally's most potent protection spells. Without this protection, Iris Temple will do more damage than she already has. She is worse than the Temple men when it comes to forcing her way. In fact, she has all of Savannah scared of her for one reason or another. Mostly because of that Book of Secrets that the different Temples have kept for over a century.

If I had my way, I'd destroy that old book, she thinks. Then the Temple reign over Savannah could end. But she doesn't have her way. Without work at the Temple's, she couldn't survive.

"Grandma's spells get rid of evil spirits," Violet says to Rose. Her eyes widen as she says, 'evil spirits.' Then she shakes her head to get her beaded braids to agree.

Old Sally gets a saltine cracker tin from the cabinet that is now filled with homemade oatmeal cookies. She gives the girls two each and Queenie three.

"Mama's medicines help people get rid of ailments and such," Queenie says to Rose. She wraps her cookies in a napkin and puts them in the pocket of her dress. "Back in the old days, illnesses were cured with roots, herbs, and teas," she adds.

Queenie looks at her mother like she's proud of how much she knows. What she doesn't say is that illnesses caused by hexes or spells can only be cured by magic. And in the Sea Islands, those islands and coastal regions along the Georgia and South Carolina coast, magical medicines are created using feathers, bones, fingernails, hair clippings, and sometimes blood. Materials that are mixed with other natural elements such as roots, sand, and leaves. Since the white slave owners feared the use of Gullah magic, these conjuring practices were kept secret, although Old Sally has never kept anything hidden from Rose. Old Sally doesn't believe in secrets. They just give the darkness something to feed on. She'll tell anybody anything they want to know.

Violet puts her plate and glass in the sink, and Rose follows.

"Can we go back to our sandcastles?" Violet asks Old Sally. "We still have work to do." The girls exchange a look as if their 'work' is of the top-secret variety.

Old Sally nods, and Violet challenges Rose to a race, the finish line being their sandcastles. It is inevitable that Violet will lose. She is a foot shorter than Rose. Yet the two girls throw their towels across the porch railing and make a mad dash through the dunes as if equally paired.

While the girls play, Old Sally and Queenie sit on the top step together, looking out over the Atlantic Ocean. The sun is just beyond the house, and the porch is shady now. It feels good to rest a minute before Old Sally has to get ironing again.

Violet and Rose build a new sandcastle in the distance right next to the old one. If not for the differences in the color of their skin, they might pass as sisters.

"They call themselves the sea gypsies," Queenie says. "They've decided they want to live together when they grow up."

Old Sally laughs. "Imagination, it be a powerful thing," she says.

"I get to be their Queen," Queenie adds, rolling her eyes.

Old Sally puts an arm around her daughter and squeezes a dose of love into her. "You be a queen to me, too."

Queenie lowers her head. Her hair is clipped short. Otherwise, it will take over her entire head. She wears colorful headbands that Old Sally makes from fabric she finds. Today's is bright yellow. The color of a bright, shiny lemon. Queenie has always liked bold colors. The bolder, the better. Old Sally gives her another squeeze like the lemons she uses to make lemonade.

"So, what be on your mind, baby?" Old Sally asks. "Not like you to be so quiet."

Queenie's brow furrows. Whatever she's thinking about has steered her into deep waters that she's not so sure she can navigate.

"I need to make a decision, Mama. Mister Oscar wants me to move into the house and be Iris's companion."

Now Old Sally is the quiet one. Mister Oscar has other reasons for wanting Queenie there. But she can't think about that right now. Sheets are waiting, and her memories of Maya weigh heavy on her today.

"You have to make a living some way, baby, and since he be offering room and board." Old Sally's voice trails off.

Queenie huffs and pulls away. No one in their right mind would want to be a companion to Iris Temple. Old Sally can barely stand working for her as it is. But Queenie hasn't found work yet, and Old Sally hardly makes enough to support Queenie, Violet, and herself.

Silence stretches in front of them like the long stretch of beach along the coastline. Old Sally searches for the truth inside her. When she thinks she has found the words to say, she takes a deep breath, and her words come out soft.

"Daughter, I be a strong woman in many ways," Old Sally begins. "I be good at cooking, cleaning, and raising children. And I be especially good in the invisible arts of our people."

Old Sally pauses, asking for courage from her ancestors to keep going. The truth isn't always an easy thing to see, much less speak. Queenie, patient in her waiting, stares out at the ocean that is so quiet it looks like a sheet of dark blue glass.

Old Sally takes another deep breath and wrings her hands together to calm herself.

"Something else be true, though," she begins again. "I still be just a colored woman whose whole life been spent taking care of white people and their children just like my mama did and her mama before her." She pauses, thinking through what she'll say next. "Sometimes history and the times be bigger than a single person," she continues, her voice softer. "And I think this be one of those times. Honey, I don't know how to tell you to do anything different than I did with my own life. I wish it weren't so, but it is, and I'm sorry I can't do better."

Queenie is the daughter of Iris Temple's father, Edward Temple, III. The fact that she has a different father than her older siblings has never been a secret to Queenie. Edward Temple was a powerful man and used to getting whatever he wanted—this included Old Sally. No love involved. Old Sally needed to keep her job so she could support her family since her husband was long gone.

Children fathered by landowners and servants were not that unusual in those days, and in some ways, the old days are still going on. The Temple blood has been mixing with Old Sally's ancestors for centuries now. Her grandmother, Sadie, carried and raised a Temple child, too, although this secret was swept into the shadows because he was a boy child. This is what Old Sally means when she tries to explain to Queenie about fighting the tides of history. Sometimes those currents just run too deep and too strong. And sometimes those tides even have an undertow.

Yet Old Sally has been getting the message for a while now that something is about to change. She's not sure when. She's not sure how. But change is coming. The tea leaves say it. The wind whispers it. And the voices of her ancestors confirm it.

. . .

WHEN OLD SALLY opens her eyes, the scene fades. She goes inside to get a shawl and pauses in front of her large picture window. A worn, comfortable chair sits next to her front window overlooking the sea. Old Sally spends more and more time in this old chair praying over the collection of souls that are hers to look out for. Usually, they are people who have been handed a challenging life, like Rose. The sensitive and creative ones often need her the most.

Every object on Old Sally's large window seat stands in for one of these people. Pieces of coral sit next to eyeglasses, alongside two blue robin's eggs, as well as other things. Each object has a story.

At the center of the window seat sits the most special object of all: a small sculpture of a sandcastle. Old Sally thinks of Rose as she holds it. Rose is one of her exceptional cases that could have gone either way. The dark side wanted her just as much as the light. Every day of Rose's life, Iris Temple sent a message to that child that she wished she had never been born. Nothing you can do to a person is worse than cursing their existence.

The vibration grows stronger in Old Sally's chest. "I waiting for you, baby. It won't be long now," she says to Rose.

Old Sally shivers and pulls her shawl close. Earlier that day, her ancestors told her that Rose is in danger again. Her return to Savannah has made her vulnerable. Old Sally's work is not yet finished. She walks out onto the porch again. These days she feels every single one of her hundred years. Her bones creak and talk to each other like they are saying, *Can you believe this old woman still be alive?* Old Sally talks back to her old bones sometimes and tells them to hang on, that it won't be long now, that they still have work to do. Thankfully, her old body and the good lord have listened.

Old Sally smiles and taps the center of her chest as the hum grows louder. The salty air fills her lungs with whispers from the sea. The night is clear. The moon will be full as Iris Temple makes her passage. That means the dark forces will be at their strongest. She must prepare for what's coming. The change she predicted thirty-five years ago is finally here.

"Whenever a cycle begins or ends, it be a powerful thing," she says to the ocean breeze. "I must stay awake to what be next and not be lulled to sleep."

In the distance, two figures approach the house. She has lived a long, rich life, and when her time comes, she will be ready to go. But first, she must finish what she set out to do for Rose, as well as protect Queenie and Violet during the transition to come. Then Old Sally's work will be complete. Then she, too, will get to rest.

CHAPTER TEN

Rose

A warm breeze pushes Rose and Queenie down the
path. The beach lays out her sandy skirt in front of
them. Rose stops in the middle of the path to greet the
landscape. It will be dusk soon, and the sky takes on brilliant shades of orange and red to the southwest. Rose
wishes she had her paints with her. Something this beautiful begs to be captured. She and Queenie walk arm in
arm, as the wind playfully whips at their clothes. It is high
tide. The ocean crashes on the shore a hundred feet away.
Water birds squawk and run along the front edges of the
waves, like small, winged children daring the water to
catch them.

Rose and Queenie take the walkway through the dunes.
Rose has spent many happy hours on this stretch of coastline. It feels like an old friend she hasn't seen in twenty-five

years. A flood of memories comes with her reunion. Memories of entire days spent by the shore.

The salt spray hits her face. Moisture. Something the dry air in Wyoming doesn't possess. A substance prayed for during years of drought, given freely here. Her skin tingles as if thanking her for coming back to her moist homeland. Even though she feels like rushing, she stops to take in the scene. The horizon stretches into the distance joining the sky with a thin gray line. Seagulls hover close like beggars asking for coins. Four pelicans soar on the breeze, away from the setting sun, their wings nearly touching. Why has she waited this long to return? She could have always come here without her mother's knowledge. Or perhaps she knew the effect it would have on her to be here again.

Queenie squeezes Rose's arm as if to remind her who awaits. It was good to laugh with her in the car. The whole of Savannah seems tense, including Queenie. It can't be easy to deal with the uproar those secrets have caused. She can't imagine what good could come from collecting secrets to begin with.

They continue up the path to the house. Unlike the reunion with her mother, the anticipation of seeing Old Sally again holds great sweetness. The grand woman sits in the corner of her front porch, overlooking the ocean. She appears regal, an African goddess reigning over the sea. Goosebumps rise on Rose's arms, confirmation that she is participating in something mysterious, perhaps even sacred, although Rose has rarely thought in those terms for the last twenty-five years.

Meanwhile, nothing about Old Sally seems tense. If anything, she is a messenger of calm. Rose wishes she could be more like her. This trip home has been difficult. Nothing having to do with her mother is ever easy.

Wearing a cotton dress the color of sand dollars, Old Sally stands as they approach. Creases of age flow like soft rivers down a brown landscape. Her skin is taut as the finest leather, and she is barefoot. For some reason, this makes Rose smile. In the West, she wouldn't dream of not wearing shoes. The parched earth of the high plains produces plants with prickly spines. Not to mention rattlesnakes. Yet in this setting, Rose wants to toss her shoes in the dunes and feel the sand between her toes. Instead, she hesitates with the awareness that she is only passing through. She will need these shoes again.

Despite the fact that all the other small houses on this stretch of coast have been bought up by developers and replaced by multimillion-dollar properties, Old Sally's house has not changed. It is just as Rose remembers it: a small, old, yet spirited force, just like its owner. Over a decade ago, she tried painting it from memory and couldn't capture it.

What must it be like to live on the edge of the sea, she wonders, *instead of on the edge of the Great Plains.* She imagines all the storms Old Sally has seen and that this little house has weathered. Old Sally has probably weathered personal storms, as well. Although at that moment, Rose realizes just how little she knows about her.

A momentary shame colors Rose's face. She should know more about this woman who took care of her for the first twenty years of her life. Her wishes. Her dreams. Her challenges.

I've done what every little rich white girl has done, she thinks. She's taken Old Sally's care for granted. Never giving a thought to the fact that she was a woman with a family of her own that she went home to every evening. A woman with needs and sorrows, as well as joys. If she were going to be there for more than a couple of days, she would make an effort to get to know her better.

After climbing the dozen or so steps to the house, Rose pauses at the top. Every window of the house is open to let in the sea breezes. Three large windows reveal a living space filled with things brought in from the outside: driftwood, large shells, roots left drying on the ample window sills, as well as the eclectic collection of objects on the window seat that have grown in number since the last time Rose was here. Objects she studied with fascination as a girl. Rose recognizes the small sandcastle sculpture she gave Old Sally before she left for college.

Queenie walks over first and hugs her mother. Although keeping an eye on Rose, Old Sally exhales a laugh, as though seeing Queenie gives her immense pleasure.

"Oh, child, I do love them hugs," Old Sally says to Queenie. Old Sally then turns her gaze to Queenie alone and holds her face between her hands while looking deep into her eyes. "How you be, child?" she whispers. "In your heart of hearts."

"I'm well, Mama," Queenie says, and then gives Rose a wink.

Old Sally looks into her eyes again as if to confirm what Queenie says. "I guess you be telling the truth," the old woman says. She kisses her daughter on both cheeks before returning her attention to Rose.

"I've missed you, girl," Old Sally says and laughs like her happiness can't be contained.

Rose's face grows hot as they embrace, and she receives a gift she's not so sure she deserves. At the same time, Old Sally's strength surprises her. She is thinner than Rose remembers as though her body has intentionally shed some weight to make it easier to carry.

As she did with Queenie, Old Sally holds Rose's face in between her wrinkled hands. They are soft and cool, despite the heat of the day. Rose looks away as Old Sally looks deep into her eyes. Although this loving attention is probably what Rose longs for the most, to receive it in such abundance causes her awkwardness to come out in a brief laugh. Not even Max looks at Rose with this level of intensity. He still notices when she makes an effort to look nice for him, and he seems appreciative of her body, but he has never looked into her eyes for any length of time. Nor, to be honest, has she looked into his.

"Oh my, child. You not be doing too well," Old Sally says to Rose. "It be your mama, I think, haunting you again." Then she whispers to Rose, "You be all right pretty soon, though. Just wait and see."

Old Sally kisses Rose lightly on each cheek, as she did with Queenie. Rose can't remember the last time she was kissed on the cheek. Perhaps it was the last time she saw Old Sally when she was leaving Savannah to move to Wyoming. Old Sally's lips are as cool and soft as her touch. Her gesture brings tears to Rose's eyes. Returning to the Georgia coast has brought unexpected moisture into her life again.

"Good girl," Old Sally says when she sees Rose's tears. "Now, don't be brushing those away. I need to capture them."

Old Sally reaches for a dark brown bottle sitting on a small wooden table bleached white by the wind and sand. She unscrews the top and uses the eyedropper to suck up the tears on Rose's cheek and put them into the bottle. Having lived with Old Sally the first two decades of her life, Rose doesn't question any of it. Back then, Old Sally was always gathering roots or collecting tears or strands of Rose's hair to be used for one of her spells. Looking satisfied,

Old Sally screws the cap back on the bottle and puts it in her pocket.

"Sit down, you two. Let me look at you," Old Sally says.

Queenie and Rose, though mature women, do as they are told. From the other end of the porch, they pull up two rocking chairs that have seasoned to the color of the dunes. Meanwhile, Old Sally sits and takes in every nuance of them, nodding as if taking an inventory of their every movement and emotion. It's almost as if Old Sally is about to paint their portrait.

"Yes, there's still work to do," Old Sally says, more to herself than to them. "But it's nothing I can't handle." She smiles and rocks in her chair. "Would you girls like some lemonade and pound cake?" she asks.

"We'll get it, Mama," Queenie says.

Rose follows Queenie inside, noting how little the living room has changed with its one worn sofa and two side chairs. On the way to the kitchen, they walk down a hallway that contains a wall of family photos. As a girl, Rose stared at these photographs for vast periods as if the brown faces and bright smiles might reveal the secret of happiness to her. The pictures at her mother's house weren't photographs, but portraits of long-dead white people with serious looks on their faces, as though interrupted from counting their money. She knows much less about Old Sally's family.

"I'd forgotten how powerful she is," Rose says, once they are in the kitchen. "But in a good way," she adds. Rose touches her check, remembering Old Sally's kiss.

Queenie laughs. "Yes, Mama is a force to be reckoned with, that's for sure," she says.

Old Sally's attention is the opposite of anything Rose's mother would have offered, even if she weren't in a vegetative state. No judgment resides in Old Sally's gaze, only love, and concern. The mystery to Rose is how love given so freely can feel more threatening than criticism.

Old Sally's kitchen is a celebration of primary colors and is painted the color of lemonade. Ample windows overlook the dunes and coastal grasses. Treasures rest on the window sills: shells of all sizes, small pieces of driftwood that look like earthen sculptures, a variety of stones, as well as fossils of the most intricate creatures, their spirals imprinted in history. Her mother would never dream of bringing the outdoors inside, except for expensive flower arrangements. However, Rose wonders if her own desire to collect stones, fossils, and bones at the ranch is Old Sally's influence.

Queenie uncovers the old cake tin that has been in Old Sally's kitchen since Rose was a girl. She cuts three pieces of pound cake while Rose pours the lemonade. Slices of lemon twirl inside the glasses as she stirs the sugar in the bottom.

"Homemade lemonade is a lost art," Queenie says.

"Old Sally is a lost art, too," Rose says. "I don't know anybody else like her."

Queenie agrees.

When they return to the porch, Old Sally rocks her chair slowly as if keeping time to the waves. Evening is coming on, and a hint of coolness floats on the breeze. The three women eat cake, drink lemonade, and watch the ocean like it might reveal its secrets at any moment. The water's grayness extends to meet the evening sky. The sea churns up memories for Rose that she can almost taste. Old Sally always had a snack ready whenever she came home from school: oatmeal cookies, chocolate pudding, cheese and crackers. No matter where Rose returned from, the kitchen was always the first place she went. It never occurred to her to find her mother.

Back then, Old Sally, Queenie, and Violet were Rose's life

preservers in the choppy Temple seas. They were safe. They listened when she spoke and responded. They laughed, told stories, and included her. Those moments in the kitchen taught Rose everything she knows about love and relationships.

In contrast, Rose's parents were Savannah society. Dressed in formal attire, they attended dinner parties and events full of people parading like show dogs to display their breeding. Ultimately, Rose decided that they were the poor ones, with their insincere friends and emotionally bankrupt marriages. Their children were commodities, possessions. Their value measured by their return on investment.

Rose shudders with the awareness that her mother will never know who Rose really is. To her credit, she walked away from that world twenty-five years ago and hasn't looked back. But what Rose also walked away from was Old Sally, Queenie, and Violet. Now she realizes how big a loss that was.

As night falls, Old Sally lights two large candles protected by hurricane globes. The quality of the light is intimate and warm. The floorboards of the porch creak with three melodies as the three women rock into the evening. Rose breathes deeply, filling her lungs for the first time in years. Her shoulders relax.

"That be good, child, that be good," Old Sally says. "This pain be over soon," she adds. "Your mother be about to make her transition." The reflection of candlelight dances across her face.

Rose sighs. Her mother's approaching death elicits only a vague sense of regret. After being sober for nearly two decades and having had what feels like a lifetime of psychotherapy, she has reached a point where she has made peace with her life. Nobody escapes unscathed. Some people have easier lives, some have harder. Rose takes life one day at a time, as the AA motto goes. The woman sitting on the porch next to her played a profound role in her early life, and for this, she feels thankful.

Waves surge and crash in the distance. Rose relaxes into her tiredness, embraced by sea breezes and the moonlit night. Candles flicker yet hold their light. Rose, Queenie, and Old Sally don't speak. It is as though their conversation is just below the surface, dipping and diving with the carefree motion of the dolphins often seen offshore.

CHAPTER ELEVEN

Violet

At least the phone calls have stopped, Violet thinks as she dusts the phone in the sunroom. For the last few hours, Violet was answering calls every ten minutes. At first, she answered, saying, *Temple Residence.* Then later, she responded with: *Just say what you need to say.* Unfortunately, most of the calls involved people cussing her. All the calls were anonymous. Made by cowards. Miss Temple would hate what people are saying about her. Who knew a bunch of old secrets could cause such a mess? And how in the world did someone get their hands on a book locked in a bank vault?

After Violet returns to the kitchen, she prepares a fresh cup of coffee and a bowl of strawberry shortcake for Lynette, the nurse upstairs. She cooks whenever she doesn't know what else to do, and with Miss Temple so gravely ill, she is definitely at a loss. What will her job entail after Miss Temple dies? Will she even have a job?

Violet hums, as she often does when the house is quiet. A tune comes to her from a long time ago. It has a melancholy tone, somehow linked to the past.

Violet's mother was a nurse, and something about the uniform always causes Violet to entertain the *what if's* of life. *What if* her mother hadn't died when her tire blew out on the island, and she crashed into a three-hundred-year-old live oak tree? *What if* she had grown up knowing her mother, instead of only seeing pictures of her? How might her life have been different? Unfortunately, she will never know. And the one ghost she would hope to see is totally absent.

When Violet returns upstairs with a piece of shortcake, Lynette lifts a fork and takes a bite. "Oh my, this is wonderful." She moans and takes two more bites. "The Temples are very lucky to have you," she adds.

At least for now, Violet thinks. Both turn to Miss Temple like she might have something to add to the conversation. But there is no movement, only the sound of the ventilator pushing air into her lungs.

Earlier that evening, Queenie asked Violet to stay later than usual so she and Rose could pick up Old Sally and bring her back to the Temple house. Tonight is the night Jack teaches a class, and the girls have basketball practice, so she can be flexible. Although it is nice to see Rose again, Violet wishes it were a happier reason for her to visit.

Every family has broken places, but the Temples seem to have more than most.

Violet has never known Miss Temple to be content, and because of this, Violet has sometimes felt more fortunate. She pauses to assess the different vibrations in the room and thinks how interesting it is that someone unconscious can still radiate such a chaotic buzz.

Miss Temple's force is like static from a radio station not quite tuned in. It reminds her of that Peanuts character, Pigpen, who has a cloud of dirt that follows him everywhere he goes. Miss Temple is similar, except her cloud is chaos.

Lynette finishes her shortcake and pats her vast stomach, complimenting Violet again. She walks over to the window as though the view might aid her digestion.

"Why are those people gathered in front of the house?" she asks Violet. "Two groups have come by in the last two hours."

Violet joins her at the window. "We're on Savannah's ghost tour," she says. "The Temple Mansion is the main event."

"Ghost tour?" Lynette says. "Oh my. I had no idea." She glances around the room like she's searching for evidence.

Violet doesn't mention that the secrets in the newspaper have caused the groups of tourists and gawkers to swell to three or four times their usual numbers. While Miss Temple has always craved attention, she would not be pleased with this level of scrutiny.

"Every night around dusk, tour guides show up with their groups to watch the house for signs of the ghostly Temples," Violet says.

In Violet's experience, this is precisely when apparitions go away. Ghosts never show themselves when people want them to.

Lynette's eyes widen. "You really have ghosts?" she asks.

"We have our fair share," Violet says, though, in truth, the Temple house probably has more than their fair share.

"How do you know?" Lynette asks, looking uneasy.

"Footsteps on stairways," Violet begins. "Things moved

an inch or two from their original positions. Blasts of cold air sending shivers up your spine when entering certain rooms. Things that can just as easily be attributed to an overactive imagination, if not for the sensations that accompany them."

Lynette's eyes have changed from full moons to crescents as if squinting might reveal the hidden entities in the room.

"Miss Temple's dead husband, Oscar, likes to rattle bottles at the bar in his study," Violet begins again. "Her mother always brings a camphor smell when she's around and often lingers in the upstairs bedroom that was hers. Miss Temple's father prefers to communicate by heavy foot-steps on the stairway like he's just home from one of his business trips. Or he'll come into the kitchen to look for my grandmother who used to work here."

Lynette's white face turns even whiter.

I shouldn't enjoy shocking people this much, Violet thinks.

Yet she has to admit, as the mother of teenagers and the wife of a busy husband, she doesn't always have the gift of a captive audience.

When the doorbell rings, Lynette jumps as if goosed by Oscar himself. Before excusing herself to get the door, Violet reassures Lynette that everything is fine. On her way down-stairs, she glances at her watch long enough to wonder who would be visiting after nine o'clock.

Violet opens the door, and a very-much-alive Edward Temple brushes past her, entering with so much authority that Violet is surprised that he even rang in the first place.

I prefer spirits to men like Edward any day, she thinks.

"I want to see my mother," Edward Temple says.

"Weren't you just here this afternoon?" Violet asks, wondering what Edward is up to now.

"Did you see this?" Edward asks. He holds a placard he

found in front of the gate that has a big red X over a photograph of Miss Temple taken at a fundraiser.

"No, I didn't," Violet says, although she and Queenie have been busy for days taking down dozens of signs with even stronger sentiments.

Edward towers over her and has a habit of always standing too close. Although Violet hasn't seen him in several years, he looks the same, except his dark hair has begun to gray. He wears a look of superiority he's had since adolescence. His gray suit—probably worth six months of Violet's salary—is accessorized with a charcoal gray shirt and a tie that matches to perfection.

Edward twists a large gold ring on his right hand that contains a red stone.

He cools his gruffness and flashes a smile that Violet believes is intended to charm her. Instead, it makes her more uneasy.

"I just thought I'd give the old broad a proper send-off," Edward says as if crassness is the only language she might understand. "Bet you'll be glad when she finally kicks off."

Violet debates whether to tell him that nobody should talk about their mother this way. From her perspective, people are fortunate to have mothers at all, even if that mother is Miss Temple.

When Violet doesn't respond, Edward rolls his eyes and adds a smirk at the end, as though to say, *we can play it that way if you want.* He isn't usually this crass, and she wonders if he is worried about the *Temple Book of Secrets* going public.

Edward steps into the living room and glances around as if taking a mental inventory of the antiques in the room. Inheritance, in families like these, means a great deal. But he isn't giving any clues as to what he might be scheming.

"The old place hasn't changed much. It still has as much charm as a funeral parlor."

Edward smiles and twists his ring again.

Is he nervous? Violet wonders if he might lose his fortune if all these threatened lawsuits come to pass.

She tries to remember the last time Edward visited. It was probably Mother's Day, three or four years ago. Before that, he came more often. Now he's here for his third visit of the day. A record by any means.

While Violet stands in the center of the large Oriental rug in the hallway, Edward surveys his father's study and then walks into the dining room. On the dining room table is a stack of photographs Rose brought of her ranch in Wyoming. He picks them up and studies each picture as if to assess the ranch's net worth.

"Surely you realize she's shown up again just in time to cash in," he says.

"That doesn't sound like Rose," Violet says.

"She's not who you think she is," Edward says, his tone soft now as if this softness might convince Violet of its truth. "She's taking advantage of the situation."

"Not everyone is like you, Edward," Violet says.

"Have you forgotten who you're talking to?" he asks.

She has never had much patience with him or anyone who looks at her like a landowner overlooking his property. This is precisely why she will never let her daughters do domestic work.

"Miss Temple is my boss, Edward, not you."

"At least for now," Edward says with a grin.

It occurs to Violet that if Edward inherits the Temple mansion after his mother dies, she'll for sure be looking for a new job.

Seconds later, he moans and bends over.

"Damn ulcers." He takes a bottle of antacid tablets from his jacket pocket and pops two into his mouth. He crunches them while Violet waits. She seems to always be waiting these days, and she's not sure why.

"Tell Rose I know what she's up to," Edward begins again. "And tell her she won't get away with it. She gave up her right to any Temple money when she moved to that Godforsaken place." He tosses the photographs back on the table before going into the sunroom. Then he opens a drawer to the wicker table Miss Temple uses as a desk and shuffles through his mother's papers as if looking for something he's lost.

"I don't think you should be doing that," Violet says.

"Who's going to stop me?" Edward asks. "You?" He winks at her.

A cold chill ignites a memory that haunts Violet as surely as the Temple ghosts. At fourteen, she was making a little money helping her grandmother during one of the Temple's charity events. Edward was home from college, and she had stepped outside to take a break from serving. It was hot. The peepers were croaking their little hearts out in the fountain on the other side of the garden. She didn't even realize Edward was there until he grabbed her and pulled her into the garden shed. When she screamed, he covered her mouth, and she bit him hard until she tasted his blood in her mouth. Edward pushed her aside and cussed her all the way to the kitchen.

Violet inhales sharply and reminds herself that the event was twenty years ago.

"What is it?" he asks, stepping back into the foyer.

"Ghosts," Violet says. She forces herself to look him in the eye. She will bite him again if she needs to. All the way to the bone.

"Call an exterminator," Edward says with a laugh. He goes into the study that was his father's office. She can hear him going through the desk drawers and wonders if she should tell Queenie.

That night, twenty years ago, was the first time Violet realized the role women in her family played with the Temples. Edward acted entitled to her and seemed surprised when she fought back. In a way, it was like they were both actors playing the roles their ancestors played.

Right after, her grandmother had known what happened without Violet saying a word. She's always been like that. She knows things without being told. That night her grandmother doctored the bite on Edward's hand and used an ointment that she laced with chili pepper. Edward's scream was just as loud as Violet's had been in the garden shed. He left Violet alone after that. She always wondered if her grandmother put one of her spells on him to keep him away. If so, she hopes the spell is still working.

Clearly agitated, Edward returns to the foyer. Whatever he is looking for, he hasn't found it. He smells of expensive musky cologne. Has Edward forgotten about his mother's aversion to scents? Or perhaps he doesn't care.

"I guess I've put off seeing her as long as I can," Edward says. He makes a grimace that seems almost boyish.

Edward follows Violet upstairs, and they enter Miss Temple's bedroom.

"Hello, Mother, how are you feeling today?" he asks cheerfully.

Does he not realize she's in a coma? Violet wonders.

Edward walks past Lynette like she is invisible and kisses his mother on the forehead before sitting at the foot of the bed. He crosses his hands on his lap as though a position honed and polished at a school for deathbed etiquette. Violet feels certain Edward will play the good son until he gets what he wants, which seems to be whatever he was looking for downstairs.

"Mother, are they treating you all right?"

He glances at Violet and talks to his mother like they are having a polite dinner conversation. He fills Miss Temple in on his work and tells her how horribly busy he has been. He asks if she received the flowers he sent to the hospital and waits a beat for her to answer.

A crowd has gathered that has nothing to do with a ghost tour. Someone rattles the gate. Who knew secrets could get people so riled. Violet wonders if she should call the police, and she and Lynnette exchange concerned looks. The ad in this morning's paper questioned the wrongful conviction of a long-ago murder. None of the parties are still alive, except for a few descendants who seem to want revenge.

Edward describes to his mother in detail about what is going on outside. Something Queenie had suggested they never mention to Miss Temple in case she can hear. Every few minutes, Edward reaches over and pats his mother's hand with four quick taps, as though patting the head of a bunny at a petting zoo.

Surely, even comatose, Miss Temple can see through her son's performance, Violet thinks.

Meanwhile, Lynette hovers over Edward like he might turn off the life support machines while she isn't looking. She also peers occasionally out the window where the crowd is building.

"Well, Mother, I must be going," Edward says finally. "I need to go outside and deal with the rioters. They're very upset about those secrets in the newspaper. Whoever is doing this must be very angry with you," he adds. "There's certainly plenty of people that fall into that category." He leans over and kisses Miss Temple on the cheek.

As soon as Edward steps away from his mother's side, Lynette double-checks the machines.

"Would you like me to show the gentleman out?" Lynette asks Violet, sounding like one of the bouncers at the jazz clubs she and Jack went to before the girls were born.

Edward turns and looks at Lynette like he's just now noticing her. He wastes no charm on her. "I can show myself out," he says. "I used to live here." He then stops in front of a full-length antique mirror to straighten his tie before leaving, perhaps to irk Lynette. Violet and Lynette follow him to the second-floor landing where they watch the door to make sure he goes. Without looking back, Edward crosses the foyer, walks out the door, and then slams it.

"Who died and made him king?" Lynette stands with her hands on her ample hips.

"That was Edward Temple, Miss Temple's son," Violet says.

"I know," Lynette says. "When he was in here before, he was absolutely rude to his sister. Didn't even speak to her. He just laughed and stared." She scoffs. "Forgive me for saying so, but I don't think he cared one bit about his mama laying there. I think it was all just a show for us."

"I couldn't agree with you more," Violet says.

The lights in the old house flicker as if the ghostly Temples agree, too.

"Is that them?" Lynette asks, looking more than a little alarmed.

Violet nods.

All day the house has been more psychically alive than usual. Like the people outside, the former Temples are riled. Violet glances at her watch again. She is ready to be home, where the only spirit in their apartment is a bottle of rum in the kitchen cabinet used to mix with honey, garlic, and lemon whenever she and Jack are getting colds.

The noises outside grow, as Miss Temple's energy builds. The whole house is humming along like a Hoover vacuum cleaner. In the meantime, Violet's shoulder confirms that something big is about to happen.

CHAPTER TWELVE

Old Sally

O ld Sally stops her rocking and listens to the message on the wind. Except for the light of the full moon, the beach is dark.

"It's time," she tells Rose and Queenie. "We best be going now."

Old Sally stands, ignoring the pain in her hip, and walks inside. Urgency accompanies her movements as she gathers items in the cloth bag she uses to tote ingredients for her spells.

"What is it, Mama?" Queenie asks, following her inside.

"You two wait in the car. I'll be right there," Old Sally says. She needs to not forget anything. Every ritual requires certain sacraments.

Queenie and Rose return to the car. A few minutes later, Old Sally joins them.

"Tonight, Iris crosses over into the next world," Old Sally says to them, "and I'll do my best to help her."

As they drive into Savannah, Rose is quiet in the back seat. Even Queenie isn't talking much. When death is close, people often get quiet. Life's biggest mystery requires respect.

Rose leans forward with a question Old Sally has been expecting. "Have you used Gullah magic on my mother?" she asks.

"Mostly protection spells, so others don't get hurt," Old Sally says. She always knew she would never lie to Rose. "Whenever your mother gets puffed up with meanness, it doesn't sit right in her belly."

"You mean Iris could have stopped all that stomach upset herself if she'd just been nice?" Queenie asks.

Old Sally nods.

"Lord, have mercy," Queenie says. "I wish Iris had figured that out. Then Violet wouldn't have to carry those tinctures around."

"What most people don't know," Old Sally begins again, "is that Iris has her reasons for being the way she is. Your mama was a sweet thing at first," she says to Rose. "She was a good girl and tried to do everything right, so her mama and daddy might praise her. But they be too busy to even notice her. The only thing that got their attention was meanness," she continues. "That's when they sat up and noticed because they be worried that Savannah's rich folk might judge them. Edward inherited this meanness, too, just as sure as if it had passed down like the Temple family china."

"I forget Mother has her reasons for being the way she is," Rose says.

"That be true," Old Sally says. "But just like any of us, your mama could have chosen to be something different if she wanted. She had a heart of gold, too. She just lost track of it."

"Is that the only spell you used on her?" Rose asks.

Heaviness sits in Old Sally's chest. Sadness older than her and passed on from an earlier time. "There be another spell," she begins, her tone softer. "This spell be started by my grandmother, Sadie, against the old slave master Temple for sending away the children of the slaves to work other places, never to be seen again."

"Oh, that's horrible that he did that." Tears sparkle in Rose's eyes, but Old Sally has no time to capture them. "That would be my great-great-grandfather?" Rose asks.

Old Sally nods and pulls a burlap doll from the pocket of her dress to show Rose and begins again. "This spell requires a special root that can only be found deep in the swamps of southwest Georgia. The root is ground up and put inside this doll."

Rose takes the doll and looks at it for a long time, and then sniffs it. "It smells like molasses and marsh water," she says. Rose starts to pass it to Queenie, who holds up a hand and says *no, thanks.*

"Every year, I put new roots in the doll to keep the spell fresh," Old Sally begins again. "This is a revenge spell, pure and simple. It makes any Temple sick to their stomachs when they are the master over people. That's why you've never had a stomachache in your life, Rose, and why your mother has more than most."

"I don't think it ever occurred to Iris that life had anything to teach her," Queenie says. "Or that she may be the cause of her own discomfort."

"That be right," Old Sally says.

The messages Old Sally has received from the other world confirm that Iris Temple's time on this earth has ticked

down to a matter of hours instead of days. For decades Old
Sally has known that she would be present for Iris's death.
Her family and the Temple family have been entwined for
generations like a sweetgrass basket woven and bound tight
enough to hold water. Old Sally's family carries the secret
elixir to cure the dark parts in the Temple's history. Centuries
have passed where Old Sally's family has mingled with the
Temple bloodline. Old Sally's mother was a result of this
mixing, as was Queenie.

The closer they get to Savannah, the more Old Sally feels
pulled into the agitation of Iris Temple. It confirms that this
crossing will not be an easy one. Some souls are ready to
leave this earth and embrace the transition feeling their work
is complete. Others fight it with everything they have. They
are the ones who have unfinished business.

And if anyone has unfinished business, it be Iris Temple, she
tells herself.

Within a mile of the Temple home, Iris's edginess makes
Old Sally clutch her cloth bag and pray for the strength she'll
need for the battle ahead. She hopes there is enough strength
in her hundred-year-old body to do her part in the ritual.

When they enter the house through the kitchen door, the
Temple spirits rush forward, clamoring for Old Sally's attention. In the center of the room, she stops and waits. To Old
Sally, the Temple ghosts are like youngsters that can't sit still
and get into mischief all the time. When she worked in the
house she was always telling those ghosts to behave. They
listened, for the most part. But now it seems those youngsters—with the help of the Temple secrets—have grown into
something much older and darker.

"What is it, Mama?" Queenie asks. "You look
frightened."

"The spirits. They all riled up," Old Sally says. Shadows

dance in the room, but with no precise shapes. Old Sally points to a note on the kitchen table. "That be for you," she says to Queenie.

Queenie reads the note from Violet aloud:

DEAR QUEENIE,

Edward was here again tonight. Creepy, as usual. There was a crowd at the gate earlier, too, but the police came and made them leave. I've gone home for the night, but Lynette is upstairs watching after Miss Temple. I hope all goes well. V.

OLD SALLY FEELS the imprint of Violet's earlier distress. She is glad that her grandchild went home to be with Jack. Jack will never let anything bad happen to her. Like Rose, Violet is a special child, too, but in a different way. After Old Sally is gone, Violet will make sure the Gullah traditions don't get lost. The safer she stays, the better.

"Why was Edward here again?" Rose asks.

"Sometimes, the spirits of the living get riled up with the spirits of the dead," Old Sally says. "That's why so much happens on a full moon. The veil is thinner between the two worlds."

"I forgot there's a full moon tonight," Queenie says.

"A blessing and a curse," Old Sally says. "There be no turning back now."

The color leaves Rose's face.

"You'll feel better once your mother passes," Old Sally says to her. *We all will,* she thinks. She squeezes a bit of reassurance into Rose's hand.

Old Sally isn't surprised that Edward has shown up three times today. Everything happens in threes right before a significant change. He's been waiting a long time for this moment. Once his mother is out of the way, Edward gets to do whatever he wants with the Temple estate. But Old Sally will have to deal with him later. For now, it is his mother that requires her full attention.

Rose and Queenie follow Old Sally through the dining room and into the foyer. She spent sixty years of her life working in this house and could walk through the rooms with her eyes closed and never run into anything. Her mother worked here before her, and her mother's mother before that. As a girl, she explored it when the Temples weren't around. In some ways, she knows the Temple house better than her own. She certainly cleaned it many times over. And though she hasn't been here for twenty years, she hasn't missed it one bit.

The ghost of the third Edward Temple stands halfway up the stairs as if waiting to greet her. Old Sally sees him clear as a sunny day, though Rose and Queenie don't appear to. This is Queenie's father. Wooden arms and legs used to hang on various hooks in his office in the Temple home. The sight of them always shocked Sally. Sometimes he would make the wooden limbs dance for her like he was a puppeteer, and they were his puppets.

The second Edward Temple, in specter form, stands at the top of the stairs. A surgeon in the Civil War, he was said to have lost his mind as a result of the mountain of arms and legs he amputated. He still wears his officer's uniform. Even as a ghost, his eyes are open wide, still witnessing the horror. Old Sally's grandmother, Sadie, had a boy child by him who was sent away before the war to a plantation in Virginia. They never knew what happened to him, and they never saw him again.

Old Sally's family tree is so gnarled she can barely keep it straight herself. Patterns have played out for two hundred years like they have all been puppets to the same puppeteer. In the past, she's thought of their intertwined history as a Gullah spiritual with different verses.

But now it be time for a new song, she tells herself.

For over three decades, Old Sally has known a change was coming that would end the dark pattern. The other world has sent messages foretelling the change for years, in dreams, tea leaves, and inner knowing. All speak a language Old Sally understands. Yet the messages lately all point to danger.

The *Temple Book of Secrets* showing up makes sense, too. All sorts of darkness releases before the light comes, that's why people always say it's darkest before the dawn. Old Sally caught sight of that old book many years ago. Before Edward the 3rd died, it was kept in a desk drawer in his office.

Once when it was on the top of his desk, she looked inside. It was a fancy ledger, covered in leather, where each wealthy family had a page with a list of bad things they'd done. Pages filled with different inks made from different pens, the dates going back to when her Grandmother Sadie was a girl. Some families had died out or didn't even live in Savannah anymore. But others still lived here.

Notations of who beat their wives or had mistresses. Notes about fathers who messed with their children. Heavy drinkers. Barren wives. Addicted sons and daughters. Slaves who disappeared. Illegitimate children. Secrets that even generations down the line make a family look bad. Old Sally had never seen anything like it.

It be like the devil keeping track of all his people's evil deeds, she thinks. Nothing at all about anything good.

Queenie offers a hand, and Old Sally holds it as she

climbs the spiral staircase. Rose follows a few steps behind. Old Sally rarely climbs steps anymore. Her house is on one level.

"White people just keep building up and up," Old Sally says, "reaching for the sky instead of earth." *Makes no sense,* she thinks.

The second Edward Temple laughs like what she said is ridiculous. They don't want her to succeed. They want Iris to stay with them. As long as Iris stays behind, the past has more power and keeps people down. She pauses, and Queenie asks if she's okay. She says she is.

"Are the spirits still active?" Rose asks.

Old Sally nods. "Like a fancy party where everyone is in attendance."

The Edward Temples in the past were not especially mean men, but they chose women who carried their meanness for them.

"Is my father here?" Rose asks.

The question from Rose doesn't surprise her. It broke Rose's heart when her daddy died so young. Though feeling rushed, Old Sally turns and touches Rose's cheek.

"Mister Oscar be a better man than several Temples combined," Old Sally begins. "Your daddy's ghost doesn't hang out with the other Temples. He stays in his office on the main floor."

Rose glances in that direction.

At the top of the stairs, Old Sally holds Queenie's arm to steady herself. It feels like she's walking into a strong wind. A wind that wants to steal her breath. The closer Old Sally gets to Iris's room, the more Iris's spirit shoves her away.

When Old Sally enters the bedroom, Iris Temple laughs from the in-between world. She will not go to the other side without a fight. The forces are stronger than Old Sally expected. Her head lowered, she pauses and asks Queenie and Rose to give her a moment to think. Her mind races like a general putting together a plan before going into a battle where the enemy is twice as big as anticipated. All the crossings she attended have been tame compared to this wildness.

Queenie and Rose both carry Temple blood and will be useful in their fight. But based on Iris's resistance, Old Sally needs more help than she thought. She debates whether to call Violet, but it seems her granddaughter has dealt with dark forces enough for one night. Another presence in the room calls for her attention, and Old Sally raises her head. A large white woman in a nurse's uniform stands next to the bed. In that instant, Old Sally knows this stranger is the additional help she needs.

Lynette smiles at Old Sally like somehow she recognizes what they will do together. Her ancestors have chosen her. A hard-earned kindness surrounds her, as someone strong enough to overthrow the dark and claim the light.

As Old Sally approaches Iris's bed, she senses Iris gathering strength in the in-between world. Being back in the Temple house is giving Iris power. For the longest time, Old Sally thought everyone heard voices from the spirit world. The first time dead people talked to her, she was still a girl and thought she was making up the voices in her head. But the older Sally got, the more she realized that she could communicate with people in the spirit world. What she didn't know is that people in a coma are in this in-between world, too. She thinks of it as a waiting room where people are waiting to be called. Except it isn't a room, it's a way of being.

A conversation commences between Old Sally and Iris that no one else can hear.

I'm here to help you transition, Iris.

I'm not ready to go, Iris says. *I need to set something right.*

The spirit world thinks you be ready now, Old Sally says.

You and your stupid voodoo magic, Iris says. *You're nothing but a fake.*

Then how am I talking to you? Old Sally asks.

Iris pauses like Old Sally may have a point. *What's she doing here?* Iris asks, her words aimed at Rose.

Old Sally glances at Rose, who has regained some of the color in her face. *She's come to say goodbye to you.*

It's just like her to crawl back on her hands and knees, Iris says. *All she wants is my money.*

Iris's stomach revolts in a loud grumble, revealing to Old Sally that her spell is still at work.

You did this to me, didn't you, Iris says to Old Sally.

You did it to yourself, Old Sally says.

Shut up, old woman. Iris laughs.

Within seconds, Iris's smugness changes to weeping, now a helpless child. Whenever a spirit is threatened, it takes on many disguises.

You don't fool me, Old Sally says.

Come close and comfort me, Iris says, in-between bouts of crying.

But Old Sally refuses to fall for Iris's trick. This childlike part is the most dangerous. It will do anything to get its way. Not stopping until it wraps its arms around Old Sally's neck and chokes the life out of her.

Lynette pulls a chair close to the bed and encourages Old Sally to take a seat. Old Sally thanks her, sits, and places her cloth bag on her lap. The room is quiet except for the sound of the machines.

"Mama, do you need anything?" Queenie asks from behind her.

"A glass of water, please," Old Sally says. "And a clove of garlic from the kitchen," she adds.

Queenie leaves for the kitchen, and Old Sally turns to Rose, "Gather me a piece of your mother's hair."

She pulls a pair of kitchen shears from her bag and hands them to Rose, who walks over to her mother. Rose's hand trembles as she holds the scissors.

"You can do it, Rose," Old Sally says. "Your mother needs your help."

I don't want her touching me. Iris says. *She deserted me.*

While ignoring Iris, Old Sally encourages Rose to cut her mother's hair.

Iris screams at Rose and forbids her to touch her.

Unable to hear her mother's pleas, Rose clips a small strand of hair and then gives the scissors and the hair back to Old Sally. Old Sally thanks her, not letting on at how much her mother is cursing Rose in the spirit world.

From her bag, Old Sally pulls out a small black iron bowl that looks like a miniature cauldron. She places the hair inside, along with ingredients she gathered earlier that day. In the background, Iris pleads, sobs, and then insults everyone in the room.

When a person's spirit is disturbed, sometimes the best thing to do is to turn a deaf ear. Old Sally is good at hearing only the things she wants to hear.

Queenie returns with the garlic and glass of water. Old Sally takes the water and drinks it. Water always helps ground her.

"I thought garlic was to keep away vampires," Queenie says, handing her mother the bulb.

"Oh, I don't need it for a spell," Old Sally says. "I need it for a recipe tomorrow."

The women laugh, which serves Old Sally's purpose.

Laughter clears fear out of a room. However, Iris isn't laughing.

"I need your help with the transition," Old Sally tells the three women. They stand at attention, three soldiers enlisted in Old Sally's army.

"What can we do, Mama?" Queenie asks, speaking for all of them.

"Iris Temple be putting up all sorts of resistance," Old Sally begins, "because she knows she hasn't done right in this life. But she won't take care of that old business, either. She needs to go fully into the spirit world. Right now, she's stuck in-between, and she not be going to the next world without a fight."

The three women exchange looks like they are wondering what they got themselves into.

"I think my grandfather had trouble transitioning, too," Lynette tells Old Sally. "I wanted to help him, but I didn't know how. That's part of the reason I became a nurse."

"You be right, honey," Old Sally says. "And your grandfather wants you to know you did all the right things back then. He appreciated the help."

"How do you—" Lynette begins.

"Your Old Sally just knows," she says. "Now, let's be getting down to work."

Iris's right hand shakes like she's pointing a finger to condemn their actions. Rose and Queenie take a step back, while Lynette steps forward and holds Iris's wrist.

"Her pulse is fast," Lynette says.

"That's because she be putting up a fight," Old Sally says.

Worry creases Rose's forehead like she's already had one too many battles with her mother.

"Nothin' to be afraid of, child," Old Sally says to Rose.

"This be a good thing. Not only for you, but for your mother, too. Unfortunately, she not see it that way. Not yet, anyway."

"Just tell us what to do," Queenie says. She holds her head high, ready for the task.

Even though Queenie has never studied the healing arts on Old Sally's side of the family, she has never questioned it, at least not to Old Sally's knowledge.

As Old Sally stands, her bad hip sends a shooting pain down her leg and into her foot.

Most people don't realize that there's an invisible world that is just as real and complicated as the visible one. Old Sally has a foot in both worlds.

"First, we need to form a circle and hold hands," Old Sally says to the women. They do as they are told and form a half-circle around Iris's bed.

"What I be telling you tonight will sound crazy," Old Sally says, "but even if you question it, I need you to pretend you believe." She looks each woman in the eye to get their agreement. "We need to use our imaginations now," Old Sally begins again. "That be one of the languages used in the other world. We need to imagine a circle of light surrounding the bed. This light be creating the opening for Iris to leave."

Of the three women, Rose looks the most uncertain. Soon, Old Sally will know how much Rose trusts her. Meanwhile, Queenie knits her brow as though intent on creating the light while Lynette's efforts sit heavy on her broad face. Old Sally waits for Rose, who inhales deeply and finally nods.

"Your job be to make the light so attractive and filled with goodness that Iris can't resist going toward it," Old Sally says to them. "Then imagine an opening at the top of the ball of light that Iris's soul can go through and leave this world."

Old Sally thinks of herself as a midwife, except she helps people leave this life instead of enter it. She's helped dozens of people make this crossing, and though everyone is different, many things are similar. People who have a peaceful passage are usually the ones with no regrets. These people feel complete, and even though some have had hard lives, they have made peace with what their lives have been. It is the ones with resentments and disappointments who go kicking and screaming into the next world. In Old Sally's experience, the ones who resist life in all its fullness of light and dark also resist death.

"It be over soon," Old Sally says to the women, at the same time reassuring herself. After this, Old Sally can finally rest, and Queenie and Rose can carry forward a new legacy as the next generation of Temple women.

Iris laughs as if amused by Old Sally's thoughts. *You'll never get to relax, old woman,* Iris says. *You're nothing but a servant. My servant. Who worked for sixty years for my family for next to nothing.*

Iris's words are meant to weaken her, so she won't be able to fulfill her task.

I've come to set you free, Iris, Old Sally says in the spirit world. *You've been locked into being a Temple, just like those secrets have locked people into doing your bidding. You never tried to get free of this prison, except for that one time with Mister Grainger. That boy was sent to set you free, too. But you were too scared and stubborn to go with him. If you had gone with him, your ending would be totally different. Life is like that, Iris. Sometimes it comes down to a single choice.*

Iris's struggle grows stronger. *You don't know what you're talking about,* she says.

The spirits on both sides are in a tug-of-war as Iris tries to pull Old Sally into her world. Yet Old Sally stands firm. To anyone walking into the room, it might look like an ordinary gathering of a family around a deathbed. But it is much more than it appears. Many years before, the stage was set for this final scene to play out.

Death calls Iris Temple to the journey we all must make. Old Sally is a witness to this call. Iris's life energy wanes. Her soft moan grows to a scream, loud enough for Old Sally to want to cover her ears. After several seconds, the screaming fades to a quiet weeping. Iris refuses to give up easily. Old Sally calls on her ancestors for more help. After a few moments, her grandmother Sadie appears in spirit form and stands at one shoulder and her mother at the other. In the far corner of the room is an old black woman in tribal dress she has never seen before. Is this Sadie's mother, who never left Africa? Old Sally closes her eyes to concentrate on the task at hand. Her past must not distract her.

To Old Sally, death is the next great birth, and it is the grandmothers who are needed for this task.

Death be women's work, Old Sally thinks, *just like birth be women's work.*

Rose's gaze drops, as though her mother's latest surge of anger has weakened her. Queenie puts her arm around Rose, keeping the circle intact. Old Sally can count on Queenie to watch after Rose. Just like she did when Rose was a girl. At the same time, Lynette stands steady, her large legs like the trunk of a live oak anchored to the ground. Her attention hasn't wavered.

Never underestimate the power of a large woman, Old Sally thinks, and then thanks the spirit world for sending Lynette to help.

Old Sally speaks, her voice growing in power with each

word. "It won't be long now, children. She be almost ready to go." She says what the women need to hear.

Three generations of Temple women have carried the darkness that Old Sally's grandmother experienced first, back in the slaveholding days. After her son was sold off, her grandmother wept nearly every day, crying out to God to make it right. Grief bound them to the Temples for all these years. Tonight, if Old Sally succeeds, that grief will finally stop, as the ancestors foretold. If she is unsuccessful in helping Iris transition, then it will have to be healed in the next generation. Or the generation after that. Like those secrets in that old book, someday the grief will find a way to come out.

Only Old Sally hears the torment coming from Iris's unmoving lips. The machines continue to breathe for her and monitor her heartbeat. Nothing, as far as anyone else can tell, has changed. However, an invisible war is playing itself out in a final battle.

At Old Sally's suggestion, they hum to make their bond stronger while still holding hands. Iris's resistance grows like a hurricane coming ashore. A roar fills Old Sally's ears. Chaos crackles in the spirit world. Old Sally's body quakes in the storm. For the first time in all her years of doing this, she feels all might be lost. Instead of Iris dying, it is she who might die.

Like a vessel at sea riding the giant waves, Old Sally and her ancestors rock with the current. She reminds herself that she is not alone. Queenie asks if Old Sally is okay. She says she is, and at the same time, wonders if this might be her transition, too.

"Keep holding hands," Old Sally says, "and hum louder."

The women hum and sway as the hurricane passes

through them and between them. Seconds later, they stop humming, and a calmness spreads over the room. They have stepped into the eye of the storm. Then to the complete surprise of the four women standing hand-in-hand, Iris Temple opens her eyes.

CHAPTER THIRTEEN

Queenie

"Good Lord in heaven!" Queenie shrieks. The four women stare at Iris like she is Lazarus walking out of the tomb.

Queenie had thought for sure they were successful in helping Iris to the other side. She'd never concentrated so hard in her life. But it appears that all they've helped her do is open her eyes.

Too bad the newspaper isn't here to take photographs for the society section, Queenie thinks. She imagines the headline: *Savannah's Grandmother Cheats Death!*

All this while amid the biggest scandal in Savannah's history. A secret a day hasn't kept the doctor away, it is making her sicker. Every day Queenie wakes and wonders if today is the day that all of Savannah knows her most tender confidence.

Iris's eyes take in the room, but the rest of her doesn't move. Her lips tremble as she tries to speak, and she emits something like a frustrated groan. Rose's mouth drops open, and even Old Sally looks surprised. Lynette picks up the telephone and has an animated discussion with someone, probably Iris's doctor. Evidently, Iris has done something miraculous by waking up. According to Lynette, Iris should be dead now. Even the machines say so. But Iris is as alive as any of them.

Iris opens her mouth, but nothing comes out.

Queenie thinks of all the times she longed for Iris to shut up. Yet as awful as Iris can be, Queenie wouldn't wish this helpless fate on anyone.

Old Sally leans close to Iris's ear and whispers something. Iris's eyes blink and then blink again. Queenie doesn't begin to know how her mama talks to spirits or even near-spirits, in Iris's case. All she knows is this is weird.

Lynette gets off the phone and steps over to Iris. "Hello, Miss Temple. I'm Lynette Fielding," she says, a little too loudly. Does she think Iris's muteness has also made her deaf? "I'm an RN, and I need to check you over a little bit, okay?"

Lynette, who makes Queenie look petite in comparison, shines a small penlight into each of Iris's pupils and then checks her reflexes.

When Iris looks down at her body, her eyes widen. Queenie can only imagine her half-sister's horror at wearing a light blue backless hospital gown, the ultimate in bourgeoisie.

"The doctor will be here in about an hour," Lynette says. "I can't believe he wants to come out. Doctors don't do house calls anymore. Can I get you anything?" Lynette offers a toothy smile and pats Iris on the hand.

But as Queenie can attest, doctors do make house calls for Iris. They always have. And they will continue to do so as long as she might dedicate a new wing to their hospital.

Old Sally nods like Iris is giving her an ear full. Everyone turns to Old Sally, waiting for a translation of the unspoken conversation.

"She's asking for Edward," Old Sally says.

"Do we know how to get in touch with him?" Rose asks.

"Only Iris would know that," Queenie says.

Iris looks at Rose as if to push her out of the room with her gaze. Queenie has never understood why Iris hates Rose so much. Perhaps even Iris doesn't know. A whisper of gas escapes into the room, evidence of Iris's unspoken thoughts. Queenie wishes she had some of Violet's essential oils.

"Oh my, did you have a little accident in your diaper, Miss Temple?" Lynette says in a whisper as she pats Iris's hand. "Don't worry, sweetie, I'll take care of it."

Iris's eyes ignite in a primal—yet silent—scream.

Lynette rolls Iris over and pulls open the back of Iris's gown. She peeks inside. Queenie imagines Iris would rather jump off the widow's peak of her house than wear adult diapers.

"Nothing there," Lynette reports. "Maybe it's just gas. That seems to happen to you a lot." Lynette turns to the others. "We had a phrase for that when I was a girl," she whispers with a wink. "'Silent but violent.'"

Lord, in heaven, Queenie thinks, *Lynette's lucky Iris can't move, or she'd be in traction before she even knew what hit her.*

Old Sally stands close to the bed as if listening to Iris's thoughts. "What's she saying now, Mama?" Queenie asks.

For Iris to have to rely on Old Sally to convey her wishes must feel like Iris's version of hell.

"She be agitated," Old Sally says. "She keeps saying to

contact Bo Rivers. Something about a key to a safe deposit box."

It must have something to do with the Book of Secrets, Queenie thinks. Yesterday the newspaper ran another secret accusing a prominent family finance company, led by an equally prominent patriarch, of embezzlement. His wife is one of Iris's so-called friends at the Junior League. If Iris had been awake to read it, she might have had another stroke. And if Queenie's secret ever shows up, she may have to take a bed next to Iris.

"Does she have anything to say to me?" Rose asks Old Sally.

Old Sally listens for a long time, her face unable to mask her disappointment. Iris must be telling her things she can't or won't repeat. In response, Old Sally begins to hum an old Gullah melody to calm Iris.

But Queenie can't imagine anything calming her half-sister while in this paralyzed state. Seconds later, the machines in the room scream out in alarm. Lynette rushes toward the machines but then stops. She looks at Iris and then back at them.

"Do something," Rose begs Lynette.

Lynette's expression reveals her helplessness. "I can't. Miss Temple has a *do not resuscitate* order."

"She does?" Rose asks. "That doesn't sound like Mother."

"Edward had her sign some papers a few months ago," Queenie says. "I delivered them to Bo River's office myself."

At the time, Queenie wondered why Edward would make his mother sign such an order. Perhaps he was preparing for a moment exactly like this, so his mother's death wouldn't drag out.

Iris's eyes dart around the room as if finally realizing

what is going on. The women join hands again without Old Sally saying a word. They circle the bed and hum again. Queenie imagines a circle of light and goodness calling her half-sister home. When that doesn't seem to work, Queenie imagines a bucket of the Colonel's secret recipe chicken in the center of the circle. To her surprise, Iris begins to calm. Queenie smiles briefly and wonders what would get her to go toward the light. She imagines Denzel Washington calling her home to the Promised Land and smiles. Although Oprah would be tempting, too.

Old Sally sits at Iris's side holding her hand. Perhaps her mama is encouraging Iris to let go and telling her that everything will be okay. Rose has tears in her eyes. Queenie leans closer to Rose. She can't even imagine having to say goodbye to her own mother and pushes this thought away. Finally, Iris closes her eyes. Queenie waits for them to pop back open, but they don't. Then just like on the television shows where the patient flatlines, the urgent sounds of the machines become a single tone.

After Lynette turns off the machines, the room goes silent. She looks at her watch. "Time of death, 11:54 p.m.," she says.

Old Sally releases Iris's hand and moves to a chair in the corner. She rests her head in her hands.

"What is it, Mama?" Queenie asks. "Iris has crossed over, right?"

"It didn't work," Old Sally says.

"What do you mean?" Rose asks.

"Iris's transition," Old Sally says. "I wasn't able to help her complete it."

"You mean she's not dead?" Queenie asks.

"She be dead all right," Old Sally says. "But her spirit be stuck in the in-between world."

"Does that mean I still have to run errands for her?" Queenie asks. The other women turn to look at her. "Just asking," she adds.

Iris's body gets the last word with a final, triumphant hiss.

CHAPTER FOURTEEN

Violet

Miss Temple *would want me to use the silver serving dishes instead of the China,* she thinks.

Violet has worked since six a.m. preparing food for the funeral reception and still has things to do. Every edible sea creature known to Savannah is spread out on the kitchen counters in serving dishes that she is now covering with cellophane to store. A knock on the kitchen door pulls her away from the task, and she opens the door to find Spud Grainger holding a plastic bag full of fresh scallops.

"I couldn't have done this without you," Violet says, giving him a quick hug.

"Happy to help," Spud says, but he doesn't look happy at all. In the other hand, he carries several posters pulled from the ornate ironwork surrounding the house.

"You look exhausted," Violet says, feeling worn out

herself. She hasn't had time to consider how Spud might be affected by Miss Temple's death.

"I've been up all night," he says.

In a suit and bow tie, Spud is already dressed for the funeral later this morning. For his sake, she hopes there isn't a scene. If polled by Savannah's upper class, Miss Temple's approval rating would be in the negative numbers. However, popular opinion appears to be changing. At least a little. Two posters she pulled off the gate yesterday had a different message and portrayed Miss Temple as a kind of folk hero.

Spud helps Violet carry the serving dishes to the spare refrigerator next to the laundry room. In the last bit of space, she stores the scallops to prepare later.

"Would you like a cup of coffee?" Violet asks, putting the posters in the trash.

Spud accepts her offer. "Iris would hate all those terrible signs on the fence. Does anybody know who's putting those secrets in the newspaper?"

"We have no idea," Violet says. "We were hoping it would stop after Miss Temple died, but they haven't."

Spud takes a seat at the table. "Iris would be so disappointed about how the Temple legacy is being tarnished," he says.

Thirty minutes before, Rose and Queenie left the kitchen to get ready for the funeral, and Violet was looking forward to some uninterrupted time. She has a thousand things to do, but she can tell Spud needs to talk.

Ten years ago, Spud began delivering Miss Temple's exotic meat—bringing only the best cuts, trimmed to perfection, carefully wrapped in single servings—as if Miss Temple herself might receive these gifts. But since her employer rarely stepped into the kitchen, Spud began coming to see

Violet. Not in a romantic way. He is old enough to be her father. Perhaps that was part of the initial draw since Violet never had one.

After pouring him a cup of coffee, Violet cuts two slices of banana bread, a small one for her, a bigger piece for Spud. She sits at the kitchen table, almost expecting her chair to still be warm from when Queenie and Rose were there.

Violet has often thought that more healing goes on around kitchen tables than in churches. At least it always felt that way at her grandmother's kitchen table when Violet was a girl. Meals were celebrations that not only included good food, but laughter, tears, singing, love, and conflicts— all aspects of life. To Violet, kitchens are where community happens.

In a way, it makes sense that her dream is to open a tea shop and bakery in downtown Savannah for an even bigger community to enjoy. But her dream can wait. She returns her attention to Spud.

"What did you think about all night?" Violet breaks off a piece of banana bread and eats it. It's delicious if she does say so herself.

"Mostly memories," he says. "The time when Iris and I were together."

"How did you meet her?" Violet asks. She's curious why she never thought to ask this before.

Spud smiles and pauses like he's gathering his thoughts.

"I played saxophone in a small jazz band called the Grainger Quartet," he begins. "We played local clubs and wedding receptions and various engagements with the Savannah Historical Society."

Violet has never heard this story, and it seems important for Spud to tell it.

"I first laid eyes on Iris in the mid-seventies at one of

our gigs for the Historical Society." He looks out the window into the garden as if reliving the moment. "Her presence captured my imagination, the part that's prone to improvisation. She was older, of course, and a privileged member of Savannah. Iris was everything I wasn't supposed to want or have. Perhaps that was part of the attraction." He turns away from the window and smiles at Violet. "Love doesn't always abide by the rules of social order," he concludes.

"My grandmother worked here then. Did you ever meet her?" Violet asks. "She goes by the name Old Sally."

Spud narrows his eyes as if searching the past. "I do remember her. She was very regal looking."

Violet likes to think of her grandmother as regal.

"Whenever my quartet played one of Iris's events, and we were on a break, we went to the kitchen, and your grand-mother fed us," Spud says. "She took a liking to me. One time she asked if she might have something of mine to add to some kind of collection. *Something small,* she said. I didn't really understand why she wanted it," he continues. "But I didn't want to refuse her. She was quite persuasive if you know what I mean."

You have no idea, Violet thinks. And if her grandmother's personality isn't persuasive enough, there are always her spells.

"The only thing I had on me that night was a box of brand new saxophone reeds," he says.

Violet remembers a small rectangular box with gold lettering. "Oh, that's where those came from," Violet says with a laugh. "My grandmother collects things. I always wondered what those were."

"I'm sorry, I'm confused," Spud says.

"It means she chose you," Violet explains. "She kind of

watches out for certain people. People that she feels need her for one reason or another."

"Well, I was always struggling in those days," Spud says. Then it seemed my luck changed. Maybe that was your grandmother's doing," he adds with a chuckle.

"Maybe," Violet says.

"Is she still alive?" Spud asks. "That must have been forty years ago."

"Alive and well," Violet says. "We just celebrated her 100th birthday last January."

"Impressive," Spud says. He pets his mustache. "Next time you see her, please tell her how much I appreciate her looking out for me."

Violet promises she will as Spud straightens his tie again.

Several years ago, Violet counted how many times Spud straightened his tie over coffee. The result was seven, but today he seems to have doubled his efforts.

"My quartet played for Iris's daughter's wedding reception," he begins again. "I can't remember her name."

"Rose?" Violet asks.

"Yes, Rose," he says. "We played 50-minute sets, with a 10-minute break to rest our lips and grab a smoke. Rose was marrying a young man from somewhere out West. I remember this detail because it was the first and only wedding my quartet played where the groom wore a cowboy hat. I don't think Iris liked that. She always worried about appearances in those days."

Violet doesn't tell him that Miss Temple probably died with the same concerns, the *Book of Secrets* being her biggest worry. She glances at her watch. Violet won't have time to go to the church now, with all she has left to do, but maybe the graveside service.

"Oh my, Iris was beautiful in those days," Spud continues. His gaze drifts. "I wasn't so bad-looking myself. People used to say I looked like James Dean."

He turns his profile for Violet to see the resemblance. She nods, even though she has no idea who James Dean is.

"I never deluded myself into believing that I had anything to offer Iris," he says, sadness showing in his eyes. "I've been replaying the past for days now, ever since you called to tell me that Iris had passed. The news hit me hard, Violet. I couldn't even work the next day."

She reaches over and squeezes his hand, and he returns the squeeze.

"What I keep remembering is that first time we got together," Spud says. "Can I tell you about it? I've never told anyone before."

"Please do," Violet says. She has to admit she's curious. She can't imagine her former employer in the throes of a passionate love affair. It's hard to imagine Miss Temple passionate about anything except perhaps elevating the Temple's social status.

"It was after her husband, Oscar, died. Iris was planning a charity house tour, and I came here to talk about the music. She asked if I wanted tea and when I said yes, I was surprised that she went into the kitchen and made it herself. For some reason, your grandmother was gone."

"I didn't think Miss Temple ever stepped foot in the kitchen," Violet says. *Except for leaving her critiques,* she thinks.

"Well, I'd never had anything other than sweet iced tea in my entire life," Spud says. "So when she served me a cup of hot tea from a silver tea service, I had no idea what I was doing. I'd watched enough British movies to know how to hold up my little finger when I drank from the fancy cup," he says, with a laugh. "Can you believe I was that naïve?"

Violet touches his hand again. "I can relate to being naïve. It took me years to get used to the day-to-day excesses of the wealthy," she says. "Especially while Jack and I watched every penny."

Spud nods as though he's watched a few pennies himself.

Violet imagines what a handsome man Spud must have been earlier in his life. Photographs of a younger Miss Temple always surprise her. At times, even Miss Temple looked softer and prettier.

Spud continues with his story. "Iris and I were in the sunroom when she asked me if I was familiar with the free love movement. I can't say I had any idea what she meant. It's not like Savannah had hippies in those days. But that was the first time I realized that Iris wasn't just a Temple, but a woman with desires."

His eyebrows rise as he lowers his head. "Since I was much braver back then, I asked if I could kiss her. Keep in mind I was a musician. Who was I to think I could kiss someone like her? Savannah bowed at her feet."

Violet's face grows warm with the thought that Miss Temple would not like her housekeeper and cook knowing something so intimate about her.

"Afterwards, she led me upstairs to her bedroom," Spud says without looking up. He stops here, as if, as a gentleman, he has gone far enough. Then he looks at her. "She refused to call me Spud, you know. She called me Henry. She said the name Spud, sounded common, like a French fry."

They laugh. Violet can imagine Miss Temple's inflections while saying this, the emphasis on *French fry*. However, her actions are much harder to visualize. In a way, Violet wishes she had known this side of Miss Temple. The side that allowed herself to be swept away by a jazz musician.

Violet touches his arm. "How long did it last?" she asks.

"Several months," he says. "To keep it private, we spent weekends on Hilton Head. Those times were some of the happiest of my life."

His eyes redden, and he pulls a handkerchief from his suit jacket.

"Why did it end?" Violet asks, genuinely curious.

"Iris called it off," he says, blowing his nose. "I'll never forget the day her letter arrived, telling me that our love affair was over. She threatened to sue me for everything I had if I ever told anyone, and I haven't told a soul until now."

"I'm so sorry, Spud."

"Me, too," he says. "But the most difficult part was that attached to the letter was a check for 180,000 dollars. I think Iris was reimbursing me a hundred dollars for every day of our six months together. I still have the letter," he adds.

Spud blows his nose with vigor now, as though all these years later, he is still insulted by Iris's actions. "I never cashed that check."

"Oh, Spud," Violet says, "love is hard no matter what the circumstances, but this sounds devastating."

"What I want to know is, why do rich people always think money is the solution to everything?" Spud asks.

"I have often wondered the same thing," Violet says, thinking this is one thing she'll never have personal experience with.

"Iris changed after that," Spud begins again. "She was always proper but never cutting. I changed too," he adds. "I disbanded my group, and I took a full-time job at the Piggly Wiggly as their butcher." He neatly folds his handkerchief and puts it in his breast pocket. "Then years later, she started coming to the Piggly Wiggly to order her exotic meats," he continues. "I knew it was more than that. I knew she wanted to see me. To see how I was. You don't travel across town to get something you could have delivered from anywhere in the world right to your doorstep. You don't do that unless you want to see someone and want to let them know that you still care. Right?"

"I wish she could have told you how she truly felt," Violet says. "We all deserve that much."

He sighs and agrees. "I think the most hurtful thing was that Iris required that it be kept a secret," he says. "She was convinced our affair would ruin her."

"What is it about the Temples that attracts so many secrets?" Violet asks.

"I know. It's such a mess, isn't it?" Spud says. "By the way, I saw the *Book of Secrets* once that everybody's talking about. Iris showed it to me. She said that whoever had that book could bring Savannah to its knees."

"Well, I'm not so sure about bringing Savannah to its knees, but it has certainly brought Savannah to our gate."

Spud gives a brief smile. "You know, now that I think about it, Iris mentioned that there was a second book that nobody else knew about."

"A second book?" Violet doesn't know if she has the stamina to withstand the fallout from more secret books.

"She didn't say much about it," Spud continues. "Just that it could be dangerous if it fell into the wrong hands. Where do you think that one is?"

"I have no idea," Violet says, and she doesn't want to know.

Spud thanks Violet for listening, glances at his watch, and says he'd better get going. They hug again and say their goodbyes.

The house returns to quiet, except for the unseen entities

that offer an occasional bump and rattle. Cold air brushes past her. She rubs goosebumps on her arms.

"Is that you, Miss Temple?" Violet asks as she looks around the kitchen. "He still loves you, you know."

A heavy sadness descends. A sadness that feels more like Miss Temples than her own. She shivers again and reminds herself that she doesn't have time to be a counselor for ghosts. At least not right now. She has a reception to prepare for.

Violet retrieves the scallops from the refrigerator and thinks again of Spud. Miss Temple's time with him was like a *Get Out of Jail Free* card.

"Too bad you didn't take advantage of that," Violet says, in case the newest Temple ghost can hear her.

How would Miss Temple's life have been different if she'd made decisions based on what her heart wanted instead of her head? How would any of our lives be different?

"This is what happens when books of secrets are more important than relationships," she tells her deceased employer. But it seems Miss Temple is gone. Perhaps to make it to the church on time for her own funeral.

CHAPTER FIFTEEN

Rose

M other would like this, Rose thinks.
      The street in front of the Catholic Church has
been blocked off for her mother's funeral, which promises to
be well-attended. Do people want proof that the grand
matriarch of Savannah is finally dead?

People gather outside to chat, and some even smoke. A
cacophony of smells rises from the crowd, as though every
fragrance ever denied them at her mother's insistence is
being worn on the day of her funeral.

Talk of secrets is everywhere as she overhears several
people suggest that this will be the end of the daily reveal in
the newspaper. But isn't that assuming her mother was
responsible for them? That just doesn't make sense. Besides,
Queenie told Rose the secrets showed up in the classifieds
every morning the entire time her mother was in a coma.

Rose wonders if the person or persons responsible are in the crowd of mourners. She surveys the guests and decides that they all look guilty of something.

It is a sweltering day, even for Savannah. The air is thick with humidity as if the clouds might burst at any moment, releasing the rain. The thickness holds the scents close to the ground like a cloud of toxic waste hovering near the earth's surface.

As Rose walks through the crowd, she receives a few nods from old family friends, who are at least pretending to mourn. Most everybody else appears to hide their glee. Inside the door of the church, Rose grabs a program and uses it to fan the fumes. The church reeks of a hundred years of incense, which seems tame compared to what is outside.

The obituary in the newspaper that morning applauded her mother's philanthropy over the years, as well as her commitment to the betterment of Savannah. Though her mother was generous to specific organizations, to Rose it sounded like a press release written by her mother. The announcement only mentioned her brother, Edward, and spelled out in several paragraphs the Temple lineage. A lineage that made no mention of Rose and Queenie.

Rose thinks of Old Sally. Given the predominance of Temple ghosts already "stuck" in the house, Rose hopes that Old Sally is wrong about her mother's transition being incomplete. Perhaps her mother's spirit made a belated exit after all. Or maybe she's here right now.

"Rest in peace, Mother," Rose says aloud as she enters the empty sanctuary. She wears a simple black dress and heels she pulled from her closet at home and threw in her suitcase before leaving Wyoming, an outfit she hasn't worn in the seven years since Max's uncle died. Ranching seldom calls for formal attire.

Rose walks down the same aisle of the church that she walked down when she and Max were married. A platinum casket with gold handles sits in front of the altar, where her father's casket sat many years before. It didn't matter that he wasn't Catholic and may have preferred another church. Her mother was in charge of everything and—in her usual way —used the event to showcase the Temple family.

Should she view her mother's body before people arrive? Rose debates this issue while Queenie and a younger priest enter the sanctuary through a side door. Wearing a black dress with a large yellow sash and a yellow hat, Queenie waves as she and the priest discuss lighting and sound as though preparing the stage for a Broadway production. They stop momentarily to reposition several containers of flowers —full of their own scent to rival the incense—that might impede the flow of traffic. Then Queenie and the priest exit stage left.

As if stepping to the edge of a precipice, Rose inches closer to view her mother in repose. The top half of the casket is open, revealing a plush white lining dotted with gold stars sewn into the fabric, as though the person in the coffin was a president or one of the heads of state.

A bit over the top, Rose thinks, *but this is just the kind of thing Mother would have picked out for her exit scene.*

Her mother's lips form a stern, thin line like she is bound and determined not to rest in peace. Her makeup is minimal, something she must have specified in her funeral arrangements, and her white hair is perfectly styled the way her mother has worn it since Rose was a girl.

Rose's mother is dressed in an elegant black dress, as if a mourner herself, and wears a double strand of pearls, the creamy-white in perfect contrast to the black. Proof that you can take it with you, at least until after the service.

While viewing her mother's body, Rose studies her like a possible portrait subject. She notes the line of her mother's brow, the slope of her nose, her wrinkled jaw—the skin all drooping southward in a tribute to her Dixie roots.

A door opens in the back of the church, and Rose jumps like she's been caught stealing the pearls from around her mother's neck. Queenie strolls down the aisle. Despite the sobering occasion, her eyes sparkle.

Sweet Queenie, Rose thinks. *What would I do without you?* This moment would be much harder if it were Queenie in the casket or Old Sally. A thought which makes her feel guilty.

"How are you holding up?" Queenie asks as she joins Rose.

"To be honest, she seems like a stranger," Rose says.

Queenie squeezes Rose's hand. "I doubt anyone really knew Iris," Queenie says. "Including Iris."

"Do you think she was ever happy, Queenie?" Rose's voice catches on a snag of emotion.

"For a brief period years ago," Queenie says. "But it didn't last for long."

"It's like privilege robbed her of any ability to be real," Rose says. "I wonder who she might have been without the Temple money. What might she have done if she had to venture out and forge a career?"

"I guess we'll never know," Queenie says.

They gaze into the casket, as though peering into the vastness of the Grand Canyon. On the ranch, death is a mystery that reveals itself quite often. Nature makes sense in the way it takes care of things. The weak die. The strong survive. But it is harder to put humans into that model. She would have thought her mother was too strong to die.

As Rose contemplates the meaning of life—a hazard of

attending any funeral—Queenie pulls a tissue from her purse and covers her mouth overcome with emotion. Rose does her best to console her but then realizes that Queenie isn't weeping at all. In fact, she is doing everything she can to keep from laughing.

"What's going on?" Rose whispers. Her eyes widen with the question. She doesn't know whether to be alarmed or intrigued.

"Can you keep a secret?" Queenie whispers, her hand still covering her mouth.

"Of course I can," Rose whispers back. She has been bred to keep secrets. In a way, secrets are the family business. Just ask anyone in Savannah right now. But what could be so funny on such a solemn occasion?

Queenie pulls Rose toward the closed end of the casket and taps the top of the lid with a fingernail. It makes a slightly hollow sound.

"The secret's in there," Queenie says. Her voice remains a whisper.

Rose's face registers her confusion. "The secret's in Mother's casket?"

Queenie nods. Rose's thoughts jump to a letter or something of sentimental value. Perhaps a locket or a trinket. Or maybe the infamous *Temple Book of Secrets*. But this doesn't make sense. Why is Queenie fighting so hard not to laugh?

"I don't understand," Rose whispers.

Queenie leans toward Rose and whispers back, "I put something in the casket."

Rose studies Queenie's face, and she gives Rose a grin that can only be described as sheepish.

"Don't be mad," Queenie says.

"Why would I be mad?" Rose whispers.

Queenie pauses as though weighing the consequences of

her confession and then announces: "I put a bucket of Kentucky Fried Chicken at your mother's feet. Or between her knees, actually."

Queenie's whispered confession carries the strength of a Shakespearean actor projecting to the back row of the empty church. Her eyes glisten with tears and not tears of grief.

"You did what?" Rose says in full voice.

"I wedged a bucket of Kentucky Fried Chicken between your mother's knees," Queenie says in a quasi-whisper. Then she shrugs, as though disbelieving of the news herself.

Rose's shock slowly warms to a muffled laugh. Her face turns red and hot.

"It seems only fitting," Queenie whispers in conclusion. "It was, after all, her favorite food. And not the least bit exotic, I might add."

Two sets of double doors fling open in the back of the sanctuary as if orchestrated by well-trained theater ushers. The first wave of aromatic mourners enters the church. Queenie takes Rose's arm and steers her into the family pew. Rose refuses to look at Queenie in case the glance might cause a snicker to escape. Rose anticipated her mother's funeral might be difficult, but she never expected that it might be difficult for this reason. She begs Queenie to be quiet and then grits her teeth to stop the laughter that threatens to burst past her lips into the room.

Do not laugh, she tells herself. *Do. Not. Laugh.*

Rose forces herself to think of tragic things like world hunger and puppy mills. Nothing is working. Then a more urgent problem presents itself. Rose locks her knees together to stop her bladder from releasing. She reminds herself that she is at her mother's funeral, not the best venue for hysterical laughter or menopausal bladders.

"Are you angry with me?" Queenie asks.

Rose shakes her head. Queenie's defiant gesture seems mild, considering everything she put up with over the years. It is the element of surprise that has put Rose at risk of losing it on more than one level.

Luckily, Rose and Queenie's squelched laughter sounds close enough to the sounds of grief that the stares they receive are out of sympathy instead of shock. The organist, soft-pedaling their grief, begins to play one of her mother's favorite hymns, *Onward Christian Soldiers*. In response, Rose imagines an army of fried chicken legs marching off to war led by a miniature Colonel Sanders.

A snort of laughter escapes that she segues into a cough. She forces herself to count the panes in the stained glass window in the side chapel. Perhaps if she engages the mechanical side of her brain, it will override her desperate need to laugh. In the meantime, the perfumes, colognes, and aftershaves of two hundred mourners—who have undoubtedly dabbed on extra portions on her mother's behalf—consume the musty, incense-laden, flower-filled church. Refusing to go down without a fight, the aroma of fried chicken joins the other smells. The cumulative effect makes Rose's eyes water. It also makes her nauseous, which proves the most effective tool in stopping her need to laugh.

A door squeaks open in the side chapel, and Edward steps inside. He looks straight at Rose and gives what could be mistaken for a sneer. Suddenly, laughing is the last thing she feels like doing. Encounters with Edward always prove to be a bit harrowing. First, there was the brief, bizarre meeting in the garden and then Edward's macabre visit to their mother's bedroom later that afternoon.

Queenie nudges Rose and motions in Edward's direction. Rose nods that she has seen him, too. The nub of her missing pinkie throbs.

The young priest enters from behind the altar and begins the service. According to Queenie, he has stepped in at the last minute to replace the older priest, who has been ordered bed rest because of a mild cardiac infarction the day before. The young priest is probably thirty at best and is a Sunday school Jesus look-alike with shoulder-length brown hair. Her mother would not be pleased.

Will he pull out a guitar and lead the mourners in Kumbaya? As an afterthought, Rose leans into the aisle to see if he is wearing sandals. If her mother were still alive, his informality would prompt several letters to the Vatican. Long hair and guitar singing are for the lower classes. As is anything else that might hint at liveliness.

Throughout the next hour, several people from the community get up to eulogize her mother. If not for their familiar faces, Rose would think they were paid actors endorsing a product. Iris Temple was *generous to a fault*, says one. *Thoughtful,* says another. *Selfless,* says yet another. The woman described in the eulogies is not Rose's mother. No one speaks of secrets, either, yet she imagines that is precisely what is on everyone's mind.

Glancing at her mother's casket, she decides that it is ingenious product placement. Then her stomach growls. Maybe it is the smell of chicken, but she is suddenly borderline ravenous. Why didn't she eat at the house before they left? At the time, she wasn't hungry. Now she salivates as she envisions the banana bread Violet made that Rose turned down. The current speaker looks over at her, an older gentleman wearing a bow tie. Did he hear her stomach growl?

Spud Grainger gets up to eulogize her mother and introduces himself. The name sounds familiar, and Rose wonders where she's heard it before. His dark suit is accented with a pale yellow shirt and a bow tie that looks like the wings of a monarch butterfly. He has kind eyes and seems like the type that would take in stray animals, yet paradoxically he mentions he is the head butcher at the Piggly Wiggly.

Rose nudges Queenie's arm. "Who is he?" she whispers.

"Long story," Queenie whispers back. "I'll tell you later."

Rose nods.

As Spud Grainger speaks, he stops several times to blow his nose into a white handkerchief he pulls from his jacket pocket. Of all the mourners, he is the only one who appears genuinely bereaved. Rose wishes she had known the woman he grieves.

Meanwhile, the front of the church smells more and more like a fried chicken franchise. Rose fantasizes about tiny Styrofoam containers holding mashed potatoes with gravy, as well as small white dinner rolls. It doesn't help that Spud Grainger is going on and on about exotic meats. Her stomach growls again, louder than before. Sound carries quite well in the sanctuary. Unfortunately, smells do, too.

The reptilian part of Rose's brain plots out different ways to scavenge food. She fantasizes about creating a diversion so that she can make her way to the altar and grab a chicken breast from between her mother's knees. Perhaps she could do it under the guise of revealing one of the biggest Temple secrets. However, she's not sure what that would be.

She glances at her watch. Katie, Rose's daughter, is due in from Chicago any minute for the graveside service. Rose busies herself with worrying about the synchronization of Katie's different flights and landings as the next speaker rises to eulogize her mother, offering more praise for the saint-like Iris Temple.

This is overkill, Rose thinks, regretting her word choice.

Rose looks over the large crowd of Savannah's elite gathered to pay their last respects. Some of the same people attended Rose's wedding. She didn't know them then and doesn't know them now. The wealthy do this for each other. They throw parties and donate to each other's charities and attend weddings and funerals. But other than that, they are strangers. Except these strangers, who are wearing Rolexes and designer fashions, seem poised for a revolution.

The young priest steps forward to end the service, asking one final time if anyone has anything they want to say. Edward rises from the shadows and walks over to their mother's casket. He rests a hand on the top as if a gesture of ownership.

"Thank you for your heartfelt acknowledgment of the Temple family's contribution to our fair city," Edward begins as if to remind the angry mob of their manners. His words are as polished as his shoes. He exhorts the Temple brand, reminding everyone that Savannah wouldn't be Savannah without the Temples. And despite any hard feelings of late, because of a few unfortunate secrets, they should be grateful that it wasn't worse. He looks at Rose as he speaks as if to remind her who is now in charge. His hubris, like his suit, seems perfectly tailored to fit the event. His presentation would have probably made their mother proud.

THE SERVICE FINALLY OVER, Rose avoids Edward and steps into the first black limo she comes to outside of the church. Queenie follows her, a splash of color among all the black. Rose rifles through her purse and pops three cinnamon Altoids into her mouth, hoping the curiously strong mints will count as sustenance. She has a headache now.

"I'm starving," Rose says to Queenie, her mouth on fire from the mints.

"Hold on," Queenie says. "Let me see if I have something."

Queenie drapes her large purse across her even larger lap and pulls things out of her bag that look like they might belong to some kind of southern survival kit: lipstick, billfold, two different types of bug spray, a crumbled box of tissues, a paperback mystery, four crumpled packets of Splenda, a small roll of twine, a red Swiss army knife, and enough colorful headbands to set up a store display in the corner of the limo.

Queenie finally offers Rose a handful of orange Tic-Tacs that are loose in the bottom of her purse. Rose picks off the biggest pieces of fuzz before popping them into her mouth, along with two aspirin and the cinnamon Altoids. Her mouth puckers in disgusted satisfaction. As Queenie loads everything back into her purse, Rose chews the aspirin and Altoids, leaving only small pellets of orange Tic-Tacs to suck on.

"Edward was in rare form today," Queenie says.

"This is an awful thing to say about my own brother, but I don't trust him," Rose says.

"I would worry about you more if you did," Queenie says. She straightens her hat that nearly touches the roof of the limo.

"He always stays at the country club when he's here," Queenie says. "In the past few years, he's come to Savannah and not even told your mother. I would see him in town when I ran errands. I never told her, though. That would be just the thing to get your mother on the warpath."

"Why would he not tell her he's in town?" Rose asks. She crunches the last of the Tic-Tacs.

"I don't think he could stand to be around her," Queenie says. "Lord knows she would test the patience of Job."

The limo leads the procession to the graveside. At the entrance, people hold placards that say things like **Good Riddance** and **The Wicked Witch is Dead.** Queenie and Rose hold hands as if to fortify themselves against the scene.

"Why are they so angry?" Rose asks.

"They think she's a snitch," Queenie says. "They thought she was the one releasing the secrets. Now they don't know who it is, but they're still angry."

The limo passes through the wrought-iron gates leading to the section of the cemetery where the ornate Temple mausoleum stands. The last time Rose was here was when they buried her father, over two decades ago.

Thick clouds gather and block the sun. Though a bit cooler, the humidity seems to be rising. Within minutes, an afternoon drizzle begins. Edward stands on the other side of the priest. Even though it is only three o'clock, his five o'clock shadow is pronounced. He seems alone, even in a crowd, which causes Rose to wonder if her brother ever gets lonely.

As far as she knows, he has lived in the same penthouse in downtown Atlanta for the last thirty years and has never married or lived with anyone. His firm specializes in helping corporations handle scandals—another form of dealing with secrets. Rose can't even imagine the wealth he has amassed while she and Max have struggled to keep the ranch afloat. Being a Temple in the southeast can have its advantages. He probably doesn't have to work at all, but just wants to have something to do.

Despite the rain, there are smiles on the faces of several mourners. Do they think the *Temple Book of Secrets* is being buried with her mother? *Along with a bucket of chicken, thanks to Queenie,* Rose thinks. She resists smiling.

A few minutes into the graveside service, a taxi arrives.

In the distance, Rose's daughter, Katie, gets out of the cab with another woman. They share a large rainbow pride umbrella as they approach. Rose smiles at the thought of her mother turning cartwheels in her grave as her lesbian granddaughter makes a flamboyant entrance.

Rose and Queenie part to make room for the two women on the front row. Rose notes Edward's instant disapproval as his glare now includes raised eyebrows. As the *Kumbaya* priest leads them in prayer, Katie leans into her, and Rose pulls her close. The rain increases. Rose briefly greets Katie's latest girlfriend, Angela, a woman Rose has never met and has actually heard very little about. Angela's hair is short, almost shaved, and she appears to be ten years older than Katie, maybe more. Multiple piercings make Rose wonder if she wants to look younger than she is. One piercing is on the side of her nose, another through her bottom lip and yet another through her tongue. Three holes on each ear are filled with silver studs. And these are only the ones Rose can see.

How in the world did she get through airport security? Rose wonders.

Wearing a tasteful gray dress, perhaps a little too short, Katie has even donned a bit of makeup for the occasion, making Rose think that maybe she has some Temple blood in her after all.

Her daughter looks like a Catholic school girl in comparison to Angela, who could just as easily be dressed for an equality rally in Washington, D.C. She wears black leggings and black loafers with a pink oxford shirt, shirttail out.

She must be baking in this heat, Rose thinks. If her mother were still alive, she would write Angela a handwritten letter to educate her about proper funeral attire.

Katie stands next to Rose, their shoulders touching. The

four of them, including Queenie, now share the large colorful umbrella as the rain increases in intensity once again. All stare at the coffin posed in front of the family crypt.

Through the years, Katie has asked very few questions about Rose's mother, and Rose hasn't volunteered the information. Twenty-five years before, Rose moved out West with Max and started a new life. Now that the reason for her staying away is gone, will she feel the need to visit more often? She hasn't realized how much she missed Queenie and even the old house, as well as Old Sally and Violet. Not to mention the ocean and the moisture, intent on baptizing her at every opportunity, now with rain at her mother's funeral. Maybe the question now is how she is going to go back to Wyoming.

The various fragrances of the mourners have mellowed into a smell resembling an over-ripe banana wrapped in a magnolia blossom. As the misty rain continues to fall, the dry-eyed mourners now look a little bored. Violet stands at the back of the crowd in a red raincoat, her posture erect like a dancer. It feels generous of her to come to the funeral at all, given the stories Rose has heard about how difficult her mother was.

By the time the priest has finished his remarks, the rain has grown in intensity to a mild tropical storm. The skies open up and produce raindrops the size of small tree frogs and just as hard to avoid. Black umbrellas spring open with a touch, one after another, as if choreographed for a Gene Kelly musical. Quick, awkward handshakes are exchanged as everyone disperses for their cars. The wind grabs at their umbrellas and creates a spattering of muffled expletives from the mourners. A loud rumble of thunder accelerates their departure as if her mother is warning them that they haven't heard the last from her.

Rose and Queenie run for the black limo, followed by Katie and Angela. The four of them scramble into the back, laughing from the exhilaration of the run. They dry off as best they can with the box of pink tissues from Queenie's handbag. Their funeral attire makes them look like waterlogged crows. Formal introductions are made all the way around, and they exchange damp handshakes. Rose has forgotten that Katie and Queenie have never met. It seems these two important women in her life should somehow already know each other.

Angela's streaked eye-liner adds to the crow effect. Katie dabs at Angela's rogue eye-liner, a gesture that reveals a level of intimacy that surprises Rose. She thinks back to an earlier girlfriend, also named Angela, when Katie was a freshman at Smith. While home for Christmas during her freshman year, Katie announced over eggnog that she had fallen in love with her roommate—the first Angela—who at the time of the announcement was sitting in Rose and Max's living room. Rose and Max tried not to overreact. It was Smith, after all, and this could possibly be a four-year phase. But the phase did not end after Katie graduated. After many hours of discussion about the matter, Rose and Max came to a simple conclusion: they loved Katie and wanted her to be happy and would stand by her no matter what the world thought of her lifestyle choice.

Now that Rose is getting a better look at her, the current Angela looks at least forty. According to Katie, Angela is a writer of feminist fiction and has won a Lambda Literary Award, an award Rose is embarrassed to say she has never heard of.

"Who was that man standing next to the priest?" Katie says. "He looked familiar."

"That was your Uncle Edward," Rose says. "You met him once when you were very young. He had a layover in Denver, and we drove over to meet him for coffee."

"Oh," Katie says as if discovering long-lost relatives is a regular occurrence.

"We've never been close," Rose says. "He's six years older than me."

A new tattoo peaks from underneath the cuff of Katie's sheer gray blouse as she reaches to hold Angela's hand. It is a thin vine of roses around her wrist.

"What is it with young people and their tattoos these days?" Rose asks, ready to change the subject.

Her relationship with Edward is too complicated to explain on an empty stomach.

Katie pulls up the sleeve of her blouse to show her latest prize. Katie collects tattoos like charms on a charm bracelet. They all have meaning to her. Rose tries not to reveal her worry that when Katie is elderly and getting sponge baths in the nursing home, she might regret having a skull and crossbones tattoo at the base of her spine.

"They don't mind if you have those at work?" Rose asks.

Right out of college, Katie, somehow miraculously, acquired a job in Chicago working for Harpo, Inc.

"No, Mom, they encourage self-expression," Katie says. "And they're not called tattoos anymore. They're called body art. You should see Angela's."

Her daughter's new girlfriend's tattoos don't rank high on her list of must-sees. Yet Rose smiles and nods as though she will schedule it on her calendar. Angela looks at Rose like she sees straight through to her thoughts. They exchange a moment of understanding, both agreeing to suspend judgments during this initial meeting.

When they leave the cemetery, the protesters are still there, their signs now smeared with rain. To distract herself, Rose contemplates what symbol she might imprint on her aging body. Given her name, a rose would be the most obvious. Although when it comes to flowers, she actually prefers lilies to roses.

"Is this your first time visiting Savannah, Angela?" Rose asks, all the while thinking, *it can never be said that I don't make an effort.*

"It's my first time anywhere in the South, actually," Angela says. "It's, uh, interesting," she adds, as though searching for something nice to say and coming up empty.

Will Rose's birthplace ever outgrow its stereotypes? Northerners often make conclusions without ever spending time here.

Katie has a new girlfriend every six months. At this point, Rose tries to not get too attached to them, especially the ones she likes, because those are usually the ones that come and go the fastest.

"It's my first time in the South, too, Mom," Katie says.

Rose turns to face her. "Of course you've been here before, sweetheart," she says. Then she thinks back to their infrequent family vacations. Yosemite one year, the Grand Canyon, Monument Valley, then for Katie's graduation from high school, Santa Fe. "On second thought, I guess you haven't," Rose adds.

Katie gives Rose a look like *duh* should be tattooed on Rose's forehead.

"Well, you're in for a treat, too," Rose says to Katie, patting her daughter on the knee. If she doesn't get food soon, her social skills may deteriorate even more.

. . .

WHEN THEY RETURN to the Temple house, an elaborate buffet has been set up in the dining room. Violet has pulled off what Rose could never have managed. Even Rose's mother would find little to complain about given the grandeur of the presentation—a spread that has Rose salivating like one of Pavlov's famous dogs.

Fresh, local seafood is the fare of the day. Mounds of shrimp and oysters on the half-shell sit next to steaming seafood casseroles and luscious fruit plates, without a single serving of exotic meat in sight.

CHAPTER SIXTEEN

Queenie

W*hite people sure do know how to suck the life out of a funeral,* Queenie thinks.

She looks around at the elaborate reception. She has never seen this many white people wearing this much black and sipping this much booze. Most of them are hypocrites, as it is. They hated Iris, especially after those secrets started to leak. Queenie still has no idea how those forbidden tidbits got in the newspaper in the first place. If they were meant to hurt Iris only, then she thought they would have stopped since Iris is obviously no longer around. But even this morning, the day of Iris's funeral, there was a secret in the newspaper about a Savannah banker in the 1890s who bought his mistress a hotel in Paris where she lived with their illegitimate son.

Queenie sighs, feeling tired in her bones. Dealing with all

the secrets, and now Iris's death, has been harder than she realized. Not to mention that burials and receptions were never intended to be this dreary. When people die on her Gullah side of the family it's sad, of course, but also a celebration. They wear clothes with some color to them. At funerals they tell stories, dance, and clap. Queenie taps her foot as if hearing a song coming on. But even her foot knows better than to rock a boat with this much money in it.

Queenie thinks back to Iris's gravesite service—an event duller than dirt despite the fact that more than one attendee probably wanted to search the casket to see if Iris was taking that stupid book with her. A few rioters might have made the event more interesting, but they were kept at the gate. She wonders if they'll show up here now that the rain has stopped.

In the Gullah tradition, cemeteries are sacred ground. Often they enclose a grave with a small fence to protect the soul of the person who died, and they adorn the graves with conch shells to ward off evil spirits. On the tombstone, they leave a jar of water for thirst, a bag of rice for hunger, a candle and matches for light, and a collection of herbs and roots in case any spells need to be created in the afterlife.

None of that happened at the Temple mausoleum. If Queenie had thrown a conch shell across Iris's grave, it would have hit a dozen millionaires before it hit the ground. She rolls her eyes with the thought.

All that matters in this grand send-off is that all the right people attend. All the right food is served. All the right things are said. And an enormous amount of alcohol is consumed. Meanwhile, not a single story surfaces that might shake the body with laughter to release some of the boredom.

"Violet has outdone herself on the reception," Rose says to Queenie.

Queenie agrees. Violet is a gem.

However, since they returned to the house, Rose— usually uninterested in food—has been on a mission to divide and conquer the enormous amount of seafood on the dining room table. An impressive pile of shrimp carcasses rests on her plate as she goes in to load up on scallops, and then moves into the corner of the room to feast on them.

Katie stands next to her mother and nudges her girlfriend, who watches as if witnessing a lioness devouring a gazelle.

"You look surprised by your mother's appetite," Queenie says to Katie.

"For sure," Katie says. "At home, she usually nibbles."

"There's probably a lot you don't know about your mother," Queenie says.

"You've got that right," Katie says. "I feel like I just found out that she's been in a witness protection program for the last twenty-five years."

Queenie laughs, thinking: *Finally, some life is coming to this wake.*

Katie leans close to Queenie and whispers, "No wonder she's watched the movie *Steel Magnolias* over a dozen times."

A cackle comes out of Queenie that she has been holding in for hours. The crowd turns to look. Angela, no stranger to stares, turns to Katie.

"I can't believe the accents around here," Angela says. She gives Queenie an awkward smile, as though realizing that Queenie is one of these people, too. "I want to use this experience in my next novel," she continues. "Maybe a storyline about a transgender southern belle."

That should go over well, Queenie thinks, not really sure what 'transgender' means. It sounds complicated.

Angela excuses herself and goes into the foyer where she stands behind a prominent couple from Savannah and pulls a notepad from her back pocket to take notes. She should get an earful about Savannah's secrets.

"So, your mother never told you about any of this?" Queenie asks Katie.

"Oh, I knew she grew up in Georgia," Katie says. "But I thought her folks were probably rednecks or moonshiners or something. It never crossed my mind that they would be Ted Turner with old money and extra flash."

Queenie laughs again and then hushes herself when the mayor shoots her a dirty look. "We all have our secrets," she whispers to Katie, wondering if the current mayor also has connections to the mafia like the one revealed in Iris's book.

"Are you two talking about me?" Rose skewers a scallop, dips it in a crater of Violet's homemade tartar sauce, and swallows it in one gulp.

"Absolutely," Queenie says.

Violet brings another serving bowl full of jumbo shrimp, and Rose's eyes widen as if intrigued by the challenge.

"People must tell you that you look just like your mom," Violet says to Katie.

"All the time," Katie says. "I'm okay with it. Of course, I would have preferred voluptuous, instead of tall, lean, and flat-chested." Katie rolls her eyes and Queenie can see the family resemblance there, too. Violet returns to the kitchen.

"Do you want some seafood?" Queenie asks, noticing that Katie hasn't eaten anything.

"I'm a vegetarian," Katie says. "Vegan, actually, I don't eat seafood."

"Oh," Queenie says. "Violet can make you a cheese sandwich if you'd like."

"No, that's okay," Katie says, after a slight hesitation. "There's plenty of good stuff here."

Katie picks up a strawberry along with several pieces of cantaloupe and eats it as if to appease Queenie.

Queenie isn't sure what a vegan is, either, and wonders if it has anything to do with being gay. Katie is the first lesbian she has ever met, and Angela is the second.

Live and let live is my philosophy, Queenie decides. She knows what it's like to be judged. Plus, Oprah loves the gays.

Queenie excuses herself and goes into the kitchen. "You've outdone yourself, Vi," she says.

Violet thanks her but looks tired.

"Do you need any help?" Queenie asks. She's asked this question a dozen times today. But even as a little girl, Violet wasn't the type to ask for help.

"Not really," Violet says, loading the dishwasher. "I think I've got everything under control."

Queenie steps into the laundry room off the kitchen and takes an empty laundry detergent box off the top shelf to retrieve a hidden pack of cigarettes and a pack of kitchen matches from inside. She slips them into her dress pocket.

"Come get me if you need anything," she tells Violet. "I'm going to step into the garden for a minute."

Queenie smokes only on rare occasions, usually after Iris has trampled on her last nerve. This is definitely something Oprah would never do. But today, for some reason, she feels like she could smoke an entire carton. After lighting the cigarette, she blows out the match and waves the smoke away.

Although most of Savannah was waiting on Iris to die, it

still seems strange to have her demanding half-sister finally gone. Managing Iris was a full-time job. Now, she needs to decide what to do with the rest of her life. All Queenie knows how to do, really, is take care of people. She also knows Rose will be leaving again and who knows how long she will stay gone this time.

However, now that Iris is gone, Queenie is free to visit Rose. She also wants to try to convince Old Sally to move in with her here in the Temple house when it passes to Queenie, as Iris said it would.

But death has a way of reshuffling the card deck in unexpected ways, Queenie thinks. *Nothing is set in stone. Except maybe Iris.*

The rain has stopped. Mist rises from the pathway in the garden. Water drips from the leaves of the live oak and magnolia trees as steady as if it were still raining. Queenie stands near the fountain in a sunny spot to avoid the droplets that can drench someone in seconds. The stone face at the center of the basin glares at Queenie to reprimand her for smoking.

"Mind your own business," she says and flicks ash at him.

At least the protestors have left them alone for now. Queenie never imagined they would show up at the cemetery. It seems like people would have better things to do than stand in the rain and watch a hearse pass by.

From the far corner of the garden, Katie's girlfriend approaches. Water droplets christen her pink shirt like polka-dots. Queenie searches her memory for the woman's name. *Alice? Abigail? Oh, yes, Angela,* she determines.

Queenie greets her, and Angela asks Queenie if she can bum a cigarette. After lighting it Angela inhales and rolls her eyes with pleasure before a long exhale.

"I quit ten years ago," Angela says. "But I still need one every now and again. Especially today for some reason."

"This crowd could intimidate the Queen of England," Queenie says.

Angela smiles. "I thought it was just me."

"No, honey, it's not just you," Queenie says. "If we confiscated all the Rolex watches at this reception, we could feed a third world country for a year."

The two women laugh. The more uncomfortable Queenie is, the funnier she gets. But the two grow quiet. She has run out of lines.

"This is a beautiful garden," Angela says as she glances around.

"I played here when I was a little girl," Queenie says. "My father was Edward Temple. Katie's grandfather."

"Oh," Angela says as she blushes her surprise.

"It happens sometimes," Queenie says.

"For what it's worth, my father had an affair with his secretary," Angela says. "He sold insurance. I don't think any children came of it," she adds. "Although I guess it's entirely possible."

"Humans are complex," Queenie says.

"And stupid," Angela says.

"Amen, Sister." Queenie giggles.

Angela offers a cautious smile as if Queenie might be one of those Bible-thumping Baptists she's heard about. But Queenie isn't a Bible-thumping anything, and she has nothing against Baptists. Lord knows, we are all God's children, whatever we call ourselves.

"So, what do you think of Katie's family?" Queenie asks, thinking it best to leave the subject of religion alone.

"I can honestly say they are not at all what I expected," Angela says.

"What did you expect?"

"I was thinking *Deliverance*, not *Gone with the Wind*," Angela says.

They laugh again.

Queenie is curious about Angela and Katie's relationship. Love fascinates her, especially since she has minimal experience in the art. Actually, Queenie is probably the least experienced person in Savannah in regard to intimate relationships.

A persistent ray of sunlight dances off the piercings on Angela's nose and bottom lip.

Those piercings must have hurt like hell when they went it, Queenie thinks. She is too cowardly to even pierce her ears.

Queenie flips over a stone under the magnolia tree to reveal a tiny graveyard of cigarette butts. They add two more that sizzle in the wet earth.

"Our secret?" Queenie says, looking at the butts.

"Our secret," Angela agrees.

Secrets like this Queenie can handle. The ones that don't involve lawsuits or death threats. However, there is one secret that Queenie fears will make people hate her. That secret would be best left buried under a rock with a bunch of cigarette butts.

The side gate squeaks open. Queenie and Angela turn to look. Edward walks into the garden surveying the outside of the Temple property like he does the inside. Every time he is in the Temple home, he acts like a landlord trying to catch renters doing something wrong.

What will Edward do if Queenie gets the house like Iris promised? She doesn't anticipate that it will go over very well, even if he inherits the lion's share of property and investments. It doesn't matter that he hasn't lived in the

Temple house for over forty years; his sense of ownership is undeniable.

When he sees them, Edward lifts his eyebrows as though a judgment rides on his thoughts. She has never forgiven him for what he tried to do to Violet years ago. But even without that, she would still think he was an ass.

Without saying a word, Edward strides past them and walks through the back door into the kitchen.

"We'd better see what he's up to," Queenie says.

Queenie leads the way into the kitchen, where Edward has begun to quiz Violet on her qualifications for running the Temple household, as though conducting an impromptu job interview.

"I've worked for your mother for twenty years," Violet says. "I think that more than speaks for my qualifications."

Good for you, Queenie thinks. She's proud that someone in her bloodline has the gumption to stand up to Edward.

"I think I'll go find Katie," Angela says to Queenie. "I've seen way too many egotistical white men for one day."

Edward and Angela exchange looks as if they have summed each other up and are still in negative numbers. Meanwhile, Queenie keeps an eye on Violet and wonders if Edward even mourns his mother. He doesn't appear to.

"Can I help you with something, Edward?"

He huffs, as though Queenie's help is the last thing he needs. Without answering, he exits the kitchen into the dining room. A blast of frigid air follows him out the door, and Queenie can almost swear she just heard Iris let out a short laugh.

CHAPTER SEVENTEEN

Rose

Rose mingles in the living room, receiving condolences, hearing more perfunctory comments about how wonderful her mother was, knowing full well that nobody believes it. Her mother was not sweet or caring, nor will she be greatly missed. She was, as Queenie would say, a royal pain in the backside, to friends and foes alike.

In fact, it wouldn't surprise Rose if there were an after-party following the reception where these same mourners celebrated having her mother finally gone. But in the mean-time, Rose thanks them for their condolences and tells them each how fondly her mother spoke of them, proving she can lie as well as anybody.

At the same time, it strikes her as one of the few times her mother might have been proud of her for being a Temple. Rose is acting. She is onstage. She is playing the good daughter, the gracious hostess. And her mother, the foremost critic in her life, is not around to judge her for her performance. Or is she? All afternoon, she has had a distinct feeling of being watched.

Edward enters the living room, and goose flesh crawls up Rose's arm. He greets several men from the country club and shakes hands like a politician trying to win votes. He is acting, too. A slight smile remains plastic on his face, mixed with an appropriate tinge of grief. He turns and walks in her direction.

"Shit," she says, under her breath.

Her first instinct is to duck into the kitchen, but it's too late. She doesn't want to give Edward the pleasure of seeing her retreat. Not that she could make a quick exit anyway after all the food she has eaten. Her stomach feels like a shrimp trawler after a big haul.

"Hello, little sister," Edward says. His smile holds firm through capped and gritted teeth.

"Hello, Edward," Rose says with a shiver. *Is it suddenly colder in here?*

"How long do you plan on staying in Savannah?" Edward asks.

"I'll be taking an early flight out tomorrow," she says.

Edward sips his drink. Rose has forgotten how freely the alcohol flows in Savannah.

One day at a time, she tells herself. However, this is turning into a very long day.

"So, were you with our dear mother when she passed?" Edward asks. He glances around the room.

"As a matter of fact, I was," Rose says.

"I hope I didn't miss anything." Edward's gaze turns to Rose, an eyebrow raised.

"Not a thing," Rose says, without expression.

"By the way, where's that cowboy husband of yours?" Edward says.

Does he even remember Max's name? she wonders. "He's back at the ranch," she says.

Edward extends his smile as though he finds someone working on a ranch amusing. The less information Rose gives her brother, the better. Otherwise, he will find a way to use it against her. It is a gift he has. Edward even blamed Rose for the accident with the sword when they were children. He told her parents that it was Rose's idea that they play Cowboys and Indians and also her plan to get the sword from the weapons case.

Like a five-year-old would come up with such an idea? she thinks.

Goose flesh rises on Rose's arms again, and a shot of cold air brushes past her. She wonders if their mother is eavesdropping.

"Did you ever get married, Edward?" Rose asks. Her question comes out more pointed than she intends, but she offers no apology.

"I'm married to my work," Edward says. "She's a sweet bitch of a wife, too." He narrows his eyes as if to say: *Is that the best you've got?*

Ever since they were young, everything was a contest. Edward can put a spin on anything so that he comes out the winner. It doesn't matter what the truth is. It is all about winning the game.

The smell of rotten eggs causes Rose to cover her nose. Her olfactory sense is worn out from the day. Edward doesn't seem to notice the smell.

"Well, enjoy your trip home," Edward says. "I've got to do more damage control around those damn secrets. Nobody seems to have a clue who's doing it. Is it you?"

"Me?" Rose asks, taking a step back.

Edward smiles again as if Rose's defensiveness gives him the advantage.

"I'm surprised you don't have possession of the book yourself, Edward. You always were the most likely heir of the Temple weapons, including the *Book of Secrets*."

Before he has time to respond, a brick flies through a window in the sunroom. Rose ducks and covers her head. She looks for Katie. Somebody screams. Chaos follows. The crowd gathers in the hallway, forming a semi-circle around the lone brick. Whoever threw it had a good arm. The sunroom juts out from the house but is still a good twenty feet away from the gate.

Edward runs outside, but whoever did it is long gone. Several people take this disruption as an opportunity to leave. Katie finds Rose, and Angela takes notes like her new book has morphed into a crime novel. As Queenie disposes of the brick, Violet sweeps up the glass, the only real danger of anyone getting hurt. The brick was clearly a message, not a threat. The message, Rose imagines, is that people are pissed.

A man around her age, tall and impeccably dressed, approaches Rose. He asks if he can speak with her. She excuses herself from Katie and notes that one side of his mustache is shorter than the other as though his aim was slightly off while shaving that morning. He introduces himself as her mother's attorney.

Despite the recent crisis and the humidity of the day, Bo Rivers' handshake is cool and dry. He has the tan of someone who plays golf daily or spends a great deal of time on a sailboat. His aftershave is expensive and understated— one of the few fragrances in the room that isn't intentionally overdone. Unlike the other men attending the reception, he hasn't removed his suit coat, as if to further prove his inability to sweat, even after a brick is thrown through a nearby window.

"Can you come to my office next Monday, say around one o'clock?" he asks. His accent reeks of old Savannah. "We have some things we need to discuss."

"Next Monday?" Rose's return ticket is booked for tomorrow. Monday extends her stay by three days, and she is ready to be home. "Can't we do this over the telephone?" she asks. It seems a bit old fashioned to do things this way. But if Savannah is anything, it is old fashioned.

Bo Rivers takes one step closer and lowers his voice. "I think you'll want to be there in person."

"What's this about?" Rose asks.

Directness is practiced infrequently in this part of the country, but she'd like to know if it is bad news or good before she extends her stay.

"I don't think this is the time to talk about it," Bo Rivers says, his answer predictable. His glance around the room stops at Edward, who is watching them. Bo Rivers tips his chin upward as if refusing to be intimidated. "So it's settled then, Monday afternoon, one o'clock?" he asks, turning to Rose.

She nods her consent.

"My condolences again for the passing of your lovely mother," Bo Rivers says, making Rose's mother sound much lovelier than she actually was.

Within seconds of his leaving, Katie returns to Rose's side.

"What was that about?" she asks. "You looked so serious."

"Mother's attorney wants to meet with me Monday afternoon."

"Monday? I thought you were leaving tomorrow."

"I was," Rose says. "But he seemed adamant that I attend."

"Do you want me to stay, too?" Katie asks.

Her daughter has always been protective of her, and she isn't sure why. However, she now wishes someone had protected her from all this food she's eaten.

"No, honey. There's no need to stay," Rose says. "You need to get back to work, and so does ..." Rose pauses, unable to think of the name of Katie's latest girlfriend.

"Her name is Angela, Mom, and she's very important to me," Katie says.

"Sorry, honey, it's been a big day," Rose says.

"For us, too." Katie yawns, revealing a silver ball pierced into her tongue.

"You got one of those?" she asks, with a moan.

Katie smiles as if she enjoys shocking her mother. "You're so predictable, Mom."

"And *un*predictable is better?" Rose says. She thinks again of the brick.

"Don't start," Katie says, giving Rose a playful nudge. "If you're okay, I'll go mingle again," she adds. "Everybody's talking about some book your mother kept and a bunch of secrets. Do you know about it?"

"Unfortunately, I do," Rose says. "The Temples are infamous for collecting secrets of the wealthy here in Savannah. It's how my mother always gets her way. Or 'got' her way, I should say."

"Wow, Mom, your family is fascinating," she says. "I've never been to a funeral where there were protestors, and people threw bricks through windows."

"It's your family, too, sweetheart," Rose says, her smile glib.

"I keep forgetting that," Katie says.

Despite a few minor differences having to do with current cultural trends, Rose prides herself on how well she and Katie get along. They have always been close, and as an only child, Katie seemed to get along better with adults. The closest she's come to a teenage rebellion is with her latest body art and tongue piercing.

Rose glances at the familiar strangers in the room, the ones who couldn't be dissuaded by a brick. It occurs to her why they are here. Is her mother really dead? Before the funeral, she surprised herself with a good cry. In fact, she still feels a bit hungover from the emotion, although she feels better now that she has finally eaten. *Or overeaten,* she thinks.

Regardless, she is grateful to have Katie here. Like Max, Katie helps her stay calm and reminds her of her present, rather than her past. However, there are parts of her past—Queenie, Old Sally, Violet—that she has genuinely missed.

While she hasn't missed the drama, what surprises her most is how much she has missed the land—the tidal pools and tributaries, the meandering marshland, the live oaks, the Spanish moss that graces nearly every tree. She's missed the azaleas, the vibrant green moss that grows in every garden, the people rich with secrets and gossip. Rose has missed people of color most of all. People in all their many shades.

Thomas Wolfe says you can't go home again, but Rose finally feels free to do just that. It is much more than being back in her old room, or back in the house she grew up in. It is like sliding back into her skin and becoming one with the rich, moist low country of Georgia. This landscape is in her soul.

Queenie approaches with a glass of red wine in her hand.

Rose is struck again by that feeling of having someone glad to see her. Fortunately, she can return her affection.

"I'm glad your mother wasn't alive to see someone throw a brick through the window," Queenie says. "And to think I was complaining earlier about how dull the event was."

"Hopefully, that's the end of the excitement for the day," Rose says.

"We'll see," Queenie says.

Within seconds a soft chanting can be heard coming from outside. Rose listens carefully to make out the words: *Secrets, no! Book's gotta go! Secrets, no! Book's gotta go!*

"I'll drink to that," Queenie says.

Rose holds up her glass of tonic water and salutes. They clink glasses. Twenty years before, there would have been vodka in her drink. But drinking for Rose was never about celebration. It was about forgetting. And she isn't willing to forget anymore.

After entering the dining room, Violet straightens various serving trays and then picks up empty glasses and used napkins. Rose asks if she can help, but Violet declines her offer. On the way back into the kitchen, Violet stops and glances out toward the street to see the chanters and then shrugs like nothing surprises her anymore.

"By the way, did you turn up the air conditioner?" Rose asks her. "It's freezing in here."

"It's Miss Temple," Violet says, turning to face Rose and Queenie. "She's crashing her own wake."

"That sounds like something Old Sally would say," Rose says.

Queenie agrees.

"I take that as a great compliment," Violet says.

"By the way, I smelled rotten eggs earlier," Rose says. "At

first, I thought it was Edward, but maybe you're right. Maybe it's Mother."

"Oh my, this is just what Mama was afraid of," Queenie says with a tsk.

"Ignore Miss Temple if you can," Violet says. "That's what I do. Try to ignore the chanting, too."

Rose has tried to ignore her mother for the past twenty-five years, and she's not sure what good it's done. Earlier today, she finally felt free. But it seems her deceased mother isn't exactly cooperating. As if to offer commentary, another current of cold air slides across her arm. She rubs away a new crop of goosebumps.

"Well, I think Iris would be pleased with the reception," Queenie says to Rose. "I followed all your instructions to the letter. Didn't I, Iris?" She glances up as if expecting an answer from the chandelier.

"Violet did an amazing job, too," Rose says.

As they applaud, Violet gives an exaggerated curtsy. Meanwhile, the chanting outside grows louder.

"Do you really think Mother's here?" Rose asks, with a quick glance at the same chandelier. Perhaps her mother is protesting the protesters.

Violet and Queenie nod, and Rose can see a bit of family resemblance between the niece and aunt. Rose doesn't have experience with extended family. The Temple line has dwindled over the years. Her mother was an only child, as was her mother before her. Rose has often thought she was an accident and that her mother would have preferred to have just had Edward. It is obvious Edward would have preferred it, too.

Late afternoon sun breaks through the sheer curtains sending brushstrokes of light into the dining room and hallway. The Temple house always seems dark to Rose so any outside light breaking through is a welcomed change. Plus, it makes it warmer, given her mother's intent to chill.

"I'd better get back to work," Violet says, balancing dirty dishes. "I don't want to find a note in the morning from you-know-who." She smiles before returning to the kitchen.

"Did Bo Rivers approach you about a meeting on Monday?" Queenie asks Rose.

"He did," Rose says. "I hadn't planned to stay that long. But he made it sound important."

Another blast of frigid air makes them pause.

"That woman was never very subtle," Queenie says and directs a sneer at the chandelier. "It's just like Iris to be the center of attention at her own funeral reception," she continues. "She is already, of course, being that she is the deceased. But probably not in a fully satisfying way." Queenie grins.

"It must be killing her that people are protesting outside," Rose says.

"No pun intended," Queenie says with a laugh.

Meanwhile, the reception has flat-lined. Even the different scents in the room seem to be dying away. The people who are left check their watches as though counting the seconds before they can make a mass exodus after staying the obligatory hour.

"Do you know what this meeting is about on Monday?" Rose asks Queenie.

"Probably the will."

"That's fast," Rose says. "What about probate and all that?"

"Somehow, your mother arranged it. You know how she hates to draw things out."

The chanters repeat in the background: *Secrets, no! Book's gotta go!*

"It should be pretty simple, right?" Rose asks. "I'm sure

Edward gets my share of everything. I have no idea why I would be required to be there. I certainly don't look forward to watching him gloat."

"I'm sure your mother had her reasons," Queenie says in a quasi-whisper. "That woman had more secrets than anybody in that cursed book, although I'm sure she never wrote them down. She wouldn't have taken that chance. Of course, I've been known to have a few secrets myself."

Queenie's face looks playful, even devilish. Is the wine getting to her?

"Out with it," Rose says. "Did you put a quart of coleslaw at Mother's ankles? Baked beans at her feet?"

Queenie guffaws, insisting her latest secret isn't even remotely related to fast-food. Heads turn in their direction. Edward, now schmoozing with a councilman, narrows his eyes in disapproval at Rose and Queenie, who, it turns out, are dangerously close to enjoying themselves, despite the rabble-rousing outside.

"It seems we've broken the cardinal rule of white folks at a funeral reception. No laughter allowed," Queenie says to Rose. "Darker folks don't mind a good laugh, no matter what the occasion."

Before now, Rose has never heard her speak about differences in race. She has never thought of her as black or white. In her mind, Queenie transcends color. Yet it appears she hasn't felt this transcendence. Rose wonders if the people outside are white or black. Does it even matter?

Queenie pulls Rose into a corner of the dining room as if wanting privacy. "Would you like to know one of your mother's secrets?"

Secrets, no! the crowd answers.

"Absolutely," Rose says, ignoring the voices outside. She nibbles on some fruit. All these secrets are making her hungry again. Not to mention the resident ghosts in attendance and not being able to drink.

Queenie leans in and lowers her voice. "Did you meet Spud Grainger earlier today?"

"I didn't officially meet him," Rose says. "But isn't he the butcher? The one who went on and on about exotic meats?"

"Uh, huh," Queenie says. She cuts her eyes from door to door.

"What does Mother's secret have to do with a butcher at the Piggly Wiggly?" Rose asks, putting a cocktail shrimp in her mouth.

"After your daddy died, Spud Grainger had an affair with her," Queenie says. "From what I hear, it was quite passionate."

The shrimp shoots across the room and lands in a large ficus plant. Guests from the back of the foyer turn to look as if to determine the credibility of the crustacean UFO.

"I thought you'd like that one," Queenie says with a smile.

Rose asks in a whisper, "Really?"

"Your mother told me one night when she had a little too much sherry," Queenie says. "You know how she gets on holy days."

Queenie leans over the buffet table and fills a clean plate with crab legs. The chanting fades. It is raining again. While Rose attempts to process this latest piece of news, Queenie cracks one of the spindly legs and sucks the white meat from inside with the deftness of an orthopedic surgeon.

"Mother had an affair with the butcher at Piggly Wiggly?" Rose asks.

Passion is not something Rose has ever associated with her mother. It is hard to imagine her being intimate with her father, much less the butcher at the Piggly Wiggly.

"This from a woman who could make Antarctica seem warm in comparison," Rose says.

"Tell me about it," Queenie says. With a fingernail, she fishes out a piece of crab meat from one of the legs and then sucks her nail. She savors the crab like a delicious secret.

For the first time, it is Rose who feels like chanting, *Secrets, no!* This day has already been too much, but her curiosity wants more.

"How long did it last?" Rose asks.

"Six months," Queenie says.

"Are you kidding me?" Rose says. "Next you'll tell me that Mother wasn't really a member of the Daughters of the Confederacy and that our family fought for the Union."

"Now that really would be a scandal," Queenie says. "But the confederacy was definitely supported by many, if not all, of the Temples, as the family on my mother's side can unfortunately attest." She cracks another crab leg as if to add an exclamation point to her words.

Rose sometimes forgets that Queenie has lived both sides of the Temple story, and in fact is from both sides.

Violet enters the dining room again, refreshing different plates of food and then returns to the kitchen with Queenie's discarded crab legs.

"Violet's staying on, right?" Rose asks Queenie.

"Unless she decides she can't take the boredom of a house without your mother's drama," Queenie says. "Of course, if your mother decides to haunt the place, it may be like she never left."

Queenie excuses herself and goes into the kitchen, and the reception dwindles to a small collection of her mother's oldest acquaintances, most of whom treat Rose with a certain amount of caution. What story has her mother told the old guard as to why Rose hasn't been around for the last twenty-five years? When it comes to her mother, a storyline that involves mental illness or prison can't be ruled out.

Most of her life, Rose has been cast in the role of the ungrateful daughter—the child born with a silver spoon in her mouth who spit it out just to spite her generous, benevolent mother. Very few people, other than Queenie and Old Sally, know the truth behind the disconnection.

Rose looks around for Edward, who is nowhere in sight. If he isn't still snooping around, he has left without saying goodbye, which is okay with Rose. For all she knows, Edward has probably perpetuated these lies and may have renewed his campaign to discredit her at this very reception. Or maybe he has joined the protestors. *Secrets, no!* Lately, she has had enough contact with her brother to last another decade or two, perhaps even a lifetime.

By LATE AFTERNOON, the last of the mourners exit. The crowd outside finally disperses, too, leaving the five women alone in the dining room. Queenie, Rose, Katie, Angela, and Violet finish up the last of the food. Rose takes off her shoes, her feet much more accustomed to boots these days than heels. She releases a long sigh. Her mother's funeral is complete.

Katie puts her head on Angela's shoulder and looks so much like Max, at that moment, it makes Rose miss him even more than she already does.

"Angie and I have a flight back to Chicago in three hours," Katie says to Rose. "Are you sure you don't want me to stay?"

"I'm sure," Rose says. "I'll drive you to the airport, so you don't have to take a cab."

"Where are you staying?" Katie asks.

"Here, of course."

"You mean you're staying here at the house?" Angela asks.

Katie and Angela exchange concerned looks.

"Why wouldn't I?" Rose says, thinking Angela's question a bit odd. Although truth-be-told, Angela is a bit odd, too.

"Mom, this house is so, like, haunted," Katie says. "Earlier, when I was standing in the hallway, I kept getting these blasts of cold air that had nothing to do with the air conditioner vents. I checked."

"And when I was in the garden," Angela says, "someone put a hand on my shoulder. But when I turned around, nobody was there."

Rose looks at Queenie who shrugs as if deferring the secret-telling to Rose.

"I guess it's time for you to learn one of the many Temple eccentricities," Rose says to Katie. "It seems your grandmother made an appearance earlier. But there's nothing to be alarmed about. This is what Temples do. They haunt."

After two decades of watching her offspring, the look on Katie's face is one Rose hasn't seen before—a cross between horror and exhilaration. Angela appears a bit unnerved, as well, and glances at her watch as though ready to make an exit.

"It wouldn't be the first reception the spirit Temples have attended," Queenie tells them. "But they're harmless. Honest."

Is Queenie crossing her fingers behind her back with that promise? Rose wonders.

"Was it that way when you were growing up, Mom?" Katie asks.

"It's Savannah, honey. Every house has its ghosts."

"I don't understand how you can be so nonchalant,"

Katie says. The look on her face is: *who is this woman and where have you taken my mother?*

"This kind of thing happened my entire childhood," Rose says. "Every family in Savannah has crazy uncles and cousins or a few ghosts."

"And its secrets," Queenie interjects.

"And definitely its secrets," Rose says. The danger lies in both worlds and seems to have only just begun.

CHAPTER EIGHTEEN

Violet

W*hat is Miss Temple up to?* Violet wonders. She searches through the clothes in her bedroom closet to find something to wear for the meeting downtown later that afternoon. Miss Temple's lawyer sought her out after the funeral and insisted that she attend a meeting in his office the following Monday. All week she has wondered why.

"I thought you'd left already," Jack says. He carries his morning coffee into the bedroom and sits on the bed.

"I'm the last person I thought would be invited to the reading of Miss Temple's will," Violet says. "Unless she wants to embarrass me in front of a bunch of rich, white people and tell me I'm out of a job."

She pulls three dresses from her closet that are possibilities and holds each in front of her as she stands in front of the full-length mirror on the back of the closet door.

"You worry too much, sweetheart," Jack says. "Who knows, something good could come out of it."

"Must you always be so optimistic," she says, realizing how crazy this sounds. "We need this income, Jack. Your teaching job doesn't bring in that much money, and the girls will be going to college soon. It's never a good time to lose one of our incomes, but especially right now."

"Take a breath, Vi. We'll figure it out."

Violet knows he's right, but this meeting has her on edge. To her surprise, however, her shoulder hasn't warned her of anything horrible about to happen. She feels perfectly fine.

"If I do lose my job, I can probably find something else. But seriously, Jack, how much call is there for someone who specializes in how to cook rattlesnake, buffalo, and kangaroo? Not to mention the other wild things that have come through my kitchen over the years." She laughs a short laugh and Jack smiles.

"Maybe it's time to follow that dream of yours," he says. "I can get a second job or a third one if I have to. Then you can open your tea shop."

She pauses, thinking how much she loves this man before her fear clicks in again.

"Oh, Jack, people like us don't get to follow our dreams. We're too busy taking care of people who can afford to have them."

This is gloomy, even for her. Violet needs to get this meeting over with so she can think straight again. She holds up two dresses, and he points to one. She slides it on before stepping into her low heels.

"You look beautiful," he says.

"At least I don't have to wear my uniform today," she says.

"You look beautiful, even in that."

She shakes her head, thinking he should be more worried. Although it seems she carries enough worry for both of them.

LATER THAT MORNING when Violet arrives at the Temple house, Queenie is already downstairs making coffee. Everyone assumes the house and property will revert to Queenie, who has basically taken care of Miss Temple for almost 40 years.

Not a task for the faint of heart, Violet thinks.

Even Violet has heard Miss Temple's promise, telling Queenie the different things that need to be done to keep the Temple mansion in pristine shape.

Savannah owes Queenie a lot. If not for her, Miss Temple might have aimed all that spite at other people.

Above all else, Miss Temple valued loyalty, and Queenie has been more than loyal. Not only to the Temples but to Violet, too. After Violet lost her mother so young, Queenie always found time for her. Not only is she Violet's aunt, but a friend.

"Why are you so dressed up?" Queenie asks.

"The meeting later," Violet says.

Queenie gives a slow nod. She seems distracted, but Violet can't quite put a finger on why. Sometimes she can read live people, as well as dead ones, but this isn't one of those times.

"I lost sleep worrying about it," Violet says.

"Rose must have, too," Queenie says. "I heard her up early this morning."

Violet straightens her linen summer dress bought ten years before when Jack received the Teacher of the Year award at the community college. It pleases her that she can still fit into it, but the heels feel ridiculous. She excuses herself and slips them off in the laundry room before putting on a pair of her work shoes.

Not the best look, she thinks, but at least she'll be able to still walk by the end of the day.

After returning to the kitchen, she opens the fridge to look for something to make for dinner. With Miss Temple gone, she's relaxed her strict menu planning and now takes a more spontaneous approach.

"Don't be surprised if Iris drops a bombshell today," Queenie says. "Mama called this morning and predicted it."

"Then I don't doubt it's true," Violet says. She pulls two chicken breasts from the freezer to thaw.

"Coffee's ready." Queenie pours herself a cup as Violet makes some English Breakfast tea.

Queenie refuses to be waited on, and it was only after Violet's insistence that Queenie allowed her to prepare her evening meal. They trade sweetener and then half-and-half before sitting at the kitchen table. For decades now they've sat at this same table together long before Violet even began drinking tea. She tilts her head to check in on the psychic energy in the house. The haunting has calmed over the last few days, the ghosts abandoning their usual patterns. Since her death, Miss Temple's energy has come and gone like power surges flickering the lights during a storm.

Thankfully, the protestors haven't returned. Queenie doesn't know if she could take another day of that chant.

"I've been thinking about Iris all morning," Queenie says. "It's strange to not be bossed around anymore. It's like having a toothache for thirty-five years that suddenly disappears."

"You were kind to put up with her for so many years," Violet says.

"I'm no saint," Queenie says. "I had good reasons for sticking around."

"Like what?" Violet asks, her curiosity genuine. Her aunt has been acting strange lately. The more secrets that get released, the more secretive she becomes.

Queenie takes a gulp of hot coffee and then runs to sputter it into the sink.

"Are you okay?" Violet asks.

Queenie wipes coffee from her blouse that blends in with the colorful jungle pattern. "Do you want eggs this morning?" Queenie blows her coffee with gusto now, like she's trying to blow off Violet's question.

"Wait a minute. What just happened?" Violet says. "It's not like you to avoid a subject."

"I guess I'm worried about what Mama said. She's usually right with her predictions."

Violet decides to drop it for now as Queenie takes eggs from the fridge and breaks several into a bowl. A hand on her hip, Queenie scrambles the eggs in the skillet. Why won't she answer such a simple question?

"It's just so quiet without the old gal," Queenie begins again as if they were talking about Miss Temple. "By the way, I'm wearing *scented* deodorant today," she says with a wink.

Violet laughs and then looks around the kitchen for things she should be doing. Until now, she didn't realize how all-consuming taking care of Miss Temple was. For years Violet had a set routine. First thing in the mornings, after she arrived at work, she read the critique from the day before and made adjustments to the day's meals. Between cooking, she cleaned the house, a never-ending process.

"I don't think any of our neighbors will miss her," Violet says. "I've gotten an earful from every housekeeper in Savannah. None of their employers liked Miss Temple, though most everybody feared her."

"Nobody escaped those letters of hers," Queenie says. "If she disapproved of anything you did, she wrote whoever she thought was your superior a letter, whether it was the Governor, the President of the United States or the Pope. Iris took being a tattle-tale to an international level."

Queenie delivers the scrambled eggs to the table.

"Did you get the newspaper this morning?" Queenie asks. "It wasn't there when I looked."

"The delivery boy seems to have missed us," Violet says. "Either that or somebody took it."

"Are things still disappearing off the front porch?" Queenie looks concerned.

"Three potted plants yesterday," Violet says, "but they left two very full doggy poop bags. Their dogs must be Dalmatians."

Queenie grins. "Is this ever going to stop?" she asks, turning serious again.

"I hope so," Violet says. "The whole neighborhood seems effected. I've heard from more than one housekeeper on the block that arguments have increased since the newspaper started running those secrets."

The door opens, and Rose comes in from a long walk. She looks wilted, like an azalea blossom cut from the main bush and left to languish in the heat.

"An old lady in a purple bathrobe just called me a traitor," Rose says, her face flushed.

"That's nothing," Queenie says, "I've been called the a-word, the b-word, and the c-word, all in one sentence."

"Wow, that's creative," Rose says.

"I guess we're all in this together," Violet says. "In fact, this may be the perfect time to do the sea gypsy's secret handshake."

Without hesitation, the three women gather in the center of the kitchen and begin the handshake: two claps, three arm rolls, a hip bump, and then ending with arms akimbo while shaking their heads up and down. They laugh.

"Not bad after thirty years," Rose says.

"Not good either," Violet says, but the silliness is what she needs on such a serious day.

"Come to think of it, there isn't even a handshake as part of it," Queenie says. "I never noticed that before."

"I don't know how I would have survived growing up without you girls," Rose says.

"Me, too," Violet says. "Even without parents around, I felt like I had a family."

"I need Mother to show up with one of those cool blasts of air." Rose fans herself.

"Be careful what you ask for." Queenie smiles.

"Miss Temple hasn't made an appearance since the reception," Violet says. "I think she's saving up for something big."

They agree that this can't be good.

THAT AFTERNOON, Violet and Queenie ride together to Bo Rivers' law office in downtown Savannah. Violet has never been in this building before. With equal amounts of white marble and glass, it is one of those places built by rich white people to impress other rich white people. On the ground floor, they get into the elevator, the doors close, and they take a slow ride to the third floor. A secretary lets them wait in Attorney Rivers' office. They are the first to arrive.

Portraits of old white men adorn the walls in dark wooden frames that match the furniture.

"Just once I'd like to see black men and women on the walls," Violet whispers to Queenie, even though nobody else is in the room. But it is Savannah, after all, and despite its problems, she loves this city.

"I know what you mean about the white faces," Queenie says. "Sometimes I have fantasies about asking Rose to do my portrait so I can put it in the foyer of the mansion. Then my smiling face will greet everyone who enters."

"You should do that," Violet says, with a smile.

"I would, but I'm afraid Iris might do more than roll over in her grave. She might send me to mine."

Violet and Queenie sit together on a large leather sofa in front of an entire wall covered with floor to ceiling bookcases holding law books.

"Those must be hell to dust," Violet whispers again.

Queenie agrees and picks up the newspaper on the coffee table to read since theirs never arrived.

Being in Bo Rivers' office is like stepping into that walk-in cooler Queenie talked about earlier. Violet crosses her arms over her chest to hide her body's reaction to the cold. She should have known better than to dress for summer. Air conditioners in Savannah could keep an igloo from melting. The thermostat at the Temple house was guarded religiously by Miss Temple, who kept it set at 76 degrees. But this office must be set in the low 60s. Violet half expects to see her frosty breath in front of her.

Despite the frigid temperature, Violet breaks into a sweat. She doesn't want to be here. "If I'm going to be fired, I wish someone would just tell me," she whispers again. "Why make such a big production out of it?"

"You're not going to get fired," Queenie whispers back. "Iris had a wicked mean streak, but she wasn't that horrible."

Queenie turns to the classifieds and within seconds, lets out a muffled scream. "Oh, my living God." She points to the newspaper as Violet reads:

Help Wanted: People of Color,
Housekeeper willing to Slave all day
and Sleep with the Master of the House.
Call Iris Temple: 912-944-0455

"Who the hell is doing this?" Queenie says.

Violet assures her that she doesn't know, but it doesn't help that the ad is for a housekeeper. Perhaps whoever is planting these secrets knows her job is in jeopardy. Or maybe she's reading too much into it. She's been known to do that, too.

It's now weeks since the first secret was released, and they are still clueless as to who is behind it. Whoever is doing this, not only has access to the *Book of Secrets* but to the newspaper, too. Otherwise, why would they ever agree to run them? Although, she imagines those secrets have sold more than a few papers.

The door opens, and Spud enters. They exchange looks of surprise. He leans over and hugs Violet and then shakes Queenie's hand. Oddly, his outfit matches hers. Queenie's jungle motif goes with his white suit that looks like it might be a leftover from the 80s, and his shirt is lime green. They look like they are both on a safari and want to blend in with the jungle. Spud stands against the wall and except for the periodic straightening of his purple bow tie, looks about as uncomfortable as Violet feels. She has never seen him this nervous.

Queenie shoves the newspaper under a stack of *Georgia Now* magazines like the will is all she can deal with for now. Violet feels the same. This time last year, her life was totally predictable, and more than a little boring. Now, she can't imagine what might happen next.

"Where in the world does he get all those ties?" Queenie whispers to Violet. "Do they even make those things anymore?"

"They must," Violet says, thinking how Queenie and Spud are much more alike than they are different in their preference for bold colors.

"Does anyone know why we're here?" Spud asks, his voice full amid their whispers.

"Evidently for the reading of the will," Queenie says.

"Then why am I required to be here?" Spud straightens his tie, looking perplexed now, as well as uncomfortable.

The question goes unanswered. Silence fills the room while the discomfort settles.

What if her grandmother is right about Miss Temple dropping a bombshell? If so, they are all standing at ground zero.

Rose enters, says her hellos, and sits in a leather chair to the left of the desk. Since she was running late, she told them to go ahead and drove herself. Her short, thick hair still looks wet from her shower. She shakes Spud's hand and introduces herself before silence settles in again. She gives Queenie and Violet a wink as if she is familiar with their secret code.

Minutes later, the door opens again, and Edward Temple steps inside.

"Creep alert," Queenie whispers to Violet.

Violet smiles. "Let me guess. You got that from Tia and Leisha?"

Queenie nods. Violet loves the effort Queenie makes with her daughters. Not that many great aunts would be so doting.

Edward eyes the collection of people, aiming his intense gaze for several seconds on Rose as if surprised she's there. He takes a seat close to the lawyer's desk. Is it possible that the room got even colder with Edward here? Violet's teeth begin to chatter, and she clenches her jaw to stop them. She doesn't want Edward to mistake her coldness for fear. But even Edward seems agitated. Perhaps the latest secret has him on edge, too. Meanwhile, the Temple drama seems far from over.

In a trait that reminds Violet of his mother, Edward sits perfectly straight. After he crosses his legs, he runs two manicured fingernails along the crease of his pants as though wanting to perfect the perfect line. There are few people Violet dislikes, but Edward Temple tops her list.

Seconds later, the lawyer enters the room, papers stacked in hand. His smile looks fake, and he gives a nod to Edward, the other rich white guy in the room. Violet's only dealings with Bo Rivers were answering the door on the two occasions when he joined his father, who was calling on Miss Temple. He always wanted his coffee black and made comments about watching his waistline. He flirted with Violet, too. But not enough that she could actually call him on it. She imagines his preference for women to be younger and blonder, like the secretary who showed them into the office.

"Please make yourselves comfortable." Bo Rivers' accent

has the smoothness of one of Violet's meringues that always get compliments.

Yet comfort is the last thing Violet feels. Not only is she in danger of freezing to death, but other than Queenie, she is in a room full of people much lighter-skinned than her. Of course, she is used to this kind of thing by now, but somehow being in a lawyer's office makes being outnumbered more unnerving.

Every chair in the elaborate office is made of leather, and whenever somebody moves, the leather makes a raspberry sound, as if the cows themselves are getting the last laugh. If Violet wasn't so cold, she might find this funny. Unfortunately, as soon as she sat down, her bare legs adhered to the leather, anchored in place by a healthy crop of goosebumps, so she couldn't make a raspberry sound if she tried.

"Someone may have to pry me off of this sofa at the end of the meeting," she whispers to Queenie, who assures her that she will help.

Seconds later, Miss Temple's prickly presence enters the room, as if rushing in late for the meeting. Her chaotic energy hovers around Spud and has a particular pitch to it, almost like a minor musical chord. But instead of a sound, it registers on a feeling level in Violet's chest.

Sometimes Violet wishes she could return this "gift," as her grandmother often calls it. It's not like she asked for it. One day it was just there—and without a return receipt.

While waiting for the lawyer to begin, she remembers the day the weird vibrations started. She must have been six and Rose around ten. It was winter, and they were playing in the attic because all of Rose's old toys were stored there. An old white man with solid white hair appeared. Rose couldn't see him, which was strange given Rose always saw her great-grandfather out by the oak tree. But maybe that was because a tiny piece of Rose's finger was buried out under that tree.

Violet looks at Rose now, and she can see the girl Rose used to be. She wonders if Rose sees her the same way.

The ghost in the attic that day scared Violet because he didn't go about his business like most ghosts do. He kept asking her questions. Not every spirit is harmless, yet they do share some common traits. Most ghosts do the same things over and over again, like they are locked into a pattern. They walk the entire length of a hallway before disappearing. They rattle a few glasses as if pouring themselves a drink. They move through the same rooms at the same time of day. Their routine doesn't vary. But the guy in the attic didn't have a pattern. To this day, she avoids going up there.

What's unusual with Miss Temple's ghost is that she isn't locked into staying at the house. She's here this very minute. Violet scans the room, but her former employer refuses to be pinned down. She is everywhere and nowhere at once.

Grandmother always told her that the dead don't move on if they have something incomplete in their lives. If this incompleteness has nothing to do with you, you just wish them well and tell them to move on along. After Miss Temple's death, Violet has tried to move her along, but she refuses to go anywhere.

The lawyer stands behind the large mahogany desk and opens a leather-encased folder. After taking out several sheets of paper, he pauses. Is he trying to build the suspense? He clears his throat but doesn't appear the least bit nervous. If anything, he comes across as overconfident. It occurs to Violet that they are in his territory and have to play by his rules. It is a game he appears to relish.

"As you all know, you are here at the request of Iris

Temple, who specifically asked that the five of you be brought together as the will is read. It should be noted that the will was updated June 4th of this year."

"Isn't that the day she had the stroke?" Edward asks.

"Yes, it is," Bo Rivers says. "But I assure you, Edward, the updated will is perfectly legal. There's no question that your mother was of sound mind when I saw her that afternoon."

The two men exchange a look that Violet has trouble reading. Are they friends or enemies?

The lawyer puts on a pair of dark-framed reading glasses that look like they'd be sold at a specialty shop that carries lawyer accessories. He begins to read the document. Most of it is legal jargon. Violet glances at Queenie, who winks at her and gives a slight roll of the eyes that Violet translates to mean, *Don't worry.*

While Edward studies her, Rose crosses her legs and leans back in the chair, as if determined to relax. Growing up, Violet would have given anything to have a brother or sister, even a half-sister, like Queenie had Miss Temple. But having Edward as a sibling would be worse than not having one at all.

Spud straightens his bow tie again. Grief hangs around the corners of his eyes. He is the only one in the room who seems to remember why they are all here. Violet's mind wanders. Now that Miss Temple is dead, she hopes Spud will meet someone new. He deserves to be happy.

Even though Violet listens to every word, she understands only half.

Rich people make things so complicated, she thinks, *especially when it comes to their money.*

There is a trust for this, a trust for that. Trusts rest on top of trusts, housed in multiple banking institutions, along with assets of corporations and land contracts dating back two hundred years. In contrast, she and Jack have one checking account, and a savings account opened for the girls' college fund that they rob for household emergencies. They don't even have credit cards, just a debit card. Life is a struggle sometimes, but the payoff is a simple life.

As he reads the document, the lawyer's voice falls into a steady rhythm like a washing machine on the wash cycle. Already tired, Violet daydreams about the chores left to do at the Temple house, as well as the ones to do at home. The next time she looks at her watch, minutes have passed in what feels like seconds. Opening her eyes wider, she forces herself to pay attention. If her position is about to be terminated, she doesn't want to be caught unaware.

Miss Temple's energy spins across the room and distracts Violet from what is being said. Is her former employer trying to tell her something? Maybe she's worked up over the latest secret, although it never occurred to Violet that ghosts might read the newspaper. But perhaps they read the vibes of people who read the paper.

I wish Grandmother were here, she thinks. Her skills are better than Violet's when it comes to dead folks.

Meanwhile, everyone else in the room appears oblivious as Miss Temple's power grows. The vibration makes Violet's head hurt like all the air is being sucked out of the room. Then her shoulder begins to ache for the first time that day. Whatever has Miss Temple furious is also threatening to Violet. A blast of cold air confirms that whatever game Miss Temple is playing is about to begin.

CHAPTER NINETEEN

Queenie

Queenie glances around the office furnished with dark antiques and law books and then takes a quick stab at her hair, wishing she'd worn one of her hats. *If for no other reason than to add some color to this dreary room,* she tells herself. The office space is enveloped in beige, deep browns, and burgundy. The color of wealth.

Queenie chews on a fingernail and thinks about the latest secret. Is it someone in this room who is releasing them? No, she decides, this would make no sense. It has to be someone who wants to see the Temple status in the community fall. That first day that an ad appeared, she and Iris had gone straight to the bank. According to Iris, the book was right where it should be and hadn't been moved.

As Bo Rivers reads Iris's will, Queenie grasps for an understanding of the document. She has devoured enough courtroom dramas in books and on television that the lingo isn't wholly foreign to her. But still, it seems that some of the words are obscure on purpose, to sneak things by.

Last fall, Bo Rivers came to the house to visit Iris with his father, Rutledge Rivers, who was so out of it at the time that Queenie wondered if dementia had set in. Queenie, of course, was never included in any of their meetings. As Edward Temple, III's *bastard* daughter, she was treated with indifference by Rutledge Rivers, who she heard died last winter. At the time, she had to resist saying, *Good Riddance.*

Iris and Rutledge were Catholic school chums, and she confided in him quite a lot. Could he have had access to the *Book of Secrets?* If so, what would he gain from it? More lawsuit battles for Iris? With her being his most prominent client, perhaps he would have a motive for releasing them, but how would he have gotten to that ledger in the first place? Queenie hates that she hasn't been able to solve this mystery.

Secrets aside, Queenie took it as a good sign that after Bo Rivers initially entered the room, he shook her hand first. Perhaps he realizes that when the Temple house reverts to her, they will continue to have dealings together. Or maybe she was simply sitting closest to his desk.

As controlling as Iris could be, for the last decade she has turned most house-related things over to Queenie and always talked of when the house would be left to her. Hopefully, Iris filled Edward in on her plans, too. Whenever Iris spoke of the future, she referred to her eventual demise as a kind of extended vacation. Never actually using the word death.

When I go away, she would say, *you need to do* this and that.

Well, you've gone away now, haven't you Iris? Queenie thinks. *Although maybe you haven't.*

She glances around the room. Violet is shivering, and she wishes she had a sweater to give her.

Meanwhile, Edward taps a finger against the arm of the chair as if both irritated and inconvenienced. However, Queenie knows nothing short of a total apocalypse would keep him from this meeting. Edward is the oldest son—the male heir—here to collect his legacy.

Even though Queenie wouldn't dream of threatening Edward's inheritance, the house should be hers. Not just because of Iris's promise all these years but because Queenie has taken care of the mansion like it was her own for decades now. No small feat, given how obstinate Iris was about every little detail.

Her mother's warning from earlier that day causes Queenie to sit straighter, as well as feel a little queasy. If anyone knows what Iris Temple is capable of, it is her mother.

But if anyone knows how to hit curveballs thrown by Iris, it's me, she thinks. "Bring it on, Iris," she says under her breath.

While the Temples have their share of eccentricities—the males with their penchant for bedding the servants and the females with their controlling yet delicate constitutions—Rose has somehow escaped that fate, as well as Queenie. As for not being a "true Temple," as Iris reminded her daily, she responds with a hearty *halleluiah* that she isn't. It is her mother's DNA, after all, that keeps her sane.

Queenie focuses when Bo Rivers reads a clause stipulating that anyone contesting the will loses all rights to any of the monies. He glances at Edward when he reads that part. It is just like Iris to not want any talking back, even in death.

"This could get interesting before it's over," Queenie whispers to Violet, who nods her agreement, her arms folded across her chest. She hears a chattering and leans closer. "Is that your teeth?"

Violet nods again.

When it comes to the bequeathing part of the document, her name is read first: Ivy Temple. She hasn't heard her real name in so long it sounds unfamiliar to her. Remembering her mother's warning, Queenie braces herself for Hurricane Iris.

"Ivy Temple will receive a stipend of $20,000 a year for the remainder of her natural life," Bo Rivers reads.

"Say what?" Queenie says. Rose and Violet gasp. All Iris has done is extend her allowance.

Edward Temple laughs. "You were expecting more?"

Queenie looks at Edward, thinking: *You are damn lucky I don't have one of Mama's spells at my disposal.* Then she wonders how much damage she could do if she sat on him. At the very least, it might mess up his crease.

She turns her attention to her present dilemma. In the twenty seconds it took to read the part of the document that pertains to Queenie, her world has shifted into something unknown.

"Mama was certainly right about this one," she says under her breath.

Violet looks concerned.

Never mind that there is no mention of the house or other properties or any of the Temple millions hidden away in stocks and bonds. This news sticks in Queenie's throat like a wedged chicken bone. She coughs to dislodge it. Iris not only gets the last word, but she also has her revenge. Queenie has been put in her place from the grave.

A hand touches her shoulder. Queenie jumps, thinking it

is just like Iris to take a moment to literally rub it in. But it is only Spud Grainger.

"Miss Queenie, are you all right?" he asks.

"I've been better, Mr. Grainger," she says, "but thank you for asking."

Queenie and Spud have never talked that much, even though they often find themselves in the same room. For different reasons, they were both bonded to Iris, and his reason was undoubtedly the more genuine one. Iris was a difficult woman and not easy to love, but Queenie had grown accustomed to her lifestyle. She is the first in her family to not scrub floors, dust antiques, and make endless meals for the Temples.

Iris never had any intention of leaving me the house, she thinks, looking up at the light fixture. It was all just an act to keep me loyal. Her face grows hot with this awareness. Queenie is not easily duped. But duped, she has been.

While Violet and Rose express their bewilderment at Queenie's meager inheritance, Edward's eyes sparkle as if her defeat means he is one step closer to his divine destiny. Her mind scrambles to keep up with what just happened. For the first time in thirty-five years Queenie worries about where she will live. And who will the Temple house go to? Edward?

Over my dead body, Queenie decides. Living with Edward isn't even a remote possibility. Not that he would ever suggest it. For all she knows, he will probably evict her later this afternoon, and where will she go then?

Even though Queenie has spent the last three decades of her life doting on Iris, Savannah's matriarch has her revenge. Her guilt over the casket prank disappears. She wishes now she had soaked Iris's casket in chicken grease and thrown in a match. Their acts of retaliation hold no comparison. The last word is given to Iris.

Bo Rivers reads Rose's name next, and Rose crosses her legs, the leather chair responding with a sound that Queenie thought only Iris could make.

"Rose Temple will be given a one-time amount of two thousand dollars," Bo Rivers says.

Edward laughs and claps his hands like a child opening a delightful gift at Christmas. To be given such a small amount is more insulting than being totally written out of the will. In an instant, Queenie forgets her own distress and turns her attention to Rose, who has become as white as one of the monogrammed Temple sheets.

Bo Rivers holds out a hand as if a school-crossing guard at a dangerous intersection. "Wait. There's more," he says. "The will stipulates that if Rose moves back to Savannah to live, that amount will increase to twenty million dollars. However, if at any time she moves away from Savannah, the money will go to the Iris Temple wing of the Daughters of the Confederacy building."

More gasps and murmurs fill the room. The vein on Edward's forehead bulges like an alien creature might burst through his skin. They are all on a roller coaster ride that Iris has designed. Queenie can almost hear the *click, click, click* of the metal car as they ascend the next steep climb. Meanwhile, Rose's face turns from ashen to red. A tear rolls down her cheek. Queenie reaches into her purse to get Rose a tissue and hands it to her.

"I'm so sorry, sweetheart," Queenie says to her.

Conflicted feelings are written all over Rose's face. It is Iris's final manipulation. How can Iris expect Rose and Max to move to the east coast? Their whole life is out West.

As if awakening from his stupor, Edward says to Bo

Rivers: "Wait a minute, that can't be right. Rose was written out of the will years ago."

"In the latest revisions, she was written back in," Bo Rivers says.

"Mother was very troubled at the end," Edward says. "Those damn secrets getting out made her insane. Plus, I think my sister may have manipulated her. She's always been after the Temple money."

Bo raps on his desk as if to call order to the room. "Edward, this isn't the time or place—"

A gust of frigid air sweeps through the office, a current so strong that papers flutter on Bo River's desk.

"Did y'all feel that?" he asks, turning to see if one of his permanently closed windows is open.

"Iris is weighing in," Violet says matter of fact, as though ghosts attending the reading of their wills is commonplace.

Bo Rivers' gaze darts around the room.

Is he looking for his *dead* client?

"We need to finish this up," he says. Bo continues to read, now a little faster. The name, Henry Grainger, is read next.

Henry must be Spud Grainger's legal name, Queenie thinks. She finds herself relieved that his parents didn't intentionally name him after a root vegetable. Queenie grips the chair arm to prepare herself for the next surprise.

"Henry Grainger will inherit three beachfront properties on Hilton Head Island," Bo Rivers says.

From the shock registering on Edward's face, this real estate must be worth millions. Queenie covers her smile. *What a hoot,* she thinks. Iris has left one of the Temple jewels to a jazz musician turned butcher. At the same time, Edward looks like he might take a cleaver to him.

"For God's sake, that can't possibly be right," Edward insists. "He's nobody."

Even Bo Rivers looks offended. "I assure you, Edward, your mother was quite explicit in her wishes," he says.

Meanwhile, Spud Grainger has a hand across his heart like he might recite the Pledge of Allegiance to Iris Temple. Seconds pass as his hand moves from his heart to his tie as if this single action might somehow help him pull himself together. He clears his throat.

"I think there's been some kind of mistake," Spud says.

"No mistake, Mister Grainger." Bo Rivers thumbs through the rest of the will and looks at his watch as if needing happy hour to start earlier today.

The vein on Edward's forehead appears to be throbbing now. If he strokes out, Queenie knows how to administer CPR like she did with his mother. She cringes at the thought of giving Edward mouth-to-mouth.

"Mother wasn't of sound mind," Edward says. "She had trouble with her health for years. Hell, everybody can attest that she smelled like a sewage plant."

A thin layer of sweat aligns itself above Edward's top lip as he twists the ring on his finger.

"This will is airtight, Edward," Bo Rivers says. "Your mother didn't leave any wiggle-room. Besides, everyone in this office can attest that Iris Temple would never do anything she didn't want to do."

"But what I'm saying is that Mother wasn't well," Edward says to Bo. "For all we know, she was releasing those secrets herself."

"No chance," Queenie says. "You weren't with her the first time she saw them. Iris wasn't that good of an actor."

"Why else would she give millions in property to a damn butcher?" Edward asks. He turns his glare to Queenie and then back at Bo. "She was manipulated, Bo, and for all I know, you may have been in on it."

They meet each other's gaze. "Careful, Edward," Bo says as if to remind him whose turf they're on.

Their exchange reminds Queenie of a game of H-O-R-S-E in basketball, where each player tries to make a shot from the same location. Except with Edward playing, a better name for the game might be J-A-C-K-A-S-S.

Even though everyone in the room appears visibly shaken, Bo Rivers is intent on finishing the reading of the will. Edward's name is read next. He repositions himself in his chair like his coronation requires proper posture. He takes a deep breath, and the vein relaxes on his forehead.

Queenie anticipates that Edward will receive the Temple mansion. In which case, she might have to move in with her mother at the beach tonight, considering what $20,000 a year buys these days.

But instead, Bo Rivers reveals that Edward will inherit a collection of real estate properties in Atlanta.

"Wait a minute," Edward says, his look disbelieving. "Those are junk properties. They aren't worth anything."

"Sorry, Edward," Bo Rivers says, in a tone that reveals he isn't sorry at all.

But what about the house? Queenie wonders. Maybe she gave up too soon.

Edward's face is an unnatural shade of red. She waits for his head to explode. Instead, he folds his arms tightly against his chest and looks like he did as a little boy whenever he didn't get his way, which wasn't very often.

Except for Violet—who appears to have slipped into hypothermia—they all wait to hear who gets the central jewel in the multi-jeweled Temple crown.

The reading continues. Large dollar amounts pass to several different charities, the Daughters of the Confederacy and the Junior League being the biggest winners in that category. Then Bo Rivers announces the last item of business, the Temple mansion.

Queenie leans back as Edward leans forward. The only thing missing is a drum roll as the winner is announced.

"The historic Temple house in downtown Savannah, Georgia," Bo begins, "is to be left in its entirety to Violet Stevens."

The news hits Queenie like a cymbal crash at the end of the drum roll. She does what comes naturally and giggles.

Everyone turns to look at Violet. "What did I miss?" Violet asks as if shaken from a daydream.

Bo Rivers rereads the news for Violet's benefit.

Iris, I never knew you had this in you, Queenie thinks, barely unable to contain her glee. Meanwhile, Edward strides out of the office, his fists clenched. A blast of cold air follows him out, along with an invisible contrail that smells strongly of rotten eggs.

"Edward's true legacy," Queenie says, covering her nose with her handkerchief.

Queenie turns to congratulate Violet, who suddenly keels over on the sofa in a dead faint.

CHAPTER TWENTY

Violet

V iolet opens her eyes to see several people standing over her. Spud, on his knees, gently pats her hand and tells her everything will be all right. To counteract her dizziness, she focuses on his tie.

"Welcome back," he says. "We lost you there for a while."

"Thank goodness you're okay," Queenie says to Violet. She's on her knees, too—something Violet has never actually seen her do—and she looks relieved to see her awake. She fans Violet with what looks like Miss Temple's will, evidently grabbed from the lawyer's desk. The breeze makes her even colder than before.

"Did I imagine it, or did I just inherit the Temple house?" she asks Queenie.

"You didn't imagine it," Queenie answers. "Iris has

surprised us all." Queenie smiles as though not the least bit upset.

"You mean I'm not fired?" she asks.

"Not by a long shot," Queenie says.

Violet remembers the seconds before she fainted: the collective gasp, everyone looking at her, Edward Temple's face frozen in controlled fury. Then she remembers feeling warm for the first time in Bo Rivers' office right before the light-headedness hit, like the time she tried to stand up too soon in the hospital after giving birth to her daughter, Tia. The room became a washing machine on the spin cycle and then faded to black.

While Spud continues to pat her hand, Queenie leans over and asks if she's okay. For a second, Violet imagines what it must be like to have parents. Meanwhile, Rose takes on the role of the first responder and helps Violet sit up. She holds three fingers in front of Violet's face.

"How many do you see?" Rose asks, her expression serious.

Violet answers the correct number. She's never seen Rose act like this before.

"Who is the president of the United States?" Rose asks. She widens her eyes as if to offer a clue.

"Rose, I haven't lost my mind. I just passed out." Violet still feels a little light-headed and definitely confused, but she doesn't think her current state is a result of a concussion, only the shock of a lifetime.

In the background, the lawyer is on the phone to the paramedics. His secretary stands in the corner, videotaping the entire event as if to cover him if a lawsuit arises.

With the help of Rose and Spud, Violet stands. Her knees feel shaky, and for the first time since Violet fainted, she notices the energy in the room has shifted. Iris isn't there anymore.

"Are you sure you're okay?" Rose asks.

"It was just such a shock," Violet says. But, in reality, 'shock' doesn't begin to describe what she feels.

Violet assures Bo Rivers that she is okay and that paramedics are unneeded. "I just fainted," she says. "Wouldn't you if you just inherited a mansion in downtown Savannah?"

He chuckles and agrees he probably would. Then he tells his secretary to turn off the video recorder, and everyone returns to their seats. Without Edward and Iris, the room feels different. Almost peaceful. They could be a party of friends, except no one seems to know how to proceed, including Bo Rivers.

"Now, where were we?" Violet says with comic flair, which sounds like something Queenie would say instead of her.

"You had just inherited the Temple mansion," Queenie says with another smile.

A new blast of cold air brings chill bumps to Violet's arms. Miss Temple is back. The vibration registers in Violet's solar plexus. It accelerates and grows more chaotic. New frequencies emerge, and Violet doesn't understand what these new energies mean.

Her grandmother has offered to teach Violet more about the Gullah tradition. But with Violet's full-time job and caring for Jack and the girls, she just hasn't had time to pursue it. But maybe she should make time for it. After all, her grandmother won't be around much longer. Weirdly, Violet feels her presence in the room, too, as if here to protect her.

Miss Temple's energetic charge bounces around the room

like a four-year-old after drinking a 16 ounce Mountain Dew.

But why would Miss Temple be angry about something she put in her own will? This doesn't make sense. Violet tries to detect what's going on below the surface of the meeting, but there are so many layers of chaos she can't get a clear reading.

"Did Miss Temple give any explanation for why she would leave the house to me?" Violet asks Bo Rivers. "Because I think there's been some kind of mistake."

He looks at Queenie and then back at Violet. "I thought you knew," he says to Violet.

"You thought I knew what?" Violet says. She looks at Queenie, too, who is somehow in on this.

"What is it, Queenie?" Violet asks.

Without answering, Queenie bows her head as if the moment calls for earnest prayer. Violet looks back to the lawyer for an explanation. He hesitates. He doesn't strike Violet as someone who is at a loss for words very often.

"Well, since I'm the Temple family attorney, it isn't a breach of confidentiality to tell you, Violet," Bo Rivers begins. "Can I call you Violet?" he asks, turning up the volume of his southern charm.

"But I'm not a Temple," Violet says.

"Actually, you are," he says. He speaks softer as if wanting to avoid another call to the paramedics.

"I don't understand," Violet says. "How could I be a Temple?"

Spud takes her arm as if also anticipating the worst.

"Let me explain," Bo Rivers begins. "My father, Rutledge Rivers, was the Temple attorney for many years, which included Iris Temple's husband, Oscar Bell. After my father's death earlier this year, the client files passed to me. Upon reviewing the files a few weeks ago—when all those lawsuits started showing up because of the secrets in the newspaper—I found a letter written by Oscar Bell in the back of one of the files," he continues. "I immediately called Iris Temple to the office to view the letter, and she confirmed that it was indeed from Oscar Bell. In this letter, Violet, he confirmed that you were his biological daughter."

"But that's not possible," Violet says. "My mother didn't even work for the Temples."

Rose and Spud look just as confused as she is. Everyone looks at her except Queenie, who is digging in her giant purse as though making room to crawl inside

"Someone, please tell me what's going on," Violet says to the group. "If this is true, why am I just now finding out?" Violet hates that her voice is shaking.

Silence.

"I have no idea why the letter came to light so late," Bo Rivers says, "except that it was simply misplaced all these years. It's amazing that we found it at all. Like I said, if it hadn't been for all the fallout over the *Temple Book of Secrets*, I might never have found it."

Violet remembers Mister Oscar coming into the kitchen when she was a girl and him bringing her small gifts after he returned from business trips. Sometimes it would be a pink diary with a lock and key or a book. She never questioned why she might receive a gift. She just thought he was a nice man.

"But this doesn't make sense," she says, to no one in particular. She wishes Jack were here. She could use some of his ceaseless optimism right now.

"Certain facts and requests were revealed in the letter that Iris Temple took to be true," Bo Rivers continues. "It seems that Oscar Bell is your biological father. And upon Iris's death, he specifically wanted the house to go to you.

Per his deathbed request, Iris Temple changed the will that day."

Violet rubs her forehead to help her brain take it all in. "Oscar Bell was my father?" she asks. "But that still doesn't make me a Temple."

"There's more," Bo Rivers begins again. "The letter also reveals your biological mother."

"But I know who my mother was," Violet says. "She died in a car crash on Tybee Island when I was a baby."

"Not according to Oscar Bell," Bo Rivers says. He pauses and glances at his watch as if happy hour cannot come soon enough.

"According to Oscar Bell, my real mother didn't die?" Violet asks. She's never felt so confused. Bo Rivers glances at Queenie again, who has given up on her purse and is staring into the palms of her hands on her lap as though reading her fortune and the news isn't good.

"Violet, *I'm* your mother," Queenie says, finally looking at her.

For the second time that day, Violet feels like she might faint.

CHAPTER TWENTY-ONE

Rose

Rose lingers in the hallway of the attorney's office after Violet leaves in tears.

"I had no idea the secret was going to come out like this," Queenie says, also close to tears. "I feared that it would show up in the newspaper some morning. I never dreamed it would come out this way."

"Queenie, why didn't you tell Violet you were her mother?"

"It's complicated," Queenie says. She pulls a box of tissues from her purse. She offers one to Rose, who declines.

Rose is confident Queenie must have had her reasons for sitting on this secret. She isn't the type to be cruel.

"Oh, Rose, I'm such an idiot," Queenie says.

At this moment, Rose is inclined to agree. "Violet's very

upset," Rose says. Should she be comforting Violet instead of Queenie?

"She has every right to be upset." When Queenie blows her nose, it sounds like the honk of the Canada geese that migrate to their field back home. Rose wishes she was on her way there right now.

The events of the last hour have shaken her. Her father is also Violet's father? Queenie is Violet's mother? Not to mention the biggest shock of the meeting. Is she really being offered twenty million dollars to move back to Savannah?

One crisis at a time, she tells herself, as her thoughts return to Violet.

"I always wanted a sister," Rose says, deciding to look at the positives. "But you have to admit, you don't usually find out that you have one after forty years."

"I need to find Violet and explain," Queenie says, biting her bottom lip. "There are reasons for all of this."

Rose has never seen Queenie this off-balance. Her mother always had a knack for making a mess of things. What Rose didn't expect was that she could create such a mess after her death.

"I've got to make this right," Queenie says, giving Rose a quick hug. She takes the elevator in search of Violet.

Alone now, Rose thinks to call Max but then decides to wait. It is still early in Wyoming, and he will be out checking the cattle. Besides, she needs time to think about what just happened.

She walks through the parking garage, grateful that she was running late this morning and drove her rental car. Riding home in a vehicle with Queenie and Violet and all this drama is the last thing she needs. But what to do next? Her flight is later tonight. She has hours to wait before she can make a proper escape. Since she doesn't know when she'll be back on the coast again, Rose decides to take a walk on the beach to clear her thoughts.

Her heels click across the concrete parking lot. She can't get the look on Edward's face out of her mind. His cold expression makes her shiver in the Savannah heat even now. It isn't news that her brother hates her. She just didn't realize how much.

Mother must have been livid when she found out about Daddy and Queenie, Rose thinks.

If her mother had known beforehand, she would never have let Queenie live in the house, nor would she have ever hired Violet. Not to mention that if her father had been faithful to her mother, none of this would be happening anyway. She tends to forget his culpability in all this. Yet, if she's honest with herself, she must have known something was going on. Once, when she was around twelve, she walked into her father's office and found him and Queenie there. Nothing was going on, but they were startled by her intrusion.

After pulling the rental out of the parking lot, Rose drives toward the shore. Even though she drives the speed limit, her mind races to process the last hour. She stops at a convenience store to get a cup of coffee and grabs a newspaper to read on the plane. It's too hot for coffee, but it's what Rose drinks when she really wants a glass of wine.

"How's life treating you?" the cashier asks, who is barrel-chested and middle-aged. A space between his teeth offers a view of his pink and gray tongue.

Rose forgets how friendly people are in the South, even strangers, and decides to answer truthfully. "Well, my father's been dead for twenty-seven years, but I just found out that he had an affair with our housekeeper's daughter and fathered the girl that became my best friend while I was growing up. So I now have a half-sister that I never knew I had."

"I've had days like that, too," he chuckles and hands Rose her change.

She thanks him, thinking how nobody in Cheyenne would have been so understanding. Things happen in the south that don't happen anywhere else. This is one of the things that makes her birthplace interesting.

With no idea of where she wants to go, Rose returns to her car and just drives. Before long, she finds herself on the way to Old Sally's house. Even though it is hot and humid and the coffee is making her hotter, she has the windows down so she can smell the sea.

The island has changed dramatically since she was a girl, but when she turns onto Old Sally's road, everything looks the same. Rose parks at the back of the house and gets out of the car. She isn't dressed for the beach—she's wearing the same dress she wore to the funeral—but being here feels right.

Despite all the history, Rose has come to the conclusion that her time back in Savannah has been good for her. She hasn't realized how much she missed the coast. After Rose married Max, she left all that was familiar to start a new life. She succeeded in that part, at least. Moving from Savannah to Cheyenne is about as different as a person can get without leaving the country. Until now, it never occurred to her that she might not spend the rest of her life in the West.

Rose leaves her black pumps in the car and walks barefoot through the dunes to Old Sally's house. She didn't anticipate that her quick trip to get closure with her mother would stretch into a week. Rose needed more clothes for a more extended stay, including shorts and sandals. At the same time, she's ready to be home. Ready to be with Max.

The Atlantic Ocean stretches into the horizon. Rose stands at sea level, as opposed to roughly 6,000 feet in the high plains of Wyoming. The sun feels much softer here than on the plains. The temperatures in Wyoming can easily hit one hundred degrees for several weeks every summer. But it is a dry heat, where a hundred degrees feels very different due to 10 percent humidity, not 90 percent. Coastal summers are sticky and steamy. The winters are chilly, yet mild.

When she turns toward the house, Old Sally is waiting at the door. Though this should surprise her, it doesn't. Old Sally gives a brief wave, and Rose returns the greeting. For some reason, this simple welcome makes Rose's eyes mist.

"I was expecting you," Old Sally says, as Rose climbs the steps.

"I know you were," Rose says.

She opens her arms, and Rose lets Old Sally hold her. Her embrace is as solid and strong as ever, and Rose sobs as if it is the most natural response in the world to all that has happened. Old Sally rubs Rose's back like she did when Rose was upset as a girl and says Gullah words that Rose doesn't understand, but that comfort her nonetheless.

Finally empty of tears, Rose pulls out several unused tissues she stuck in the pocket of her dress for her mother's funeral. She blows her nose. "I'm a mess," she says.

"You be a beautiful mess," Old Sally says as she smoothes Rose's hair.

Old Sally directs Rose to sit on the top step and then joins her, her body slower and more careful. For several seconds, Rose stares at Old Sally's bare feet—her long, brown wrinkled toes. Sturdy feet that have served Old Sally for a hundred years.

What must it be like to be this old, in a culture where people half her age are given senior discounts?

"I've just come from the attorney's office," Rose says. "Mother's trying to get me back to Georgia. In her will, she offered me a lot of money if I live here again."

Old Sally listens like this is no big surprise.

"I would dismiss her offer just on the principal of the thing," Rose says, "if I hadn't noticed these last few days how much I miss Savannah."

Old Sally leaves plenty of room for Rose to talk.

"The last time I was here, it was just so awful," Rose continues. "Mother and I had this horrible fight, and she accused me of only visiting because I wanted her money." Rose sniffs back new tears that threaten to come. "Then she said that she wished I'd never been born. Can you believe that?" Rose asks. "What kind of mother wishes their kid had never been born?"

"A bitter one," Old Sally says, her voice soft. "But you need to know that no matter what kind of person you turned out to be, your mother would have felt the same way about you."

"But she wasn't hateful to Edward," Rose says. "She worshiped the ground he walked on."

"Edward paid a high price for that," she says. "He still be paying."

Rose pauses while her shoulders slowly relax. "I guess I never thought of it that way," she says.

"Let's take a walk," Old Sally says. "The wind be good for blowing away muddy thoughts." Her toes wiggle as if ready to go.

Rose helps her stand and holds her arm as they go down the steps. Old Sally is frailer than Rose wants to admit. When they reach the beach, Rose continues to hold her arm, not knowing if it is Old Sally who needs support or her. As they walk, Rose tells Old Sally the details of what happened in Bo River's office, although she doesn't seem surprised by any of it.

When Rose tells her about Violet finding out about her real parents, Old Sally stops walking and turns to look at the sea, like she sees something play out in the past.

"Secrets be no good for anybody," Old Sally begins, still staring at the horizon. "It's the truth that sets people free. I just wish I'd been brave enough to tell the truth when I could."

She lowers her head as though disappointed in herself. For a second, Rose wonders if it is Old Sally who is releasing the secrets to the newspaper. But the thought seems so far-fetched, she doesn't entertain it for long.

"I lied to Violet," Old Sally continues. "It was wrong to let her think that my daughter Maya was her mother. But Queenie be convinced we'd all lose our jobs if people knew."

"You mean you knew, too?" Rose never thought Old Sally capable of lying.

"I'm not proud of going along with it all these years," Old Sally continues. "I left it up to Queenie to say whatever she thought was best, and I stayed out of it. But I owe Violet a big apology, and I hope she can forgive me."

"Violet needs an apology from Queenie, too," Rose says.

"She and Queenie got some mending to do, for sure," Old Sally says. "We've all got mending to do."

Betrayals are commonplace in the Temple lineage. In fact, you could almost say they are a Temple family trait. Yet it seems that Queenie, as well as Old Sally, were not without their reasons.

"We humans be on this planet for about a minute and a half," Old Sally begins again. "And all that time we be struggling with ourselves and each other, trying to be something that we're not. Even this old, I still don't understand why we do that," she continues. "It seems like we spend our whole lives sleepwalking. Not noticing the love and beauty all around us."

Old Sally continues to look out over the sea, like the answers to her lifelong questions might ride in on the waves. The old woman takes a deep breath, and Rose does, too. They stand in silence for a long time, Rose digging her toes into the moist sand of the rising tide. Even though she has never been comfortable with the quiet, something about this moment feels different. Rose always thought silence was empty and lonely, but while standing next to Old Sally, she realizes how full it is.

Old Sally begins to walk again, and Rose joins her. "What do you think you'll do?" Old Sally asks.

Rose almost regrets the end of the silence. "I can't imagine how Max will react to all of this," she begins. "We're always worried about money, but he isn't the type to be bought. The ranch is his life. Besides, we're too old to start over."

Old Sally laughs. "Nobody ever be too old to start over," she says. "I may just start over myself one of these days." She laughs again as if the idea tickles her.

Their walk is snail-paced compared to the vigorous walks Rose has done for exercise since she's been here. Yet this rhythm feels more natural. It occurs to her that if she walked this way every day of her life, she might finally arrive at contentment.

The ocean breeze blows in her face. The grasses among the dunes wave at her in the breeze. Rose stops and picks up a sand dollar in perfect condition. She runs a finger along the raised petal-like design on the shell's back.

"Violet and I used to collect these as girls, do you remember?" Rose asks.

"Like it was yesterday," Old Sally says. "You hid them in the roots of that old oak in the garden. You thought I didn't know your hiding place, but I did."

Memories clamor for Rose's attention. "Do you remember that day we tied our entire collection onto the lower limbs of the oak with white kitchen string that you gave us?"

Old Sally smiles. "It looked like a Christmas tree covered with beautiful white ornaments," she says.

Rose smiles. "Violet and I lay on our backs looking up at that tree for hours until Mother told us to take those tacky things down. Of course, we shot up like rockets," Rose continues. "Violet got scared and ran into the kitchen to find you and left me standing there to face Mother alone. That woman scared me to death."

"Nobody be forcing you to take anything down now, baby. You free," Old Sally says.

Rose looks into Old Sally's eyes, the brown having more flecks of gray than she remembers. "Am I really free?" she asks.

Old Sally nods. "The door to the jail cell be open. Now you just got to walk through."

Rose picks up a pebble and tosses it into the ocean. How many times has she walked this same coastline with Old Sally? She wishes now she'd kept count. As a girl, one of the biggest treats of her life was getting to spend the night at Old Sally's house. Old Sally would move all her special trinkets and make a bed for Rose in the window seat where she could watch the ocean in the moonlight. Sometimes Rose awoke at dawn, and dolphins would be playing on the waves. Later, she would wonder if she'd dreamed it.

After wandering down the beach, they turn around and

walk back over their own footprints. An unexpected calm flows through Rose.

"I've missed this place." She breathes in the sea air.

"This place has missed you, too," Old Sally says.

Rose feels ready to come home to Savannah now. She's tired of running from the past. Tired of pretending that she doesn't miss the people and the land here. Her mother's bribe has helped her take an honest look at where she really belongs. It has everything to do with who she is at this moment and what she needs in life.

But Max will never leave the West, she tells herself. It is his home just as surely as the Georgia coast is hers.

CHAPTER TWENTY-TWO

Queenie

"Holy heaven, what a disaster," Queenie says to herself. She places the keys to the Town Car on the hook in the kitchen. Her secret is out and not at all how she wanted it to be. After Iris died, she gave herself a month to tell Violet. The plan was to take her out to dinner some night and spill the secret she'd bottled up all these years. She has to admit, though, it will be helpful to get some sleep again. She's been worried for weeks that this very secret would show up on people's doorsteps all over Savannah and everyone in town would know. Not that anybody would even care, except Violet.

The drive home from Bo River's office with Violet was the longest ride of her life. Violet's silence proved fertile soil for Queenie's shame. Queenie apologized, but her apology was met with more of Violet's silence. She then attempted several more apologies with the same result. Once they were home, Violet insisted that Queenie stop apologizing. Then she got out of the car, slammed the door, and ran inside.

The moment called for something more than Queenie had. A better reason. Better words to explain. In all honesty, it felt inevitable that she would have a child by Iris Temple's husband. Wasn't that what history expected of her?

The phone hasn't stopped ringing in the foyer, even though she had it changed to a private number. It is unreal how many people have called looking for a job after this morning's ad. Did they really think it was real? Queenie unplugs the telephone and goes upstairs. She doesn't have time to worry about phone calls or the handful of protestors outside. She seeks refuge in the green armchair in the corner of her bedroom. She pulls out her journal and pen from the side table drawer where she keeps it hidden. The last thing she needed while Iris was alive was Iris finding all her private thoughts. They might fill a whole other book of secrets.

Journaling is something Queenie picked up from watching Oprah, and she is faithful to the practice of documenting her feelings and thoughts. In the margins, she writes the three things she's grateful for every day. But she is not ready for gratitude yet. Too much is in the way. Queenie picks up a pen and begins to write the story she never shared with anyone until now, not even her journal.

I was sixteen when Mister Oscar first invited me to his study. I hated him for suggesting it, but another part of me liked the attention since I'd never really had a daddy. Not having a parent is like having only half of a road map in life, one torn right down the middle, so you never fully know where you're going or where you've been. Of course, I always knew that Iris and I had the same father. But he never acknowledged it. Not once. Sometimes I would sneak looks at him to see if I could recognize parts of me that came from him. As far as I could tell, we had the same nose, but other than that we could have been total strangers. He was tall and thin and very white. Did I mention he was very white!? Maybe the most significant thing we had in common was how well we could keep a secret!

What secret, you may ask, dear journal? Well, when I was a girl, my mama would disappear from time to time into his bedroom, and I knew not to ask where she'd been. It was just the way things were. Other girls I knew had mothers who did the same thing. All housekeepers for Savannah's upper class. Afraid to lose everything they had if they refused to do what the Misters wanted.

So, actually, going into Oscar's study that first time when I was sixteen was like being initiated into the secrets that my mother knew. But unlike the Sea Gypsies that Rose and Violet created, I never enjoyed being a member of this secret society.

Don't get me wrong. Oscar was a nice enough man. He wasn't cruel. Sometimes Oscar was even sweet. But I hated the way he smelled, a combination of liquor and cigars. To be honest, I think we were both playing at a game we hated, but a game that was expected of us.

QUEENIE PAUSES and recalls the smell of Oscar's cigars and his bittersweet breath and thinks: *Funny how smells can bring back memories so strongly.* It's as if Oscar stands right next to her this very moment. She looks around like maybe he is. At this point, the dead outnumber the living in the Temple mansion.

More than once, Iris accused Oscar of making her sick to her stomach with all his smells. He let Iris use him as a doormat on more than one occasion. At times, her harsh treatment made Queenie feel sorry for him. Didn't he know that men—white men—ran the world?

It never occurred to her that Iris didn't know about the affair, just as it seemed that Iris's mother must have known what Queenie's father was up to. *How do you deny children running around the house who are a light brown version of your husband?*

The Temple features are distinct: a nose just a bit too pointed, eyes just a bit too small, yet with kindness around the creases that don't necessarily match up to the personality —facial features that most people would find hard to miss. However, the denial in the Temple family is powerful enough it could power all of downtown Savannah. Denial that's served up in their shrimp and grits every morning, as if to fortify them to keep the secrets. Secrets that are now showing up all over Savannah.

It feels good to confess, even if it's only to her journal. She begins to write again:

WHEN I WAS FIFTEEN, Oscar would come into the kitchen all the time. I wasn't a great beauty—I was already what you might call FULL figured—but my complexion often got me compliments. Of course, Oscar was no spring chicken and was already worn around the edges. He liked to make me laugh, and made jokes about boys beating down the Temple door to get to me.

"Don't be silly, Mister Oscar," I remember saying to him. "That door's too old and heavy."

Then he'd say how he'd break a door down to get to me if he had to.

At the same time that I hated the attention, I also craved it. Mama watched his subtle advances and didn't say a thing. Not one thing. She just stayed busy, refusing to look up from her work. I waited for weeks for her to say something. I kept thinking she would stop Oscar from flirting with me and tickling me right under her nose. Maybe Oscar was waiting for that, too. But when Mama turned a blind eye to it, I hated her with every bit of my teenage vengeance.

Since then, I've learned that nobody's mama is perfect, but this was the first and only time she ever disappointed me. And I think she disappointed herself, too.

Then over the years, I resigned myself to what was expected of me. I wasn't proud of what I did. But there were consequences to saying no, and who knows, I may have loved Oscar a little bit, too.

QUEENIE PUTS DOWN THE PEN. "How could Violet possibly understand how things were back then?" Queenie says aloud.

History pulled at Queenie from every direction and created a dangerous undercurrent of shame in which she thought she might drown. She didn't have the strength to choose anything different from what her mother and grandmother had done. *Hadn't we been taught our whole lives to take care of the needs of white people? And didn't that include the bedroom needs, too?*

If her mother had stood up to Oscar, she might have been fired and never worked again. That's how things were. One word from the Temples, and you could be blackballed forever. Blackballed from Savannah, the whole state of Georgia, and maybe the Carolinas, too. Then how would her mama support herself?

Today, keeping servants in their place is much more covert. Messages are sent by innuendo, a wink, a glare. Yet they are just as potent. She thinks of Violet downstairs and wishes she could go to her. But Violet made it clear she isn't ready to talk.

W.W.O.D? she writes in her journal. What would Oprah do?

She thinks for a few seconds and decides her hero would give Violet the time she needs. Then take responsibility for the pain she's caused. Queenie sighs. Sometimes making Oprah proud isn't the least bit easy.

Thanks to Oscar, Queenie found an alternative to spending her life in a kitchen and cleaning until her shoulders froze up, and her knees went bad. For years, she's been saving up the puny allowance Iris gave her so that Violet can stop working here and finally open that business she's always wanted.

It was Oscar's idea for Queenie to become Iris's companion. But even this so-called luck came with a price tag on it. She was never to tell anyone that Violet was their child, especially not Iris. And when her older sister, Maya, tragically died a short time after Violet was born, Oscar dreamed up the story to go with their deception, saying that Violet was her sister's child. Maya was several years older and was already married by the time Queenie was in grade school.

"Just so you know, Iris, I don't miss you one bit." Queenie points her finger at the overhead light fixture. "I don't miss your bitterness. I don't miss your constant criticism. Nor do I miss your not-so-subtle reminders, every day of my life, that I was servant stock and not a true Temple. And those errands you used to send me on? What a ridiculous waste of my time. All I've got to say is that you sure didn't trouble your imagination very much."

Queenie huffs and remembers all the times she was told to mail a letter at the downtown post office, even if their regular postal carrier was expected to deliver and pick up

within minutes. Then an hour after Queenie returned from
the post office, Iris would decide she needed stamps.

Her huff is followed by a yawn. *This delving into the past is
quite exhausting,* Queenie thinks.

After hiding her journal again, she puts her feet up for a
quick snooze. Within minutes, she settles into a sweet dream
about Denzel Washington giving her a sexy foot rub and
then is startled awake by a knock on her bedroom door. In
her imagination, she asks Denzel to come back later and then
shuffles toward the door to find Rose.

"Sorry to disturb you, but I have to leave for the airport
in a couple of hours," Rose says.

Sometimes Queenie can see the young girl Rose used to
be. Shy. Awkward. Serious. "Did you have a nice walk on
the beach?" Queenie asks.

"I spent some time with Old Sally, so yes, it was wonderful," Rose says.

At Queenie's invitation, Rose sits on the end of the bed.
"Have you thought about what you'll do?" Queenie asks.
She's been so into her own crisis she hasn't even thought
about Rose's.

"I'll have a long talk with Max, I suppose," Rose says. "I
haven't told him yet. I left a message that I had something to
talk to him about once I got back. I guess I want to think
about it more and decide how I feel. Mother sure knows how
to shake things up, doesn't she?"

"Your mother was a force of nature," Queenie says, "and
in some ways she still is." She looks at the chandelier again,
as if daring Iris to disagree.

"I doubt Max will have anything to do with Mother's
blackmail," Rose says. "This whole day has just been unreal,
hasn't it?"

Queenie nods, her thoughts returning to the meeting in

Bo River's office. She expected surprises from Iris, but not from Oscar.

Why did he write that stupid letter? she wonders.

Queenie was prepared to go to her grave without anybody knowing. Except that after Iris died, it just didn't make sense to keep it a secret anymore. What she didn't expect was that finally telling the truth would feel like such a huge relief, despite the fact that Violet may never forgive her. It reminds her of those girdles she tried to wear in the 60s. Her ample body pinched and contained until finally released in the evening, so grateful to be unencumbered. Having that secret out feels a little like that, too. Like finally she can breathe again.

"How did I not know that you were Violet's mother?" Rose asks.

"I'm very good at keeping secrets," Queenie says. "But keeping this one was selfish. I know that now." She joins Rose at the end of the bed. "What I want to know is how I could have been such a coward? For years I convinced myself that Violet was better off not knowing the truth. She had this image of her dead mother that comforted her. A perfect mother who died too soon. How could I compete with that, Rose? I'm not a perfect anything, and I thought that if Violet found out the truth, she'd be disappointed."

Rose takes Queenie's hand and squeezes it. "When are you going to talk to her?" Rose asks.

"As soon as she'll listen. Although I'm not sure what I'll say."

"You need to explain what it was like for you and why you felt the need to keep the secret," Rose says. "She needs to hear the truth, Queenie. In AA they call it making amends."

Queenie remembers Rose's attempt to make amends with

Iris twenty years before. After the letter arrived at the house, Iris read it aloud to Queenie. It was a lovely letter. Heartfelt. Sincere. But Iris dismissed it. Then she marked the letter *return to sender, recipient deceased,* and ordered Queenie to return it to the post office. Even for Iris, the response was especially mean-spirited. Her whole life Iris never knew how to apologize. To her, apologies were a sign of weakness, not of strength.

"Promise me you'll talk to Violet today," Rose says. "I don't want what happened between my mother and me to happen with you and Violet."

"I promise," Queenie says and rests a hand on the shelf of her bosom to offer a solemn swear.

Rose squeezes Queenie's hand again and stands. "I've got to pack," she says.

"Can I take you to the airport?"

"I'd appreciate that," Rose says. "I need to drop off the rental car, but if you want to wait with me in the terminal, we could have a little more time together."

For the first time that afternoon, Queenie feels like everything might be okay again. She has amends to make, but maybe Violet will forgive her.

"If you're hungry, we can stop by Kentucky Fried Chicken on the way," Queenie says with a grin. "I haven't been back since the day of the funeral."

"I still can't believe you put a bucket of chicken in Mother's casket," Rose says.

"Original recipe," Queenie says. "You know how your mother had a thing for tradition."

Rose laughs, as Queenie turns serious again.

"I have no regrets, Rose. Especially after that stunt your mother pulled today." Her head upturned, Queenie waits for Iris to comment, but the room is quiet.

"I don't think she's been around since the reception," Rose says. "Maybe that's a sign that she's finally ready to go."

"We should be so lucky," Queenie says. "Truth be told, I've had enough of your mama to last at least two lifetimes, maybe three."

Rose leaves to pack, and Queenie goes downstairs. When she enters the kitchen, Violet jumps. "You scared me," she says with a frown.

"I didn't mean to scare you, baby, and I certainly didn't mean to hurt you either."

Violet's face softens, and she bites her bottom lip as though willing herself not to cry.

"I was wondering if we could talk about all this after I get back from taking Rose to the airport," Queenie says.

Violet looks away and doesn't answer.

Queenie's shame feels full-bodied now as if a literal person standing in the room. She doesn't like this person.

"I need to tell you what happened," Queenie says. "You deserve to hear the facts."

Violet wipes a single tear from her cheek and then agrees. At this point, nothing can keep Queenie from telling the truth. She owes Violet that much. This secret has stayed hidden way too long. Unlike people, secrets never die. Look at that stupid book. Just when you think two hundred years of confidences will be buried in a bank vault forever, it resurges, refusing to be forgotten. It's in their nature for secrets to surface in one way or another, and Queenie is counting on it being in Violet's nature to forgive her.

CHAPTER TWENTY-THREE

Violet

Once the house is empty again, Violet looks at the kitchen ceiling and calls Miss Temple's name. It's not like spirits to come when called, but she wants to know if Violet getting the house is what Miss Temple really wants. After all, the note on Miss Temple's nightstand said she was going to change the will, and then her agitated spirit showed up at the will reading.

Violet leaves the kitchen and stands in the foyer listening to the tick of the grandfather clock, the heartbeat of the house. Having no time to process anything, she isn't sure what she feels. It is a mixture of shock, sadness, and exuberance. None of which she has much experience with.

As if moving through a dream, Violet walks from room to room. Could this house really be hers now? She walks out the front door and down the front steps, something she rarely does since she always uses the side entrance. The Temple house is one of those mansions with a gold plaque on the front giving the date it was built.

A house with a pedigree, she thinks.

Violet has often thought that their apartment would fit into the Temple carriage house with room to spare.

After opening the gate, she steps onto the wide sidewalk, looking back at the house. She covers a smile, embarrassed by her good fortune. For years she's wanted to get away from this house—specifically from her duties as a housekeeper and cook. Liberation was her goal. Yet even as a girl, she loved this place. While Rose complained about its formality, Violet always thought it was like a castle in a fairy tale. A castle that would never, ever be hers.

Further down the sidewalk, posters are taped to the tall wrought iron fence, their messages scrawled in dark markers. **Iris Temple is a Traitor**, says one. **Keep Your Secrets to Yourself!** says another. **Who Do You Think You Are?!** says a third. Miss Temple worked so hard to make the Temple name mean something. She would hate how ordinary folks are reacting to the scandal.

A black Buick with darkened windows is parked at the end of the block. It has sat there for several days. She can make out the figure of a man inside. It reminds Violet of a scene from one of the crime novels Queenie loans her. A suspicious-looking character lurks in the shadows, though you don't find out who they are until the end of the book. The smoke from the stranger's cigarette exits out of a one-inch gap at the top of the window. The car is running, probably for the air conditioner. A soft beat of bass comes from the car radio. Rhythm and blues. She likes the music but not the stranger.

Violet shudders, adding fear to her list of mixed

emotions. She lowers her eyes as she passes, and then walks through another gate to a stone pathway that leads to the side entrance. The kitchen entrance is typically the servant entrance, although nearly everybody uses it to come and go, except for Miss Temple. While the front entrance is formidable, the garden entrance is open and inviting.

To rid herself of the fear, she focuses on her surroundings. The courtyard and garden always have a magical feel for Violet. She spends her breaks out here whenever she can. A large oak dominates the center of the garden, the ground nearby covered in a carpet of moss. It is the kind of spot that invites a picnic, or perhaps a nap, no matter what season or time of day. Not that she ever has time for such a thing. Except her grandmother used to make picnics for her and Rose to have under this tree when they were girls. Sometimes she would join them and tell them stories about their ancestors. Queenie was nearby. Always.

What did she think about when she watched me? Violet wonders. She can't imagine standing by and watching Tia or Leisha and not claiming them as her own. It would break her heart to do so. She pushes away the betrayal she feels. It is too big to face. Too dangerous.

A wooden bench sits under an arbor next to an ivy-covered wall of the house. Blooming flowers are everywhere. In the far corner, a twisted crepe myrtle tree stands, its blossoms scattered on the ground, releasing the last moments of their scent. The breeze pushes the aroma of the blooms in Violet's direction. She drinks in the garden's perfume, feeling intoxicated by the events of the day, as well as nauseous.

Will she keep the gardener? But how will she afford him? She has heard of people who are house-rich and cash-poor.

This is definitely her now. Although, she can't believe she's even thinking this way.

A warm breeze rattles the leaves of the crepe myrtle tree. Even though it is only April, the evenings are already hot and will continue to bake them to the end of October.

The squeak of the garden gate alarms her until she sees it is Spud. Now dressed in casual clothes, he is without his bow tie. Violet has never seen him without a tie. He carries an armload of posters he's pulled from the fence.

"What kind of people do this?" He rips the posters into pieces.

"People with nothing better to do, I guess," Violet answers. "Which reminds me, did you see that black Buick out there?"

"I did. Who is that?" Spud asks.

"No idea," Violet says. "Queenie walked up to rap on the window yesterday, and he drove off when he saw her coming. At least we assume it's a 'he.' With those dark windows, it's hard to tell."

"Do you want me to talk to him?" Spud asks, sounding braver than he looks. Something about being able to see the tiny tuft of gray hair at the V of his polo shirt makes him seem overly exposed. It occurs to Violet that earlier today, they were regular, hardworking people, relying on a weekly paycheck to get by. Now, they are wealthy. All because of Miss Temple. A woman he obviously loved. And a woman Violet worked hard not to hate.

"I think if you try to talk to him, he'll just drive away again," Violet says.

"Have you called the police?"

"We did," Violet answers, "but since he isn't breaking any laws, they can't do anything."

"Doesn't it scare you?" Spud asks.

"I guess I have a higher scare quotient since I deal with ghosts every day," Violet says. With that, she gets Spud to finally smile. "Besides, the Temple mansion is like a fortress with all the security systems on," she adds, thinking she probably needs to learn how to operate them. Of course, Queenie knows how, but she doesn't want to talk to Queenie right now.

Violet invites Spud inside, and he takes his usual place at the kitchen table. "We both got quite a shock today," he says.

"I think I'm still reeling," Violet says. It strikes her odd that an older white man would be such a good friend. A friend she can say almost anything to. A friend that if not for Miss Temple's eccentricities, she might never have met. "Jack keeps calling to see when I'm coming home," she adds, "but I can't seem to leave."

"How do you think he'll react?" Spud asks.

"I honestly have no idea," Violet says. "He'll probably be in shock just like I am." She pauses. "Is it alright with you if we don't talk about that right now?"

"Whatever you need is fine with me." Spud starts to straighten his tie, but his hand hangs there a moment when he realizes it isn't there. An awkward grin crosses his face, as though going casual will take some getting used to.

"I was in the middle of making turnovers," she says.

While he pours himself a cup of coffee, she turns her attention back to the biscuit dough she left on the countertop when Rose and Queenie left. She rolls out and cuts several pieces—shaped like the sail of paper boats—and folds the strips of dough over sliced peaches before placing them on a baking sheet.

"You're as good as Julia Child," Spud says.

Violet thanks him. She always gets compliments on her cooking. At church socials, people line up in front of whatever she brings, so they don't miss out. With Spud watching, she makes a dozen peach turnovers, one after another.

"I bake when I don't know what else to do," Violet says.

"Lucky for me," Spud says.

Violet smiles. Flour dots her arms and forehead, and she wipes it off. Silence follows.

"Here we are together, a butcher and a baker," Spud says. "All we need is a candlestick maker." He pauses like he's waiting to see if she thinks he's clever.

Violet smiles. She used to read the nursery rhyme to Tia and Leisha. When Violet was young, Queenie read them to her. She claps the memory away, along with the flour. It seems she has to rethink her entire life.

"Tell me something I don't know about you," Spud says as if wanting to fill the silence until she's ready to talk.

Violet looks at him, reminded of how often she appreciates his kindness.

"Well, let me think," Violet says, glancing out the kitchen window that overlooks the garden. "In 1980, I was a runner-up in the Miss Georgia pageant." Her face tingles with warmth. She hasn't told anyone this fact in twenty years.

Spud reacts like this news requires a standing ovation. "Well, it doesn't surprise me one bit," Spud says. "What did you do for talent?"

"I sang Amazing Grace," she says. "A blues version. It was my grandmother's idea."

"I bet it was beautiful," he says.

"I don't know about that, but for years people walked up to me on the street and told me how moved they were by my performance. One of the judges even confided that if I'd been a little lighter-skinned, I would have won the title."

"Will you sing it for me someday?" Spud asks.

"I've kind of given up singing," she says, "but maybe

someday." She pauses, wondering why she gave up singing. Did she just get so busy working she didn't have time anymore?

The smell of turnovers calls her back to the oven where she takes them out and places them on a cooling rack, their perfectly browned crusts glisten with a light sugar glaze. Despite her recent windfall, she still wants to open her Tea Shop and Bakery. She wants to have something to pass along to her girls. Of course, a mansion might be a nice thing, too.

With a peach turnover on a plate for each of them, she adds a scoop of vanilla ice cream. Then she refills Spud's coffee and makes a cup of tea for herself. Although Spud and Violet have sat together many times, this moment feels different.

Spud takes a bite of turnover, and his eyes close. This pleases her. Her own turnover sits untouched. Vanilla ice cream forms a moat around the pastry to create an island of sweetness.

"I can't believe dear Iris left me real estate," Spud says. "I feel like I won the lottery."

"Me, too," Violet says. "But I can't help wondering if there's been some huge mistake."

"It wouldn't be like Iris to make mistakes," Spud says.

"But she gave you up," Violet says.

Spud pauses, as though his peach turnover is trapped behind the lump in his throat. He swallows, and she can hear his gulp. "I think that's the kindest thing anyone has ever said to me," Spud says.

Violet rests a hand on Spud's arm. "It's the truth," she says, watching him blush.

"Have you talked to Queenie yet?" he asks like there's truth to be found there, too.

"We're supposed to talk later tonight," Violet says. "I

don't know whether I'm angry or sad or relieved. Rose seems to think that Queenie had to keep it all a secret so I wouldn't lose my job, and she could still live here and be close to me. It makes sense, in a way. But, honestly, I don't know what to think."

"That's why it's important to talk about it," Spud says.

As if summoned, the door opens, and Queenie walks into the kitchen. "Sorry for the intrusion," she says.

Violet pretends interest in the soggy turnover.

"Would you like some coffee and dessert?" Spud says to Queenie. "Violet has outdone herself with the peach turnovers."

Queenie thanks Spud and serves herself. The tension in the room feels like a tightrope stretched between two Savannah mansions. When Queenie takes a seat at the kitchen table, Violet has to resist leaving the room. Her muteness accompanies the tension.

"Shall I leave you two alone?" Spud asks.

"No!" Violet and Queenie answer in unison. Their awkward laughter waits for a beat before filling the room. The tightrope quickly relaxes.

The last six hours have felt like a roller coaster ride at Six Flags. Violet's emotions have ranged from intense anger to confusion, with moments of compassion thrown in. On the one hand, she wants to hear what Queenie has to say. On the other hand, she'd prefer never to speak to her again.

"Rose will get to Denver around ten tonight," Queenie says. "Max is driving from Cheyenne to pick her up."

Is she hoping the small talk will rescue her from the big conversation we need to have? Violet wonders.

"I guess they'll have a lot of talk about," Violet says. *Like we do,* she wants to add. Which one of them will have the courage to speak first? Meanwhile, she's tired. Her day started early, and now it's eight o'clock. The hurt she feels lies just underneath her skin like a splinter that refuses to work its way out on its own. She wants to scream: *How could you lie to me all these years?*

"I'm so sorry I lied to you," Queenie says as if she's read Violet's thoughts. They have this kind of connection sometimes. A connection where they know what the other is thinking. Now Violet knows why. In the womb, she nestled just inches from Queenie's heart. With this thought, her breath catches in her throat. She refuses to cry. She's cried enough for one day.

Violet stands and puts her uneaten turnover into the kitchen sink. She wants to go home but stands frozen.

"Just listen to what she has to say," Spud tells Violet, his voice soft.

Despite his awkwardness, she is glad Spud is here. "I'm willing to listen for a little while," Violet says to Queenie. She leans against the kitchen counter to anchor herself in place. "But if I say 'stop,' I need you to stop."

"Absolutely," Queenie says. But then she hesitates as though her courage flounders.

Violet and Spud exchange a look. His eyes open wider. Is he reminding her to stay open to what Queenie has to say?

"At first, I thought that if the Temples knew, they might try to take you away from me," Queenie begins. "Then later, I thought they might say I couldn't live here anymore." She looks into Violet's eyes, who turns away. It is too much to deal with her pain, as well as Queenie's. "Perhaps it's not a good enough reason to live with a lie all these years," Queenie continues, "but it's all I knew to do. To complicate things, Oscar made me swear that I would never tell. He was convinced that nothing good could come of it. But it seems that nothing good has come from keeping the secret, either."

A long pause follows. Spud taps his coffee cup as if to remind Violet to speak. But she hasn't a clue what to say. *Go to hell? Get out of my house? I forgive you?*

Queenie bows her head. If she's waiting to be forgiven, she's going to have to wait longer. Violet isn't the type to give angry outbursts, but sometimes she wishes she were.

"I've been afraid that you would hate me, not that anyone could blame you," Queenie begins again.

"I don't hate you," Violet says, her voice raised. She doesn't want to let Queenie off this easy, but she is telling the truth. Violet doesn't hate Queenie. Maybe if she did, it wouldn't hurt so much.

Queenie's relief comes out in a rush of words. "You don't know how good that is to hear."

"Well, I'm glad one of us feels good," Violet says, her voice elevated again. "How could you lie to me every day for the last forty years?" Her voice breaks with emotion.

As Queenie takes a step closer, Violet holds out her arm to stop her. Queenie lowers her eyes. "I've done unforgivable things," she says, her voice contrite.

Violet can't believe how messy life sometimes gets, even when people mean well. "I need some time to get used to this." She steps back like even a few inches might help create the time. "What would you do, Queenie? What would you do if you thought your mother had died when you were a little girl, and now you're told that your real mother has been sitting right across from you all these years?"

"I honestly have no idea." Queenie stands and puts a light hand on Violet's shoulder that Violet shrugs away. "Please don't touch me. Don't speak to me and stay out of my sight," Violet says. She looks straight into Queenie's eyes that fill with tears. Perhaps she is the type for angry outbursts after all.

Queenie's lips tighten as if trying to hold back the sobbing. She leaves the room to give Violet what she wants. Now it is Violet's tears that begin again.

AFTER A GOOD CRY, Violet goes home to their small apartment. She's put off telling her family as long as she can. Tia and Leisha are watching television in the living room as Jack walks out of their bedroom.

"I was getting worried about you," Jack says. "How was the meeting with the lawyer?"

She turns away from his kiss. "I need to call a family meeting," she says, loud enough for the girls to hear her in the living room. Both girls moan. Family meetings usually mean there's a problem, and something needs to change.

Reluctant, the girls turn off the television and sit at the table. Jack does, too. All three look worried that they've done something wrong, but she is too tired to reassure them.

"Something really big happened today," she begins. "Something really, really big." In the moments that follow, she tells them about the meeting at the lawyer's office and what she learned while she was there. When she finishes, all eyes stay on her. She can't remember the last time she had her family's full attention.

"Queenie is my grandmother now?" Leisha asks. "How come we're just now finding out?"

"I think Queenie was afraid I might lose my job if Miss Temple knew." Violet's voice trails off. She is so tired of thinking about all this.

"Well, I don't think people should lie," Leisha says.

At sixteen, Leisha makes all A's and is one of the youth leaders at their church.

"I don't think she felt that she had a choice," Violet says.

She surprises herself with her willingness to defend Queenie. It helps that they've been so close over the years. But isn't this what makes the betrayal hurt even more? Violet wonders again why Queenie never told her the truth.

"I love Aunt Queenie," Tia says. "She's funny and cool."

Tia is fourteen and looks just like her father. Tall and lean, she plays center for the girl's basketball team in high school. Unlike her outgoing sister, she is shy.

"I love Queenie, too," Violet says.

"So, are we going to live there?" Tia asks. Tia and Leisha share one of the bedrooms in their two-bedroom apartment.

"Yes, I suppose we will," Violet says, "if your father agrees."

She has thought about this possibility all afternoon. She can imagine the Temple house full of teenagers and life, where homework is done on the large dining room table, enough room for both girls to have at least six friends over.

"All of this will be up for discussion," Jack says. "Let's not go counting chickens," he adds.

"Your dad's right," Violet says. "None of this is a done deal."

Violet imagines how Jack's life might change, too, if he finally has a home office to do his class preparation, instead of taking up the whole kitchen table. He can have two offices if he wants. Not to mention the thousand square foot workshop located at the very back of the property that currently serves as a garden shed of sorts, but could easily be converted. The biggest question, of course, is whether or not he minds sharing an office with the ghost of Mister Oscar. *My father,* she reminds herself. She remembers as a little girl riding on his shoulders in the garden. She blinks away more tears that threaten to come. It is still too much to take in.

"I can't leave my high school," Leisha says. "All my friends are there."

Despite their phenomenal good fortune, Violet's older daughter looks upset. Geographical changes don't sit well with teenagers. So much change is going on in their bodies that to throw in a literal geographic change, even if it is only a few miles away, is too much to ask. Leisha's best friend moved to Atlanta over the Christmas holidays, and it's been hard on her. Violet reassures Leisha that everything will work out. It's too soon to make any decisions, anyway. The house isn't officially Violet's yet, and maybe it won't ever be. *Especially if Edward Temple has any say about it,* she wants to add.

For the first time that day, she realizes Edward is her half-brother. The thought makes her queasy. Violet was Leisha's age when he attacked her. She never told Jack about the incident, and now she wonders why.

Violet yawns. It is after midnight by the time she and Jack crawl into bed.

"God works in mysterious ways," Jack says.

"Do you really think this is God's doing?" Violet asks.

"You never know," Jack says.

Jack always has more faith than Violet that things will work out and that God is watching out for them. Violet isn't so sure.

"I don't even know how to think about Queenie being my mother," she says.

"I've always liked her, though," Jack says. "If you were going to have a surprise relative, she's a great one to have."

Sometimes Jack is so easy-going, Violet wishes she could get a rise out of him. He looks like a giant teddy bear, and he acts like one, too.

"You're not upset that she lied to me for all these years?" Violet asks.

"It sounds like she had her reasons," Jack says. "Besides, she's been so generous to you and me and the girls over the years. Now it all kind of makes sense."

"So, what's your reasoning about Miss Temple leaving her house to me?" Violet says. "Even if her dead husband, *my father,* did leave a letter telling her to do it, that's just too unreal."

"Maybe she grew a conscience," Jack says. "Your family has been working for her family forever. Let's face it. You haven't been paid what you're worth the whole time you've been there, and it's doubtful anybody else did, either. Maybe it was time for her to give something back. Maybe, at the end of her life, she realized that."

"But this just doesn't happen in real life, Jack. No matter how many maybes you throw in."

He gives her a quick kiss on the lips and rolls over. "Just accept it and be grateful," he says.

Her anger at Queenie threatens to bleed over to Jack. She stops herself from voicing it. Besides, she doesn't have the energy to fight.

Within minutes, Jack begins his low snore. Violet questions briefly how he can sleep with all that has happened, but that is Jack. He's unflappable. He won't let this windfall go to his head. It simply goes in the blessing column, and a requirement of accepting blessings is to have gratitude. But Violet hasn't made her way to the gratitude column yet.

Her thoughts return to Queenie. She'll need a place to live. Violet can't imagine throwing her out. If anything, it's more Queenie's home than hers. Despite her anger and hurt, she has to admit that Queenie's reasons for withholding the truth make sense. Miss Temple could be vindictive. If she found out the truth, she might have thrown Queenie out of the house and probably Violet, too.

But why give Violet the house? Did she really feel that strongly about honoring the last wishes of Mister Oscar—Violet's father? Something doesn't add up. Unfortunately, it seems, everybody who could clear up the mystery is dead.

I might as well give up on sleeping tonight, she thinks. Violet rolls over in bed and for the first time that day, her shoulder throbs. Edward. The last thing she needs is to have him seeking revenge for something she didn't even ask for. If she's right about him, and she's almost certain she is, he will do anything to get back whatever he feels belongs to him. Her shoulder confirms the danger. But there is already something suspicious going on. Someone in a black sedan is watching the Temple house. Not to mention that long-buried secrets are popping up everywhere.

CHAPTER TWENTY-FOUR

Rose

The landing at the Denver airport is bumpy. Wind currents dance along the Front Range of the Colorado Rockies like bucking broncos refusing to be tamed. Rose gets off the jet and has to resist getting on her hands and knees to kiss the azure blue carpet at the unloading gate. She makes her way through the familiar airport feeling a combination of fatigue, hunger, and shell-shock from the reading of her mother's will.

At the baggage claim, she looks for Max. He is probably parking the truck by now. At least she hopes he is. Rose feels weary from the day and wants to see him. It's hard to believe a few hours earlier, she was in the office of her mother's attorney. Yet Savannah feels a world away now. She wants to be home. She wants to sleep in her own bed. And tomorrow morning, Rose will get back to her regular routine and check in on the new calves that were born while she was away.

As she waits on Max, she tries to adjust to being back in the West. She remembers when she first arrived here. After growing up on the east coast, relocating to Cheyenne was like moving to another planet. The average rainfall is 13 to 15 inches in Wyoming. Savannah receives fifty inches or more. Cheyenne is high plains, semi-desert—Savannah is low country, sea level, and marshland. The first few years, it felt like the wind on the edge of the Great Plains nearly lifted her off the ground. She made jokes about being Dorothy in *The Wizard of Oz*. Now, like Dorothy, she wants to find her way back to Kansas, but in Rose's story, that is Savannah. She clicks her heels together three times but is too tired to smile.

A man next to her announces it is snowing outside, as he retrieves his skis from a second baggage area. Winter in Cheyenne has an element of life and death to it. Becoming stranded on the highway in an unexpected blizzard in April or May can be dangerous. A woman she knew from the co-op froze to death during a May snowstorm. Her body wasn't found until the snowdrift finally melted in mid-June. It is April now, one of the most unpredictable months of the year. It can be raining one minute, hailing another and snowing heavily the next. The Rocky Mountains create their own weather system, and the Front Range has a front-row seat to the drama. Meanwhile, Rose isn't even wearing a coat. It is packed in her suitcase.

"Where are you, Max?" she whispers, scanning the crowd for a familiar face.

"Are you from around here?" a young man asks, perhaps college age. If not dressed in blue jeans and a sweater, Rose might think he was a Hare Krishna. He seems much too friendly and peaceful to be an average guy. *Do Hare Krishnas still hang out in airports?* she wonders.

"I've lived in Wyoming for twenty-five years," Rose says.

"Wow, that's a really long time," he says. Rose is grateful he doesn't add that he wasn't even born yet or one of those comments that the young say to accidentally bring attention to how ancient she is. "I'm from D.C.," he adds. "Is it true that it's still wild here?"

"In Denver?" she asks.

"The West, in general," he says.

"It's true," she says. "We have coyotes that roam outside our ranch and pronghorn deer, descendants of the African antelope."

"Wow," he says again with a grin.

Rose doesn't really have the energy to be friendly, but in a way, it's a nice distraction while she waits on Max. On the ranch, there aren't many opportunities to *wow* people. "Of course, our biggest worry out here is the rattlesnakes." She adds this part solely for the shock effect.

"Really?" the young man says. His smile has not wavered.

"We find them in the garden all the time and under the house and in the barn, and sometimes they'll just be sunning themselves out on the road or next to the mailbox."

No wonder I miss Savannah, she thinks. The Georgia Coast has its own species of rattlesnake, as well as water moccasins. But in all the years she lived there, she never actually saw any. The wildness in the South has an easier time keeping itself hidden in the undergrowth than creatures in the stark, open plains. The people on the coast keep their wildness mostly hidden, too. Especially when it comes to their secrets.

Rose remembers the look on Edward's face when her

part of the inheritance was read. If he had been holding a sword, he might have lopped off her head instead of a little finger.

The luggage conveyor springs to life. Everyone turns to watch luggage surge out of the terminal's inner bowels and circle on the baggage carousel.

"Hey, nice talking to you," the Hare Krishna says, with an even bigger smile to go with his blond hair and peaceful blue eyes.

"You, too," she says with what she decides is a western wave—quick and noncommittal. Rose and the young man are separated as people in the back move forward to get their bags.

As usual, Rose forgot to tie a red ribbon around the handle like Max always tells her to do, so that her common-looking black bag can be more easily recognized. She grabs one off the conveyor belt, sees it isn't hers, and then hoists it back. Too tired to be coordinated, Rose bangs her knee in the process. Wincing with pain, she eyes another.

"There you are," Max says, arriving at her side. He grabs Rose's bag off the conveyor belt just as it is about to pass and sits it at her feet. Help has arrived.

Rose hugs him and takes in his smell, his shape. At six feet, two inches, he is a half a foot taller than her, and when he's wearing his cowboy hat, it seems even more. Max has cleaned up for the occasion. He wears the shirt she loves and his best pair of blue jeans. His face is also clean-shaven. Rose hasn't realized just how much she missed him until this moment.

"You look good," he says.

"You're lying," Rose says. "I caught a look at myself in the airport bathroom and nearly scared myself to death. But thanks for saying so anyway." She squeezes him again.

These days, her face always reveals her tiredness. She can't rely on the resiliency and elasticity of youth any longer, the only help she gets is from Revlon.

"How was the flight?" Max asks.

"Bumpy, as always," Rose says with a grimace.

Rose hates turbulence. It ranks right up there with stomach flu and a pinched nerve in her back. Except for the quickness of getting places, there isn't anything about flying that she actually enjoys. By car, the trip from Wyoming to the Georgia coastline would take 28 hours of nonstop driving. She would still be somewhere in Tennessee.

"Let's get you home, little lady," Max says in his faux western voice. His attempt to sound like John Wayne isn't even remotely close, but Rose plays along as his damsel in distress.

"Why, thank you, kind sir," Rose says in an exaggerated southern drawl she reserves only for him.

Max reaches for her carry-on full of books and magazines for the trip—she always takes enough to read for a year— and swings it lightly over his shoulder. Life feels easier whenever Max is around. Rose wraps her arm around his as they walk in a comfortable, welcoming silence to the parking garage.

After Max puts her things in the back of the truck, he pays the parking attendant, and they hit the open road. Despite her weariness, she resigns herself to the two-hour drive home.

Even though it is dark, Rose can feel the vastness of the landscape stretching out in front of them. It is snowing hard now. Max has his wipers on high. On I - 25, they have a straight shot home to Cheyenne. Rose's thoughts drift to where normal life awaits her. The next morning she will make her favorite coffee and glance at the morning newspaper before diving into the bookkeeping for the ranch that is undoubtedly piled up on the desk in the den. Then as soon as the sun is up, she will go out to the barn. *If I can make it to the barn,* she thinks, as they pass a snowplow.

The windshield wipers take frantic swipes to keep the glass clear. Her shoulders are tense. The weather is a topic of daily conversation at the ranch. Part of Rose's job is to monitor the cable weather channel, so nothing storm-related catches them by surprise.

"Do you want to tell me what happened?" Max says, breaking the silence. He keeps his eyes on the road.

Rose called him earlier that day and told him there was big news, but that she wanted to tell him in person. This also bought her time to decide how she felt about it. Max, in his infinite and sometimes maddening patience, hasn't pushed it. Now she feels too tired to go into it.

"You've kept me in suspense all day," he says as if sensing her hesitation.

Rose pauses, pulling forward what feels like her last bit of energy. "Well, it seems Mother has an interesting proposition for us," Rose says, "and I don't know if you'll even consider it for a second."

Max gives an inquisitive grunt, cowboy-ease, for *'what might that be?'*

"If I move back to Savannah, I inherit twenty million dollars," Rose begins. "If I stay here, I get two thousand."

This time, Max's grunt has more energy to it—a kind of nuanced *'what the hell?'* A long pause follows as he takes this news in. He doesn't talk much, but when he does say something, it is usually worth waiting for. Rose waits. She and Katie used to make jokes about Max being E. F. Hutton, from those stock brokerage commercials that aired with the slogan: *When E. F. Hutton talks, people listen.*

Max takes off his cowboy hat, worn on even the darkest of nights and the cloudiest of days. The lights on the dashboard reveal the crease from the brim that always brands his forehead, along with the rancher's version of a golfer's tan. Max grunts again.

A three-grunt conversation, Rose notes. *That's a new record.*

Rose doesn't know how to tell him that she'd like to go back. Maybe after she's rested, she'll have the energy to bring it up.

The wipers keep to their task and begin to drag against the glass. The snow slows. Max turns down the wipers, and Rose relaxes her shoulders.

"How soon can we pack?" Max says, finally.

Even in her tiredness, Rose's gasp is full volume. "Excuse me?" she asks.

This isn't the response she expected at all. She never considered that Max might actually give up the ranch. Four generations of his family have lived in Wyoming. Most of his extended family are still here, except for one wild cousin—considered disloyal by the rest of the family—who moved to Austin and works on radio.

"I say, let's do it," Max repeats, sans grunt.

"Are you serious?" Rose asks although she knows Max isn't the type to kid around.

"For twenty-five years, I've watched you try to fit in here," he says. "You've tried. You've really tried."

"But this is our home," she says.

"I know." He goes silent again like he's giving the possibility more thought.

For several minutes Rose is hypnotized by the wipers pushing the snowflakes to the edges of the windshield. She doesn't want to get her hopes up. If they stay in Cheyenne, she'll be fine. They have a good life here.

Max clears his throat and pulls her out of her daze.

"It's not a decision to take lightly, Rose, but I turn fifty this year. Before I know it, I'll be seventy, with no one to turn the ranch over to."

"What about Katie?" Rose asks.

"You know Katie doesn't want to come back here. She's not the ranching type."

Max is right. Katie wasn't happy in Cheyenne. She survived high school by pouring all her energy into making good grades so she could be accepted at a college back east.

The evening after the funeral, Rose gave Max a detailed description of Angela on the phone. Their daughter's lifestyle has not caused Max to waver in his devotion to Katie in the slightest. Their only hesitation—the fear of any parent, especially in Wyoming after the Matthew Shepherd tragedy —is that they don't want Katie to have a difficult life.

"Besides," Max begins again, "we're practically bankrupt. So twenty million dollars sounds very attractive at the moment."

They pass Fort Collins, an hour from home. The snow has slowed even more. A full moon emerges from behind the clouds. It fills the entire side view mirror and looks enormous. It suddenly occurs to Rose that if they move, she will miss seeing the moon and stars with such clarity on the open plains. But there is also something magical about seeing a full moon through trees laden with Spanish moss accompanied by the smell of magnolia blossoms wafting through the air.

"I can't believe you're even considering this," Rose says to Max.

"I can't believe I'm considering it, either," Max says. "But I think I'm ready for a new adventure. I'm definitely ready to stop working so damn hard. But mostly, I want you to be happy, Rose. We've lived for the last twenty-five years where I wanted to live. Let's live the next twenty-five years where you want to."

Emotion catches in her throat. She has never loved Max more than she does at this moment. Like every couple, they've had their issues, but nothing they didn't work hard to get past. She reaches over and takes his calloused right hand and presses her love into it.

"Are you sure?" she asks.

"I'm sure," he says.

Their eyes meet briefly, and he squeezes her hand again before returning it to the steering wheel.

The weariness around Max's eyes is as tangible as the calluses on his hands. She has spent hours of her life trying to rub the pain out of his back and shoulders after a long day. Ranching is hard on an almost fifty-year-old man. It's hard on anyone. She's had her share of aches and pains, too. But this is the first time she's heard him voice his willingness to walk away from the ranch.

Rose tries to imagine Max in Savannah. He's only been there twice. Once for their wedding and then a second time at Christmas, a year after that. Rose pauses to let this new possibility seep into her tired body. She thought moving back to Savannah was not even an option. She thought that Max wouldn't want to leave their home, nor be manipulated by her dead mother. But evidently, Rose thought wrong.

As they pass the last exit for Fort Collins, the snow begins again in earnest. She hopes they don't close I-25 down before they get home. She thinks back to her walk on the beach earlier that day. It was nearly 80 degrees in Savannah. She doesn't have the heart to tell this to Max.

Snow drifts form along the highway. Max isn't talking now. He's putting all his attention into getting them home before the road closes. Even though Max seems certain, they will probably need to have many more conversations about her mother's proposition before they sell the ranch. But Rose feels a spark of possibility come alive inside of her. Can she really go home again?

CHAPTER TWENTY-FIVE

11 Months Later
Queenie

The one year anniversary of Iris's death is a month away, and the *Temple Book of Secrets* is still in the news. Reporters have joined the crowds out front, and Queenie has even dealt with paparazzi while doing her errands. Paparazzi—Savannah style—which consists of a couple of acne-faced teenagers taking snapshots of her picking out lettuce in the produce aisle of the Piggly Wiggly. Why anyone in the world would want a picture of Queenie threatening to throw produce at her stalkers is beyond her.

After a court injunction stopped the newspaper from printing the secrets, they began to show up on flyers delivered to downtown mailboxes and stapled to light poles and trees. Not to mention community boards in almost every grocery store and coffee shop. The mystery continues as to who is planting the secrets, and Queenie has heard that there are even bookies who are laying odds as to who it might be. Queenie, Edward, and Rose are suspected. Even Violet has been named. But what would they have to gain from all this? If she had to guess, she thinks that whoever is planting the secrets is someone outside of the immediate family, but also someone who knows a tremendous amount about the Temples and somehow got access to the book. But how?

Queenie is usually good at figuring out *who done it* in the murder mysteries she reads, and it is often the last person you would ever suspect. But this is one mystery that has her totally stumped. She is even starting to wonder if it is the deceased Temples who are doing it, to somehow free themselves.

Whoever is doing it has not tired in their quest to expose every last secret. It doesn't matter if a secret is two hundred years old and contains information about a family that has long since died out, it shows up somewhere and is reported upon. Savannah is getting a history lesson about its past.

However, Queenie prefers to focus on the present. Earlier that day, she received a phone call from Rose that they sold their ranch and were now in the process of packing up everything to move to Savannah. At Violet's insistence, they will live in the Temple house with Queenie, as well as Violet and her family, who plan to move in as soon as school is out in June.

"How do you like that, Iris?" Queenie looks up at the light fixture in the sunroom. "This old mansion is becoming a halfway house for recovering Temples."

As always, Queenie's laugh comes out as a cackle, but then she stops herself with the thought: *No need to rub it in.* Even dead, Iris can still make Queenie regret it. For months now, she has carried a sweater with her everywhere she goes to combat the icy blasts of Iris's disapproval. But at least the odor has gone away.

For Queenie, life without Iris isn't what she expected. As much as she yearned not to be ordered around and criticized, she has yet to find something to fill the yawning gap that Iris left behind. In her weaker moments, she even wishes Iris was still here.

For months, Edward kept things interesting with his team of lawyers contesting the will like a team of Georgia bulldogs fighting for a touchdown from the one-yard line on a fourth down. However, Bo Rivers assures them that Edward doesn't have a case and that the entire dispute should be settled in the next few weeks.

Queenie walks into the dining room and looks out the window to see the black sedan parked in its usual place. It shows up as regularly as a Temple secret. She wonders if they are somehow related. Queenie goes into the kitchen where Violet is polishing the silverware at the kitchen table.

"What are you doing?" Queenie asks. "Nobody's going to fire you if you want to relax for a change."

"The silver still needs to be polished," Violet says. "What am I going to do, hire someone?" She laughs.

Queenie tells her she has a point and takes a polishing cloth and starts on the knives.

A day doesn't pass without Queenie writing in her journal about how grateful she is that Violet forgave her. It took several months and many talks and tears on both parts, but they reached the conclusion that they needed to forget the past and focus on the future.

Now, if these damn ghosts would just do the same, Queenie thinks. "Rose called this morning," she says to Violet. "They'll be here this time next month."

"I'm so glad they'll be living here, too," Violet says, going to town on a gravy boat. "At least then, the ghosts won't outnumber the people anymore."

"It's about time," Queenie says.

Violet's girls, her granddaughters, as Queenie is now finally free to call them, have already claimed two bedrooms at the east end of the house. Queenie and Violet have been getting them ready for weeks. Not only have they taken down draperies and cleaned windows, but they have also moved furniture from other parts of the house to accommodate two teenage girls.

"I like that this old house is coming alive again," Queenie says.

"I'm not sure the rest of the Temples like it," Violet says. "Have you noticed how quiet it's been on the ghost front lately?"

"Come to think of it, I haven't needed my sweater all day," Queenie says.

"It's like when children get quiet," Violet says. "It means they're up to something."

"It wouldn't be the first time," Queenie says. "By the way, Mama called with another warning. She says to be careful around the anniversary of Iris's death. Evidently, anniversaries create openings between the visible and the invisible worlds."

"That's the last thing we need," Violet says.

"Tell me about it." Queenie polishes the salad forks, wondering how many of her ancestors have done this same thing. Except now, these salad forks belong to her daughter. She smiles her glee.

"I think Rose and Max should have the back two bedrooms," Violet says. "They look out over the garden, and they can convert one of the bedrooms into a den."

"That's a great idea," Queenie says, "those rooms will

be perfect for them." She remembers a summer when Violet and Rose were girls. The older she gets, the more vivid her recollections. "Do you remember saying as a little girl that you wanted to live with Rose when you grew up? Mama and I just rolled our eyes. But it seems you got your wish."

Violet smiles. "I'd forgotten all about that," she says. "Maybe the seed got planted then, and the possibility has been growing all these years."

"In that case, I should have planted the seed that I'd be wealthy in my old age," Queenie says with a wink. "But, I guess there's still time."

Queenie has talked to Violet about Old Sally may be living here, too, someday. Not that it will be easy to convince her to leave her house. Violet was totally open to the idea. Old Sally is getting frail—something she didn't think was possible a few years ago—and Queenie worries about her.

"By the way," Violet says. "Spud is coming over later to help with some things."

"He's been coming around a lot these days," Queenie says. She's not sure how she feels about this. In a way, she hates sharing Violet, now that they get along again. But she doesn't want to be selfish.

"I think he's lonely," Violet says. "That's our good luck because he's incredibly helpful, too."

"I'll see him today," Queenie says. "I've continued Iris's tradition of going to the Piggly Wiggly every Wednesday. He always seems glad to see me." What Queenie doesn't admit is she likes seeing him, too.

"Spud is a real sweetheart," Violet says. "Maybe you should get to know him a little better. How long's it been since you had a man in your life, Queenie?"

She pauses long enough to count back the years.

"Would you believe in 1973?" Queenie asks. This shocks her as much as it appears to shock Violet.

"Time to get back on that horse," Violet says.

"That horse turned into a jackass and died a long time ago," Queenie says with a chuckle.

"I have an idea," Violet says. "Why don't you invite him over for dinner? He's a vegetarian, you know, so how about picking up some Portobello mushrooms at the store, and I'll make Portobello burgers."

"I could never be interested in a man who doesn't eat meat," Queenie says, her tone dismissive.

"Don't make excuses," Violet says. She hands Queenie the car keys and gently pushes her toward the door.

As Queenie walks down the aisle toward the meat section, she remembers following Iris down this same aisle. At the counter, Spud Grainger wraps a package of ribs for a customer. When he sees Queenie, he smiles, and she nods in return. Lips pursed, she studies him from the back of the line.

He's a tad scrawny, as men go, she thinks, *yet still handsome.* It doesn't seem to matter that he's about a dozen shades lighter than Denzel. But how does he feel about full-figured women? Iris was scrawny as a Q-tip. Queenie puts her hands where her waist used to be. A waist that disappeared sometime in the 1970s. *Lord, have mercy,* she thinks, *if things ever got amorous, I might accidentally crush him.* She smiles at this thought and catches Spud Grainger smiling back.

When it is her turn, Queenie tells Spud of Violet's invitation to come to dinner that night, all the while trying not to gag at the thought of mushroom burgers.

Yet Spud accepts the invitation and then straightens his

tie, which prompts Queenie to straighten the red wrap she's wearing around her hair. Instead of two peas in a pod, they are more like a zucchini and a watermelon growing on different vines altogether.

A flash goes off near the dairy section, and she rolls her eyes at the same kid who got a photo of her getting out of the Town Car. Does he think she's delivering a Temple secret to the butcher?

"If it's okay with you, I'll bring some shrimp," Spud says, unaware of the camera. "We just got in some beauties this morning. Do you like shrimp and grits?" he asks. "I make a mean shrimp and grits."

"I thought you were a vegetarian," Queenie whispers, in case he doesn't want his customers or the paparazzi to know.

"Not a strict one," he says. "I also eat seafood."

Queenie smiles, thinking there may be hope for him after all.

"Six o'clock?" Queenie asks. She flutters her eyelashes, wondering who she's trying to fool. She hasn't flirted with a man since Elvis Presley wore blue suede shoes.

"Is something irritating your eye?" Spud asks. "I have some eye drops in the back."

Queenie assures him she's okay and swears off flirting for another forty years, as they say their goodbyes.

While in the area, Queenie gets her hair done at the Gladys Knight and the Tints beauty parlor, as she always does. It feels strange to drive on these outings, instead of being Iris's unwitting passenger. However, she likes the thought that pedestrians are safe in Savannah again. She half expects a public service announcement to run at the bottom of her favorite television programs to document this change. Along with the latest Temple secret.

In Iris's honor, and because she's hungry, Queenie goes through the pick-up window at Kentucky Fried Chicken. Another acne-clad teenager—minus a camera, yet with an Adam's apple the shape of a chicken gizzard—sticks his head out the window.

"Hey, isn't this the car of that rich old lady who used to come through?" he asks.

If I needed further proof there it is, Queenie thinks. "I'm afraid Iris Temple died almost a year ago," she tells him.

The teenager sniffs as if genuinely saddened, and starts to pick at one of his pimples. "She was kind of interesting, you know?"

"Yes, Iris Temple was definitely interesting," Queenie says.

He leans further out the window and whispers, "She used to tip me. Can you believe that? Nobody ever tips."

Queenie smiles. Iris could be generous when she wanted to be.

After he takes her order, the teenager gives Queenie a free side order of slaw as condolence. After parking at the back of the lot, she eats three chicken strips and a biscuit, along with the bereavement cole slaw. It is still a mystery to her how Iris could devour an entire bucket all by herself. As delicate as Iris's digestive system appeared to be, she must have had an iron stomach.

Queenie thinks back to the bucket of original recipe she placed in Iris's casket the morning of her funeral. *Not my finest moment,* she thinks, realizing that with all the preservatives they put in things these days, the chicken will probably stay crispy for the next thirty years.

She pauses with the regret that sweeps over her occasionally, but it's not like she can take it back. Queenie's feelings for Iris have softened over the last months, like a mother who forgets the pains of childbirth. Although she has a vivid memory of giving birth to Violet at her mother's beach house in the middle of the night on the 13th of August. Violet was a perfect baby, and it broke Queenie's heart to not claim her as her own. It was a death of a sort, too.

After she finishes the chicken, Queenie drives back to the Temple house, where the black Buick remains at the end of the block. On this particular day, the driver has changed shirts from the one he wore earlier. At least the sleeve sticking out of the window is different. The windows are tinted so she can't see his face.

"I'm going to get to the bottom of this once and for all," she tells herself.

Queenie parks the Town Car in the carriage house next to the big house and then sneaks back toward the gate so the anonymous driver won't see her in his rear-view mirror. She tiptoes down the sidewalk, wondering when she might have last tiptoed anywhere. Hiding behind a forest of pink azalea bushes, Queenie then scoots along the edge of the hedge. Finally, about twenty feet from the sedan, she begins to half-run, half-pounce toward the driver's window.

"Who are you?" she demands. "Why are you watching our house?"

The driver jumps and says, "Holy shit! Where'd you come from?"

The element of surprise has worked in her favor. She looks into the sunglasses that shield his eyes and sees her own reflection. She has to resist fixing the bow in her hair.

"What are you doing here?" she asks.

The driver turns on the car and quickly closes the window. She pounds on the dark glass. "Tell me who you are," she insists. "Are you the one releasing the Temple secrets?"

He guns the motor but waits until she is a safe distance away before he races off.

Her heart racing and still huffing from the exertion, Queenie retrieves her groceries from the car and goes inside to find Violet, who, despite her windfall inheritance, works every day as she always has. With everything in limbo until probate is over, Queenie has been paying her salary from her own savings, although she told Violet that she is using some money Iris left behind for household expenses.

"What's up with you?" Violet asks. "Why are you panting?"

"That guy's still out there," Queenie says. "I walked right up to his window this time, and I think I scared him to death."

"Did he say anything?"

"Nothing," Queenie says.

"It's not like we're doing anything worth watching," Violet says.

"Exactly," Queenie says. "But that makes twice I've tried to get a look at him and haven't been able to."

They agree that maybe Queenie should leave the sleuthing to someone else.

Everything from the refrigerator is on the counter, and Violet is wiping down the shelves. For the last couple of weeks, Violet and Queenie have done the spring cleaning of a lifetime. After taking down the heavy, lined curtains that covered every window of the house, they donated them to one of the black funeral homes in town. Every day the rooms get brighter. Queenie and Violet have also cleaned the inside windows, hiring a man to help with the outside. As her lower back can attest, they have scoured everything that can be scrubbed. She likes to think that they are cleaning out all the secrets that were ever hidden in the Temple house.

"Oh, I almost forgot, Spud will be here at six," Queenie says. "He's making shrimp and grits." She hands Violet the Portobello mushrooms.

"I'll marinate these and make some fresh collards," Violet says.

Collards are one of her mama's specialties, and her mouth waters just thinking about them. For some reason, Queenie has been thinking about her Gullah ancestors more than usual lately. She has a few ghosts to deal with on that side of the family, too. She thinks again of the man in the sedan. Even though she saw only a sliver of him through the window, there was something about him that seemed familiar.

LATER THAT EVENING, Queenie sets the kitchen table with regular plates, stainless steel cutlery, and worn cloth napkins —the ones the servants always used when she was growing up. No bone china. No silverware polished to a high gloss. No crystal water goblets. While incredibly casual in comparison to the fancy dinners Iris insisted on, Queenie loves the informality of her meals now. She has not missed the exotic smells that always hovered around the dining room one iota —including the ones coming from Iris.

From the kitchen, they hear a crash in the foyer. They exchange surprised looks before Queenie rushes into the dining room toward the noise, with Violet a second or two behind. A sizeable tropical plant in the hallway has fallen on its side with dirt scattered everywhere.

"Maybe our toddlers have shown up again," Violet says. "This kind of thing happened a lot right after Miss Temple passed."

Together they right the container, sweep dirt onto a dustpan and return it to the pot.

"Maybe she isn't happy with the changes we've been making," Violet says.

"Iris never did like change," Queenie offers.

Violet stops in the foyer and tilts her head to listen. "Oh my, Miss Temple is definitely worked up over something."

Will Iris ever be at peace? Queenie wonders. It's sad to think of her half-sister rattling around this old house, dragging her unfinished business through the rooms like an invisible steamer trunk, knocking over whatever gets in her way.

"We should tell Mama about it," Queenie says. "I hate to worry her with stuff like this, but maybe there's a Gullah spell that's like Valium for ghosts."

"Or maybe she can conjure up something for the humans who have to put up with them," Violet says.

Queenie smiles. "Now there's an idea," she says.

Violet pauses. "You know, Queenie, I've been thinking that it's time that I learned the Gullah secrets. Old Sally's been offering to teach me for years."

"She'll be thrilled to hear that, Vi, provided she doesn't already know through her tea leaves or something," Queenie says. "The minute you were born, she was convinced you had the family sensitivity. She even thought your gift might be stronger than hers. And, as you know, that's saying a lot. She'll be thrilled to hear your decision."

As far as Queenie is concerned, the family 'sensitivity' skipped a generation, leaving Queenie with a tone-deaf instrument. Not that she minds that much. Having the family gift seems as much a curse as a blessing. If she were as sensitive as Violet is to the entire goings-on in this house, she would probably be popping Xanax like after-dinner mints.

They scoop the last of the dirt back into its ornate pot, and within seconds someone bangs on the front door. They jump.

"Maybe it's that man watching the house," Queenie whispers.

"He's kept his distance for months," Violet whispers back. "Why would he knock on the door now?" The knocking continues harder and louder.

"Or maybe it's someone pissed because their secret got out," Queenie whispers again. "Did anything show up in the mailbox today?"

"Not that I know of," Violet says.

They exchange a look. Thankfully, the protesting out front has all but stopped. But they've received packages of rat poison in the mail. A brick through a carriage house window closest to the gate. Not to mention, they pull enough posters off the fence every week to build a bonfire. But who knew that that crazy *Book of Secrets* contained enough confidences to release one every day for over a year.

Violet approaches the door with Queenie close behind. As she passes the ornamental stand by the door, Queenie grabs one of the large black umbrellas.

"I'm not afraid to use this," she says. "In fact, I welcome the opportunity."

Queenie pulls back the umbrella like it's a bat, and she's winding up to hit a baseball out of the ballpark.

"Let me in," a voice demands.

Every muscle in Queenie's body tenses as she recognizes the enraged voice of Edward Temple.

CHAPTER TWENTY-SIX

Violet

V iolet's shoulder throbs as Edward Temple pounds the ancient beveled glass. If he breaks the glass, it will be next to impossible to replace. She and Queenie hide behind the door. Edward is furious, and Queenie looks about as terrified as Violet feels.

Before opening the front door, Violet takes a deep breath and tells herself to stay calm. Edward's face is red, and he smells of alcohol. Behind him, Spud has arrived for dinner and strides up the walk, looking alarmed. Violet appreciates his timing. They could use reinforcements.

Unfortunately, Edward has at least twenty pounds on Spud, but Edward's anger makes it seem like even more.

Spud asks Violet if she's all right. She says she is, but in fact, she's been better.

"Can I help you with something?" Spud asks Edward.

Edward narrows his eyes at Spud as if attempting to focus. "Oh, it's you," he says, "the family butcher. Making another delivery?" Edward smiles as though he finds himself funny. Then he turns and glares at Violet like she has something he wants.

"I suggest you calm down, Mister Temple," Spud says from behind him.

"I suggest you go screw yourself, Mister Grainger," Edward answers, not taking his eyes off Violet.

A sharp pain shoots through Violet's shoulder, and she grabs the door jamb to steady herself. Meanwhile, Queenie holds up the umbrella like she's ready to swing for the fences if Edward takes another step forward.

Weeks ago, Violet heard that Edward's case against Miss Temple's will wasn't going in his favor. This is the part about having money that Violet doesn't like. It can make people greedy and not think clearly. She has no idea why Miss Temple didn't take better care of Edward in her will, but she is certain she had her reasons. Miss Temple always had her reasons.

"Perhaps we should speak about this in the lawyer's office," Violet says. She crosses her arms, getting a ghost of a chill.

"Those asshole attorneys don't know what they're doing," Edward says, as a spitball of saliva hits her cheek.

Violet hates cussing as much as she despises Edward.

Edward's eyes are red like he's had too many martinis. A piece of toilet paper clings to a small dot of blood on his neck.

"I need to look for something in the house," Edward tells Violet. "It's imperative."

Even if he is her half-brother, Violet isn't about to let him in and resists telling him it isn't his house anymore.

Seconds later, a police car arrives, flashing lights twirling but no siren. Edward cusses under his breath. In Violet's and Jack's neighborhood, the police would have sirens blasting and two or three squad cars. Yet here they don't seem to want to disturb Savannah's wealthiest citizens. For the first time Violet realizes that because of inheriting this house, she is now part of the wealthy, too.

One of the police officers walks up to the front door, and Edward straightens his clothes like he's getting in character. He turns to greet the cop.

"Are you sure you're all right?" Spud asks Violet and Queenie.

"A bit shaken, that's all," Violet says.

Violet and Queenie hold hands, and Spud looks at them like he's seeing the family resemblance for the first time. It is still odd for Violet to think of Queenie as her mother. But she looks forward to getting used to it.

"Who called?" one of the police officers asks. He looks barely old enough to shave. A drop of mustard christens his shirt to the right of his identification tag. Violet's first inclination is to grab the spot remover from the laundry room and get that stain out before it sets.

Violet looks at Queenie, who shrugs, her umbrella still poised. "I'm not sure who called," she says.

"Ma'am, I need you to put that down," the officer says to Queenie.

Queenie glances at the umbrella she forgot she was holding. Then she returns it to the stand just inside the door, and the officer thanks her.

Edward steps forward and introduces himself, holding out his hand for the young officer to shake. The officer puts his hand on his holstered gun instead.

"Step over here, sir," the second officer says. He is older, with a substantial middle-aged paunch.

"Don't you know who I am?" Edward asks the officer, his voice raised. "Who is your commanding officer? I could have you fired, you know."

Edward may know how to talk to a high society crowd, but you don't speak this way to regular people. Especially if they work for law enforcement.

"Yes, sir, I'm sure you could get me fired," the officer says. "And my wife would be all for it, too." The officer leans next to Edward and sniffs. "Is that alcohol I smell on your breath, sir? Did you drive here?"

"For God's sake, go catch some real criminals," Edward says.

Within seconds, the officer has Edward walking a straight line and touching his nose. A test he appears to fail. What prompted Edward to lose control like this? In the distance, he points at Violet and Queenie like they are the real criminals.

"Those women have something I need," Edward says. "They are thieves. They are living in my house under false pretenses. They must be removed immediately."

Edward holds his stomach and releases a burst of gas like a warning shot over the bow of a ship. Violet cringes, feeling mortified for Edward. But Edward doesn't seem embarrassed by it at all.

"Good heavens, man." The older officer covers his nose with his sleeve.

Edward points his finger at Violet and Queenie. "It's my house. Not theirs. Look at them," Edward continues. "Do they look like they belong here?"

The older officer looks at Edward, then at Violet and

Queenie. He shakes his head like he's sick and tired of dealing with people like Edward.

"I think we'd better take them all downtown," the older officer says to his partner. The younger officer agrees.

Edward turns toward the house. "But I need to find the key," he says.

Violet's shoulder throbs again. The younger officer takes Edward to the squad car as Edward keeps yelling about needing to find a key. Does he mean a key to the front door? Then the older officer walks up to the porch to escort Violet and Queenie down the walk.

"Excuse me, officer," Spud says. "Do you mind if I drive these women to the station? We could follow you."

The officer hesitates but then agrees.

"It's just a formality," Spud says to Violet and Queenie, as he opens the door of his small Toyota. Queenie eyes the back seat like she's wondering if she can fit.

"Would it still be a formality if we weren't a darker color than them?" Violet asks.

Spud says he doesn't know, but he hopes that isn't the case.

Meanwhile, Queenie falls into the back seat of the Toyota and says, "Heaven help me, this car is made for midgets!"

Violet laughs and gets in on the passenger side.

"Why was Edward making all that noise about a key?" Spud asks.

"This is the first I've heard anything about a missing key," Violet says. But her shoulder confirms that it is something important.

"Maybe he's trying to find the key to the safe deposit box," Queenie says from the back seat. "That means there's probably a whole lot more in there besides the *Temple Book of Secrets*. For all we know, there may be secrets about people that don't even have ties to Savannah. Senators. U.S. Presidents. Iris's grandfather dealt with foreign heads of state," she continues. "The possibilities are endless as to what the Temples—what *we*—have lorded over people."

It is still strange for Violet to realize she is even remotely related to the Temples.

"But I thought this last year of being in the spotlight would be the end of it," Violet says.

"We may be closer to the beginning than the end," Queenie says.

The pain in Violet's shoulder intensifies, confirming that whatever has Edward worked up has placed them all in grave danger.

CHAPTER TWENTY-SEVEN

Queenie

"Happy Anniversary, Iris."

Queenie addresses the chandelier in the dining room, which always shakes with the cold blast of Iris's presence. She and Violet clear dinner dishes from the dining room table, which hasn't been used since Iris's stroke. But they wanted to have a special dinner to celebrate Rose and Max's arrival earlier that afternoon. They had driven for three days and have already retired to a guest room upstairs to get some rest. The moving trucks are scheduled to arrive next week.

"I'd forgotten how handsome Max is, in a rugged cowboy sort of way," Queenie says. She follows Violet into the kitchen and wonders if Denzel Washington has ever made a western.

"Max seems quiet but nice," Violet says. She stacks dishes next to the sink.

"He certainly loved your roast," Queenie says, "and the apple pie."

Violet smiles and then rubs her left shoulder. "Something isn't right," she says.

"It's bothering you again?" Queenie asks.

"Maybe I'm just getting old," Violet says.

"Nonsense. I've got pantyhose older than you. Besides, that shoulder is better than having a crystal ball."

Violet frowns. "The last time it did this was the night Edward showed up at the door, and we ended up at the police station," she says.

Queenie and Violet spent nearly an hour explaining their relationship to the Temples to a police sergeant who took notes like he was writing a screenplay. Finally, Queenie thought to call Bo Rivers, who showed up in the middle of the night to clear things up. As much as she tries to resist it, there is something about him that she likes. Bo asked for a temporary restraining order against Edward, which she is sure didn't go over very well. Edward wasn't charged with anything, and luckily neither were they.

After that night, Queenie and Violet began a diligent search for the key to the safe deposit box that holds the *Temple Book of Secrets*, and no telling what else. So far, they've found nothing.

"Surely Edward won't show up tonight," Queenie says, addressing the concerns of Violet's shoulder. "He doesn't even know Rose is here. Plus, we've got a cowboy in the house, and I don't think Max will let Edward get away with anything."

Violet doesn't look convinced. "All I know is that as soon as Rose and Max arrived, Miss Temple's ghost started throwing fits," she says. "Then the others got on the band-wagon. I've never heard them this high-spirited."

"Maybe it's because of the anniversary that Mama warned us about," Queenie says.

Anniversaries of deaths don't usually bother her, but for some reason, this one has her biting her nails. Queenie is nowhere near as sensitive as Violet, but even she can feel a tension in the air.

"I guess it could be a false alarm," Violet says. It sounds like she's trying to convince herself, as well as Queenie.

"*I guess* I could be a size six," Queenie says with a laugh, thinking the last time she was a size six was probably when she was about six years old.

Violet rolls her eyes, and it reminds Queenie of how Violet did this as a girl.

"Well, I'm going to leave the dishes until the morning," Violet says. "I've got to get home. Jack will be wondering what happened to me. Will you be okay?" she adds.

"Don't worry about us. I'll keep an eye on things," Queenie says. "And tell my son-in-law hello."

As they hug, Queenie feels grateful again for Violet's forgiveness. Life is much more enjoyable—not to mention simpler—without so many secrets to keep. Although she has a feeling the Temples have a few more hidden away.

After Violet leaves, the house is quiet. Almost too quiet. The kind of quiet that makes people use clichés like *the calm before the storm*. It doesn't help that Queenie has been reading a new murder mystery in the sunroom, now dark except for a single Tiffany lamp near her chair. The room itself looks staged for a murder, and it helps to remember that Rose and Max are upstairs.

The sound of rattling glassware comes from Oscar's old office. Queenie gets up and walks toward the noise.

I'm acting like every nitwit in every horror movie I've ever seen, she tells herself, but this awareness doesn't stop her.

She opens the door to his study and turns on the light. Nothing is out of place. No shadows grace the corners. Except for Iris, who doesn't seem to mind being blatant with her gusts of cold air, it's hard to catch the Temple ghosts haunting the place. She pulls her sweater closer. Her attention is drawn toward the leather couch against one wall, the scene of more than one secret.

"Are you getting in on the excitement, too, Oscar?" Queenie asks. She looks at the large leather chair behind the desk, where he often sat nursing a glass of bourbon. A photograph of Iris glares at Queenie from the desk. "You stay out of this," she says, pointing at Iris's framed stare.

Violet is right, Queenie thinks, *the knocks and creaks in the old house are turned up on high tonight.*

Maybe, without her knowledge, a family reunion of dead Temples has been called. Queenie shivers with the thought, then returns to the sunroom to get her book before going upstairs. Despite the extra noises, Queenie anticipates sleeping better tonight with Rose and Max nearby. She hasn't liked sleeping in the house alone since Iris died. Violet didn't want to move her family until it was clear Edward would lose his legal challenge. She also didn't want to disrupt Tia and Leisha's school year, which Queenie could understand.

In bed now, Queenie finishes another chapter of her book. A murderer stalks within the pages of the novel she's reading, and she can't help feeling that someone is stalking here, too. Certainly not Rose or Max, but it is a big house with plenty of room for murderers to hide. Not to mention, most of Savannah has it in for them right now.

Queenie reaches into her nightstand to retrieve a hefty

stack of letters. She hasn't told Violet how many death threats she's received in the last eleven months. At first, they were all addressed to Iris, but since her death, they aren't sent to anyone in particular. They arrive anonymously. No return address. The threat typed on plain white paper as if they all watched the same television mystery. Some say they are watching, and when we least expect it, they will get us. Others say to stop telling secrets, or we'll live to regret it. Threats are rarely very creative. At least the lawsuits have been dropped since Iris's death.

Queenie takes comfort in the fact that the Temple mansion is practically a fortress with its security alarms and locked gates. She also knows that most threats are simply that—threats. It is a bold move for a bully to actually take action on what they say. She sighs, too tired to entertain her fantasies. It takes forever for her to fall asleep, yet when she does, it is deep.

THE TELEPHONE RINGS several times before Queenie is awake enough to answer it. When she picks up the phone, she hears her mother's voice: "Get out of the house, baby. Bad things be happening."

Queenie, in that fuzzy place between wakefulness and dreaming, keeps wondering which world is real. She opens one eye and glances at the digital clock by the bed. It is 4:34 in the morning.

"You hear me, baby? You be in danger," her mama says. "Get out of the house!"

Old Sally's frantic message finally breaks through the fuzziness. Queenie sits straight up, and her eyes pop open like she's just had a double espresso. It's not just her in danger, but Rose and Max, too. She sniffs and smells smoke.

"Mama, call the fire department!" Queenie tells her before slamming down the phone.

A crackling comes from downstairs that sounds like bacon frying. Hundreds of strips of bacon. The whole downstairs is the pan. Queenie sniffs and smells smoke. She remembers a recurring nightmare from her childhood where the same thing happened: a frantic call from her mother, the crackling fire, the desperate need to get out of the Temple house. She has an odd feeling of going through the same motions. The dream always ended before she got out, as though the real ending is being left up to her.

Queenie stands and throws on her yellow bathrobe. She pauses long enough to wonder what she should take with her as she flees. She thinks of her dozens of journals, too heavy to carry out. Then her gaze falls on the framed photograph on her bedside table taken years before of a young Violet and Rose on the beach. Clutching it to her chest, she runs to her bedroom door. She unlatches it and then stops. Like she saw in a movie once, she touches the outside of the door to see if it's hot. The door is cool to the touch, so she opens it. Smoke wafts up the stairs. She coughs and pulls her bathrobe over her nose to keep out the smoke.

Queenie makes her way to the bedroom where Rose and Max are staying. The smoke hasn't reached here yet. Yelling their names, she bangs on their door. Max opens the door wearing boxer shorts and his cowboy hat.

"Fire!" Queenie manages to yell, which sounds like something a prankster would yell in a crowded movie theater.

Max turns and yells to Rose to wake up. Within seconds, they have thrown on clothes and shoes as if they've practiced this scenario before. Then the three of them set out for the stairs. The darkness is illuminated with a nightlight of flames. In the shadows, Queenie sees someone fleeing downstairs. Fearing Violet may have returned to the house, she calls out. But the figure is too tall to be Violet. Whoever it is runs through the dining room and into the kitchen, disappearing so quickly Queenie wonders if she imagined it.

The crackling of the fire increases as they descend the stairs. The flame's intensity dwarfs any heatwave Savannah has ever experienced. The nightgown underneath her robe is soaked with sweat. They descend the spiral staircase and Queenie hesitates at the bottom, long enough for Max to yell out that they can't stop.

The inferno roars and swallows his words as soon as he shouts them. Rose's eyes are wide with terror. Max takes both of them by the arms and leads them toward the door, yelling at them to keep moving. All of a sudden, dark smoke billows out of the kitchen. The door between the kitchen and dining room is now covered in flames crawling toward the ceiling. Queenie doesn't see how anyone could have escaped through the wall of fire.

"Shouldn't we try to save something?" Queenie yells, but the flames swallow her words, and no one hears her.

Priceless artwork and antiques fill the house, as well as Temple memorabilia dating back to the Revolutionary War. She glances at the extinguished Civil War torch in the Temple foyer and wonders if the ghost of one of those Union soldiers—or perhaps General Sherman himself—has shown up to finish the job. She hears her mama's voice tell her to keep going, to get out of the house. It's like a secret passageway has opened between their minds, and Queenie hears her mother's thoughts. She tells Queenie to run and then orders Edward out of the house, too. Is Edward here? Could that be who she saw in the house?

Smoke billows across the high ceilings, unwilling to

waste any time. The whole back of the house is already engulfed in flames. A smoky orange glow illuminates the contents of the house.

Two thoughts occur almost simultaneously: *How has the fire spread so quickly? And why haven't the alarms gone off?*

They move now as if in slow motion. Everywhere they turn, there are more flames. The floor grows hotter under her bare feet. She wishes now she'd thought to grab a pair of shoes. Sweat drips into her eyes and stings. They pause in the foyer. The floor gets hotter, as though the cellar underneath her has turned into a furnace. Queenie sidesteps the embers that begin to pop and fly from the walls. With Max's help, they make their way to the front of the house and he flings open the heavy wooden front door. The moist air of the Georgia coastline fills her lungs as they run toward the street.

"The dogs are in the carriage house," Max yells over the noise of the flames. He runs in that direction as Queenie and Rose wait on the sidewalk in front of the house. Queenie puts an arm around Rose, who appears stunned, as anyone would. She glances down the street for the black sedan, but it isn't there.

"I'm going to go next door and call the fire department," Queenie says.

Rose nods, her gaze transfixed on the burning Temple house.

Since Queenie hasn't run anywhere since Jimmy Carter was in office, her awkward jaunt across the street to the Bennett house takes her breath away. Pebbles stick to the bottom of her feet. Every few steps, she stops to brush them away. Mister Bennett lives there with his new wife, who moved in two years before. They are an American cliché. The new Mrs. Bennett is thirty years younger than her husband and used to dance in a chorus line on Broadway. Soon after she moved in, Iris dismissed the woman as *trailer trash* and wrote a letter to the head of the historical district to insist that they weed out the riffraff. Queenie isn't even sure what *'riffraff'* is, but Iris would probably put her into the same category.

From the looks of things, I'm homeless riffraff now, Queenie decides.

As she pounds on the Bennett's door, she remembers Edward's pounding from weeks before. Was he the one who started the fire? Is Edward the type to burn down a house out of spite? She pounds on the door again and tries to remember if the Bennetts have had any secrets revealed about them. If so, they might slam the door in her face. She can't remember. Maybe something about his first wife, who was addicted to painkillers and went to the Betty Ford clinic? She realizes how silly secrets are when it comes to life and death issues like fires.

The *riffraff* dancer answers the door in a red teddy that pushes her ample breasts toward heaven.

Mercy, Queenie thinks, *those things will have every heterosexual man in Savannah puckering up.* Queenie has to remind herself not to stare.

"Our house is on fire!" Queenie yells. She turns and points to the illuminated skyline. The teddy-clad dancer runs back inside and calls for her husband to telephone the fire department. Before Queenie has time to thank her, the first fire truck rounds the curve that her mama must have called.

The teddy-clad dancer invites her inside. Queenie thanks her, but then explains that she has to check on Rose, Iris Temple's estranged daughter who has moved back to Savannah with her cowboy husband and their two dogs.

Sometimes when Queenie is stressed, she gives too many details.

"It would be helpful if you could call my daughter, Violet, and tell her what's happening," Queenie says to the new Mrs. Bennett. Queenie writes down the number on a piece of paper Mrs. Bennett provides.

Violet will be heartbroken that her surprise inheritance is going up in flames. But what if the fire had broken out while they were all living there? Maybe not all of them would have gotten out.

Sirens pierce the night air as red and white lights bounce 360 degrees around the square. Firemen jump off trucks and run with hoses toward the house. It is exhilarating, in a way, to watch such heroic actions. Flames climb the outside of the building like red wisteria vines. Within seconds, two of the dining room windows burst outward, causing the firemen to duck and cover their heads. Just as another fire truck arrives, flames surge out of the broken windows like a dragon whose fury has been unleashed.

From the Bennett's driveway, Queenie watches the scene in disbelief. She has always enjoyed fires in fireplaces. Fires with carefully confined blazes that take the moisture out of a room on the handful of cold days in Savannah when the temperature nears freezing. But this blaze is a different beast. It roars its power and jumps from one surface to the next while eating everything in its path. Yet miraculously, it stays contained to the Temple house. Multimillion-dollar mansions on either side remain untouched.

A small crowd gathers as Queenie rejoins Rose and Max a hundred yards away from the burning Temple home. Their two border collies, Lucy and Ethel, howl to the chorus of fire trucks. Queenie stands barefoot on the sidewalk, her feet aching from her flight across ash and ember. Flames shoot out of Iris's bedroom window and stretch into the sky. For a split second, Queenie sees the figure again in the window. She squints to make out who it is.

"Did you see that?" she asks Rose.

They stare at the window. "Maybe it's a Temple ghost," Rose says.

"Or maybe it's Edward," Queenie says.

"Edward?" Rose asks. "You think Edward might be in the house?"

Rose runs to a nearby fireman. "I think my brother may be in there," she calls to him over the noise of the fire and spraying hoses.

With a look of alarm, the fireman runs to his superior. Both men study the flames. Seconds later, the inferno explodes outward. Everyone cowers to avoid flying debris. The front of the house is now engulfed. The fire chief directs the hoses to address the latest surge and walks over to Rose and Queenie. "I'm sorry, but I can't send my men in there. It's just too dangerous," he says.

Rose and Queenie look back at the house.

"What was Edward doing in there?" Rose asks her.

Queenie tells her she doesn't know.

Meanwhile, a crowd has gathered in front of the house. Some of them are people she recognizes from protesting the secrets being released. At least they aren't chanting while the house burns. She doubts any of them would have had the nerve to start the fire if it was arson.

Max returns and holds Rose in his arms, two leashes in hand. The dogs are quiet now. Everyone is.

CHAPTER TWENTY-EIGHT

Old Sally

"It be time," Old Sally says. The dream woke her out of a sound sleep. In it, the ancestors told her that today is a day of reckoning. It is also the anniversary of Iris's failed crossing. This told her that Iris may be trying to go again.

Old Sally believes dreams are always a step or two ahead. Sure, they speak in riddles most of the time. But they are riddles that Old Sally takes the time to decipher. After more than a half-century of listening to her dreams, Old Sally believes they have wisdom deep as a gold mine, but only if you take the time to dig out the gold. These days, they come to her crystal clear. She will make her own crossing soon enough.

In this most recent dream, the Temple house was on fire. Edward wore his great grandfather's Confederate uniform and set fire to the draperies in his mother's room while all the Temple spirits urged him on. Iris laughed as the flames increased as if this was the only way to take back her power. Edward acted out his mother's bidding.

Awake, her heart still races while she calls Queenie and then the fire department. Then she calls Kenny, the son of a friend of hers who lives nearby, to get a ride into Savannah.

As she gets dressed, Old Sally remembers the night Iris died and how Iris cursed her as Old Sally tried to help with her transition. She's been waiting to see how that curse plays out. Being on the other side, all mysteries are revealed, so Iris Temple knows the spells she's put on her over the years. This knowledge, no doubt, fueled Iris's need for getting even. Now it seems her revenge is to put Queenie in danger. The worst way to hurt a woman is to harm her children.

Old Sally goes out of the kitchen door and down the back stairs to wait for Kenny. The moon is so full it makes her eyes widen. Its power pulls the tide high, as the waves crash on the other side of the dunes. She's seen many storms on this beach and a hurricane or two, but tonight feels much more dangerous. Old Sally asks again for their ancestors to intercede and keep Queenie, Rose, and Max safe. Headlights turn off the main road, and she makes her way to the end of the walk.

Kenny stops the car and runs to the passenger side to open the door for Old Sally. He is in his thirties now, but he was in some trouble as a teenager. Nothing that serious, but he stayed with Old Sally until he got his life back on track. Kenny is the color of night and is sweet as an angel if you treat him nice. He drives a bit reckless, and as soon as they take off, Old Sally grips the door. She puts up with Kenny's driving because her child is in danger. It doesn't matter that her child is in her sixties.

"I left there around midnight, and everything was quiet,"

Kenny says.

Kenny is out of work right now and agreed to keep an eye on Queenie and Violet after Old Sally saw in the tea leaves that Edward and Iris might try to hurt them.

"This not be your fault, Kenny," Old Sally says. "Bigger forces at work."

The world blurs by Old Sally's window as they ride in silence. *That's what it's like to get this old,* she thinks. You look up one day, and your whole life has rushed past so fast you barely caught a glimpse of what's passing. Then before you know it, you're at the end of your life and wondering how you got there.

Old Sally shivers with the awareness that Queenie and Rose are still in danger.

"Can you get there any faster?" Old Sally asks Kenny.

"Are you sure?" he asks.

Old Sally nods.

"Well, hang onto the Jesus bar," he tells her.

"The what?" Old Sally asks.

"The handle above the door. You hold it and say, *Oh, Jesus!*" Kenny laughs.

"You was always a cut-up, Kenny, even when you was a little boy." She grips the handle, thinking *I'll take all the help I can get.* Then as Kenny accelerates, she closes her eyes.

WHEN THE CAR finally comes to a stop, Old Sally opens her eyes again and waits for her stomach to catch up. A block away, the Temple house is in flames. The sight makes her want to close her eyes again, but she reminds herself that sometimes total destruction is the only hope for things to change.

Kenny comes around and opens her door. Ash flies

through the air and is all she can smell. When Old Sally gets out of the car, she realizes how tired she is. Not just from being up in the middle of the night, but from all the years of battling the dark side of the Temple family. She is ready for this to be over. It started this time last year when all those secrets got released. It was the beginning of gaining power over the darkness.

Her heart pounds as she finally sees her daughter. Queenie crosses the street and walks into Old Sally's arms. Old Sally hangs on tighter than she usually would. Only she knows how close she came to losing her daughter.

"Are you okay, baby?" Old Sally asks.

"I've been better," Queenie says. "It looks like I don't have anywhere to live anymore."

"You know you can always live with me," Old Sally says.

"At sixty, moving back in with my hundred-year-old mother isn't that appealing." Queenie's laugh dies quickly like an ember shooting from the house.

While Queenie holds her arm, Old Sally watches the fire.

"A dream woke me up," Old Sally says. "I saw the flames, and I saw you and Rose and Max still in the house. I be so frightened," she adds. "I thought the Temples had finally won."

"They almost did," Queenie says. "But I don't think Edward was as lucky."

Old Sally looks up at the burning house.

Sacrifices are often required before things can change, she thinks. She lost her daughter Maya way too young. Now there is Edward.

"Shame on you, Iris, for poisoning your son and creating this mess," she says aloud. Iris poisoned Edward with bitterness just like she tried to poison Rose. But unfortunately, Edward liked the poison.

Old Sally turns away from the fire. The way she sees it, all those years when Rose was out of the picture, Edward was glad. It meant more for him. But when he heard that Rose was coming back, he plotted on how to get his way. Just like he cut off a piece of Rose's finger when she was a little girl, he thought nothing of cutting her out of the picture forever.

Yesterday, Old Sally spent all day putting together another protection spell for Rose on her return to Savannah, using the tears she collected when Rose came to visit her at the beach. She renewed a protection spell on Violet, too, since Edward already came after her once when she was young.

There was another Edward, Queenie's father, who Old Sally wasn't strong enough to resist, so she got pulled into history repeating itself, as did Queenie. But Violet was unwilling to go down that road. Old Sally is proud of her granddaughter for that. She may be the strongest of Old Sally's line yet.

"I want to see Rose," Old Sally says.

Queenie helps her cross the street. "Mama, who brought you here?" Queenie asks, glancing back at the black sedan.

"That be Kenny," Old Sally says. "You remember Kenny, Evelyn's boy? He was away for a long time but came back a year ago."

"That tall black man is little Kenny who used to come to the house with Evelyn?"

"He's not so little anymore," Old Sally says.

"All this time, I thought he was one of Edward's goons," Queenie says.

"No, he be one of my goons," Old Sally says, the word 'goon' giving her pleasure. "Did I ever tell you about the time Iris accused me of being part of the Gullah mafia? I said to her, '*Iris, I not part, I be the head!*' Iris didn't know what to say to that, but I think she kind of believed me."

"I guess nothing should surprise me anymore," Queenie says. "I certainly never expected you to have Kenny spy on us for nearly a year."

"I needed to protect you from Edward, and anybody who might be upset about their secrets being told," Old Sally says. "But the one time Edward did show up a few weeks ago, Kenny had gone to take his mama to church. He felt awful about that, too. Of course, Kenny has to sleep, so he goes home around midnight every night."

"But how could you afford to hire someone to watch the house?" Queenie says.

"It not cost a thing," Old Sally says. "Maybe you don't remember, but I helped his mama heal her cancer a few years back."

"Why didn't you just put a spell on Edward?" Queenie asks.

"I have two spells on him already," Old Sally says. "But since his mama died, she joined forces with him, so I needed a little extra help."

"I'm glad you called when you did, Mama. You saved our lives."

Old Sally and Queenie join Rose and Max in front of the house, and she gives Rose a big hug.

"Edward was in there," Rose says, her voice shaking with emotion. "Was he waiting for me to come back to do this?" Rose asks. "How did he even know?"

"He probably had someone watching the house, too," Old Sally says.

Max extends his hand, and Old Sally shakes it. The last time she saw him was the Christmas after he and Rose married. *Some men be afraid of them hugs*, she thinks. *But give me time. I'll win him over.* Regardless, she can tell he is a good man.

"Mama, when we were fleeing the fire, I heard you talking to me in my head," Queenie says.

"I know you did, baby."

"But how is that possible?"

"There be all sorts of mysteries playing out all the time," Old Sally says. "Besides, you may have more of me in you than you think."

"Maybe I do," Queenie says.

Violet and Jack arrive, winded from running from where they parked their car. Violet gasps when she gets close, as though swallowing a scream. Then tears begin, and Queenie pulls her close. To see Violet hurting makes Queenie cry, too. Old Sally is so happy they get to be mother and daughter again.

"It be alright, Violet," Old Sally says. "Important things can't be destroyed. They be yours forever." Now it's her turn to give Violet a hug. The four women stand witnessing the sacred flames, while the men talk.

"My shoulder predicted this was going to happen," Violet tells Old Sally. "After I got home, it got so painful I walked into the emergency room. But the doctors couldn't find a single thing wrong, and now it doesn't hurt at all."

"That shoulder kept you safe and sound," Old Sally says.

Violet agrees.

"I'm sorry about the house, sweetheart," Queenie says. "But Mama's right. We haven't lost the important things."

Meanwhile, Old Sally pictures all those secrets going up in flames with the Temple ghosts and the Temple house. The fire purifies and wipes clean all the sins and secrets of the Temple family.

A blessing can often be found in the center of a tragedy, she thinks.

Despite the firefighters' efforts, the blaze continues to burn through the early morning hours, fueled, she imagines, by a century's worth of lemon oil massaged into the ancient wood of antiques. Some of that polishing came from her. She can still smell that lemon oil on her hands sometimes, like a ghost at her fingertips.

A fire always draws people to it. It seems all of Savannah is here to watch the Temple house burn. Iris Temple spent most of her life trying to leave a legacy that people would respect, but she also saved secrets to threaten people with if she ever needed to get her way. With the Temple secrets purged and the house destroyed, the Temple family might be able to rebuild on a new foundation.

Old Sally senses her mother and grandmother watching the scene. Their spirits finally liberated from the past. Both women worked at the Temple house, their tears and sweat embedded in the history of this place. Meanwhile, the scene holds them all captive, as they are called to witness the end of an era.

"I think Edward was in the house because he was looking for the key to the safety deposit box," Queenie says, the first to break their silence. "Maybe he found it and started the fire. Or maybe the fire was an accident. But that safety deposit box held the *Book of Secrets*, as well as a bunch of other things that would make people nervous."

Old Sally startles at Queenie's words. Could there be more in that box than the *Book of Secrets*? Things Old Sally doesn't know about? She forces herself to believe that it is finished. She doesn't have the strength to do more. Either way, her part is over. She is certain of this. Only one ritual remains.

"Was the key somewhere in the house?" Rose asks.

"Nobody knows," Queenie says. "Iris died without telling anyone where she kept it. At least as far as I know."

Old Sally remembers where the key used to be kept. She found it one day while she was cleaning, probably thirty years before. Among the old objects on the dresser, there was a new box there. She had opened it to see what was inside. The key was there on a small gold chain.

"But why would a key be so important?" Rose asks.

"The keeper of the key has the power," Old Sally says. For everyone's sake, she hopes that the key is never found.

"Mama, did your dream show you how the fire got started?" Queenie asks. "The fire alarms attached to the security system didn't work, even though I just had them tested last month."

"It be Edward," Old Sally says. "With the encouragement of Iris."

"You mean on purpose??" Violet asks.

"Yes," Old Sally says. "I don't have proof, but I think Edward be a prisoner to the old ways, too, and needed things to change."

Old Sally stands between Violet and Queenie near the old oak that holds court in the Temple garden. Like the houses nearby, it remains untouched by the fire. A slight breeze blows from the east, carrying the smell of the sea. The crowd has dwindled, leaving only a few firemen and family behind.

"Old powers claim people every day," Old Sally says. "The Temple house burning to the ground be a fitting end to the old way. Now the cycle can be broken."

Her words are soft, and everyone leans closer to listen. It's times like this when Old Sally becomes the elder of her clan, chosen to pass on messages from the ancestors. As if anticipating the final ritual, Violet asks everyone to hold hands, and they form a small circle. Moonlight scatters at their feet.

"Now the dance between the masters and slaves can end," Old Sally tells them.

"May it be so," Violet whispers, and encourages the others to repeat it.

Old Sally feels no need to rush. She's waited a century to fulfill this task. The task of letting go of the past. "Now all that hurt between the Temples and us be turned into ash," she begins again. "That old way be gone. Now, something new be coming."

"May it be so," they say together, and it is Jack who adds an "Amen." She is glad Jack and Max are part of the circle, too. If they are uncomfortable in any way, they don't show it, which speaks well of her granddaughter's and Rose's choice of mates.

Silence follows. Still holding hands, Violet begins to hum a Gullah melody that Old Sally taught her and that her Grandmother Sadie had taught Sally. The tune sounds sad and haunting at first, but then it rises and lifts on Violet's pure tone as if carrying a moment of grace for each of them. Old Sally rubs the goosebumps on her arms. Goosebumps tell her Spirit is close. As she sways with the rhythm, she looks up through the tree's branches. A lone star peeks through. She has waited a hundred years for this one moment—the moment when her life follows the full circle of the moon. Gratitude fills her. There is nothing more powerful than knowing that you did with your life what you were meant to do.

They stand together until dawn. An orange sun, the same color as the dying flames, rises behind the Temple house. The scene is oddly beautiful, as a new day rises above the smoking ruins.

CHAPTER TWENTY-NINE

One Year Later
Rose

V ibrant green moss grows where the Temple house once stood. Palm trees have been planted and dozens of camellias. A color palette of pastels spreads before her. Rose wants to come back and paint this scene. Sunlight pours through the garden, the only part of the Temple property that remained untouched by the fire. In the months afterward, Violet donated the land to the city of Savannah, and city planners extended the original garden over to where the house once stood. A gold plaque that reads *Temple Garden* hangs on the wrought-iron gate that opens into the small park in honor of the Temple family. No posters or protestors are anywhere to be seen. It is as if the burning of the Temple mansion satisfied everyone's need for revenge.

Rose opens the gate. She likes to think that all the Temple

ghosts are buried here, along with all the secrets. The investigation into the cause of the fire was inconclusive. Arson was not ruled out, but there were questions about some of the wiring in the basement. After the fire, the leaking of secrets from the Temple book stopped. Did the person releasing them take pity on the Temples? Or was there another reason?

Shortly after the fire, Rose remembered something from her childhood. When she was maybe seven or eight years old, she came home from school one day and Old Sally wasn't in the kitchen. When she went looking for her, she found her sitting at the Temple desk, a ledger in front of her that she had been reading for some time. Old Sally had told her that it was the *Temple Book of Secrets*. This was when it was still kept in the bottom drawer of her father's mahogany desk that had been Rose's grandfather's desk before that and her great-grandfather's desk even before that. Her mother would like that Rose remembers the history of it.

Old Sally hadn't scolded Rose when she found her but had said something peculiar that Rose can still remember because it was like a riddle she could never figure out. Old Sally said: *There will come a time, Miss Rose, when this old book will spill all its secrets and then the Temples will be free.*

Would Old Sally be capable of revealing those secrets if she thought it would release the past? For all she knows, Old Sally might have copied out every secret in that book in all those years she worked there. Yet this makes no sense either.

As Rose steps into the garden, her memory jumps to the night of the fire and the transformative moment with Old Sally under this same tree. The melody Violet sang plays again in her mind. That night marked a beginning for Rose. Although, if pressed to explain, she isn't sure she could express what she means by that. Perhaps it wasn't a beginning at all, but the ending of her exile from Savannah.

Something moves in the shadows. At first, Rose wonders if it might be her great-grandfather haunting the old tree, but it is someone else, someone alive. The well-dressed African-American woman is statuesque and is dressed like she might work on Wall Street. She stands underneath the live oak that has been in the garden for as long as Rose can remember. When the woman sees Rose, she looks away, but not fast enough for Rose to miss the sadness in her eyes.

Rose calls across the garden: "I didn't mean to disturb you."

"It's lovely here," the woman says as if this might somehow explain her sadness.

Rose agrees. The garden, now a mixture of new and old, has never looked more scenic. She wonders if it approves of its new purpose. The crepe myrtle that stood outside her bedroom window was scorched by the fire, but it came back the following season with the most astounding blossoms she has ever seen. Like the phoenix rising from the flames, the garden has risen to a new level of beauty. No longer in the shadows of the house, every plant and tree appears to have new growth.

Should Rose leave the stranger alone? To answer her question, the woman walks over to her and introduces herself as Regina.

"It's my first time in Savannah," she says, "though I've wanted to come for years."

Rose notices a gold ring with a red stone on her left hand. Her eyes widen as she stares at it because the ring is just like Edward's, except smaller.

"I'm wondering if you knew my brother," Rose says. "Edward Temple?"

The woman looks at her as if to determine her level of trustworthiness.

"I'm Rose," she says. "Edward's sister." She extends her hand, and they shake. The woman's handshake is firm, confident.

"Your brother and I were very close friends." Regina places the emphasis on *close*.

Rose tells her how sorry she is for her loss. "Were you friends for long?" she asks, although from the rings she thinks they are much more than that.

"Twenty years," Regina says. "We met on one of his trips to California, and then I moved to Atlanta." She pauses. "Actually, we've been married for ten of those years," Regina adds.

Rose tries to hide her surprise. Edward was married? The knowledge of her brother keeping someone he loved a secret for so many years, causes a poignant throbbing in her little finger. At that moment, she wonders if she ever knew him at all. She can only imagine what her mother might have done if she knew that Edward was married to a woman of color. She might have required Edward to get a divorce before he received his inheritance.

"We didn't know about you," Rose says.

"Edward insisted that we tell no one in his family," Regina says. "He was always afraid that his mother would disown him. I never even met her." She hesitates and offers an awkward smile like tears might come next. Tears she doesn't want to shed.

A breeze rattles through the Palmetto palms as Rose recalls Edward's insistence at their mother's funeral reception that he was married to his work. How sad it is that Regina wasn't included in the gathering.

"It's hotter here than in Atlanta," she says as she rolls up the sleeves of her blouse. "I didn't think that was possible."

"People like to say you get used to it, but I don't think

you ever do," Rose says. "I suppose it's the price we pay for living in paradise."

Regina nods as if she likes the idea of paradise. "Oh," she says. "I almost forgot. Actually, I was hoping to find you." From her purse, Regina pulls out a small priority mail envelope and hands it to Rose. It is addressed to Edward and has their mother's name as the sender. "I found this the other day and thought you might like it."

Rose thanks her. She glances at the envelope and sees that it is postmarked the day before her mother's stroke.

"Well, if you don't mind, I think I'll go seek out some air conditioning," Regina says.

Rose turns toward her, not wanting their meeting to end. "We're in the process of moving, or I'd invite you over for dinner," Rose says.

"Oh, that's all right," Regina says. "I'm just passing through. I wanted to see, you know, where it happened and where Edward grew up. I had no idea the neighborhood was this lavish, but there was a lot I had no idea about." Regina pauses and steps closer. "By the way, I didn't think Edward should publish those secrets in the newspaper."

Rose gives a half-gasp, half-laugh. "It was Edward? But why would he release the secrets?"

Rose is genuinely confused. Her thoughts race. It makes no sense that her brother would want to tarnish the Temple brand. Yet she remembers how half-hearted his eulogy was.

"But why?" Rose asks again.

"A few years ago, when Edward went to visit his mother they were having dinner at a restaurant downtown," Regina begins. "Evidently, an interracial couple came in, and your mother was appalled and said some ugly things. Edward was furious over that for months. Then after she mailed him the key to the safe deposit box a few months before she died,

Edward decided that releasing the secrets would be his way of destroying the Temple legend—the secrets, the racism, all of it. He has a lot of connections in Savannah, you know, and different old school buddies helped him arrange things, as long as he kept their secrets out of it."

Regina pauses as if remembering the sequence of events.

"In the letter from your mother that contained the key, she also mentioned a second safe deposit box and a second key," Regina begins again. "This was news to Edward, and evidently this second box contained secrets that stretched beyond Savannah to include the entire world. After that, Edward became obsessed with finding the second key," she continues. "That's why he made that last visit here. He wanted to find that key before anybody else did. I'm not sure what he was going to do once he found it. I guess now we'll never know."

Regina looks at Rose and begins to cry, enough tears that Rose embraces this stranger who is also her sister-in-law. After guiding Regina to a nearby bench, Rose pulls a clean tissue from the pocket of her shorts and hands it to her. If she were Old Sally, she might try to collect these tears. But perhaps the time for protection spells is past.

As quickly as they began, Regina's tears stop and she announces that she has to leave. She walks away, and Rose calls after her. "Regina, did Edward leave everything to you?" she asks, hoping she doesn't find her question rude. "I mean, I hope he did, you know?"

"Actually, I'm now the landlord of several Atlanta high rises in need of renovation," she says with a wry grin and turns toward the gate.

"I'm happy to have met you," Rose calls after her again. "Whenever you come back to Savannah, I hope you'll look me up."

"I will," she says, turning to wave. But Rose wonders if she actually will. "Good luck with your move," Regina adds, before exiting through the gate.

Rose can't imagine that her brother was easy to live with, but she likes to think that perhaps he found some happiness. Though in Temple fashion, it was all a secret.

ALONE IN THE GARDEN AGAIN, Rose digs in her purse and pulls out the sand dollar she found in a box of her childhood memorabilia while she was packing. After tying the shell onto one of the oak's lower branches, she stands back to admire it, remembering the day she and Violet laid in the grass looking up at the tree adorned with sand dollars. Like all childhoods, there was a mixture of good and bad, but she chooses now to remember the good.

Today marks the second anniversary of her mother's death. They purposely chose this auspicious day to move into their new place. According to Old Sally and Violet, who can see these things, her mother's spirit has been at peace since the fire. For her mother's sake, Rose hopes this is true. Her mother would like the idea of a park being created in honor of the Temples. In a way, it redeems the mess those secrets caused.

Before leaving, Rose bows to the garden of her childhood.

"Goodbye, Mother. Goodbye, Edward. Goodbye, old tree." She pats the rough bark of the live oak that watched over her all those years. Her best wishes extend to all her lineage, descendants, as well as ancestors, the best and worst of the Temple clan.

· · ·

STOPPED at a traffic light on the way out of town, Rose opens the envelope that Regina gave her. Inside is a small key on the end of a gold chain. With the key, is a letter written by her mother on Temple stationery.

Dear Edward,

Enclosed is the second key to the second safety deposit box at the bank. For some reason, it feels wise to send it to you, now that the Book of Secrets is being released. You must use all of your resources to find out who is doing this and make them stop. Our family has always had enemies, but this is someone who is especially devious. You must make them pay.

Nobody else knows about this second key or the contents of the box, and it should stay that way. The Book of Secrets is nothing compared to the ledger in the second vault. Use it whenever you see fit, and by all means, don't let Rose or Queenie get their hands on either of the keys. They don't understand the world the way we do.

By the way, did you know that Violet Stevens is your father's child? I only just found out. Oscar left a letter saying he wanted her to have the house. Since it was his final request on this earth, I will honor it. My last request to you, which hopefully won't need to be followed for many years, is that you accept my decision.

Love from your devoted mother,
Iris Temple

P.S. I called earlier. Was that one of your servants who answered the telephone? I'm not sure why she was working so late, but I hope you didn't have to pay her extra.

*P.P.S. This may come as a surprise to you, Edward, but I've been
thinking a lot lately, and I wrote Rose back into the will. Please
don't contest it. I've been so unforgiving of her over the years.
Perhaps it is because your father was much fonder of her than me.*

A CAR HORN honks behind her. The light is green. Rose
drives but then pulls off the road as soon as she can and
turns off the car. Two keys? Two safety deposit boxes full of
secrets? Even for her family, that seems excessive. If her
brother was in the house the night of the fire looking for the
second key, was it merely his misfortune to be in the wrong
place at the wrong time, as the saying goes? Or did he actually set the fire? These are questions that will never be
answered.

Shaking, Rose rereads the letter while tears spring to her
eyes. She has come to expect moisture these days, in its
many forms. However, this final word from her mother is
totally unexpected.

TRAFFIC IS light across the Talmadge Bridge and up the South
Carolina coast. Rose anticipates the next chapter of her life. If
two years ago, someone had told her that she would be
living in Savannah again on Old Sally's property, she would
have thought them crazy. But a lot can happen in two years.

The original structure of Old Sally's house remains,
though it has been expanded and totally renovated in ways
Rose never imagined. Before, it was like a tightly closed bud
that now has blossomed into a spacious, lovely flower with
many petals. Even Old Sally, who knows most everything
before it happens, seemed surprised by the overall transformation.

During the construction, Old Sally lived near the renovation site in a Winnebago that Rose bought for her so she could remain near her beloved beach. Old Sally made friends with the construction workers, and they ate lunch with her every day on two picnic tables they set up outside her camper. For months, Violet cooked hamburgers and hot dogs on two large grills for the workers and made huge bowls of potato salad and baked beans. Other times, she made dozens of ham and cheese sandwiches with home-made sweet potato chips and gave them large slices of lemon meringue and peach pies. As a result, they finished the house in record time and promise to visit whenever they can. According to the workers, they have never known a project to go so smoothly.

Rose turns off the main road and takes the sandy drive to the beach. In the distance, their new home resembles one of the elaborate sandcastles Rose and Violet built when they were girls. There are enough bedrooms in the big house for Old Sally, Queenie, Violet, Jack, and the girls, as well as Katie and Angela. Rose and Max have the guest cottage in the back with a wrap-around porch that connects to a wooden walkway leading to the main house. In their new compound they have a combined total of three dogs—Rose and Max's two border collies and Katie's small mutt. In addition, Angela has two cats, and Violet's girls, Tia and Leisha, have a pet turtle but have already asked for a dog.

Nearly home, Rose pulls into the driveway of Spud Grainger, who now lives a quarter of a mile down the beach. He waves from the second story deck of his new house and heads down the steps to her car. Officially retired from the Piggly Wiggly, Spud has traded in bow ties for colorful Hawaiian shirts. As he opens the car door, she thinks how odd it still is to see him without a tie.

"You ready?" Rose asks.

"I'm always ready, now that I'm a man of leisure," Spud says. He smiles.

"It's nice of you to help with the move." Rose has enjoyed getting to know Spud over the last year.

"Did Katie and Angie make it in?" Spud asks.

"They arrived last night with a full U-Haul," Rose says. "We were up until midnight unloading it."

Katie and Angela are the most surprising addition to their complicated living situation. Six months ago, they had a commitment ceremony in Chicago that Rose and Max attended, and just last month, Katie announced she was pregnant. Rose doesn't question the details—a grandchild is a grandchild. Although what surprised her even more was Katie's announcement that she wanted to raise their child in Savannah among family. Luckily they have plenty of family —in a traditional and non-traditional sense—to go around.

"I was in Hilton Head last night, or I would have helped with the U-Haul," Spud says.

Spud converted one of his Hilton Head properties into a retirement village for jazz and blues musicians. Having taken up the saxophone again, Spud spends every Saturday night attending a jam session in the lobby. People from all over the Carolinas and Georgia come to hear them.

"Did Queenie enjoy herself?" Rose asks.

"Oh my, yes," Spud says with another smile. "That lady can really dance."

Over the months, a budding romance has developed between Queenie and Spud. She goes with him on Saturdays to hear him play the saxophone.

The Temple clan looks different these days, becoming inclusive instead of exclusive. A mixture of black and white, married and single, straight and gay. If her mother is somehow privy to these events, she is probably writing a letter of protest to God at this very minute. But Rose doesn't care. She is happy to let her mother have the last word.

Three moving trucks of various sizes are in different stages of unloading as Rose pulls her car into their new eight-car garage. Moving men carry boxes and furniture out of the different trucks like bees coming out of several hives. Rose and Spud dodge movers as they walk the wooden boardwalk to the front of the house. At one point, Spud takes her elbow and steers Rose out of the path of an over-stuffed armchair.

Like she paused that day she first saw Old Sally again, Rose stops on the walkway to take in the ocean. It is high tide. Sandpipers skirt the edges of the waves, as they always do.

"I could look at this view every day for the rest of my life," Rose says to Spud.

"And the good news is, you will." Spud's smile is almost as bright as his shirt.

Rose laughs. "You know, Spud, you're absolutely right."

The renovated house is at least four times bigger than Old Sally's original dwelling. It has two stories now, with a large porch attached to the kitchen and a sunroom facing the ocean. A dozen wooden rockers rest on the front porch, and a large wooden picnic table is built in so they can eat outside if they choose. While Rose takes off her sandals at the top of the stairs to go barefooted, Spud excuses himself and goes inside.

Max stands at the ornate double wooden doors looking like a native. He no longer wears his cowboy hat and boots but opts instead for a ball cap, shorts, and flip flops. Having relaxed like a pro into their financial freedom and subsequent early retirement, Max gives Rose a quick embrace. The envelope Regina gave her crinkles in her pocket, and she wonders briefly what to do with it.

"Happy?" he asks, before directing a mover who has stopped in the doorway to ask where to put a box.

"Definitely," Rose says, realizing it's true. She's never felt so full of possibilities.

They have walked through the house many times at different phases of the construction, but now it is finally complete. Floor to ceiling windows grace every side of the house. Ceiling fans in every room spread the ocean breeze around whenever they choose not to run the air conditioning. Everyone had input into the original plans, and with Violet's blessing, they have created a kind of collective dream house. Life is never perfect, of course. There have been a few bumps in the road, but something about this new adventure and new family feels right to Rose. They will get through the rough spots together.

"Someone's waiting for you on the side porch," Max says.

"Who?" Rose asks.

"Just go," he says as if intent on being mysterious about it.

The inside of the house is organized chaos. Tia and Leisha giggle with two girlfriends by their side and carry boxes to a different wing of the house. Violet, Queenie, and Angela are in the kitchen fixing everyone's lunch. Angie smiles at Rose. Her hair is longer, and her face is minus the piercings. She appears more relaxed and lighter than when Rose first met her.

Spud greets Queenie with a kiss on the cheek. In response, she pats him on the rump and laughs.

Violet has her hair braided with beads like Old Sally used to do when she was a girl. Mother and daughter sing

Michael, Row Your Boat Ashore, swaying to the melody, their shoulders touching as they cut up peaches. Rose remembers when Queenie sang this in the car and hopes she won't throw in a primal scream to go with it. *Although this crowd could probably handle that, too,* she thinks.

Violet rolls out dough on the countertop for a peach pie and then transfers it onto the pie plate and crimps the edges. In three months, Violet will open a new business called *Violet's Tea Shop* in downtown Savannah. The day before the fire, Violet's shoulder had warned her to move her money from where she kept it in the Temple mansion kitchen.

Rose stops to eat a piece of peach from Violet's bowl. The taste is so completely delicious, she takes another piece and then another.

There's nothing in the world as rich and soulful as Georgia peaches, Rose thinks, as peach juice runs down her chin.

"Welcome home," Queenie says, and her words sound as sweet as the peaches. They exchange a hug full of history.

Rose and Queenie have waited a long time for a moment like this. A time when neither of them is haunted by secrets or shame, and they can completely be themselves. After Violet worked through all the hurt feelings with Queenie, the two women became practically inseparable. Violet spends part of every day learning the Gullah family traditions from Old Sally, as well as creating some special teas and tinctures she plans to sell at her shop.

On her way to the side porch, Rose admires Old Sally's new window seat that has replaced the table and been expanded to her specifications. Colorful cushions have been added for Old Sally to sit on while she nurtures her collection of beautiful and ordinary things, as diverse as the people they represent, including the ones who now live in this house. The sandcastle Rose gave Old Sally nearly thirty years before sits in the center, and next to it, Rose puts the second key.

Later, she plans to talk to Queenie and Violet about what to do with what's in the safe deposit box at the bank, but she has a feeling a big bonfire on the beach may be in their future. She will also tell them that it was Edward who was releasing the secrets and why he felt the need to do it. She likes to think that her brother had good intentions at heart. She only wishes she had known this side of him.

After admiring the view again, Rose walks out the side door to find Old Sally and Katie sitting on the wraparound porch. At almost 102 years of age, Old Sally reminds Rose of the tree in the Temple garden. She has watched over all of them over the years and has also been one of the biggest blessings in Rose's life. When she sees Rose, Old Sally smiles, igniting the love Rose has for this woman.

Rose flashes back to herself as a girl, leaning into Old Sally's wide hip, her strong, brown arms wrapped around Rose. *Those memories make up for everything her mother did or didn't do. As long as you feel love from somewhere, it's enough,* she decides.

Katie holds Old Sally's hand. Seeing the two of them together makes Rose smile. This must be what Max wanted Rose to see. Several times upon waking, she has told him about a recurring dream. In the dream she is living in a house by the sea. A house filled with people who love her.

This is what family is all about, she thinks. Generations all under one roof, honoring and appreciating each other.

"Old Sally's going to teach me some of her spells at the same time she teaches Violet," Katie says.

"That's terrific," Rose says. She wonders what her mother would have to say about Katie learning what she considered "voodoo."

Katie lets go of Old Sally's hand and walks over to Rose to kiss her on the cheek. "I'll leave you two alone and go help Angie," she says.

Rose nods, noticing how pink Katie's cheeks have already become. *This move is going to be good for her, too,* Rose thinks.

As Katie walks away, Old Sally stands to greet Rose. She moves more slowly these days. On the night of the fire, she seemed to pass the mantle to Violet. Yet her eyes remain bright. They embrace. For years whenever she and Old Sally embraced, Rose felt like a little girl in the arms of the Great Mother. This is the woman who not only baptized her with the sprinkler bottle while doing the ironing when Rose was a girl, but also the woman who sprinkled her with love throughout her life. But it's her turn to take care of Old Sally now, with the help of Queenie and Violet, who were also raised in the shade of this grand woman.

Old Sally relaxes in Rose's arms. Confirmation comes from somewhere deep inside that Rose has been moving toward this moment her entire life. A new feeling washes over her like a gentle ocean wave. She is home. She is finally home.

THANK YOU FOR READING!

I hope you enjoyed *Temple Secrets*. It was great fun writing this book. I loved creating these characters, especially Queenie and Old Sally. Now that they have journeyed out into the world, I have actually missed spending time with them.

As an author, I love hearing from readers. It completes the circle when the story travels from writer to reader and then back again. To be honest, you're the reason I write. So feel free to tell me what you liked, what you loved, even what you wish I'd done differently. You can also tell me your favorite characters.

You can write to me at susan@susangabriel.com or contact me through my website: www.susangabriel.com.

Finally, if you enjoyed the Temple story, please consider leaving a review on Amazon, Nook, iBooks or Goodreads.

Your review can be short and sweet. You can tell potential readers what you liked most about the book, what interested or surprised you, or whatever you feel like writing.

Reviews help readers who aren't familiar with my books take a chance on my work.

Thanks so much for reading *Temple Secrets* and for spending time with me. A sequel is now available and continues where *Temple Secrets* leaves off. It is called *Gullah Secrets*.

In gratitude,
    Susan Gabriel

P.S. If you want to be notified when I publish new books, sign up for my newsletter on my website: www.susangabriel.com. Also consider joining me on my facebook author page: SusanGabriel, Author.

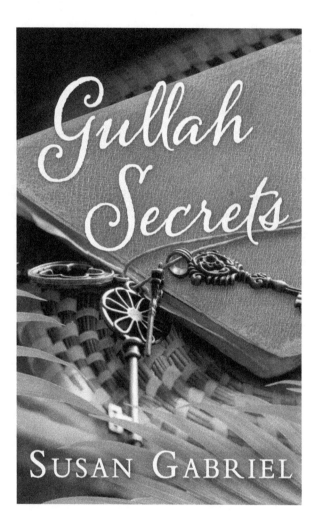

Gullah Secrets: Sequel to Temple Secrets

**A family legacy in danger. A stranger in their midst. Do they
have the strength to survive the gathering storm of secrets?**

For the Temple women, the winds of change are blowing. And if they're not careful, it could sweep them all away...

After rising from Temple servant to tea shop owner, Violet finally feels in charge of her destiny. While learning Gullah folk magic from her aging grandmother, she worries much of her cultural heritage will be lost to the grave. Is there enough time for Old Sally to pass down all her special wisdom?

Bride-to-be Queenie has never felt younger at heart. Engaged to the man of her dreams, the feisty sixty-year-old won't let anything ruin her big day—not even ancestral ghosts or a mysterious wedding crasher.

Rose's southern roots run deep. Even after three decades away, she can still feel the shadow of her deceased high-society mother watching her every move. Can she shake her ghost and find a place among her family?

With a storm of trouble brewing across the island, the Temple women will have to survive more than a force of nature to put their ghosts to rest...

Gullah Secrets is the sequel to the bestselling novel *Temple Secrets*. If you like Southern gothic literature, characters you won't want to close the cover on, and locations steeped in history, then you'll love this hilarious and warmhearted saga.

ACKNOWLEDGMENTS

I am grateful for how stories—wherever they come from—enrich our lives, and for books that inspire me to be a better writer. I am grateful for my readers, who have told me what my books have meant to them and encouraged me with such heartfelt reviews and emails.

For information on the Gullah culture, I am indebted to Bill Moyers' story on the PBS show, NOW, as well as an article called Gullah: A Vanishing Culture, by Paige Williams, in the Charlotte Observer, along with lots of other research online.

I am grateful for my first readers: Anne Alexander, Krista Lunsford, Josephine Locklair, Jeanette Reid, Ann Bohan, Liz Gunn, Kendrick Wronski, and Jane Kennedy. Thanks to Nancy Purcell and the Quotation's writers group in Brevard, NC, who gave me feedback on the first chapter of *Temple Secrets*. I also appreciate the feedback given to me by my literary agent, Mary Grey James.

Of momentous importance to my writing life is my business manager, Anne Alexander, who creatively and masterfully does all the marketing and technical things that are so absolutely foreign to me as an author. Holly Adams, my audiobook narrator, is also a treasure.

To my family and friends, thank you for all your support for the last two decades as I acted on this crazy dream of writing novels.

Finally, to my writing assistants Emma and Jack, who are the sweetest mutts in the world, and who spend their mornings in my office at my feet while I write.

P.S.

Insights, Interview & Reading Group Guide

About the Author

Q & A with Susan Gabriel

13 Things I Reveal About Myself in the
Writing of *Temple Secrets*

Reading Group Guide

ABOUT THE AUTHOR

Susan Gabriel is an acclaimed southern writer who lives in the mountains of Western North Carolina. Her novels, *The Secret Sense of Wildflower* (a Kirkus Reviews Best Book of 2012) and *Temple Secrets* (2015) are Amazon and Nook #1 bestsellers.

She is also the author of *The Wildflower Trilogy* (*The Secret Sense of Wildflower*, *Lily's Song*, and *Daisy's Fortune*). Other books include *Trueluck Summer*, and *Grace, Grits and Ghosts: Southern Short Stories*. Find out more about Susan and her books at SusanGabriel.com.

f

Q & A WITH SUSAN GABRIEL

Tell us a little about yourself.

I've been writing novels for twenty-five years. Before that I was a marriage and family therapist with a private practice in Charleston, South Carolina. I grew up in the South (Knoxville, TN), and for years I swore that I would *never* ever write southern fiction. I had enough crazy "characters" in my gene pool to not want to spend any time there. But as they say: *never say never*. It was after living in Colorado for three years that I discovered what a Southerner I actually am.

Now, I live in the mountains of North Carolina, ten minutes from a national forest that has a river that I love to walk along. I have two grown daughters, two rescue dogs, and two cats.

How did you get the idea for *Temple Secrets*?

Right after I returned from Colorado with my newly

reclaimed Southern identity, I wanted to write another southern novel. I had already written *The Secret Sense of Wildflower* several years before, which I considered a fluke, as in my "only" southern novel. This was back in my "never" stage. Sometimes our destiny keeps tapping us on the shoulder until it finally throws a brick.

The seed of the idea occurred to me decades ago when I lived in Charleston. A dear friend who lived South of Broad told me about a housekeeper she knew who still worked for the same family who had enslaved her ancestors. This fact intrigued me. Since I had recently completed a novel set in Charleston, I decided to have *Temple Secrets* take place in Savannah. Savannah is a sister city to Charleston and is somewhere I've always enjoyed visiting.

With the setting in place, I began to write. The characters showed up full-fledged as if they'd been waiting for me all those years to tell their story: Queenie, Iris, Violet, Rose, Spud, and Edward. And of course, Old Sally. I watched and wrote as their lives played out in my imagination.

To me, the ending is symbolic of what I think our culture needs in order to heal. Acceptance of all kinds of family. Diversity in age, lifestyle, ethnicity, as well as experience.

Who is your favorite character in *Temple Secrets*?

I loved all of the characters, even Iris and Edward, who were quite dastardly at times. But they had reasons for being who they were, as we all do. I loved that Edward got some redemption at the end.

I guess I would say that Queenie was my absolute favorite. I just loved her sense of humor and her resilience. Most of all, I loved writing her dialogue. *Sweet heavens!*

Old Sally was also a favorite. We desperately need wise

old women in our culture, so the least I can do is put them in my stories.

Of course, I also loved Violet and how she wanted to be an agent of change and open a tea shop. I love tea, by the way, and make a pot of it every morning when I write. (Organic Assam is my favorite at the moment.) Rose was the prodigal daughter returning, and she carries some of my experience of moving from the West back to the Southeast. I adored Spud, too, the vegetarian butcher. We humans are fascinating with all our paradoxes.

So, yes, I loved them all, even with their flaws. When you work on a manuscript for several years, it is crucial to find the story and characters compelling. Otherwise, it's easy to lose interest. I never lost interest in this story, and I am honored whenever anyone chooses to read it.

When are you the most creative?

The mornings are my most creative time. I am usually alone, and I am generally working on whatever my current novel is. A typical morning for me is to write from around 9 am, to around 1 o'clock. Then in the afternoons, I might meet friends for tea or paint in my art studio. For many years I taught writing classes and edited novels to support my writing habit.

Share a favorite quote.

It is hard to only pick one. I love quotes. Here are two by Carl Jung: "Small and hidden is the door that leads inward."

And: "You must go in quest of yourself, and you will find yourself again only in the simple and forgotten things. Why not go into the forest for a time, literally? Sometimes a tree tells you more than can be read in books."

And then one from Maya Angelou: "There is no greater agony than bearing an untold story inside you."

What creative project are you working on now?

Having just completed the Wildflower Trilogy (2019), I am about to start working on a novel that I've already been tinkering with for seven years. It is in a first draft and needs to be revised. No title for that one yet, but it takes place in the lowcountry, near Charleston. I also have several characters hanging out in my imagination that are waiting for me to get to them.

What were you like as a child?

Very shy and outdoorsy. Some might say a tomboy. I stayed outside riding my bike, playing games with my brother, or playing golf. I rarely read but did well in school. (How is that even possible?) There weren't that many books in our home. It wasn't until I was out of college and having my first child that I began to read children's classics, trying to make up for what I had missed. I am a late-bloomer in many ways. Now I read voraciously. I haven't stopped.

Is there somewhere you've traveled that has influenced your creative life?

As I've mentioned before, I lived out West for a few years, which is about as different from the moist, shady south-eastern United States as you can get. I loved exploring this new terrain and the wildlife that resided there. It was in the

West that I finally claimed my southern soul. I missed shade. I missed deciduous trees. I even missed kudzu! But I missed moisture most of all. Now I'm back in the southeast living in an area of the North Carolina Mountains known for its waterfalls. Life is good.

13 THINGS I REVEAL ABOUT MYSELF

...in the Writing of Temple Secrets

1. Ancestors are important to me. The sense that we aren't alone; that people came before us; that some may even be watching over us.

2. Secrets intrigue me. They make people do strange things. Everybody has them. Sometimes we even keep secrets from ourselves.

3. The spirit world or the invisible world (think ghosts, spirits, the secret sense), fascinate me and are underestimated.

4. Female characters and female voices are underrepresented in our culture. My mission is to get more female characters out into the world who are courageous and have integrity and humor.

5. I think characters over forty are the most interesting.

6. I think happy endings are possible in life, and that it's only to the level that we've experienced sorrow that we can experience joy. Readers have told me that my books make them laugh and cry.

7. I love to make people laugh, so my books are often humorous. When I was younger, I wanted to be a stand- up comedian. As a girl, I would sneak into the den late at night to watch Joan Rivers on the Johnny Carson show. Since my comedy act never hit the road, I became a writer instead. Well, first, I became a teacher, then a psychotherapist, and then a writer. It was by no means a straight path to writing. I grew into it.

8. Old wise women show up in nearly everything I write because I hope to become one.

9. I am fascinated with death, so there is usually at least one death in my stories. To me, it's just the natural end of living. However, I rarely kill off an animal, especially a dog. (The exception was a dog dying of old age in one of my other books. I'm still sad about that.)

10. I think reading novels opens us to a deeper emotional experience.

11. Sometimes when people are consistently obnoxious to me, I create a character in a novel with some of the same characteristics and then have them be found out for who they really are in the course of the story. I am very good at disguising these real people in the skins of my fictional characters. Novelists do this all the time.

12. I always write about things that interest me. I write the story that I would love to read, trusting that other people will enjoy it, too. Since I spend years writing a book, I have to love the characters and understand them. After I release a book, I often grieve the loss of not having the story in my life every day.

13. I think we are all trying to find our way "home," in one way or another. Home being a place where we feel the most authentic.

~

Does anything surprise you? I love hearing from readers. You can email me at susan@susangabriel.com.

READING GROUP GUIDE

1. Who was your favorite character? Why?

2. What do you think motivated Iris? On the one hand, she could be cruel and dismissive to Queenie, yet she had loved Spud Grainger for decades. Do you think she is a sympathetic or unsympathetic character? Why?

3. How much of a person's character would you say is shaped by what has happened to them in the past, or what happened in past generations?

4. Did it bother you that Queenie was willing to overlook so many of Iris's faults to live with Iris? Why?

5. Do you believe that keeping secrets is sometimes justified? Should Queenie have told Violet who she really was from the very beginning? Why?

6. What do you think of Rose coming home to see her

mother on her deathbed? In what situations might estrange-
ment from one's family sometimes be necessary for self-
preservation?

7. The author paints Old Sally with a quiet grace and an aura
of wisdom about her. How do you think she does this? Have
you ever had a wise old woman in your life? If so, what was
meaningful about your relationship with her?

8. In what ways do you think racism still shows up in relationships where people of color work for people who are
white?

9. How was the Temple Book of Secrets an agent of change
for the entire family?

10. How did you feel about Edward's seeming redemption at
the end of the novel? Discuss people in your life who have
appeared totally one way and then who surprised you with
something you never knew about them.

11. What role do you see Violet playing in the novel? What
did you think of her ability to perceive ghosts? How might
her children end up different from her because of her
choices?

12. In the final scene, were you hopeful that all of the characters could live together peacefully? If you were to write a
sequel for this novel, what do you imagine happening? (P.S.
There is a sequel now called *Gullah Secrets.* It continues
where *Temple Secrets* leaves off.)

The Wildflower Trilogy

The Secret Sense of Wildflower

Named a Best Book of 2012 by Kirkus Reviews. Small southern towns have few secrets in Appalachia, 1941. When thirteen-year-old Louisa May "Wildflower" McAllister is targeted by the town's teenage bully, she may need more than her "secret sense" to survive.

Lily's Song

A mother's secrets, a daughter's dream, and a family's loyalty are masterfully interwoven in this sequel to *The Secret Sense of Wildflower*. A compelling tale set in 1956 Appalachia that captures the resilience and strength of both mother and daughter, as secrets revealed test their strong bond and ultimately change their lives forever.

Daisy's Fortune

Tennessee, 1982. Wildflower McAllister returns to the small mountain town that stole her innocence and cast her out. Can she stop a harrowing legacy from spreading to another generation? If you like strong women, generational tales, and the power of family and the land to heal, then you'll adore this compelling finale to the Wildflower trilogy.

Available in ebook and paperback.

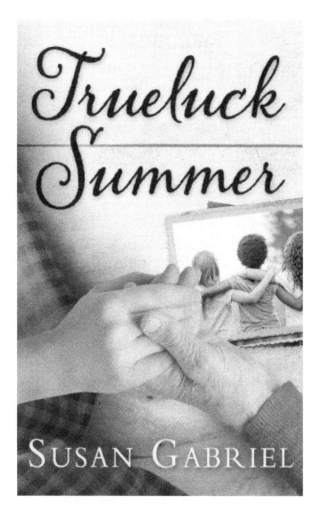

Trueluck Summer: A Lowcountry Novel

A hopeful grandmother. A sassy young girl. Their audacious summer stunt could change their southern town forever.

Charleston, 1964. Ida Trueluck is still adjusting to life on her own. Moving into her son's house creates a few family conflicts, but the widow's saving grace is her whip-smart granddaughter Trudy. Ida makes it her top priority to give the girl a summer she'll never forget.

When a runaway truck nearly takes her life, Trudy makes fast friends with the boy who saves her. But since Paris is black, the racism they encounter inspires Trudy's surprising summer mission: to take down the Confederate flag from the South Carolina Statehouse. And she knows she can't do it without the help of her beloved grandmother.

With all of Southern society conspiring against them, can Trudy, Ida, and their friends pull off the impossible?

Trueluck Summer is a Southern historical women's fiction novel set in a time of significant cultural change. If you like courageous characters, heartwarming humor, and inspirational acts, then you'll love Susan Gabriel's captivating tale.

Available in ebook, paperback and audiobook.

ALL BOOKS BY SUSAN GABRIEL

FICTION:

Temple Secrets Series:

Temple Secrets

Gullah Secrets

The Wildflower Trilogy:

The Secret Sense of Wildflower

Lily's Song

Daisy's Fortune

Trueluck Summer

Grace, Grits and Ghosts: Southern Short Stories

Seeking Sara Summers

Circle of the Ancestors

Quentin & the Cave Boy

NONFICTION

Fearless Writing for Women:

Extreme Encouragement & Writing Inspiration

Available at all booksellers

in print, ebook, and audiobook.

CPSIA information can be obtained
at www.ICGtesting.com
Printed in the USA
BVHW071912120620
581249BV00005B/148

9 780983 588276